DETECTIVE FOR THE DEBUTANTE

SAFE HAVEN SECURITY
BOOK THREE

BREANNA LYNN

ISBN: 978-1-955359-58-0 (ebook)

ISBN: 978-1-955359-59-7 (paperback)

Cover Design by: Najla Qamber, Qamber Designs

Edited by: Happily Editing Anns

Printed in United States of America

https://breannalynnauthor.com

He swore he'd never fall in love...until she become the only thing worth falling for.

Leigh Whittaker was never supposed to mean anything more than a memory—a woman I helped rescue, my friend's younger sister.

Sweet. Off-limits. A line I promised never to cross.

But then something shifted.

A glance. A touch. A feeling I couldn't ignore.

Now I can't stop thinking about her.

Being near her feels like gravity—like coming home when I didn't even know I was lost.

Her world is unraveling, and mine isn't far behind. She won't admit she's in danger, and I'm barely holding my own life together. But somehow, in the chaos, she's the calm. The light. The only thing that makes sense.

I told myself I'd never fall in love.

But what if the one woman I never saw coming…is the one I was always meant to find?

For every person who strives to see the good in people...
never let anyone or anything change you.

CHAPTER 1

LEIGH

I love weddings. I love my quaint hometown of Mistletoe Creek, Tennessee.

And I love how happy my sister is.

The final notes of Tracy Byrd's "The Keeper of the Stars" fade off, and I can't hold back the sigh that escapes as Mama and Daddy and Hannah Grace and Cole finish the dance along with half a dozen other couples occupying the makeshift dance floor. It's the same song Mama and Daddy danced to at their wedding. And now my sister and her new husband are sharing a moment with them.

I've grown up with my parents talking about falling in love in high school, and I've watched Cole and Hannah Grace morph from childhood best friends to more. Sure, they may have broken up for about seven years, but their happily ever after is back on track.

And I want mine.

But it doesn't necessarily involve a white dress and a gold band. At least not yet.

"That's an awfully heavy sigh for a happy day." My best friend, Sydney, plops down with a plate of cake and hands me one.

Or should I say another piece of cake?

"How many pieces does this make?" I ask her and slide a clean fork into the fluffy white confection.

She snorts, already on bite number two.

"Does it matter? I don't count calories in wedding cake. But this is probably number three. No, wait, number four. I had a slice earlier when you were talking to the pink ladies over there."

She thumbs in the direction of Fern, Fawn, and Merry who occupy another table as they whisper and point at the guests milling around the outside of the Mistletoe Creek Civic Building. Once the mansion of the town's founder, it was converted years ago to hold functions like my sister's wedding.

The three women Sydney is referring to are in their seventies or eighties—no one is brave enough to ask them and confirm—and are the most notorious set of matchmakers our side of the Mississippi. Which is why I've tried to stay as far away from them as possible. The fact the three of them are sporting pink hair? Not out of the ordinary.

"Merry said they were paying homage to Hannah Grace's wedding colors," I say.

"Aren't pink and mauve the same color?" The question is muffled by the cake in her mouth.

"Not according to Mama and Hannah Grace."

"Is it weird they dyed their hair to match the wedding? I mean, I've seen people with pink hair before—hello, I live in LA for Pete's sake—but it's not usually because someone is getting married."

Sydney's from California and is one of Cole's coworkers at SAFE Haven Security. She and I became best friends over the last year through summer trips, texts, and FaceTime. And one of our favorite pastimes is to pick on my sister's new husband and Sydney's unofficial big brother.

"You better not let them hear you say that. In fact, you better not let them hear you at all. We'll be next," I whisper and slide another forkful of strawberry and cream cake into my mouth.

I like Sydney's idea of not counting calories in wedding cake.

"Meh. I leave for California tomorrow." She shrugs.

Lucky.

Sydney is going back to her independent life while I am all but living with Mama and Daddy like I am still a kid when I'm not at school.

"One, I'm here for a few more weeks. And I'd like to avoid their matchmaking efforts. Two, you say that like being over two thousand miles away is protection. Those women have a long reach."

"My favorite color is black. You're saying they'll dye their hair black for my wedding?"

"Why? Getting married anytime soon?"

She barks out a laugh. "Fuck that."

I shush her and glance around, making sure nobody else heard her. If they did, no one reacts.

"You're going to get your mouth washed out with soap," I warn her.

"That's a thing?" She sits up and glances at the table closest to us like she's expecting a bar of soap to suddenly appear.

Fortunately, the family of four is not Fern, Fawn, and Merry since they have hearing like Sheldon Cooper from *The Big Bang Theory*. My lips twitch as I recall Leonard, Sheldon's roommate, yelling, "Damn his Vulcan hearing."

The three elderly women and the character from one of my favorite shows share one thing in common—always hearing something you don't want them to.

"Ivory soap tastes the worst," I tell her.

She shudders.

"I'll take your word for it. Instead, I'll enjoy this cake and head back to California without the taste of soap in my mouth."

She lifts another bite, moaning as her lips close around the fork.

"That way you eat cake is obscene," I tease her and roll my eyes.

She shrugs again, unperturbed.

"This cake is better than most of the sex I've had recently."

"Syd! Lower your voice—you can't say things like that here." Where any one of my parents' generation or older is close enough to overhear her.

The look she gives me is one of the "yeah, right" variety. She's given me a few of those while she's been out here in Tennessee this week. It's been highly entertaining to watch city-girl Sydney handle our small town. And her no-filter attitude is something I love about her. As is her no-fear confidence. When I grow up, I want to be like Sydney.

Is that weird since we're the same age?

"What? You're saying you can't say the word sex here either? Holy shit, are you a virgin? And, follow-up, if so, how did I not know?"

Thank God she's lowered her voice. Instead her eyebrows are practically at her hairline as she studies me.

A flush spreads up my chest and settles in my cheeks as I squirm in my seat.

"No, I'm not. And it's just never come up, I guess," I mumble and focus on the few crumbs left on my plate.

"Phew. I was worried for a second. Might have had to stage an intervention," she teases and pushes her empty plate away.

"Despite my parents' best efforts, they weren't able to control every aspect of my life," I grumble.

Because if it was up to them, chastity belts would still be a thing.

"Glad to hear it." She grins.

"And something tells me if you're enjoying cake as much as you are, you're not really the one to stage an intervention."

"It's not that it's not available, but I'd rather spend time with my vibrator than another round of sex where I have to give an anatomy lesson and draw a road map to explain to the man what to do. Although maybe I need to rethink that. With him. Holy shit," she says, biting her lip.

I crane my head around to find out who she's talking about, and my breath catches in my lungs.

Ink teases out of the open collar of a white dress shirt ready to bust at the seams thanks to the broad shoulders it's wrapped around. The scruff I remember accompanying the well-groomed goatee is gone, leaving a chiseled jawline I want to trace with my fingers.

Or my tongue.

My thighs clench together and my core throbs at the site of the Nashville detective who helped Cole with Hannah Grace's stalker almost a year and a half ago.

"Murphy?" I try to say his name with more nonchalance than is coursing through my body.

"That's Murphy? How did I not know he looks like that?"

I shrug, the move stiff and awkward. I'd like to turn back around, but I don't have that much willpower.

Murphy O'Connell is a beautiful specimen of a man.

"Look like what?"

"Like he just stepped out of every woman's favorite fantasy—Mr. Buttoned-Up Suit in the boardroom, inked god in the bedroom."

"I don't remember him looking like that."

Liar, liar, pants on fire.

"You better not. I'd have to hold it against you for keeping that secret."

The memories from the only other night I've spent in his company are fuzzy as I try to focus on them. Confusion, anger, sadness at what my sister's best friend had done to her. Had almost done to me. Humiliation because I had been all about Zach Nolan until that night.

"I was still recovering from the Ambien Zach put in my drink. I just remember thinking Cole's police friend was nice. He had a soothing voice."

I'd been shaking as he started questioning me about Zach and what I remembered, but I'd focused on his voice, letting it relax me enough that the shaking subsided.

When my sister's best friend turned out to be her stalker and kidnapped me as bait to get Hannah Grace to come to him, Murphy had helped Cole solve the case. He'd been Cole's backup when they both got to the house where Zach was keeping me. Murphy hadn't pressed for answers when he took my statement, but waited patiently for what I could remember—which wasn't much.

I'd had a crush on Zach Nolan. I had flirted like crazy. We'd talked and drank wine and then I didn't know anything else until Hannah Grace woke me up.

Unlike me, Hannah Grace hadn't been drugged. She was able to provide enough of a statement and then formal testimony to help put Zach away for a long time. She had saved me.

There was no way I could ever repay her for what she had done. For being my hero.

"I can't believe I thought he was cute. Zach," I clarify.

Sydney reaches over and squeezes my arm, well aware of everything that had happened since she works with Cole and helped with the case.

"You had no idea he was a creep. Nobody did."

"I should have known. I liked him. Ergo, he was not a nice guy. None of the guys I've dated have been great."

"You've been surrounded by frat boys for far too long, Laura Leigh."

"Leigh," I correct.

Maybe it should have been harder changing my name from

something everyone called me for the first twenty-two years of my life. But it wasn't. It was refreshing. A new start for a new stage of my life.

Laura Leigh was the Mistletoe Creek version of me, the University of Tennessee version of me, the debutante Mama hoped would give up the notion of finishing my law degree and move home. Leigh is the more sophisticated version. The Nashville version. The independent college graduate who has just finished her first year of law school in Knoxville.

"And that's who is in Knoxville. Frat boys all over that college campus. My options are pretty limited."

"You need to get out more."

"That's my plan. So long as Mama and Daddy uphold their end of the bargain."

A summer to live on my own in Nashville in Hannah Grace's old house. Without their almost constant hovering.

"Really?"

"Yes. I've had more than my fill of a bunch of gym bros masquerading as Greek-pledging, pre-med boys."

"Nashville is going to be so good for you," she says, her smile turning mischievous.

"I hope so."

"We need a hot girl summer. You in Nashville. Me in LA. Then we'll compare notes."

The idea holds a lot of merit. I really, *really* want a hot girl summer.

"Think about it as your reward for successfully finishing your first year at law school. You and I both know that you need this summer—in more ways than one."

She gives me a pointed look because she knows everything at stake. At the end of the summer, a decision will be made on which law students will be invited to help on Project Justice. The project helps wrongfully convicted individuals to fight their convictions. If I don't get invited, I have agreed I will take a job working at the corporate law firm of one of Daddy's golfing buddies.

I may have gotten into law school with the intent to put guys like Zach away, but the more I read about men and women who were acquitted after twenty or thirty years, individuals who had missed out on their lives because of their inability to fight, I knew where I wanted to focus.

Too bad my parents aren't on board.

Since everything happened with Zach, they are more worried than ever before. To the point where Daddy has arranged a nice, boring, corporate law job after I finish law school. One that exists in our small hometown.

"Okay," I say. "Let's do our hot girl summer."

"We're starting right now. I—"

"It's not summer yet," I hiss.

Although it is close enough—the official start of summer is only a couple of weeks away.

"Consider this your practice session. I dare you to walk over to the sexy Hemsworth cousin and offer to buy him a drink. And see where it leads."

"It's an open bar," I remind her.

"Who cares? That's just your opening line. Now go. I'm going for another piece of cake." She stands and picks up the back of my chair until I stand too.

"Enjoy your cake, Syd." I smooth the mauve satin skirt against my hips.

"Your boobs look amazing in that dress," Sydney says with a wink.

A giggle escapes and I roll my eyes.

Only Sydney.

"Thanks."

"Now go get him, tiger." She blows me a kiss and heads toward the cake table.

Ready or not, here I go.

CHAPTER 2

MURPHY

"Glad NPD could spare you," Cole says, wrapping an arm around Hannah Grace.

The two people in front of me make me want to argue against my no marriage rule. And it is more than just the beautiful words they spoke to each other during the ceremony. It's the way they are in tune with each other. The way Hannah Grace reaches for Cole who is always right there. An awareness as a result of the confidence and love I've only ever witnessed before between my parents. Between my sisters and their significant others.

And sometimes it makes me jealous. But not enough to take the plunge myself.

"They don't really have a choice."

"What do you mean?" Sawyer asks, joining us with his wife, Evie, next to him.

"I just accepted a job with the FBI. I'll be joining one of their task forces in DC."

"Task force?" Cole perks up and his wife rolls her eyes.

"I thought we weren't going to talk security at our wedding," she tells him, drilling her index finger into his side.

"I'm not. I'm talking to Murphy about his new job opportunity." He squirms away, capturing her finger and bringing it to his lips.

"Come on, Hannah Grace, we'll go get another glass of champagne," Evie tells her and the two depart after kissing their spouses.

The two men wait until their wives are gone before turning to me expectantly.

"Task force?" Cole repeats.

I nod, not hiding the smile as I explain.

"I'll be working with the behavioral analysis division, profiling crimes committed against women. When I was working on my degree a few years ago, I focused on the psychology of violent crimes against women."

With a mother and two sisters—one of whom had dealt with an ex who wouldn't leave her alone—my focus had been singular. And with this new job, successful.

"Like Hannah Grace and Laura Leigh?" Cole asks.

"It happened to my sister Riley too. But not like..."

I don't need to say Zach's name. There's a hard edge to Cole that wasn't there before. But sometimes the crimes against women were worse. Hannah Grace and Laura Leigh had been lucky. Riley had been lucky.

Some women weren't. I'd worked on those cases as well, and they were the reason why this job was one I couldn't wait to start.

"Well, fuck," Cole says.

"What?" I ask.

"I was going to ask you to check in on Laura Leigh this summer. She accepted an internship with the public defender's office and will be in the city starting in a few weeks."

My big brother instinct roars to life at the memory of the petite blonde whose blue eyes were unfocused because of what some asshole had done. At the slight tremor of her hand when she had reached out to steady herself on the wall when we spoke.

"My job doesn't start until September 1st. I'm happy to keep an eye on her."

"Thanks, man, I appreciate it." Cole claps me on the back and he, Sawyer, and I end up talking about some cases they've worked on recently.

I'm half focused on them and half focused on how to head out so I can do some research tonight when a blonde walks up to where we stand on the edge of the dance floor. All of my focus is now homed in on her, on the way the soft lights reflect off the honey-colored highlights in her hair, turning the color to spun gold.

Blue eyes that are a mix of curious and confident catch mine, and it's the jolt back to reality I need.

Holy fuck.

"Hi," she says, coming to a stop next to me.

"Murphy, speak of the devil. You remember Hannah Grace's baby sister, Laura Leigh, right?" Cole asks.

The manners my parents taught me are second nature and the only reason I can nod and reach out to shake her hand while my brain is scrambling to latch on to the little sister thoughts now scattering like leaves in a breeze.

"Laura Leigh."

She slides her palm into mine, and I attempt to ignore the electric sparks that zip up my arm and then head to an inconvenient part of my body where my blood seems to have gone. Because nope. Women at weddings are off-limits. But little sisters at weddings?

That's a whole other level of forbidden I'm not entertaining.

"It's just Leigh. I go by Leigh now," she explains, shooting a glare at Cole.

Let go of her hand, dumbass.

Belatedly, I realize while I've been trying to figure out the exact shade of her blue eyes—more of a Caribbean blue than her sister's cornflower color—I've still been shaking her hand.

Letting it go, I stuff my traitorous hand and its partner in my pockets.

"Sorry. You'll always be Laura Leigh to me. Or Lee Lee."

"Cole, if you ever use that nickname again, I'll sic Sydney on you," she warns.

"Lee Lee?" I ask, unable to help myself.

"A childhood nickname. It really is just Leigh now." Her tone is soft, husky, the slight drawl pulling me in like the Pied Piper.

What would my name sound like breaking on her lips?

You're not going to fucking find out. Little sister, remember?

"Leigh," I say, trying out the name.

She tries to fight a shiver, but doesn't quite manage it as her eyes clash with mine.

"Cole? The photographer wants to get a few more pictures," Hannah Grace calls from the other side of the dance floor.

He grimaces, but salutes us before joining his wife.

"Good luck!" I call after him.

He shoots me a look over his shoulder before looking at Hannah Grace again.

"That's my cue to go find my wife for a dance," Sawyer says. "Good talking to you, Murphy. Let me know how the new job goes."

We shake hands and then it's only Leigh and me.

"Poor Cole. Guess he got the karma he deserved," Leigh says, the corner of her mouth quirking.

Fuck, she's cute.

And the mischievous grin draws my attention once more to her lips.

Are they as soft as they look?

Clearing my throat, I turn my focus to her, angling to provide a bit more distance between us.

"Should I go rescue him? Tell him there's an emergency?" I ask, causing her smile to stretch into a fuller version of the tease it was before.

It's like the sun coming out from behind storm clouds. Would she taste like the sunshine she reminds me of?

You're not going to find out. She's off-limits. She's only twenty.

No. She was before. The first time I met her. But still, that makes her what? Twenty-one? Twenty-two? Regardless of her age, she's still enshrouded by the little sister label. That label means one thing and one thing only.

Forbidden.

"I think Hannah Grace might actually murder you if you do."

I bark out a laugh.

"Fair enough."

We fall into a silence, equal parts comfortable and awkward as my attention shifts to the people milling around the dance floor.

Time to go.

"Well—"

"I… can I buy you a drink?" she asks, slicking her tongue along her bottom lip.

The lights around us reflect off the trail of moisture.

"Are you old enough to drink?" The words are out of my mouth before I can stop them.

"Are you?" she fires back.

Fuck. The spark coming to life in her gaze is attractive. What else would create that burn?

I know I look well over the legal drinking age. If there was any question, the more salt than pepper sprinkled in my goatee when I look in the bathroom mirror should prove it.

"I'm thirty-six years old, Little Bit. Well over the age to enjoy a beer if I want to. Are you really twenty-one?"

"Twenty-two." She crosses her arms over her chest, the move highlighting her breasts and yanking my attention to the impressive cleavage created by her dress.

Record scratch.

How old did she say she was?

Twenty-two. Twenty-fucking-two. I have no business looking

at a twenty-two-year-old like I want to devour her. Even if I want to.

"Fuck, you're just a wean," I groan and close my eyes, willing the attraction to disappear before I open them again.

"A what?"

My eyes pop open, and a line carves between her brows as she studies me.

"A wean. A wee one. A kid," I explain until I land on the phrase she understands.

Her eyes narrow as she glares at me.

"Well, this *wean* is going to get a glass of champagne. Excuse me." She tosses the blonde curls not in her updo over her shoulder and steps around me, stumbling slightly as she steps onto the cobblestone path.

My hand snaps out to catch her but she brushes past me and heads for the bar.

"Wait a minute." I follow her, my fingers wrapping around her bicep to turn her back in my direction.

The silk of her skin under my fingertips combined with her perfume overwhelm my senses. It's a mix of floral and musk and some sort of berry, and I drag in another lungful while I can.

I should let her go.

But I don't want to. I don't want her to be angry with me. And there's no logical reason for why I feel the way I do.

"What?" she snaps.

"I didn't say no," I tell her.

"You didn't say yes, either."

Touché.

"Isn't it an open bar?" I tease, trying to get her to smile again.

She spins around, focusing on me, her mouth open to respond with what I'm sure will be another snarky response. Instead, she snaps it shut, and her glare softens until a smile teases the corner of her lips.

"Nothing to say?" I ask when she doesn't respond.

"Since when did an open bar stop you from letting a pretty girl buy you a drink?" Her fingers walk up the placket of my buttons, and I cover her hand with mine before she can feel just how hard my heart is pounding in my chest.

Because encouraging her will only lead to something I can't give her.

But damned if I'm willing to stop talking to her.

There's something about her that draws me in and makes me want to ask questions. A warmth I feel in my soul.

"By all means." I nod behind her to the waiting bartender.

She orders a glass of champagne for herself, and I ask for a glass of Jameson. I'm digging my wallet out for a tip when she fishes two dollars out of the top of her dress and drops them into the tip jar. I don't think I've ever been envious of dollar bills before, but I am of the two Leigh pulls from the satin stretching across her breasts.

Drinks in hand, we move to a small cocktail table set up between the bar and the dance floor.

"Cole tells me you're heading to Nashville next month?"

She takes a sip of champagne and hums in response.

"Yes. I have an internship with the public defender's office this summer."

"You want to be a lawyer?" I lift my glass and enjoy the smooth slide of the Jameson as it travels down my chest.

"Yeah. After…everything happened, I decided I wanted to become an attorney. I wanted to make sure guys like Zach went behind bars."

"I hate to tell you, but the office you're working for does the opposite."

She giggles, lifting her glass and tossing back half of the champagne.

"I know. Why I got into law was one thing, but then I found out about all the individuals who get arrested and convicted of crimes they didn't commit. Did you know anywhere between four and six percent of people in jail are actually innocent?"

"Which means there are more in there for a reason. A good reason."

"If even one person has lost their freedom because they were wrongfully convicted, that's too many."

Color stains her cheeks, that fire I like once more blazing to life in her eyes.

"So you're going to work for the public defender's office?"

She shrugs. "Ultimately, I want to work for Project Justice. It's an organization to help wrongfully convicted individuals file appeals to be exonerated. The application for the project closes at the end of summer, and I thought this would look good on the application."

"I wish you luck in getting selected then. I'm starting a new job myself. With the FBI." And for the first time since I accepted the job, regret creates a pang in my stomach.

"You're leaving Nashville?"

"Not yet. In fact, you'll probably see me around your office since I have to stop by for a case occasionally."

"I hope so. I don't know many people in the city."

"How many people do you know?"

"Including you?" she asks and lifts her glass again for a smaller sip.

I nod. "Yeah."

"One."

She surprises another laugh from me, and her accompanying giggle is infectious.

"Since Hannah Grace moved to California, there's no one else there I know," she explains.

"Why Nashville then?" I ask, genuinely curious.

I take another drink of my Jameson and wait for her response.

"It's where the internship offer came from. And it made sense since Hannah Grace's house is empty right now."

"You're staying at her place?"

She nods, sending a lock of hair free from her partial updo. "Yeah."

"How long is the internship for?"

"Are you interrogating me, detective?" She lifts her hands, her fingers playing with the pendant of a necklace where it rests against the smooth skin of her collarbone.

I have to fight not to drop my gaze back down, shaking my head and blinking to avoid the temptation.

"Sorry. My mom says I do the same thing to her and my sisters all the time."

"Habit of the job, probably. Have you been on the force long?" Her body begins to move to the beat of the song the DJ is playing.

"I did the whole college thing. Studied psychology. Once I was done with school, I joined the force."

"And now the FBI," she murmurs.

"Yep. I leave for DC at the end of August."

"What does your family think of you moving?" she asks.

That's the only dark spot in the happiness I associate with this new opportunity. I don't know why, but I hadn't expected tears when I told Mom, Quinn, and Riley about my impending move. They'd tried talking me out of it. Repeatedly.

And I doubted they were done.

"They don't want me living so far away."

That's an understatement.

"Boy, do I understand that," she murmurs, her eyes searching the tables.

"Looking for someone?" I ask.

"Just my parents. There." She points to a table where a man in a tux and a woman in a navy sequined dress stand next to three pink-haired women, and they all wave in our direction.

We wave back. The song changes and the movement of her hips drags my attention to the material wrapping around her curves. The slow movement mesmerizes me.

Just one dance. What can it hurt?

It's a fast song. Safe enough.

Then I'll go.

"Come on." I lace my fingers with hers and turn from the table.

"I'm sorry?" she asks, but still stays with me as I lead us to the dance floor.

"I can tell you want to dance. You haven't stopped moving since this song came on."

"You noticed?"

I glance over my shoulder, and a pretty blush pinkens her cheeks.

"It's part of my job. Noticing," I tell her.

Yeah, because noticing her *is only part of the job.*

"Oh."

We reach the dance floor and she moves to the music in a contagious exuberance. So when the next song comes on, we continue to dance.

The third song is slower, and I'm reaching for her before I can talk myself out of it.

Her arms climb along my chest to drape around my neck, and the brush of her fingertips along the hair at my nape creates a shiver that works its way down my spine.

"You're a really good dancer," she murmurs as we pass other swaying couples.

One corner of my mouth kicks up in a smile.

"Thanks. It was something my mom had me learn. Dad knew how to dance, and Mom always said that was what caught her attention first."

She giggles and my half smile stretches to a full one.

"You're pretty good yourself," I say as we rotate around the dance floor.

"All good debutantes know how to dance."

Fuck, the sass she says those words with is enough to have me struggling to remember there's a fourteen-year age difference between the two of us.

I chuckle.

"You must have been a good debutante then."

She laughs. "God, no. I was terrible. I hated wearing all the dresses and going to all the different events. That was more Hannah Grace's thing than mine. I'm not a fan of rules. Neither are you, judging by this."

Her fingers trace the ink peeking out from my collar, setting off more of those sparks I'm struggling to ignore.

"It's allowed. So long as it's not visible." And I absolutely push that line.

The song ends and I spin her out and back before dipping her, as her fingers grip my biceps through the thin material of my dress shirt. I relish the sensation, pausing for several heartbeats before I lift her back to a standing position.

"That sounds like a story," she says breathily.

"Oh it is. A long one."

"Ah."

Speaking of pushing boundaries, I've flirted enough with the line—and with Leigh—tonight. There's no future there. Not even one I would allow with a beautiful woman. Because Leigh isn't any other beautiful woman. And she deserves more than a few weeks of amazing sex before we both move on. And spending time with her is only going to send the wrong message.

I open my mouth to say goodbye, but that's not what comes out of my mouth.

"How about I buy you a drink and tell you about it?"

"I thought it was an open bar?" she teases, throwing my own line from earlier back at me.

The smirk I give her has her breath catching audibly, and I put more distance between us and soften my expression to a smile.

"It's never stopped me from buying a drink for a pretty girl." We stop at a cocktail table. "Champagne?"

"Yes, please."

"Wait here," I demand.

Using the physical separation, I try to remind myself of every reason why I need to keep my distance. Because when I'm next to her, it's hard to remember any of them.

Because Leigh is the first woman I've met in a long time who has me curious to learn more. And I know what people say about curiosity and cats.

CHAPTER 3

LEIGH

"Your tattoos?" I ask as soon as Murphy sets my glass of champagne in front of me.

"So eager for the story," he murmurs, taking a sip of amber-colored liquid.

The light catches on the light sheen of moisture on his bottom lip and I clear my throat, taking a drink of my own as I wait for his story.

His golden-colored eyes take on a faraway look and he lifts his right hand, covering his heart.

"This was my first. I was in New Orleans with some friends."

"Spring break?"

"Mardis Gras. A very memorable trip because of this." He rubs his fingers along the spot. "But otherwise I don't remember much else."

He smirks, his gaze zeroing in on me, and my breath catches.

"W-what is it?" The words are little more than a murmur as I struggle to remember how to breathe.

"A *Dara*. A Celtic knot. It means strength. Warriors often used the symbol on their armor or weapons."

Warrior.

Murphy O'Connell one hundred percent fits that description. I can easily picture him as an ancient soldier ready for battle instead of the man dressed in the white button-down, reminiscing about his first tattoo.

"And that led to everything else?" I ask.

He nods. "There was something about the way the needle ran across my skin, the image growing as the artist did her thing. I was hooked. But by then I knew I would be joining the force. And I knew the rules. So I've had to make sure none of them were visible."

"But these," I say, reaching out, my fingers grazing the ink peeking out of his shirt collar.

There's a light charge in the drag of my fingertips against his skin, and I try to ignore the rush of awareness the touch creates and reluctantly drop my hand.

He shrugs.

"This shirt isn't as high as some of my others. And I have a really flexible captain."

He smiles and I return the easy grin with one of my own.

"Ladies and gentlemen, I've just been told Mr. and Mrs. Strickland are taking their leave from their party. Let's all get together and see them off, shall we?" The DJ's voice echoes through the small area, and everyone starts to shift toward the archway that leads to the parking lot.

"Should we go see them off?" Murphy asks, holding out his hand.

I slide my fingers along his and our fingers wrap together like they've been doing it for years.

"Let's go."

Our hands stay connected while we send off Cole and Hannah Grace, and then he pulls me back toward the dance floor. I wouldn't expect a man as big as he is to move with the rhythm he does, except he's already explained it's a result of dance lessons.

The faster song slows down to another ballad, the last of the night according to the DJ. Murphy pulls me closer, my chest resting against his heartbeat.

"Do your parents still dance together?" I ask.

"Sorry to interrupt. Laura Leigh?" Mama's voice breaks through the thud of Murphy's pulse.

We stop dancing and I open my eyes to find my parents next to us. Mama's expression is a mix of mischief and concern. The mischief no doubt from the matchmaking scheme she's already trying to concoct for her only unwed daughter, and the concern has become a near constant since Zach kidnapped me. It's a softer version of the look on Daddy's face.

The two of them were overprotective before. But now? I'm surprised I was ever allowed back out of the house.

You only have the summer to prove yourself.

"Hi, Mama. Daddy. I think you met Murphy before. He's with Nashville Police Department," I tell them.

The twin concerned faces relax and Daddy reaches out a hand to shake Murphy's.

"You're in Nashville?" he asks Murphy.

"Yes, sir."

"Good. Glad someone will be there to look after our Laura Leigh," Daddy says.

I barely bite back the groan as embarrassment crawls through my body. For a little while I had felt like Murphy's equal. Now? I feel like what he had called me earlier—a baby. But just as quickly as the embarrassment came, panic is hot on its heels.

Please don't let Murphy mention his move.

I breathe a sigh of relief when he only smiles and nods.

"Happy to, sir."

Somehow I think his definition of looking after me is

different from mine. But a small part of me hopes I can convince him my definition is the best.

Hot girl summer indeed.

"Sweetie, now that Cole and Hannah Grace have gone, we're heading home. I don't think I've sat down for more than a few minutes all day. Are you still staying at Sydney's?" Mama asks.

"Heck yes, she is!" Sydney joins us, wrapping an arm around each of my parents. "I hope you don't mind me stealing her for one more night. I head back to California tomorrow afternoon. Hi, I'm Sydney." She releases Mama to shake Murphy's hand and shoots me a covert wink at the same time.

Thank God for Sydney.

"Murphy O'Connell."

"Okay, hon, well, if you're sure. Take me home, Jake. I need to get out of these shoes," Mama says to Daddy.

"Take them off now, woman. No one is going to care."

"Jacob Whittaker, I am not walking barefoot outside in public on the day of my eldest daughter's wedding. After how many years, don't you know me by now?"

"Thirty-seven, Bethie. It's been thirty-seven years together since our first date at the drive-in. And I do. But you have to know I'm always going to try to fix whatever you need."

The two of them share a look. A *long* look I have no desire to witness between my parents because ew, they're my parents. Love is one thing. But the look they share? Didn't need to be present for it.

"Have a good night, Mama," I say and give her a quick hug before turning and giving one to Daddy. "Good night, Daddy."

"Night, Lee Lee. Let me know if you need anything," he whispers in my ear and squeezes me a little tighter.

They say their goodbyes to Murphy and Sydney and walk in the direction of the exit as Sydney pulls me closer to her in a hug.

"I'm going to head back to the bed-and-breakfast. I've got to do some work on a case. But if you end up not wanting to stay with me, no hard feelings."

"Syd!" I whisper, heat rushing to my face.

"Just remember what I said—hot girl summer. And text me to let me know for sure," she says before releasing me.

"See ya around, handsome." Sydney blows Murphy a kiss and shoots another wink in my direction before following my parents' path toward the exit.

I'm contemplating apologizing for the multiple interruptions when Murphy tugs me back into him, shifting us back to the slow rhythm of the ballad.

"I'm so sorry about them," I murmur, resting my head back against his chest.

"Don't be. I'd be the same way with my sisters. And my mom too. So, that was Sydney?"

A smile curves my lips.

"That was Sydney. How do you know about her? Cole?"

"Cole."

We say his name at the same time and I glance up, meeting his gaze.

"He says she's like the worst little sister ever. I told him he hadn't experienced Quinn and Riley when they were younger."

His response stretches my smile.

"How old are your sisters now?" I ask.

"Quinn is thirty-three now and married with two kids, and Riley will be thirty next month and is engaged. I can't believe she's getting married in just a few weeks."

"What about you?" I ask.

The song ends but we stay where we are.

"What about me?" he whispers.

"Any marriage plans for you?"

He shakes his head.

"No wife. No kids. I don't see that changing anytime soon either."

"Why not?"

"I made the decision a long time ago. My job is too dangerous to make someone have to face a future like the life my mother had—a widow with three kids."

"A widow?"

A line carves between his eyebrows, his normal hazel eyes dimming to a light brown.

"This story probably needs another drink." He blows out a breath.

It's only then that I realize we're still standing on the now-empty dance floor. A few people still mill around the tables, the bar still open even though the bartenders are packing up glasses and bottles. He interlaces our fingers, tugging me behind him until he reaches the bar.

"A glass of Jameson for me and champagne?" He turns to me and I nod.

Warmth radiates from his hand to mine, frissons of awareness traveling from the connection through the rest of my body. He doesn't let go of my hand when the two glasses are in front of him, passing me mine as he grabs his and nods toward a table.

Only when we're next to the cocktail table does he release my hand. I feel the loss instantly and grip my champagne flute to make up for the tingles still traveling along my palm. He takes a drink from his cup and sets it down, focusing on me.

"Sorry," he says.

"We don't have to talk about it if you don't want."

His smile is self-deprecating.

"I can't give you a buildup like that and not tell the story. I… I'm okay. I can tell you if you still want to hear it."

I nod.

He wraps both hands around his glass, his fingers overlapping, and clears his throat.

"My mom was widowed when I was sixteen. Dad did what he thought was a normal traffic stop for a busted taillight. Turns out the driver had two girls in the back of his car. Human trafficking. The driver of the car shot him and left him on the side of the road." His voice is strained, his gaze focused on a memory instead of right now.

I reach out, laying my hand on the soft cotton of his shirt.

"Oh, Murphy, I'm so sorry."

He moves his opposite hand and covers mine, dwarfing it where it rests against his arm.

"Thank you. It happened a long time ago. This summer it will be twenty years. Wow. Twenty years. It just hit me. Some days it feels like only yesterday. Like when something happens I want to talk to him about."

"I can imagine. How old were your sisters when he passed?" I ask.

"Quinn was thirteen and Riley was ten."

"You guys were so young."

"Mom was a rock star though, raising three kids on her own."

"She never remarried?"

He shakes his head.

"She always said Dad was her *chompánach anam*. Her soulmate."

"And you don't believe in that?" I ask, a pit forming in my stomach, a combination of sadness for the young children who lost their father and the wife who lost her husband. But there's something else there too. A sadness I can't put a name to.

He shrugs.

"I've never experienced it for myself."

"Neither have I, but I still believe in it," I admit. "My parents, Cole and Hannah Grace. How could they be anything but meant for each other?"

"I believe there are soulmates for those who want them. But for me? I won't tempt fate. I won't do that to somebody else."

"Is your job that dangerous?"

"There's always a chance," he tells me and takes another drink from his glass, dislodging our hands.

"There's always a chance with any life. You could be in the safest job in the world and still have something happen. It doesn't change the need to experience life to the fullest. You could get hit by a bus," I argue.

His lips twitch as he fights a smile.

"You're right."

"I know," I grumble.

This time he barks out a laugh and I can't hold back the giggle, the tension and sadness from his story dissipating.

"Is that why you're heading to Nashville? To 'experience life to the fullest?'" he asks.

"Partly."

"What's the other part?"

"It's somewhere new, but not. There I get to be independent. I get to figure out my life without the opinions of others."

He nods like he understands what I'm saying even though I'm not one hundred percent sure myself.

"That makes sense. I'd like to think you and I are alike that way. It's why I'm so excited about moving to DC."

He tells me about DC and what he's already learned from visiting for his interview, his new job with the FBI, and then we talk about places I need to check out in Nashville and the ones he promises to show me before he leaves. We talk about everything and anything. And before I know it, the night has worn on.

"Guess we shut this place down," Murphy says as we wrap up about a trip he's taking in a few weeks to look at apartments.

He gestures to the staff pulling the fabric cloths off the tables while others pack the centerpieces away.

Glancing around, I realize he's right. The other wedding guests still milling around earlier are all gone; the only other people left are the staff doing cleanup.

"It looks like it. I guess we should get out of here so they can finish cleaning up," I tell him.

"Are you going to be okay to drive?" He motions to the two empty champagne flutes in front of me.

It's been almost an hour since my last glass, but even that's not an issue.

"I rode over with Hannah Grace and my parents earlier. But the best thing about small towns? You can walk everywhere. What about you?" I point at the two empty glasses in front of him.

"I'm okay to drive. But a walk sounds nice too."

"Where are you staying?" I ask him.

"The Glass Slipper," he tells me.

"What a coincidence. Looks like we're headed in the same direction," I say, heat radiating through my body as I recall Sydney's words from earlier about maybe staying somewhere else for the night.

He smiles and butterflies unfurl in my stomach.

"I just need to grab my bag from the bridal suite," I tell him and motion to the building.

"I would have thought you would stay with your parents," he says, following me inside the building and up the polished wooden staircase to the room that doubles as a bridal suite for weddings.

The ornate gilt accents and cream color scheme made me feel like a princess while we got ready earlier.

I shrug and look over my shoulder to find him staring at my ass. Or at least I think that's where his gaze is.

I hurry to grab the big tote and light jacket I brought and close the distance to Murphy, the butterflies in my stomach rewarding me by swirling through my stomach and sending awareness in waves of my body. Murphy is leaning against the doorjamb, one ankle crossed over the other. The pose may be casual, but the coiled energy existing in his muscular form is anything but. This room may have made me feel like a princess, but I prefer the butterflies that flutter to life when I'm close to him.

"I am. But my Uncle Mark and Aunt Faith are using my room since they flew in from South Carolina."

"Ready?" he asks.

I nod. "Let's go."

This time he leads the way down the stairs and out the front door into the darkness, the almost empty parking lot proving what we already knew—we're the only ones left at the wedding. A light breeze kicks up and I shiver, but not from the cold. Murphy is the first man I've been alone with—truly alone with—since Zach. Sure, I went on dates when I was at school, but I always made sure we were in public venues or with a large group. It's where I felt safe. Only I feel safer than I ever have before, alone with the detective who helped rescue me once upon a time.

"Cold? Do you want your jacket?" He must have noticed my shiver.

A flush builds in my chest to settle in my cheeks, making the breeze a welcome reprieve.

"No. I'm okay."

"Here." He reaches for the tote and I hand it over, still keeping the jacket tossed over my arm.

We walk in comfortable silence until we reach the property exit and turn in the direction of the bed-and-breakfast.

"It's been a while since I've spent so long just talking. I didn't mean to talk your ear off all night," he says, a tinge of disbelief in his voice.

"Really?"

He nods and we fall back into comfortable silence for a block.

"I keep thinking how idyllic it must have been growing up here," he says, glancing around the dark scenery around us.

The rhythmic chanting of katydids mixes with the chirping of crickets and the gentle buzz of cicadas in the distance and provides a soothing ambient soundtrack for our walk. It's the sound of home.

"It was. Like a fairytale. I don't think I have one bad memory of this place."

"It's a lot different than Nashville."

"Did you grow up there?" I ask.

"Born and raised." His teeth flash white in the darkness, the streetlights casting us mostly in shadow.

"What was that like?" I ask, curious about the younger version of the man walking beside me.

"Different from here. Definitely not the fairytale, but my parents tried to keep my sisters and me protected from the world."

"Oh."

Our fingers graze in the darkness and my tongue ties for a reason I can't figure out. If I were Sydney, I'd have something witty to say or be able to banter. But the easy flow of our earlier conversation is gone. Because I'm not Sydney. I'm me. And I'm admittedly awkward and a little unsure of what to say. Except the words that push at my lips.

No. Anything but that.

I stop and after several more steps he does as well. Light notes of citrus and bergamot tease my nose, and I move closer to him and the heat radiating around us.

His hands lift, running along my bare arms, and a shiver works its way down my spine.

"Everything okay?" he asks.

"Yeah," I say, but just as quickly shake my head. "No."

"Which is it?" The amused curve of his lips is countered by the concern evident on his face even in the darkness.

"I'm fine. But...I have to tell you something."

Abort, abort. This is not the right thing to say.

Right thing or not, I don't want to hold it back.

"What?"

"I…I wasn't sure if you'd remember me. Or if you would even want to talk to me." The admission rushes out of me in one long breath.

"Why wouldn't I want to talk to you?"

"Well, the last time we talked was when you were talking to me about what happened with Zach. I saw you at the courthouse during the trial, but we didn't talk or anything."

A muscle tics in his jaw.

"It still pisses me off he managed to fool everyone. He hurt you and almost hurt Hannah Grace." His thumbs rub the sensitive skin of my inner arms.

I soak in the casual affection of his touch and fight the urge to move closer.

"I'm sure you've seen worse," I tell him.

"It never gets easier." He doesn't acknowledge my statement, and I don't envy him whatever he's experienced that flashes in his vision.

Will that be me at the end of this summer?

My bosses had discussed the types of cases I would be exposed to at length during the interview process for the internship. It was the only hesitation I had when accepting the job. Growing up in this place, and being exposed to something so different, a part of me was afraid I wouldn't be able to do it.

But I still have to try.

He continues to stare at me, thumbs running hypnotic circles and making me want to reach on tiptoes and cover his mouth with mine.

"To answer your question, Leigh, I did want to talk to you. I wanted to make sure you were okay. After…"

"After I was drugged and kidnapped?" I offer.

His hands flex against my arms and tug me closer to him. The possessive quality of the touch has my heart racing in my chest.

"I hate what happened to you," he says. "If I could change it, I would."

"I survived. And it's only part of my past. Not my entire story."

"I can see that."

"It was harder on Hannah Grace. Zach may have been a monster, but he was also her best friend."

She had grieved his loss like he had died. Because in a way, he had.

"You were so young when it happened. I worried about you." I start to lift to my tiptoes, ready to kiss him after standing here staring at each other for so long, but his next words drop me like a rock back to my feet. "All I kept thinking about was my sister. How I wanted to protect her and other girls like her."

And that's how he sees me. Like his little sister.

Clearing my throat, I step back, then turn back toward the inn. He falls into step beside me, and silence envelops the two of us as we walk. It's a mixture of past and present. Of wishing he could see me as something more—a woman instead of a victim he compares to his little sister.

But I don't regret tonight. Spending time getting to know him.

And he'll probably still take over my imagination in private moments with my vibrator. But that's all tonight was.

We're at the bottom of the porch steps of the bed-and-breakfast when he rests his hand on my arm, stopping me from ascending the stairs.

"What is it?" I ask.

"This time it's me who needs to tell you something."

"Okay?"

"I don't want you to read anything into this. But I also know if I don't say something, I'll regret it."

He lifts his hand, his fingers sliding along a piece of hair that had fallen from my updo at some point in the evening. He tucks it behind my ear, his thumb softly grazing against my jaw, close to my lips.

"Okay?" The question comes out as a whisper.

"You're hard to forget, Leigh Whittaker. You were beautiful then. But tonight? In that dress? I haven't been able to focus on anything else. You're fucking stunning, Leigh."

"S-stunning?" I ask, stammering over the word as the moment stretches between us.

"Stunning. If I were a few years younger or you were a few years older..." He closes the distance until his chest brushes my breasts. "I have to keep reminding myself I can't kiss you."

My lips tingle as his gaze fastens on my mouth.

"Can't?"

Why not? I'm absolutely on board with a kiss. With more if it turns into it.

"I shouldn't."

"Shouldn't?" I parrot, my forehead wrinkling as I try to understand what he's saying.

"Little Bit, don't look at me like that."

I try to ignore the zing his nickname gives me. It's not flattering. *Little Bit*. But it wasn't what he said, so much as how he said it. Half groan, half plea. It's his tone that has my core throbbing to life the longer we stand here with him staring at my mouth.

"Like what?"

"Confused. Disappointed. You have a line here." He lifts his finger, running it between my eyebrows.

I huff out a breath.

"You said you shouldn't kiss me."

"Yes."

"Why not?"

"Because I'm old enough to know better. Nothing can come from this. And I respect your brother-in-law too much to lead you on."

What would Sydney do?

Lifting on my tiptoes, I bring my lips millimeters from his.

"What if I want you to kiss me? What if I'm okay if nothing can come from this?"

It's not like I'm looking for a lifetime commitment from him either. Just to enjoy the attraction sizzling between us all night.

His sighs, the breath washing over my lips.

"I can't."

"Well, I guess it's a good thing I can," I murmur and lift my hands to thread through his hair as my lips fasten to his.

CHAPTER 4

MURPHY

Fuuuuck.

At the first contact of her lips against mine, my dick punches against the zipper of my slacks like a horse at the gate during the sounding bell of the Kentucky Derby.

I want the record to reflect I had tried to be good. I had tried to not kiss her. I couldn't control what she did.

And while she may have taken me by surprise at first, after a heartbeat, I take the kiss over. Lifting my hands, I cup her jaw, tilting her head and taking the kiss further. Deeper. My tongue dips in, tasting hers. A small moan works its way from her throat, not leaving the fusion of our mouths, but the small sound does ratchet the kiss up another degree. She presses against me, her breasts crushing against my chest. Fuck, what I wouldn't give to be doing this with nothing between us.

I skim my fingers down her arms, my tips grazing the side of her breasts as I travel south and find her hips to grip the warm flesh beneath the silky fabric. Flexing my fingers, I lift her to the bottom step and ease the slight crick in my neck—Christ, she's fucking tiny—but not breaking the connection between my mouth and hers.

Not until my lungs are ready to burst from lack of oxygen.

Only that burn is enough for me to rip my lips from hers, dropping my mouth to her jawline while I suck air into my deprived lungs. And only long enough to gulp several deep breaths before finding her lips again. This time her tongue finds mine and my hands shift back, squeezing her ass and yanking her lower body into mine. She lifts a leg, wrapping it around my hip and pulling me closer while her fingers grip the fabric at my arms.

A curse echoes through my body, wanting to feel the pinprick of her nails against my skin.

I want it all. To taste the silky flesh so readily exposed by her dress. To find all the hidden places that inspire her to moan my name. What would it sound like on her lips as she falls apart?

You don't need to find out. She's too young for you. She's a good friend's little sister.

Her fingers climb my chest again, and those thoughts skitter away as I lose myself to the sensation of her. Her taste. Her scent. Her touch.

I'm a hair's breadth from asking her up to my room. To take what she so willingly is offering.

It's why I need to break the kiss. To step back.

My fingers flex, unwilling to let her go, and the struggle is real until I can soften the kiss before I break it. It's even harder to put space between us, but I need the cool air that rushes in, bringing with it a wash of sanity and a much-needed reality check.

I was just making out with a woman fourteen years my junior. Cole's little sister-in-law. How would I feel if one of my friends made out with one of my sisters?

They're both either married or engaged.

That logic has no place here.

Not like you were using logic a second ago.

Her eyes blink open slowly, the light on the porch turning them to sapphires. Her lips are swollen, begging for more kisses, and her nipples are pebbled against the bodice of her dress. My hands itch to reach up, to give them the attention they're asking for so prettily.

"Wow," she whispers.

I'll second that thought.

Clearing my throat, I don't say anything. What can I say? I should have stayed firm and dodged the kiss. I shouldn't have put myself—and Leigh—in this situation.

But that horse is already galloping free. Shoving my hands in my pockets, I'm trying desperately not to yank her back against me. To claim her the way my body is demanding. I've done enough.

"Should we..." Her teeth sink into her lush lower lip, and my dick reminds me he's still ready for action. "Do you want to take this inside? Head to your room?"

Fuck. Fuck. Fuck.

Everything in me wants to say yes.

Just because you can doesn't mean you should.

I know this. Which is why when she reaches out a hand, I take another step back. Her expression goes from turned on and well-kissed to confused, that deep line bisecting her brows again and her blue eyes sharpening to focus as she studies me.

Because of me.

And what I was too weak to prevent.

"I...that kiss..." I stumble over words, trying to find the right ones.

I need the blood centered in my dick to come back to my brain to help me find the words I need to let her down gently.

"It was amazing," she says, her eyes lighting up as she reaches for me again.

"It was." I'm not going to lie. That kiss was the best I've had in a long time.

My hands reach for hers before they can connect to my chest and I hold them awkwardly between us. Because if she touches me again, I can't guarantee I'll do what I'm supposed to do.

"It sounds like there's more."

I nod. "I'm older than you—"

"Who cares?" she asks, a mischievous smile drawing my attention back to her mouth.

Focus, O'Connell.

"Not by a year or two, Leigh. There's fourteen years between us."

Her smile fades at the edges.

"Age is just a number. You're attracted to me just like I am to you. We're both consenting adults. That kiss—"

"It doesn't eliminate the age gap. And even if I didn't focus on that, I respect Cole too much to fool around with his little sister."

"He's not my brother," she argues.

"Brother-*in-law*," I correct.

"Why does he get to dictate who I sleep with?" Her smile fades, her hands dropping mine.

Part of me wants to reach back out, to tangle our fingers back together.

But I have to fight that urge.

"I have no plans to settle down—"

"Neither do I. Jeez, you act like this is a lifelong thing versus one night."

Her comment rubs me the wrong way.

Because she's not a casual sex kind of girl.

"You have your whole life in front of you. And deserve more than burning the sheets up for a few weeks before we go our separate ways." The words are hard to get out, but I manage.

"You're pretty sure of yourself," she sneers.

I let the comment slide because she's hurt. Her arms cross in front of her and wrap around her body, the rejection clear.

This is my fault.

Goddammit.

"I...I'm sorry," I say.

"Yeah, that makes two of us." Turning on her heel, she marches to the front door.

"Leigh—"

"Good night, Murphy."

"Good night, Leigh. I'm—"

The front door slams on my apology.

"That went well," I mutter, blowing out a breath as I lean my head back to stare at the star-filled sky.

I'll give her time to cool off and try to apologize again in the morning before I head back to Nashville.

There's no sign of Leigh as I step inside the B and B. It's probably a good thing since it wouldn't take much to break the control I've managed to build around myself. Leigh Whittaker is a beautiful woman. Inside and out.

Trudging up the stairs, I stop myself from checking under other doors, looking for a light to go track her down. Instead, I find my room, unlocking the door and heading for the bathroom to shower.

But the water isn't cold.

Alone in the steam-filled room, I recall the kiss with perfect clarity. I imagine what it would be like if Leigh was here with me. Pretend I was able to unwrap her silky dress and discover the smooth expanse of skin underneath.

Her name is on my lips as my hand wraps around my dick.

Which is going to stay my little secret.

Because as beautiful as she is, Leigh Whittaker is off-limits.

CHAPTER 5

LEIGH

A mix of humiliation and sexual frustration surrounds me as I stomp into the bed-and-breakfast, only quieting my steps on the polished wooden stairs to avoid waking up the owner and her husband.

I half expect Murphy to follow me inside, but when he doesn't, disappointment joins the party as well.

"What the fuck is wrong with me?" I hiss to myself as I walk down the hall to Sydney's room.

I should not be disappointed that the man who rejected me doesn't follow me inside.

"Stupid, stupid, stupid boys," I grumble, the last word leaving my lips as I burst into Sydney's dark room.

But she's not asleep. Instead, she glances up at me, the glow of her massive laptop screen highlighting the red piece of licorice dangling from her lips. Headphones cover her ears, the rock music blaring through them clear from my spot by the door.

I barely stop myself from slamming the door—I'm not at home but in a bed-and-breakfast with other guests—but still shut it with a contained force and yank my hair free of its updo. Sydney drops her earphones to her neck, presses a button on her laptop, and silences the latest album from one of our favorite bands, Just One Yesterday.

"I didn't expect to see you here tonight. You and the detective looked pretty chummy when I left the reception." She closes her laptop and turns her attention to me.

Finally managing to yank out most of the pins holding my hair in place, I shake my head and let my hair drop around me. Reaching up, I massage my scalp with my fingers as I try to find the words to explain it. But since I don't really know how to explain it to myself, how can I explain it to someone else?

I lift my shoulders and drop them with a sigh, all of my anger quickly fizzling to sadness mixed with a little humiliation for good measure.

"There are no words," I tell her.

Reaching over to the side table, she flicks on the light and snags the bag of licorice, holding it out like a chewy lifeline. I grab a piece and grip it between my teeth before turning my back on her and motioning for her to get the zipper.

"There are always words. Lots of them. Try some."

Frustration gnaws on my stomach and I chomp a bite of the licorice, talking around it.

"We were getting along. We talked a lot tonight. About a lot of stuff. Decided to walk back." The dress loosens and I hold it to my chest and step into the en suite bathroom to change into my pajamas.

"So what has you coming in here spitting like a wet cat?" Sydney calls to me.

"He kissed me!" I tug my T-shirt down and stomp back into the bedroom.

"He did? Go, detective." Her little shimmy and the waggle of her brows has the corners of my lips twitching.

"Well, actually, I kissed him. But he kissed me back," I add quickly.

Because that mattered.

Didn't it?

"I bet he's a good kisser. He gives off that vibe."

The residual sexual frustration and tingle in my lips agree with her, but I don't say the words out loud. Instead, she nods as she studies me.

"Definitely a good kisser," she confirms for herself.

"Whether he is or isn't doesn't matter. When I suggested we head to his room, he turned me down. Told me he 'respected Cole too much' and how I wasn't just some one-night stand. Even when I told him I wasn't interested in anything serious. Apparently, he's yet one more person who knows what I want more than I do."

As if I don't have that enough with my parents. As if at twenty-two, I'm not allowed to know what I want for myself. The frustration is starting to boil up again, and the roller coaster of anger and humiliation is beginning to exhaust me.

Sydney rolls her eyes and blows out a breath.

"Ugh." Her voice drips with disgust, and that emotion joins the amusement park ride in my body too.

"Right?"

"That's so frustrating. Worse than mansplaining."

I flop onto the bed, reaching for another red candy.

"It doesn't matter. He didn't want me." The sting of rejection hurts like a bitch, and I chew ferociously on the candy.

Sydney's head pops into my vision.

"Is that what he said?"

"Well...no. He said everything else. I am too young, I'm Cole's little sister—"

"He's not your brother."

"That's what I said!" I say and reach for a third red candy. "He just clarified how Cole is my brother-in-law. And I have my whole life in front of me and deserve more than to burn the sheets up for a few weeks."

"But that's exactly what you need," she says, pacing to her

suitcase to grab another bag—this one of M&Ms—from next to a pile of clothes.

"Try telling him that," I grumble and accept the bag of peanut butter candy-coated goodness when she passes it my direction. "Thank God you have junk food."

Although my stomach is already rebelling at all the sugar mixing with the drinks from earlier.

"Always."

We munch on the candy in silence. I'm in the middle of trying to decide whether I'm more angry or embarrassed when she makes a sound.

"Y'know," she says around a mouthful of M&Ms. "There's something he didn't say too."

"What's that?" I ask.

"He never said he *wasn't* attracted to you."

No, Murphy had never said that. He had even agreed the kiss was amazing. And he had talked about how great the sex would be between us—if only I wasn't fourteen years his junior and Cole's little sister-in-law.

"No, he didn't. I don't think that's the issue, Syd."

"The only issues he's creating are in his own mind," she huffs and grabs another licorice piece.

"It's dumb."

"Oh, one hundred percent."

"So what the hell am I supposed to say to him when I see him again?" I ask.

"Who says you have to? You haven't seen him in over a year."

"He's staying here too," I remind her. "And, even if I don't see him tomorrow, he promised my parents he would check in on me."

Before, the concept of running into him again in Nashville had been exciting. Comforting. A strange mix but one I wasn't mad at. Now? It feels more like I am just another obligation to him.

"Maybe he'll leave before we go down to breakfast in the morning," Sydney suggests.

"Maybe *I* should leave before *he* goes down to breakfast in the morning."

"Why?"

Sydney's question catches me off guard.

"What do you mean why? Because it's going to be awkward as fuck to have to look him in the face after kissing said face off and throwing myself at him as a one-night stand."

"Lord, is it small towns that prevent women having sex-positive imaging or something else?" she mumbles and yanks a strand of hair behind her ear.

"Huh?"

"There is nothing wrong with you kissing him. You were attracted to him; he was attracted to you. Or he wouldn't have kissed you back. There's also nothing wrong with asking for what you want. You wanted him." I don't bother to correct her that I am still attracted to him and still want him. "There is nothing wrong with taking charge of your own pleasure. Be it at your hands or the hands of somebody else. Why should you be embarrassed? You are a consenting adult, you took your shot, and he declined. That doesn't mean you need to slink out of here in the middle of the night like you did something wrong. If anything, he should because he's throwing up excuses for not acting on the mutual attraction. And stupid as shit excuses at that."

"So I, what? Pretend nothing happened?"

She lifts a shoulder and lets it drop, mischief coming to life in the tilt of her lips.

"That's one option."

"What's the other?"

"Doubling down. Flirt with him, tempt him, pursue him until he forgets every reason he shouldn't and realizes how easily he can."

"Is that what you would do?"

"Pffft. No. But for every hot guy who isn't interested in what I'm offering, there's a handful of others who are. I don't waste my time on someone who isn't after the same thing I am."

"So why is that an option then?" My head is spinning with a mix of sugar, possibility, and fear of rejection for a second time.

"Because it's your decision, not mine. To be honest, none of the guys I pick up in LA look like him. Otherwise, I might reconsider. Regardless of what you choose, neither option involves you leaving in the middle of the night."

I hold up my hands.

"You're right."

"That's what I keep telling Sawyer and Cole. As one of my besties, you have an obligation to believe me."

I nod my head seriously until we both erupt in a fit of laughter that leaves us clutching our stomachs.

"I shouldn't have eaten so much junk food," I manage to breathe out, holding my aching sides.

"When you hang with me, you build up a tolerance. Ask Jessie."

"I'm jealous you guys get to hang out with each other all the time since you live together."

"You could always move to LA. Jessie could have her brother find us a three-bedroom apartment."

Not only is Jessie Sydney's roommate, but her older brother, Jax Bryant, is a rock star who pays the lion's share of their two-bedroom apartment rent in a secure building.

It would be so fun. I can picture myself in LA hanging out with Sydney and Jessie. The three of us tackling the big city. But there's a small part of me clinging to the known. To the familiar sights and sounds of Tennessee. I need to see if I can handle Nashville before I take on something more daunting.

"Maybe after law school. I want to finish that first."

"Who said you can't? There are schools in California. Ask Jessie. She's enrolled in a music therapy program at UCLA."

"Maybe." The word comes out on a yawn as I start to crash from the sugar high.

"I'll ask her about it when I get home. Send you the details."

What does it hurt to have more information? Hannah Grace lives in LA. So does Sydney. Would it be so bad to relocate?

"'Kay." I readjust the pillow and Sydney reaches for her laptop again. "Aren't you going to get some sleep?"

She shrugs.

"In a bit. I need to finish something up. But I'll do it without the music. Don't want to keep you up. You were up early this morning to help with wedding prep."

"Too early," I grumble and burrow against the soft fabric.

"Get some sleep. We'll talk more at breakfast tomorrow."

"Holding you to that," I murmur.

It's the last thing I'm aware of as I drift to sleep and dream of the choices I have regarding a certain hazel-eyed detective I'd rather have other types of dreams about.

CHAPTER 6

MURPHY

There were three things I was certain of after a fitful night of sleep.

One, last night was an anomaly. A moment of weakness. That would have no repeats. Leigh Whittaker needs to stay firmly entrenched in the friends column with no more plans—or fantasies—of kissing her again.

Two, she is going to need a cooling-off period based on the level of pissed-off female who stormed inside last night.

I grew up with two sisters. I knew when a woman needed time before an apology would be accepted. It once took my sister Quinn two weeks before she would accept my apology when I accidentally shared her crush on one of my friends with said friend. And the murderous expression on her face then had reminded me a lot of Leigh's face last night.

And three, up until last night I had prided myself on two things—my self-control and my patience. Looks like my self-control finally recognized its kryptonite.

Leigh Whittaker.

I am not going to let my patience become collateral damage. I can wait to talk things out with her. Even if it takes until we are both in Nashville before I try to reach out.

You need a phone number to reach out.

One I don't have, but know Cole will give to me if I ask.

The time apart will not only give Leigh her cooling-off period but hopefully allow me to rebuild some of the self-control that evaded me last night.

I wanted to blame the alcohol. But I hadn't had that much to drink. I wanted to blame the setting, but I had gone to plenty of weddings before without kissing someone I knew was off-limits.

Everything about last night was centered on the petite pixie who made me feel like the sun had come out after a long storm.

Those kinds of thoughts are what got you in trouble last night.

Right. And those are the kinds of thoughts I need to stop thinking.

Nodding my head, I continue until my foot hits the last stair tread. The door is less than twenty-five feet from me when the universe throws two obstacles in my path. The first is the warm, spicy-sweet aroma of vanilla, cinnamon, and sugar. As if on cue, Elle, the owner of the bed-and-breakfast, comes from the hallway behind me leading to the kitchen balancing a large plate of steaming cinnamon rolls, and my mouth waters.

I've never been able to turn down anything sweet, and homemade cinnamon rolls? Suddenly that sounds much better than a cup of coffee and a pastry from the small shop in the town square I spotted when I drove into town.

And second? The echoes of Leigh's laughter coming from the room to my right—the dining room. The sound tickles my ears, my body already turning in the direction before I yank myself back into place, facing the front door.

"Good morning, Mr. O'Connell. Breakfast?" Elle asks, eyeing my ramrod posture as she readjusts the massive plate of cinnamon rolls.

I force my body to relax to a more normal posture and drop down that last step to the main floor.

"No, thank you. I thought I'd go retrieve my car. Get on the road to Nashville."

If she's curious why my car isn't here, she doesn't say anything.

"Of course. I could box one up for you to take with you?" she offers.

My stomach chooses that moment to rumble its approval and she smiles.

"I'll drop these off and get a fresh one out of the next batch while you're out."

"Thank you. I should be back—"

Words fail me, my attention snapping to Leigh as she steps into the doorway. Her blue eyes lose some of their Caribbean sparkle, the color reminding me of a storm-riddled ocean, as the smile curving her lips dims.

I'm only vaguely aware of Sydney behind Leigh. Of Elle moving soundlessly between us once she drops off the plate in the dining room.

"Good morning." I finally manage to get the words out around the lump of awkwardness sitting on my vocal cords. My voice is strained and I clear my throat.

"Good morning," Leigh murmurs.

"Good morning," Sydney replies from over Leigh's shoulder. "Coming for breakfast, Murphy?"

Her question creates an awkward—and frustrating—debate in my body, and it takes more time than I want to decline the temptation of Leigh and homemade cinnamon rolls hot from the oven. But she doesn't deserve to be led on. And that's what I would be doing if I said yes.

"I was actually going to head into town. Time to get home."

Leigh's gaze collides with mine before she shifts her focus.

"Hot date?" Sydney asks, popping a bite of food in her mouth.

Leigh's head turns to look at her friend so fast I would bet she's dizzy now.

"No."

Sydney rolls her eyes and her eyes bounce between Leigh and me.

"Leigh." Her name feels awkward on my tongue, but I force myself to continue. "Can I talk to you? Privately."

Sydney moans loudly as she takes a massive bite of the cinnamon roll in her hand, and my stomach growls again.

I ignore it and wait for Leigh to respond. When it's clear that she's not going to, I clear my throat.

"About last night."

"There's nothing to talk about. We kissed—" My attention snaps to Sydney and back to Leigh. "Sydney knows everything. We kissed. I made the offer for more. You declined. End of discussion."

It's an answer I should accept. Accept and move on. But instead my body tenses with the need to try to get her to understand how hard it was to turn her down last night.

Oh, it was hard last night.

Fuck. That's not what I meant.

"I want to explain."

"There's no explanation needed. I got your message. Loud and clear. What else could be left to say?"

A lot.

What? I was wrong to turn you down last night. I want to be friends.

For the first time in a long time, I'm not sure what to say, and I don't like this uncertainty rolling through me whenever she's around.

But I can't walk away from her either.

And that was what put me in this situation in the first place.

The heat of Sydney's gaze is a laser beam of intensity as she continues to shovel in bites of her cinnamon roll, and the tips of my ears grow warm under her scrutiny.

"I want us to clear the air."

"There is no air to clear," Leigh says flatly.

I should have kept to my plan to give her a cooling-off period. The pissed off radiates from her in the tension of her shoulders, the clipped tone she uses with me.

It's like I'm a stranger to her.

Isn't this what you wanted?

No. I had hoped we could be friends.

I may not be able to kiss Leigh Whittaker despite the memory of her taste still making my lips demand more. But I can keep my promise to Cole and her parents. I can look after her while we are both in Nashville.

"I promised your parents I'd keep an eye on you." Based on the way her mouth tightens to a line, that was the wrong thing to say. "I'd like to show you some of the places in Nashville we talked about last night."

There's a spark—a flash—of interest before she extinguishes it.

"Just…think about it. I'll call you," I say before she can say something else.

I still have zero clue why I'm pushing this. But I can't just go back to the way things were before yesterday.

"You don't have my number. Excuse me." She walks around me and up the stairs, not looking back.

"Leigh." I start to go after her.

"I wouldn't," Sydney speaks up, reminding me she's been there the whole time.

"Why not?" I turn my attention back to her where she's licking cinnamon roll icing from her thumb.

"She told me."

"I heard her," I say.

"Everything."

The way she says the one word has me feeling like a young boot my first year on the force and screwing up something big.

"You screwed up," she says, not needing a response from me.

"Tell me something I don't know."

"She's embarrassed about what happened."

I figured that weighed in somewhere.

"She has nothing to be embarrassed about," I tell Sydney.

"That's what I told her. How if you weren't interested, there would be other fish in the sea."

My teeth click together at her words.

Leigh isn't yours.

"Don't get all caveman. You think just because you don't want to every other guy is going to be the same way? She deserves a hot girl summer."

Two sisters and I have no idea what that even means.

"What the fuck is a hot girl summer?" I ask her.

"I don't feel like explaining it to you. All you need to know is I convinced Leigh to use this summer as one."

Guess I'm going to have to call my sisters on the way back home and ask. If they know. And if they'll tell me. The two questions are exclusive. And I stopped trying to predict their behavior a long time ago.

"You know, you remind me of my sister Quinn," I tell her.

The sass is uncannily similar, and I feel like I'm fighting with my younger sister versus a woman I just met last night.

"I'll take that as a compliment."

"Yeah, Quinn would too." My lips twitch with the urge to smile and I finally release it.

She smiles in return, her eyes staying steady as she studies me for several beats. The feeling is unnerving, like she can see every secret I keep locked away. My mother has that ability. And one of my first sergeants right after graduating from the academy. Mike Jacobs had been my dad's sergeant when he was killed in the line of duty. In a way, it was like my dad was there with me. But Mike could see through me as clearly as if I were made of glass.

Kind of like Sydney now.

I roll my shoulders under the steady scrutiny, nothing to hide when it comes to her—or Leigh.

"You ever think about being a cop?" I ask after several more moments until the sensation of being a bug under the microscope is too much to bear in silence.

She smirks.

"I sort of am. I just use a computer instead of a gun."

The way she says it has my spidey-senses tingling.

"And what did your computer tell you about me?"

"You're so sure I looked into you?"

Forget cop. Sydney could play professional poker.

But so could I.

I lift an eyebrow as my only response and she nods.

"I did."

"And what did you find?"

"You're more than just a pretty face, O'Connell."

Her comment catches me off guard and has me focusing on our conversation, not sure I heard her right and, if I did, how I'm supposed to take her comment.

"Err…thanks?"

"It's a good thing." Reaching into her pocket, she pulls out her phone and focuses on her screen for a minute.

My phone dings with a text.

"You should check that," Sydney tells me, once more glancing at me.

I pull my phone from my pocket, the text message on the screen from a phone number I don't recognize.

UNKNOWN NUMBER

You better be worth her time.

"How the hell?" My head snaps up to find Sydney grinning at me.

How the fuck did she get my cell phone number? I'd taken a lot of pains to make sure it wasn't easy to find.

"It's what I do. That and more. Leigh's important to me. So don't screw it up."

"Screw what up? There's nothing to screw up."

Her smirk is frustrating because it doesn't give away anything. And as a trained detective, I should know how to see beyond what people want me to.

"Something tells me there's more between you than either of you wants to admit. But if you're not worth her time, you'll lose her before you've even begun."

"She's not mine to win or lose," I tell her.

She shakes her head.

"And I don't have the time to explain to you why you're wrong. See you around, O'Connell."

Without another goodbye, she heads in the direction Leigh took earlier and leaves me standing alone at the door to the dining room. I'm not sure whether to be scared, impressed, confused, or all three.

Luckily, I'm saved by the decision when my phone vibrates in my hand with a Washington, DC area code. Stepping onto the porch, I click on the green button.

"O'Connell."

"Murphy, this is Rachel Park."

The special agent in charge of the task force I'll be working on.

"Ma'am. What can I do for you?"

"I got the results in yesterday for some of the background checks. We need to schedule your polygraph, but the vendor will be reaching out to you for that. Just wanted to give you the heads-up."

"Thank you, I appreciate that." Excitement fizzes through my blood. But for the first time, it's joined by something else.

Something I don't want to put a name to, but has everything to do with the woman with golden hair and sea-storm eyes.

"You're still ready to start for us in September? I'd love to have you sooner if NPD can cut you loose."

"I'd love to, ma'am. But I want to make sure I have time to close out the remaining cases I have." Not like my captain has been assigning me any additional cases once they received my notice. But I do still have some that need additional follow-up and notes to add.

"Understood." She gives me more particulars about the vendor and what to expect before we hang up.

When my phone buzzes in my hand, I half expect it to be another phone call from her.

But no.

This is a text that widens a small fissure of hesitation to something more noticeable.

COLE

Hey, man, thanks for agreeing to look in on Laura Leigh while you're in Nashville. Hannah Grace and I really appreciate it and I know her parents are super relieved too.

He includes Leigh's number below his text.

Look in on Leigh.

It's the one thing I'll allow myself to do. That job in DC is calling my name. Eyes on the prize, I can't forget that.

Absolutely. Happy to help.

One problem down. Now I have Leigh's phone number.

But something tells me I have a bigger problem. One more important than anything. Including my new job in DC.

And it involves Leigh Whittaker accepting my apology.

CHAPTER 7

LEIGH

MURPHY

Happy Monday.

Lunch?

My stomach growls as I read through Murphy's latest attempt to "check up on me." I grab the half-eaten granola bar on my desk, my teeth sticking against the hard granola and nearly as hard chocolate chips as I key in my response.

Can't. Sorry

It's not the first time I've turned him down. In fact, our text history is a hodgepodge of him offering to hang out, to show me Nashville, to meet up for food, and my excuses. It's not that I don't want to see him again—he is easy on the eyes, and the memories of the night we spent talking keep trying to make me forget the embarrassment of his rejection after the smoking hot kiss we shared.

The more time that passes, the harder it is for me to remember to turn him down.

MURPHY

I have an appointment in your neck of the woods.

There's a great barbecue place near your office.

Rain check. I have a meeting right after lunch I need to help my attorney prep for.

Putting my phone to the side, I try to focus on the flurry of email activity in my inbox on a Monday morning. Something nobody bothered to tell me when I was looking for internships. That my last summer as an undergrad, as a non-adult adult, had been my last summer of freedom. And I didn't even realize it at the time. Last summer had been a summer of picking and choosing what all I did.

This first month of my summer as an adult has been all about navigating. Traversing a quasi-friendship with the sexy-as-sin detective who keeps trying to connect with me despite every attempt I have made to avoid him. Negotiating Nashville traffic during morning and evening rush hour. Stacks and stacks and more stacks of paperwork. Long hours and alarm clocks.

Clocks, plural.

Because one thing I have learned about myself already? While I have always considered myself a morning person, that doesn't mean anything when the alarm goes off before six.

Speaking of early morning, I stifle a yawn and stand, grabbing my coffee mug and making my way to the break room. I make another cup of coffee for myself and also grab one for the attorney I was assigned to support at the beginning of summer. Lindsay Carter is the assistant deputy public defender for Nashville and one of the best mentors I could ask for. Her ability to articulate her passion for the law makes her the best kind of teacher, and I have spent the last few weeks learning all about being a woman who can succeed in a very male-dominated world.

And despite the early mornings, the traffic, and every other negative thing that tries to pop up, this is still the best experience of my life. The best summer I have had in…forever.

"Knock, knock," I say from her doorway and hold out the mug when she looks up.

Her bright blue eyes are rimmed by stylish frames, her brown hair pulled back in a tidy updo.

"You're a lifesaver," she says, reaching for the mug and humming as she takes a sip.

"Your calendar looked pretty full today. Thought you could use it."

She nods, taking another, longer drink.

"It is. No rest for the weary."

"Is there anything I should know about the meetings you added me to?"

"Most of them are pretty standard. The only one I'm not sure about is our meeting this afternoon. William got a call from Charlie Vanderweel asking to set up a meeting. He assigned it to me since Kenneth was on vacation until today."

William as in William Bailey, the Chief Public Defender for Davidson County.

Sucking my lips into my mouth, I keep my comment to myself. But it seems like Lindsay, as the assistant deputy public defender, does a lot more work than her boss, Deputy Public Defender Kenneth Scott. Lindsay hasn't given me any indication whether that comment would be welcome, and I am only an intern who needs a solid recommendation at the end of the summer for my application with Project Justice.

"Okay." I use the safest response I can.

"I would recommend you take a look at his original case file. It should be in the court legal database."

"It's weird though, right? That he would contact our office when he wasn't represented by us originally?"

She shrugs. "It is. So we'll just have to wait to see what he has to say this afternoon."

I nod. "Okay, I'll take a look and be ready."

She glances at her watch.

"Don't forget, we have our staff meeting in fifteen minutes. Do you have the files of the current caseload?"

Lindsay had given me a stack of file folders last week to review in preparation for today's meeting.

"I do."

"Great, I'll see you in just a few in the big conference room."

She turns back to her laptop, and I head back to my desk and pick up my phone to find another text from Murphy.

MURPHY

Are you avoiding me?

Despite the number of excuses I've given him, he's not outright asked me that question before.

What do I say?

Not exactly?

But today, I really do have a legitimate reason.

No. Just busy.

I take a quick picture of my half-eaten granola bar and send it to him.

Breakfast and lunch today.

My calendar pings, reminding me of the staff meeting, and I grab the folders, my coffee, and a water bottle and head to the conference room to get ready, relegating Murphy into the background so I can focus on work.

The staff meeting runs long, and my notebook is jam-packed with notes when we finish after three hours.

"Have you had the chance to read the Vanderweel file?" Lindsay asks as we step into the lobby.

I'm balancing my now-empty coffee mug on the stack of files, and my pen I brought with me shifts just enough so that I bobble the entire stack, saving most of the files.

"Oh, no!" Several of the folders and the precariously balanced coffee mug crash to the ground, and we both brace ourselves for the shatter of ceramic against the tile.

Fortunately, it doesn't break.

I bend down, wobbling on the thin heels I wore with my black pencil skirt and royal-blue top today.

"Phew," Lindsay says, relaxing next to me. "Here, let me help."

"Ms. Carter, Chief Bailey needs to see you." Another intern sticks their head out of the doorway of our office area, and Lindsays straightens with a sigh.

"Like I said, no rest for the weary," she says.

"Don't worry, I've got it."

Oh, shit.

I recognize that voice.

Embarrassment, desire, and anticipation all flow through my body like a chemistry experiment gone wrong, as if someone was just waiting to open the tap on the emotions I've tried to keep sealed shut since that night.

Polished brown shoes come into my field of vision, as does a strong hand accompanied by the peek of ink beneath the wrist of a dress shirt clinging to the muscled arm like a second skin.

I stand stock straight, hoping the warmth in my cheeks doesn't betray me as I wait for Murphy to finish grabbing the cup and errant file folders before he unfurls from his crouch like a panther rising from the jungle floor.

"Good thing this was empty," he teases, a half smile tilting his lips.

"I can take it." I reach for the mug, and the files in my hands shift again.

"Looks like you have your hands full. I can help," he offers.

The knee-jerk response to decline his offer is on the tip of my tongue, but when my gaze collides with his, the words scatter, the denial dying a quick death in the wake of his overwhelming presence.

I motion to the door on the other side of the lobby and he follows me, flashing his badge at the security guard at the front who acts as our receptionist for entry behind the locked door. I lean my hip where my badge is against the reader on the wall, the door beeps, and Murphy opens it.

"What are you doing here?" I toss the question over my shoulder quietly as he follows me to my work area.

He doesn't answer until we're at my cubicle outside Lindsay's closed office door.

He lifts a plastic bag, and the sweet, smoky smell of barbecue teases my nostrils as he sets my empty mug and the few file folders he had on my desk. My mouth waters and I drop the rest of my files, ignoring the half-empty granola bar wrapper near my keyboard.

"You said you were too busy to go to lunch, but I still had my appointment and this"—he reaches over and grabs the granola bar—"isn't lunch."

He tosses it into the trash can with a clang and hands me the bag. The smells wafting from the container are heavenly, and my mouth starts to water.

"I thought I could pick you up something and drop it off so you ate properly. I wasn't sure what you liked so I ordered the pulled pork, mac and cheese, coleslaw, and cornbread salad. I'd have gotten you a drink too—"

His sweet gesture is making him hard to ignore. As is his presence in my office. And suddenly I'm forgetting every reason I had come up with why we shouldn't be friends.

"Don't worry about it. This is much more than I expected to eat for lunch. I wasn't kidding about having another granola bar."

He produces a water bottle from his pocket.

"It's not cold, but it's wet," he says, mischief lighting a fire in his eyes.

Fuck, he's dangerous with that look. And suddenly the water isn't the only thing wet.

No, no, no.

Only trying to stop my body's natural reaction to him, the chemistry sizzling between us, is like trying to stop the earth from spinning.

I wish it didn't have to be all or nothing. But it's like my body has a switch where Murphy O'Connell is concerned. Either off where we can't be friends or on where I have to fight my attraction to him in order to be his friend. But I can keep those feelings to myself.

Friends.

Friends bring each other lunch. We're being friendly.

"Thank you," I tell him.

"Anytime. There's a fork in there too." He gestures to the bag, and I unpack the Styrofoam containers, the smells growing stronger.

"Where's yours?" I ask, dropping into my chair and opening all the containers as I start to shovel food in my mouth.

If the smells were mouth-watering, the taste is heaven on earth. The pulled pork melts in my mouth, and the mac and cheese is a blend of sharp and rich cheddar.

"I ate there before I headed this direction. I never turn down Urban Barbecue when I'm on this side of town." He leans against the edge of my desk, his presence overwhelming my space. But not in a way that's unwelcome.

"You said you had an errand? For work?" I ask around another mouthful of sandwich.

I can only imagine the picture I make as I devour the food in front of me.

He shakes his head.

"Mom needed me to pick up something for her."

As if he already wasn't a dream come true, the fact he's bringing me food while doing an errand for his mother? It just elevated him another notch.

"You didn't have to bring me food," I tell him, forking a bite of coleslaw.

"You need to eat, Little Bit. Make sure you take care of yourself."

The sweet words are countered by a fucking nickname that makes me feel stabby or bitey.

Stabby. Keep your mouth away from him!

Easy to do when I have delicious food to occupy it.

A gentle smile hovers on his lips, his muscles testing the seams of his dress shirt while his hazel eyes focus on me like I'm the only other person in the world. Despite being at my workplace, it's like he belongs here, and his quiet confidence is the biggest turn-on of all.

It's a struggle to fight that attraction. To focus on the food and not the desire unfurling like a butterfly's wings in my belly.

I do an admirable job. Mostly.

But a small part of me sits up and begs to kiss him again.

And it isn't long before food no longer occupies my attention.

"Thank you again," I tell him. "That was delicious."

"Maybe next time you won't duck my invitation?"

I blow out a breath.

"I wasn't." Today.

But it's as if I say the last part out loud for his benefit.

"And the others?"

Because there had been others. And while working in the public defender's office requires long hours, there were still plenty of other nights and weekends I could have said yes.

Instead, I hung around Hannah Grace's—my—house, absent-mindedly flipping through TV stations until I was tired enough to go to bed.

My computer dings with the reminder of the after-lunch meeting I had given as my excuse this morning.

Saved by the bell.

"I need to go."

"Mm-hmm." The deep rumble of his agreement tickles my eardrums, the sound some secret direct line to my core that throbs in response.

No, ma'am, not gonna happen.

"Can I walk you out?" I ask, proud of myself when my voice doesn't betray anything other than polite inquiry.

Mama would be proud too.

Or maybe not, considering her desire to see me married and settled.

"I suppose I should be going. Since you have your meeting." He says it like he has all the time in the world.

"Don't you need to get back to work?"

He nods, but his gaze remains laser-focused on me.

"I do. But now I can at least tell Cole I've seen you. He and Hannah Grace have been worried."

And there it is. The reminder. This is an obligation. At least on his part.

"I just talked to Hannah Grace and she didn't seem too worried. I don't think they're as concerned as they led you to believe. You don't have to keep checking up on me for them." I try to give him the out.

Grabbing my laptop and notebook, I gesture to get past him. But he takes up so much space—both literally and figuratively—his cologne surrounds me as I brush past him.

"It's not just for them. I meant what I said—about us being friends," he murmurs.

I really, really want that to be true.

And he's given me no reason to question him.

There are only two things making me hesitate.

First, how much of his desire to be friends stems from his promise to Cole, Hannah Grace, and my parents?

And second, how can you be friends with someone you're so attracted to? But how do I explain all this to him?

Try. He might surprise you.

"I—"

"Leigh, you ready?" Lindsay's door opens and she steps into the hallway.

"Yep. Just walking Murphy out now." I'm not sure whether to be relieved or frustrated I'm out of time.

"Great, see you in the conference room shortly."

We follow Lindsay to the lobby and I stop, turning to him while she steps into the conference room.

"Hang out with me this weekend," he says.

"Is that a request or a demand?" I ask, hoping for one more than the other.

"A request. I want to be friends. Will you be my friend?" He accompanies the question with a crooked grin almost impossible to turn down.

"I...I'll think about it."

His smile dims, but he nods.

"I'll hold you to that."

A shiver works its way down my spine with the determined set of his jaw as he says those five words.

"Thank you again for lunch, Detective," I say and turn to head into the conference room.

"I meant what I said, Leigh Whittaker," he calls after me.

I have no doubt he did.

"Fucking pig." The venomous words are a low growl, echoing through the lobby, and the hairs at the nape of my neck stand on end.

CHAPTER 8

LEIGH

I twist around, seeing another man in the lobby who wasn't there before. Murphy nods toward the conference room and I head quickly into the room, spinning around to watch out the door, my heart racing.

"My goodness, what was that?" Lindsay asks, standing and shifting to where I'm watching from just inside the door.

Murphy is standing in front of a man wearing baggy jeans, a T-shirt, and a flannel jacket despite the heat outside. His beard is grizzled, hair standing in every direction. Gone is the kind-hearted detective who kept me calm at the hospital as I waited for my sister to wake up. Gone is the tempting, tattooed god I've been fighting my attraction to. This Murphy is all steel and granite, his hazel eyes hard as he fixes his stare on the man in front of him. Their words are too low for me to catch, but the body language is obvious—Murphy is on guard.

"Oh." Lindsay breathes the word next to me.

"Do you know who that is?" I ask her.

She shakes her head.

"Maybe he's here to meet with someone else," she suggests.

"Not anymore."

As we watch, Murphy escorts the other man toward the exit, waiting inside as he leaves and three other men in suits enter. The tension in Murphy's face tightens impossibly more as he and the taller of the three men meet face-to-face.

The shorter man says something to the Theo James look-alike who smiles at Murphy before following the other two toward the conference room. The three men catch us staring and we step back from the door, heat traveling to my cheeks at being caught. Even without a mirror, I have zero doubt they resemble a cherry-red tomato.

Lindsay recovers first, her face taking on her professional demeanor rather than the interested woman watching what had just happened in the lobby.

"Gentlemen, please come in."

My attention darts toward the door where Murphy still stands, his hazel gaze locking on mine and creating a shiver of awareness despite the length of the lobby between us.

"And you are?" The Theo James look-alike stands in front of me, hand at the ready.

Holy crap, I've been so preoccupied with Murphy I missed introductions. The look-alike, other two men, and Lindsay all stare at me as if questioning my ability to speak.

Mentally shaking my head, I focus on the man in front of me.

"Leigh. Leigh Whittaker."

His hand glides along mine, the graze of his fingers skimming my palm in an almost ticklish sensation before he confidently grips my hand.

"Leigh, a pleasure. Charlie Vanderweel."

If I thought his smile was nice before, the one he gives me up close is lethal.

"Mr. Vanderweel, nice to meet you."

"Charlie, please. My father, Charles, and our attorney, Marvin Crosby."

We all shake hands and I follow Lindsay's lead and take my

seat next to her on our side of the conference table. Once we're all seated, she flips open a thin file and shuffles through the meager contents.

"Mr. Vanderweel, I'm not sure I understand the reason for this meeting. We have no record of representing anyone with your last name—"

"You didn't," the other attorney jumps in.

Charlie gives the other man a look and holds up a well-manicured hand, drawing attention back to him.

"You may or may not recall I was wrongfully accused and convicted of murdering my fiancée three years ago. I served eighteen months in jail until the real killer was caught and confessed to her murder."

Now I really wish I had read through Charlie's file. I don't know what I was expecting, but it absolutely wasn't the bomb he just dropped. Hopefully my surprise doesn't register on my face.

Lindsay's expression doesn't change, and it's obvious from her continued focus on Charlie she's aware of the case.

"I do have to admit, I recognized your name from that murder case. I'm so sorry about your fiancée."

He nods his head.

"I appreciate that, thank you. Selene was a beautiful soul taken from us far too soon."

My heart breaks for the distress crossing his features, the sudden downturn in his eyes as he speaks about his late fiancée.

"I'm still confused by the desire to meet with us?" Lindsay asks gently.

"I was fortunate I had the money for private legal counsel to continue the investigation until the real killer was found. And I know many who use your services are not afforded the same opportunities."

"Our resources are stretched—"

"It's not a judgment, Ms. Carter. Just an observation. One I'm hoping to remedy. I'd like to create a fund that would allow those who use the public defender's office and are wrongfully accused to be able to continue their fight. I am willing to donate an original three million to the fund, my father has also decided to donate an additional five million, and Marvin and his firm offered to bring the fund up to an even ten million dollars."

Lindsay sucks in a swift breath and my own heart pounds in my chest. I haven't been around for long, but even I know that's a lot of money for the financially burdened office. If that's true, this project would rival what Project Justice does nationwide for just Nashville.

"I-I…that's very generous of you," Lindsay finally says.

Charlie's dark brown gaze swings to me before he turns back to Lindsay.

"Obviously it may mean hiring additional staff. Or rededicating some current resources," he says.

Lindsay clears her throat, recovering some of her poise.

"I will need to confirm with Mr. Bailey that we can accept your generous donation and put the fund into action."

If so, I wonder if I can request to work on the fund while I'm here. This experience would be the perfect addition to my application, and I write the reminder to ask Lindsay later.

"Of course, of course." Charlie nods, spinning a shiny gold pen in his hands.

"And how will we determine who to allow access to the fund? What happens if they are still found to be guilty? What—" Lindsay asks, clicking her pen now poised above her notebook.

"You'll find most of the answers to any questions you may have in here." Marvin passes over a stack of papers Lindsay places on top of the file folder.

Is Charlie Vanderweel for real? He was wrongfully accused and wants to donate money to help others like him.

The rest of the meeting is brief, every question Lindsay asks either given a very vague response or she's directed back to the paperwork she already has. But it's the other attorney who is doing most of the talking. Charlie has gone silent, leaning back in his chair, fingers poised in front of his lips as he studies me. But that's not the right word.

Stares.

The attention is somewhat unnerving. The back-and-forth conversation fades, and I struggle to pay attention to them while being the center of Charlie's focus.

My lips twitch with a smile I can't quite contain despite dropping my attention to the notebook beneath my fingers.

Lindsay stands, followed by Mr. Vanderweel and his attorney, catching me off guard as I stand. My ears grow warm and I hope they're not as red as they feel.

How did I miss the end of the meeting?

"Gentlemen, I'll be reviewing this with my boss and getting back with you on this proposition."

"Of course."

We all shake hands and Charlie lingers in the doorway with me.

"I look forward to working with you, Leigh."

"Don't you think that's a bit premature?" I ask him.

"There's something to be said for wishful thinking. And admittedly, we may have just met, but I get this sense I've known you forever."

I don't have the same impression, but keep that thought to myself.

I follow him out of the conference room.

The three walk off and Lindsay's posture relaxes.

"That was...interesting," she says after a beat.

I nod.

"You had no idea that's what they wanted to meet about?"

"It's not often people schedule a meeting and want to give us money. It's typically the other way around. I'm going to go see if I can get on William's calendar to discuss this." She lifts the folder.

"Okay."

"How about you make several copies of this so we can take a deep dive into it?"

I take the folder from her, just realizing I managed to leave my notebook behind when I followed Charlie out.

"Can do. I'll just grab my notebook and go make copies."

"I'm going to go get with William's admin and get on his calendar."

Lindsay heads back to the office area and I step back into the conference room.

Grabbing the forgotten notebook, I glance up, jumping to find Murphy filling the doorway.

"What the hell was that?" He steps into the room, closing the door.

"I'm sorry?"

What the hell is he talking about?

"Why were you meeting with Charles Vanderweel? That guy is a psychopath. He murdered his fiancée."

"What I was meeting with him about is none of your business. And he is not. And they found the real killer."

He snorts and drags a hand through the short strands at the side of his head.

"Some homeless drug addict they paid to take the fall. All the evidence was there. It was him. I worked on that case."

"First of all, how could they pay him if he was in jail? And what do you mean you worked on the case? You should know better than to talk to me about any of this."

"I wasn't primary on the case, and I'm not sharing anything from the case file. And you didn't represent him. The walking, talking windbag he was with today did."

"It's still none of your business," I tell him, stepping closer.

The fact I need to crane my neck to meet his gaze at this angle just makes me more irritated with him than I already am.

"You're not meeting with him again," he growls, crossing

those muscled forearms across his chest as if he's laying down some law I'm required to follow.

In the famous words from a movie I watched with my sister when we were younger…as if.

"You are not the boss of me, Murphy O'Connell. I am doing exactly what you do—my job. And if you don't like it, well, too damn bad. You don't have to like it and you certainly don't need to stick around and watch."

Stepping around him, I hold my head high and walk through the door and across the lobby, not breathing again until I'm at my desk.

Just who the hell does Murphy O'Connell think he is anyway?

CHAPTER 9

MURPHY

At some point are you going to be able to communicate with Leigh without pissing her off?

I made progress earlier.

One step forward and a mile backward isn't progress.

I know better than to follow her though. Much like the last time she stormed away from me, now is the time I need to keep my mouth shut.

Even more than I need Leigh to believe me.

Charlie Vanderweel is dangerous.

Dropping into the nearest chair in the now abandoned conference room, I huff out a breath. Very few cases still get to me after over a decade on the force.

Dad's. For obvious reasons.

Leigh's, because I had become friends with Cole and Hannah Grace by extension.

Uh-huh. It has nothing to do with the beautiful blue-eyed blonde who just stormed off.

But then there was Selene Gordon's story. No matter how many cases I had seen, that one still bothered me.

The notoriety. The media coverage as one of Nashville's

prominent families came into the spotlight in a way no one expected.

Charlie Vanderweel is a violent, psychopathic killer. He is a trust fund baby on steroids. Which is why Leigh needs to stay the fuck away from him.

How someone like him could come from an upstanding citizen like his father never failed to surprise me. Vanderweel Senior is known for his community involvement and donations to local charities and first responders. The two couldn't be more opposite if they tried. But as good as Vanderweel is, he turned a blind eye to his son, and the two worked to get his conviction overturned.

And when they succeeded, they released a murderer back on the streets.

Leigh needs to stay far away from Charlie, whether she wants to believe me or not.

Pulling out my cell phone, I scroll my contacts until I find the one I'm looking for.

I put the phone to my ear and wait for the connection.

"O'Connell. Long time no talk to. What's up?" Cole answers the phone, his slight southern drawl at odds with the speed of his LA speech.

"Cole. How's married life, man?"

"It's good, great even. I'm actually hoping to cut out early today and take my wife out to dinner." The smile in his voice is evident, and my own lips twitch.

"I'll keep my fingers crossed for you then. And I won't keep you too long."

"I'm hoping you're calling with news about Laura Leigh."

He probably doesn't want to hear how I managed to piss her off again.

Again? It's not like he knows you pissed her off before. Or why.

Nerves swirl in my belly.

Yeah, because you kissed his little sister.

Fuck off. She isn't his little sister.

Close enough.

I clear my throat. "Yeah. I ran into Leigh today. Brought her lunch since she was too busy to break away."

"Is she doing okay? Nashville is such a change from Mistletoe Creek."

"She's fine."

You spelled pissed off wrong.

"We really appreciate you checking in on her."

"It's no trouble."

Because being around her is easy. It's the fighting not to kiss her again that is harder than I want it to be.

"Hannah Grace worries about her. We all do."

"I'm keeping my eye on her. Some of the people she runs into here... well, I'm sure you know they're not always innocent."

The image of Zach Nolan sitting in the courtroom as I testified in his case flashes through my mind.

Another psychopath.

Maybe I need to double-check my sisters' pepper spray canisters again.

Although both of them are married now with husbands who could do the same, it's my job as their big brother.

Cole huffs a humorless laugh.

"You don't have to tell me. I still don't quite understand why she took that job with the public defender's office."

"She's a smart woman. I'm sure she has her reasons."

She had shared so many of them with me already.

Cole snorts. "That's exactly what she told me the last time we talked and I asked her."

I open my mouth to tell Cole about Charlie Vanderweel—my intent behind calling him—but second-guess myself. I don't want to worry him when I'm more than capable of keeping an eye on Leigh. I've honed relying on my gut to a science. And my gut is telling me Cole doesn't need to know about this.

At least, not right now.

"I'll make sure to keep an eye on her," I tell him.

"It's a big city."

I bark out a laugh.

"I'm well aware. But the house is in a quiet neighborhood, and you said the neighbor across the street kept an eye on Hannah Grace?"

"Braeden, yeah. He and Hannah Grace still text, and he told her he's keeping an eye on Laura Leigh as well."

Jealousy flares like a hot spike in my chest. Cole continues before I can respond.

"But he bartends most nights. And every time we talk to Laura Leigh, she's at home watching reruns."

Liar, liar, pants on fire.

Leigh had said she'd been busy every time I tried to see her.

But now I am hearing the real story.

And that somehow reinforces how much I intend to look out for her. Not Braeden, not anyone else. Me.

"I promise you, I'll look after her. Like what I would want if I was farther away from my sisters."

I swallow hard with the realization of how soon I'm going to have to leave watching after my sisters to their husbands. And everyone will have to look after Mom.

But for the time I have left, I will look after everyone. Leigh included.

Even if you don't think of her as a sister?

That doesn't matter.

What I think isn't going to see the light of day. I'm not going to act on the chemistry still bubbling under the surface. It doesn't change the fact that Leigh is fourteen years younger than I am.

She is still the little sister—at least by marriage—to someone I consider a friend.

Last, and by no means least, I am never planning on getting

married or settling down. And Leigh has her whole life in front of her.

"Thanks, O'Connell. I appreciate it." Cole's phone beeps. "Shit, this is Sydney. I gotta grab it for a case she and I are working."

"Grab it. I'll talk to you later."

"See ya."

The phone beeps and I pull it from my ear and check the time.

I'd like to head home given how close it is to the end of the day, but the mountain of paperwork on my desk isn't going anywhere unless I go back to work. And I promised Captain Overton I would clear my desk to the best of my ability before I leave at the end of August.

It's not like I have anything or anyone waiting on me tonight.

Or most nights.

My molars grind together as I attempt to ignore the dig.

So what if most of my nights are spent wrapped up in paperwork at my office? Or with it spread over the coffee table in my living room? The only one who ever comes to my apartment is Mom. My apartment is my sanctuary. Hookups are conducted elsewhere—sometimes her place, sometimes a hotel, sometimes somewhere a little more public. But never at my place.

But tonight, I have an itch to head back to the office. I want to look at the notes I have on the Vanderweel file. Seeing him again was enough to spark that interest.

Seeing him with Leigh?

Fanned that spark to a flame. One I can't ignore.

Pocketing my phone, I step into the lobby, heading quickly for the door to head back to the office.

"Officer."

I pause and turn toward the voice, barely containing the groan when I realize who it is.

Kenneth Scott is the reason most cops consider the public defender enemy number one. We spend days, weeks, or months on a case only to have lawyers like him do everything they can to undermine our hard work, to release criminals despite the evidence we compile.

"It's detective," I remind him. Even though I know he knows. We've met each other in the courtroom a time or two.

The Barbie boyfriend look-alike narrows his eyes at me.

"Do you have business here?" Kenneth asks.

"Is that any business of yours?" I counter.

"It is when you bully my client out the door. I had a meeting with Mr. Ellis. A legitimate one. After speaking with our receptionist when my client didn't show up, I understand you showed him the door."

Fuck, I'd forgotten my earlier run-in with Vinny Ellis. Between trying to chase Leigh down and then coming face-to-face with Vanderweel, he had completely escaped my mind. Not that I'll let Kenneth Scott know that.

Crossing my arms over my chest, I stare at the weasel-eyed attorney in front of me.

"Did your receptionist share with you that your client approached me with vulgar language?" I ask, keeping my voice calm.

He tsks and shakes his head. "First amendment protections apply, Detective. Unless you'd rather not follow the laws you're charged with upholding?"

And this is why I try to avoid this asshole at all costs.

"You may want to advise your client if he wants a good perception in court, he'll want to clean up his mouth."

"And you may want to recognize this is not your property and unless you have a legitimate business reason for being here—"

"I was meeting with Leigh Whittaker." The words are out before I can stop them.

"Ah, yes, Ms. Whittaker. She's one of our more promising interns..."

The look on his face turns from angry to contemplative to

lecherous in the span of a heartbeat, and suddenly I want to rip him limb from limb.

"She's a friend of mine." The words are innocent on the surface, but my tone is meant as a warning.

Instead he looks amused.

"So not a legitimate reason to be here. Stay away. Otherwise..."

My temper snaps at the chain I have it tethered by.

"Is that a threat?" The words are practically a growl.

"Temper, temper, Detective. Merely a reminder. One if you don't want to follow, I'm sure I can get your captain to help remind you of as well."

He doesn't scare me. And even if he does call Captain Overton, she'll say the same thing—this guy is the stereotypical lawyer. There's no love lost between us and him.

"That's what I thought," he says, taking my silence for agreement. "Goodbye, Detective. I trust we won't be seeing you outside of the courtroom."

"You'll definitely see me if you're representing Vinny. You would think by now you'd be tired of representing scum, but I guess water always finds its level."

I don't wait for a response, but walk outside, the door drowning out his sputters as he attempts to fire back.

Asshole.

Not only do I need to protect Leigh from Vanderweel, but from douchebags like Kenneth too.

Because I'll be damned if either of them touches her. Not on my watch.

CHAPTER 10

LEIGH

Friday night and I'm just now pulling out the thick manila envelope I've been adding to all week. Not only do I have the case file from when I pulled it for Lindsay, but different news articles, pictures, anything else I could find about Selene Gordon's disappearance, her death, and even her relationship with Charlie before her disappearance.

The TV is on a low volume—background noise—as I lean back into the couch cushions and scan through the first page.

Selene Gordon hadn't been from Charlie Vanderweel's world. Charlie—and his dad—were from old money in Nashville. The Vanderweels *were* Nashville. Selene, on the other hand, had grown up in a middle-class family. With her blonde hair and blue eyes, her resemblance to Hannah Grace and me in the picture is striking enough I take several moments to study it. The article it accompanied is one that detailed her disappearance. There are so many pictures of her and Charlie posing together at charity and other social events. The two of them might as well have been models. Or Nashville royalty living a fairytale after he met her while she was working for his father's investment firm. When he proposed, the entire city was anticipating their wedding.

But their story didn't have a happy ending.

Reaching over, I grab my wine glass, taking a drink as I start the account of her disappearance.

A week before the wedding, Selene had disappeared. No note. Phone and purse left in her apartment. Charlie had reported her missing when he showed up at her apartment for a date and found her door unlocked, her phone on the kitchen counter.

No one had heard from her.

A missing person's report was filed.

The wedding day came and went.

Poor Charlie.

With a sigh, I lean my head back against the couch. I couldn't imagine living through something like that.

"Courtney, will you accept this compass as we continue to search for love?" The question pulls my gaze to the TV, and I watch the contestant on *Searching for Love* hug the recipient of one of his compasses.

With a sigh, I refocus on the papers in my lap.

A tip line had been set up, and while there were hundreds of thousands of tips, with extra officers assigned to the case, plus a quarter of a million dollars offered by the Vanderweel family for any information leading to her being found, there was nothing.

It wasn't until almost a month later that an early morning paddleboarder called 911 to report a body washed up on shore near the East Bank Landing. And Selene's case had been moved from missing persons to murder once the coroner confirmed her identity with the remains.

Tears burn my nose and I blink the building moisture away. Selene was my age when she was found dead. Goose bumps ripple down my arms and legs as I compare her situation with mine. The biggest difference is Hannah Grace had rescued me. And no one had rescued Selene.

Her official cause of death was first ruled an accidental drowning, but why would Selene have been out without her cell phone and purse? Why would she have been near the Cumberland River wearing a pink dress better suited for a high-end restaurant and her date with Charlie?

The case was destined to remain a mystery. Until a neighbor returned after three months abroad. He reported hearing Selene and Charlie arguing in her apartment the day before she went missing.

I fidget against the cushions, trying to reconcile the cool, charismatic man in the designer suit I met earlier this week with the one the neighbor described.

With the neighbor's information, Charlie's alibi about being home alone was called into question. And his answers to questions about his relationship with Selene—that he had talked to her an hour before he showed up at her apartment, and he had found her door unlocked—changed. His new answers said that he had talked to her on the way over to her apartment and the door to her apartment had been open. The difference in stories led to more digging.

GPS and phone records were pulled. Charlie hadn't called Selene the day she had disappeared. And his car had been near the East Bank Landing six hours before it showed up at Selene's apartment complex. Which was enough for a warrant to search the car.

I suck in a breath, holding it as I read through what was found in the trunk.

Selene's hair, a pink thread from the dress she had been found in, and a single high-heeled shoe Charlie tried to explain as her having left behind after a trip they had taken the previous weekend.

Charlie Vanderweel was arrested for second-degree murder, and it took the jury less than two hours to find him guilty. Closing my eyes, I can picture the courtroom. Charlie standing there next to the attorney I had met, hearing the verdict being read.

When I open my eyes, I'm surprised to find the show replaced with an early morning infomercial. The contents of the folder are scattered along the floor, the manila folder itself tucked under me where I'm curled up on the couch. I sit up, rubbing the sleep out of my eyes and trying to remember how I ended up on the couch.

The last thing I remembered was reading about Charlie's conviction while *Searching for Love* played in the background. My body aches, my muscles tight as I try to figure out what woke me up besides the darkness that had followed me into dreams.

I was running from something. Terrified.

"It was just a dream," I mumble to myself, grabbing the remote and turning off the TV.

More like a nightmare.

But one fuzzy enough I don't fully understand it. The same sort of fuzziness from the night when I woke up on a dirty mattress to my sister's panicked face. Stumbling to the shower, I try to clear away the cobwebs of sleeping on the couch and the remnants of the dream, before dressing in a tank top and shorts. Before I leave, I grab my camera bag out of the hall closet and the small can of pepper spray, pocketing it before grabbing my keys. The small metal canister has been a staple in my stocking for the last few years, not that I minded. In fact, just having it gave me a little more confidence in facing a world where the likes of men like Zach Nolan still existed.

Yellow rays wash into the hazy mix of pink, purple, and blue as the sun crests the horizon. This morning's early morning wake-up wasn't planned, but I'm not going to let it go to waste either. Today is Saturday, and I am going to explore through the view finder of my camera. It's creative therapy.

Is it coincidence I pull into Centennial Park?

The park Murphy kept texting you about.

I shake my head, dispelling the reminder, and pull into the parking lot. He may have told me about the park in several of his texts, but that wasn't why I had chosen it. One of the online photography boards about Nashville had recommended it.

My photography class had come after Zach, after his trial, and I had found something I hadn't realized I'd been missing—creative therapy. Peace in the quiet moments to myself. It was a welcome reprieve from the near-constant anxiety after Zach kidnapped me. Not that I remembered much thanks to the Ambien and alcohol. But taking pictures soothed the anxiety in a way nothing else could. While some photographers preferred sunset, I had found sunrise suited me better. The sights and sounds as the rest of the world woke up, waiting for my camera lens to find it.

There are other cars in the parking lot this early, and some of the tension between my shoulder blades eases. While the pepper spray and camera both help, I also like to know I am not alone.

I start off down a shadow-dappled path closest to my car, the cool air a tease when the temperatures are going to skyrocket later today. The shadows change shape as I get farther down the trail, the light filtering through less and less until the way the light envelops the green of the foliage catches my attention—and that of my camera lens. I stop several times while two women run past me with a nod, exercising in the still cool air. A little farther along the trail, I indulge in the affection of an overweight goldendoodle and his patient owner before I'm alone again to wander the winding path.

The silence reminds me of the stillness in the mountains surrounding Mistletoe Creek. For the first time since coming to Nashville, it feels like home. Taking a deep breath, I sigh it out and round the sharp bend in the path.

The view in front of me freezes me in my tracks where two trails converge to one on a sharp bend.

"Oh."

The word is a whisper, not enough to do justice to the vista of the sunrise reflecting off the small body of water, the Parthenon in the park rising like a sentry from the sea of manicured green bounding the water in front of it.

I kneel down as I lift my camera, changing several settings until the image becomes clearer through the view finder. Until it's exactly what I want. Holding my breath, I depress the button in an attempt to capture the magic enveloping me in this exact moment. I'm five or six shots in and nowhere close to being done when I'm tackled sideways into the still damp grass, my breath whooshing from my lungs and making it impossible to say anything, let alone scream. I'm a tangle of limbs with someone else, my heart pounding against my breastbone as the fight-or-flight reaction holds firmly in the fight reaction. My elbow raps sharply against the ground, pins and needles traveling my entire arm as I struggle to get free.

The sound of my own heart hammers through my ears, making it impossible to hear anything as I continue to struggle. Fear and adrenaline fight for supremacy, and it's as if time is both sped up and slowed down at the same time. Like I'm fighting molasses as I gain control of my limbs.

Fuck. Run. Get away. Move. Do something. Anything.

It takes more time than I want to gain control of my legs, a deep curse wrapping around me when my knee connects with something solid.

"I'm so sorry. Are you okay? Here, let me help you up."

My brain is too busy panicking for the words to register, and it's only after several breaths that the throbbing of my heart clears from my hearing, allowing me to process the repeated apology.

"Leigh?"

Another breath and I recognize the brown eyes searching mine as he leans over me, surprise and concern changing the timbre of his voice.

"Charlie?"

He reaches out a hand to help me up. An aftershock of adrenaline surges back through my body, and I'm not sure whether to take off running or stay stock-still. I'm still trying to decide when his hand grasps mine and helps me up. As soon as I'm standing, I drop his hand, unsure of who the person in front of me is.

The grieving almost widower? The angry fiancé who murdered the person he loved the most? Someone entirely different?

I'm not sure, and my muscles lock as I try to quickly excuse myself, glancing around to see if anyone else is close by.

My stomach sinks as I realize not only are we alone, but we're shielded somewhat by the trees and the way the path curves where we're standing.

"What are you doing here?" he asks.

A lie that I'm meeting someone perches on my lips, but his next question scatters the words.

"I didn't break your camera, did I?" He motions toward the camera hanging around my neck.

Shit. I'd forgotten all about it. The camera had been a present a few Christmases ago from Mom and Dad—neither of whom would be happy to learn it got broken while I was alone in a park. Lifting it up, I study it carefully, relieved when there are no obvious signs of damage.

"No, I think I took most of the impact," I tell him, the pins and needles receding from my arm at last.

"I'm so sorry. I didn't see you. Usually no one is out this time of morning when I jog."

Only then do I realize he's dressed in athletic shorts and a T-shirt, a pair of well-worn sneakers on his feet. Some of the tension eases from my shoulders, but a small part of me still wonders if this was truly an accident or on purpose.

Yeah, because he's been watching you for the last week, saw you leave for the park at the butt crack of dawn, and just so happened to have exercise clothes for jogging in his car. Get over yourself.

Easier said than done. Especially given what I had fallen

asleep to and the remnants of the nightmare still rattling around. But the least I can do is apologize, because I had been leaning down, not visible for anyone who wasn't looking down.

"No, it's my fault. I was kneeling down for a picture."

"You're a photographer?" he asks.

"Just for myself. You run here?"

"I do. Almost every day. It's one of my favorite places in Nashville." His words help relax some more tension, and I can take my first full breath since being full body tackled to the ground.

"Do you live around here?"

Nosy, much?

He shakes his head.

"I used to. It's a great park to jog. Selene must have thought the same thing because this is where we met. She was jogging there"—he points to the other side of the water—"when we met and I proposed there." He points to the larger area of green near the Parthenon. "I'm sorry, you didn't ask for my life story."

The words tell me one thing, but grief is visible in the hollows of his cheeks, in the slight hunch of his shoulders despite his ramrod-straight posture.

Has he ever talked to anyone about what's so obvious to me?

"Maybe it's weird I still come here—"

"Not at all. I…it's sweet," I say at last, landing on the closest word.

And I mean it. Because Charlie Vanderweel doesn't strike me as a killer. There's a deeper emotion at play. One that breaks my heart to witness.

"It's just…where I feel closest to her still." He shrugs, and the struggle to swallow his grief is visible.

"You still miss her?" I ask.

Instead of chastising me for my obvious question, he nods, his chest shifting as he inhales and exhales deeply.

"She was my person." The words are simple, but filled with so much emotion, it's tangible in the air around us.

"I'm so sorry for your loss." The words are automatic, but feel trite in the wake of the grief he still wears around him.

"Thank you."

"I should probably get going. Let you get back to exercising," I say, moving back to the path to follow it closer to the Greek look-alike building.

He follows me, reaching out a hand, his fingers brushing the elbow I rapped on the concrete earlier.

"Wait. I…I should apologize about the way I acted Monday. It was incredibly rude."

The mental picture of him I had painted—the arrogant, rich, frat boy from the other day—melts in the light of this different person. He's shy. Unsure of himself. Awkward to a certain extent. And I'm having trouble reconciling all the versions of him—our initial meeting, how the media painted him, and this morning—into who he actually is.

But something in my gut tells me this uncertain version of him is closest to the real him.

"You weren't rude. I'd say you were assertive, but not rude," I assure him.

One side of his mouth twitches with a smile.

"You look a lot like her. Selene," he explains. "And have several of her mannerisms. It was a bit of a shock. Still, no excuse. I am sorry if I gave you the wrong impression."

The impression I had gotten was he might be interested. And for no good reason, my ego deflates. The attention had been nice, but it wasn't like I was interested in him either.

Murphy's serious hazel gaze flashes through my memory, and I force the image into the box it came out of. I need to focus on Sydney's words about a hot girl summer instead, but not with Murphy. And not with Charlie Vanderweel either.

"You didn't give me any impressions, wrong or otherwise."

I smile at him, and this time his smile stretches across his face before he nods to my camera.

"Have you gotten your picture of Taylor's bench yet?"

"Taylor? Like Taylor Swift?"

He must hear the adoration in my voice.

"Swiftie?" he asks.

"Um, duh. Now what about this bench?"

He laughs. "The mayor dedicated a bench to her the last time she had a concert in town. Selene was a massive fan too. I think it would have been her favorite spot in the whole park. Want me to show you?"

I hesitate, still not one hundred percent sure I want to go somewhere in a park I don't know with someone who may or may not have murdered his fiancée.

Make up your mind; either he did or he didn't.

"Um..."

Three other people whiz by us on bikes, heading in the direction he had pointed to a moment ago.

"People wait to see it for hours. I tend to run elsewhere to avoid the crowds."

I perk up at the word crowds, but still check my pocket for the thin canister, feeling it roll in my fingertips.

"Lead the way." I gesture for him to precede me, falling into step beside him.

So he does. More and more people join us the closer we get to Taylor's bench and her willow tree, and we navigate the growing crowd as he asks me about my photography. I grab my pictures, and he recommends several other spots he thinks I might like for pictures as we reach the edges of the crowd.

"I should let you get back to your run," I tell him, the temperature climbing higher around us.

He wipes his temple and nods slowly.

"Yeah. Probably. I'm heading that direction," he says, gesturing in the direction of the parking lot where my car is parked.

"Okay."

"Can I walk you back to your car? If you're heading out," he offers.

The early morning light is already melting under the heat of the day and it's not even eight a.m. yet.

"I am, but don't worry about it. I can find my own way back."

Maybe it's my past, maybe it's Charlie's past. But I don't trust him. Not yet.

"Humor me? Please." The words are light, but the expression in his eyes—a mix of regret and concern—have me biting back the polite no.

There's another small group on the trail ahead of us, and their presence is the final encouragement I need to agree.

"Okay." I let my camera hang loosely around my neck and tuck my hands in my pockets, my fingers gripping the pepper spray.

Just in case.

We follow the trail back to the parking lot and we land on the subject of the Wrongful Conviction Fund and my interest in Project Justice. By the time the trail ends back at the parking lot—where a lot more cars surround mine—my fingers loosen, releasing the security blanket. Charlie Vanderweel didn't murder Selene Gordon. He couldn't have. I wouldn't become friends with a murderer. Not after Zach.

"Thanks for walking me back. You probably want to get going before it gets much hotter," I tell him, a bead of sweat rolling between my shoulder blades.

"Yeah. I'll end up just running home to finish my workout."

"You want a lift?" I offer.

It must be a good sign when my conscience doesn't rebel as soon as the words are out of my mouth.

He shakes his head. "Can't work out unless I do the work. But thanks for this morning. I would say it was nice running into you—"

"Not literally," I say.

He chuckles.

"No, not really. Even if it gave us the chance to get to know each other a little better."

"That part was nice. I don't know many people in Nashville. People at my office. My neighbors."

"Just be careful. It's a big city," he tells me, and I'm reminded of Murphy's similar words.

"I will."

"I'll see you around, Leigh."

"Bye."

He heads off in the direction of a different path, and I put my camera back in its bag in the backseat. My spine tingles, the sensation of not being alone overwhelming me.

"Forget something?" I ask, backing out of my car, the smile on my lips fading when I realize Charlie isn't standing beside my car.

Instead he's facing away from me, running farther down the trail.

But the sensation of being watched still has my hair standing on end, and I rush into the driver's seat, locking the car doors.

"No more true crime before bed," I mumble and crank the ignition, the cool blast of air conditioning creating gooseflesh along my skin.

But even as I drive out of the parking lot and make my way home, the sensation of being watched doesn't fade.

It grows stronger.

CHAPTER 11

LEIGH

"Can I get an iced caramel macchiato with an extra shot and extra caramel, please?" I ask the person at the coffee counter in the courthouse first thing Monday morning, stifling a yawn.

She's the one I see all the time when I'm here. Probably the person I see the most often.

Libby.

Is she the owner?

I'm just about to ask her when another voice interrupts.

"I've got it." The rich baritone is accompanied by an inked wrist I know well, as a credit card exchanges hands without my participation.

Spinning around, I nearly plow into the impressive chest of Murphy O'Connell. He's wearing a green button-down shirt, a tie loose around his neck.

Why is he here?

"You don't have to," I tell him and try to ignore the flutter in my body being this close to him creates.

Traitorous body. It's not like I've heard from him since last week. I shouldn't still be attracted to him.

But you are.

As if to prove my point, the corner of his lips twitches and lifts, a cross between a smile and a smirk. Damn him. I doubt he realizes just what that look does for my panties.

"I know. I want to. Consider it a peace offering."

"Peace offering?"

But I already know why he's making the offer. The anger is residual, a sticky residue left behind since so many days have passed.

He had warned me away from Charlie Vanderweel. Who wasn't dangerous. Even if I did get the sensation of being watched off and on throughout the weekend. It was only when I was at the grocery store and running other errands, other people all around me. I made sure to keep other people around me, staying inside the house with the doors locked when I was home.

I was relieved when the sensation hadn't followed me to the courthouse this morning.

"I almost called you this weekend," he says to me before turning to the barista. "Dark roast, please?"

His smile has the same impact on her it initially did on me—he dazzles her. But she manages to ring up his coffee and grab it before working on my order.

"Why?" I ask, slightly grumpy at being ignored while the barista makes eyes at Murphy.

How obvious could she be?

Can you blame her?

"I wanted to apologize." He continues to stay focused on me, ignoring the coffee worker, despite her attention staying focused on him.

"Apologize for what?" I ask. Sighing, I shift my weight from foot to foot, already regretting the high heels for today's court appearance for one of Lindsay's clients.

"You already know. I realize it too. I overstepped. I don't have any control over who you choose to spend time with." His tone may be full of resignation, but the way his jaw clenches tells me what he really thinks about the idea—he doesn't like it. His gaze focuses on the board next to the coffee counter listing the drink options instead of meeting mine.

"No, you don't. I'm curious, though, what made you realize that?"

I get my drink and blow on the lid before gingerly taking a sip.

He shrugs, the move nonchalant enough I want to stomp my foot against the polished marble floor.

"My sisters."

The comment I had locked and loaded to fire at him for his indifference scatters.

"Your sisters?" I ask, taking a big swallow of my drink and nearly burning myself on the hot liquid.

He gestures toward the exit, but I point in the direction of one of the courtrooms and he falls into step beside me.

"I realized if I did to them what I tried to do to you, I'd have likely been on the receiving end of a fist to the gut or a knee to the groin. Or both, knowing Riley."

I like his sisters already.

"Oh, really?"

He hums his agreement and takes a drink from his cup before responding.

"I may not like it and I can give you my reasons why—"

"You don't have to like it. But you will respect it."

"You're right. In the grand scheme of things, it is your choice."

His gaze collides with mine, the hazel depths holding genuine contrition and something more. I can't quite name the emotion, but it makes me feel like he sees me. The real me. Not the young girl I was when I met him. But like I'm an equal. Like he does actually respect me.

It's a heady sensation, a warm buzz fizzing through my blood that isn't the result of my sweet coffee.

"So you came to the courthouse to tell me all this? You couldn't just call me up this weekend?"

"Serendipity. I had planned on calling you later today. I was supposed to testify today. But the perp took a plea deal from the DA."

"Is that what this is for?" I ask, reaching out and tugging on the loose tie.

A fire glows deep in his gaze, and my lips go dry at the somewhat hidden expression. On my next blink, the desire I know I saw is gone, replaced by one of resignation.

"When we testify, they like us to look professional," he explains, making air quotes around the word professional.

The light green of his dress shirt covers up more of his tattoos than others, as does the fact that it's buttoned all the way up. His khaki-colored dress pants do little to hide muscular thighs. In short, he looks like sex on a stick. Exactly like he has every other time I've seen him.

How is it fair?

"What are you doing here?" he asks, interrupting my ogling.

"Lindsay has a prelim hearing this morning. She wants me to get some exposure to the courtroom side of things."

A shiver works its way down my spine and I hold it off, taking another sip of my coffee as I glance around, the sensation of being watched having returned. For a moment, I consider telling Murphy about it. About how it's come and gone all weekend.

But I have no proof. Just a rock sitting in my stomach. I move closer, basking in the warmth he exudes. If he notices, he doesn't say anything.

"What'd they do?"

"Who?" I ask, taking another sip and doing another covert sweep of the coffee area and lobby. Nodding in the direction of the courtroom, I start to walk away, trying to keep my gait slow when I want to rush away.

"The perp. The one—"

"Perp sounds terrible. Like you already know they're guilty," I say, not hiding my frown as I stare at my cup.

"What would you call them?" His question is tentative, almost a whisper.

Like he doesn't want to disrupt whatever truce we've established over a few sips of coffee and a short walk from the coffee shop to the courtroom.

"By their name. Or... they're clients, I guess." I shrug the shoulder not weighed down by my large bag that doubles as both a purse and a briefcase.

He makes a noncommittal sound.

"We just see things from different perspectives. For example, I could see you as my enemy." He says the words so matter-of-factly, I nearly drop my coffee.

"What? Why?" I knew relationships between attorneys and police officers were contentious, but enemies?

"You help free the people we arrest."

"But sometimes those people are innocent," I argue, meeting his gaze again. "Life isn't always as black and white as you want it to be. Sometimes there are reasons things happen, situations spiraling out of control. Not every crime deserves the same consequence."

"You're right," he says.

His admission surprises me.

"The world is full of gray. Sometimes people are innocent. Sometimes there is more to the story. But the odds of that are rare, Little Bit."

Gone is the sensation of being watched, anger and frustration blocking everything else out.

"I hate that nickname," I grind out between my teeth.

He barks out a surprised laugh that echoes off the hallway around us.

"All of that and that's what you focus on? My nickname for you."

Heat climbs into my cheeks.

"I heard everything else too. But the nickname is terrible."

"I didn't realize how badly you disliked it."

"It makes me stabby," I admit.

"Well, we can't have that, can we?" he asks, still smiling.

"You could call me Leigh," I offer.

"I like having my own name for you. Everyone calls you Leigh." The words are innocent enough, but the intense way he studies me, the fire banked within his golden gaze, creates a responding heat in my body that has nothing to do with embarrassment.

Danger! This line of thinking did not do you any favors before.

Memories of the rejected kiss pop up.

I groan, as much to dispel the memories as in response to his statement.

"Not everyone. Most people still call me Laura Leigh. Like my sister. And Cole. My parents. Everyone except who I work with. They call me Leigh. So does Sydney."

"So your friends call you Leigh?" he asks.

I nod. "Yes."

"Am I your friend, Leigh?" I try to ignore the way his lips wrap around my name.

Try and fail.

My breath stalls in my lungs. I want him to say it again.

Are we friends?

"I...I'm not sure. Do you think we are?" I turn the question back around on him, wondering what he'll say.

The smile he had moments ago was nice. This one? This one is devastating to my sanity.

"I want to be your friend." He says the words slowly, testing them out.

Like I told Charlie the other day, I don't have many in Nashville. When Sydney and I had talked about me moving to Nashville, we had talked about me going out more, experiencing the city. I had thought I would have other interns to go out with. Maybe form some friendships there.

But the office is more cutthroat than I anticipated, and not one of the interns seems interested in anything more than office politics and getting a leg up for more internships or even associate opportunities.

I had been spending more and more time bingeing *Searching for Love* on my couch. Maybe with a friend I would have something else to do. I could have someone to check out the city with. And what better person than one from Nashville?

But what about how hot you find him?

Maybe it's the wrong choice, maybe it isn't. But I want to be friends with Murphy. Attraction and all.

"I could use a friend," I say, as much to myself as to Murphy.

The embarrassment of the rejected kiss, the desire I still feel for him? I can shove those to the side. No, not can. Will. I *will* shove those away.

"How about I show you the city then? As a friend. Do you like pool?"

"Pool?" I ask.

My brain is whirring, trying to keep up with the conversation while also trying to force the haze of attraction into a box entirely too small for such big emotions.

"Yeah, you know. The game with the balls and sticks." One corner of his lips kicks up in a smile at his double entendre.

"Oh, yeah. I used to play with balls and sticks all the time." If he's going to use innuendo, so can I.

He sucks in a harsh breath, caught at his own game, before he releases it.

"How about we hit up my favorite pool hall on Friday? What do you say? Pizza and pool?"

It beats another night binge-watching *Searching for Love* on TV. Thank God one of the streaming services has all the previous seasons. If I am not going to live my hot girl summer—

and it is looking more and more like that isn't going to happen —I can at least live vicariously through the reality dating TV show.

"Okay."

"Six o'clock. I'll pick you up at your place." Neither statement is a question.

"I'm at Hannah Grace's," I remind him.

"I know."

"How—"

"Leigh, there you are. We start any minute now. Are you ready?" Lindsay pokes her head out of the courtroom and my attention whips to her.

Shit. Shit. Shit.

How is it when I'm with Murphy, everything else disappears?

"Yeah. Sorry, I went to grab coffee and ran into Mur—Detective O'Connell," I explain, taking a step away from Murphy and closer to the courtroom.

"Detective." Lindsay nods.

"Counselor." Murphy's attention is only on her for a heartbeat before he shifts back to me.

"Sorry, I have to go," I tell him.

"No apologies. I need to head into my office. I'll text you."

"O...okay."

He turns and walks back down the corridor, and I can't help but drop my attention to the way his dress pants hug his ass like a sports car on a mountain road.

Something tells me you're not supposed to admire the asses of your friends.

"That is one fine-looking man. Is he single?" Lindsay whispers, opening the door to the courtroom.

I shrug. He was at the wedding.

"I'm pretty sure he is." Otherwise, how would his girlfriend feel about him inviting me to play pool?

"Even better," she says with a wink.

A possessiveness builds in my chest, and I want to stomp my foot and tell her no. He's mine. But he isn't.

He's a friend. Not my boyfriend.

With a glance at her watch, Lindsay slides a professional mask into place. "Ready?"

I take another drink of my coffee. I wish I could shift into professional mode as fast as she just did.

"As I'll ever be."

Only as much as I try to pay attention, I can't help but replay my conversation with Murphy earlier. Are we friends now? Can we be? The awkwardness from the kiss is gone. Even if the attraction is still there. At least on my part.

But I can ignore that. I've been attracted to other guys without acting on it.

Ever been friends with one you found as attractive as Murphy?

But that question isn't fair. Murphy isn't the same caliber as most of the frat boys I had been exposed to in college. The attorneys at the office and the ones I run into in the courthouse aren't much better. And there is a strict no-fraternization policy with other members of the public defender's office.

None of your other "friends" create a four-alarm fire in your body like the chemistry you have with Murphy.

Doesn't matter. It can't. I can ignore it.

Whatever you say.

Luckily, my lack of attention isn't noticeable to anyone but me. The preliminary hearing full of different motions is through relatively quickly and I am familiar with the different requests, having helped Lindsay prep the motions.

While she heads to another meeting, I go back to the office. By the time I get back, I've lost count of how many times I waffle back and forth.

Murphy is my friend. We're not friends. We cannot possibly be friends and I keep my sanity.

And for now I'm leaning firmly in the friends camp.

I don't care what people say. Guys and girls can be friends with each other. Sydney is friends with Cole and her boss, Sawyer. Hannah Grace had been friends with Zach. Although theirs was not the healthiest example to look at.

I'm sure there are others if I think about them.

Does my budding friendship with Charlie count?

Turning the corner into my cubicle, I set my bag down when my phone rings.

"Hello?"

"Hi, Leigh. It's JoAnna. Kenneth was wondering if you had a few minutes. He had something he wanted to talk to you about." JoAnna is Kenneth's paralegal and also the middle-aged woman who on-boarded all the interns when we first started.

But why does Lindsay's boss want to meet with me? I've been assigned to Lindsay since I started and had no interaction with Kenneth until now.

"Did he say what about?" I ask, curious.

She clucks her tongue. "I'm sorry, he didn't."

I think about having her ask. But can I?

Can you really turn down the request?

"Okay. I'll be right there."

Kenneth's office is on the opposite side of the building next to Chief Bailey's office, and nerves jump in my belly as I make my way from my work area to the other side of the building. Have I done something wrong?

JoAnna gives me a soft smile as I approach her desk. The blue tunic-style top she's wearing highlights her blue eyes, her copper-red hair styled and shellacked with the hairspray still lingering in the air around her.

"Go on in, honey. He's expecting you." Her words are gentle, encouraging, like she can spot the tornado of emotions on my face.

Taking a deep breath, I release it, then return her smile with a shaky one of my own.

"Thanks."

With a step toward the door, I twist the handle and walk in, hovering in the doorway while he wraps up a phone call. Lindsay and Kenneth's polar-opposite personalities are reflected in the decor of their offices. Lindsay's reflects a warm, inviting environment. Kenneth's is all dark, heavy wood. Intimidating.

Does he mean to do that?

His wide desk takes up one end of the room, with a table and three chairs located closest to the door. In between the two formal setups is a less formal seating area, a couch and chair in cream leather occupying the space between the two.

"Ahh, Leigh. Thank you for coming to see me. Why don't we have a seat?" He walks out from behind the desk, gesturing to the couch and chair.

His dress shirt and pants have sharp lines ironed into them, not a wrinkle daring to make an appearance. His blue eyes are sharp, belying the wide smile, and there's not a hair out of place on his head. He reminds me of what Barbie's boyfriend would look like if he was older.

Maybe the hairspray scenting the air was his, not JoAnna's, and I have to suck my lips into my mouth to hide my smile. He's still standing, gesturing to the small seating area, and I take the chair while he sits in the corner of the couch closest to me, leaning forward, his elbows splayed on his knees.

"JoAnna said you wanted to talk to me?" I ask.

"I did. I wanted to give you the good news. William approved the Wrongful Conviction Fund. We're able to get started on it next week."

"We?" I had figured since Kenneth didn't take the meeting that Lindsay would be overseeing the project.

"Lindsay's plate is overly full right now. William wants me to handle it to ensure the project gets the attention it deserves."

There's an undercurrent in the condescending way he says that, creating a defensiveness that has me biting back the comment forming on the tip of my tongue in support of my boss. But there's a power play and I have nothing I can say to the second in charge of the public defender's office.

Right?

"Oh." I want to say so much more, but hold myself quiet.

Anger courses through my blood, but so does sadness. I had been excited to work on a project like that. Had hoped I would get the chance because I knew how good it would look for my application with Project Justice. I slouch, unable to hide my disappointment.

"I was actually hoping you'd be willing to work on the team I'm putting together for the project. Seeing as how you met with the Vanderweels and their attorney when they came in."

"Really?" I lift my gaze to his face and wish I hadn't.

There's something more there than just the professional conversation we're having, and a pit forms in my stomach. He's not asking me because I was in the meeting.

There's a glittering in his eyes that wasn't there before.

One almost...predatory. Like a snake trying to catch prey.

Ew.

Fuck.

I want to be wrong. I want this to just be me misunderstanding the situation. But after Zach, I honed my intuition. And the vibes Kenneth is giving off are reminiscent of the five-alarm blares of the drunkest frat boys at parties I attended with my sorority sisters.

"I've noticed you, Leigh. You have a bright future ahead of you. I know you're still in law school, but what are your plans after you graduate?" He leans back in his chair, crossing his foot over his knee. The charcoal pants strain at the seams, the dark blue shirt making his eyes bluer. But instead of warmth, they chill me to the bone.

"I...I haven't decided yet," I say, crossing my legs at the ankle as tension starts to lock my joints.

There's a power disadvantage here. One I'm at the losing end of.

I want to get up and walk away, but what will that mean for my internship if I do?

"You're at Tennessee, right? A Volunteer?"

Surprise ripples through me, followed swiftly by unease. How does he know where I go to school? Had Lindsay shared that with him?

"Did you go there too?" I ask.

He laughs, but the sound isn't genuine.

"Roll Tide." He shifts forward again.

I lean back, more to the opposite side of the chair, trying to put more distance between us and to turn the conversation to something more superficial than my career.

"We're rivals," I say, mentioning the contentious relationship of college football and hoping he focuses on that.

He smirks. "Only on the football field. I think you've been a great addition to our team. And once you finish law school, I'd love to see you come back here."

Why? I want to ask the question, but recognize the situation I'm in right now.

"Really?" I try to keep my tone light, and a small part of me is excited by the prospect of having a job directly out of law school.

One my parents have nothing to do with.

One in a field I want to focus on.

But there are strings with this job. And that's becoming crystal clear.

"Of course it will depend on passing the bar and your grades, but something tells me those are foregone conclusions." He reaches out and squeezes my knee, invading my personal space.

My leg jumps, but he doesn't move his hand.

"We should grab a drink sometime. Discuss some of the classes you'll have and a continued internship while you're at school."

My skin crawls as he continues to lightly grasp my knee, his fingers almost rubbing, but not enough to be certain if I'm only imagining it. I know some of the attorneys will go to happy hour together. Lindsay even shared there are networking expectations for full-time employees. But I haven't gone, despite being invited a few times.

His index finger shifts against my leg, and revulsion ripples down my body as the alarm bells sound off again. The urge to stand is off the charts, but I stay seated.

Why? Get up. Walk away. This guy is a creep!

Clearing my throat, I glance down at where his hand rests against my skin, hoping he gets the clue.

He doesn't.

"There's a happy hour on Friday. At Cue Craft. We could talk more about your future then. A few of our junior associates will be there, and you can pick their brains about their experiences with law school."

I don't think I've ever been gladder to have plans in my life.

"Oh, um, shoot. I already have plans."

His hand tightens painfully on my leg and I stand, dislodging it. Finally.

Where's my pepper spray when I need it?

You shouldn't need it at work.

He rises from his seat, closer to me than I had expected given where we were seated.

"Plans?" His breath is a mix of coffee and something else. Whatever it is, it's foul.

A mix of garlic and onion and I try to hold my breath and put some distance between us.

"Mmm. I've been so busy with work, I haven't had the chance to explore the city and it seems like an amazing place to live." My words run together and I try to add a little more space between us without looking too obvious about it.

Kenneth has been anything but subtle. His attraction is as

clear as the windows making up two sides of his office. But I'm not interested. Job or no job.

"There are a lot of things to show you," he says.

Yuck. My stomach somersaults at the hidden meaning of his words, the coffee I had earlier threatening to make a reappearance.

"That's what Murphy says too," I say, trying to yank the conversation back into safer territory.

"Detective O'Connell? How do you know him?"

"I met him a couple of years ago. He actually helped my brother-in-law with a case his security firm handled. He's a really good friend."

Kenneth's face morphs like he tastes something sour.

"Maybe you'll be able to grab drinks another time then," he says, his gaze narrowing as he studies me.

Not if I can avoid it.

"That sounds…" I stop myself from using the word terrible. "Sure. I, um, I should get back. I have some work I need to do after this morning's court appearance."

"Of course, we'll talk soon. It's been a pleasure, Leigh."

Why does it feel like there's a veiled threat to his words? On the surface, they seem innocent enough, but the way he says them creates a fight-or-flight response I've never experienced at work before.

His attention centers on my chest despite the fact that the top I wore today doesn't show any hint of cleavage. Instead it goes all the way up to my neck.

I'm not sure what I say, but I don't breathe again until I'm back at my desk.

Kenneth Scott, with his intimidating behavior, scares me. But the more I analyze the situation, the more I wonder how much I really have to tell anyone. And if I say something and he's able to talk his way out of it? I've effectively blackballed myself out of my internship and experience that would look good on my application for Project Justice. I want that job more than anything else.

I spend the rest of the day debating with myself, studying Lindsay—a woman in a man's world if there ever was one. Both of her bosses are men. I've never met Chief Bailey, but if he's anything like Kenneth, I wonder if she's dealt with the same sort of behavior I experienced today.

I want to ask her, but a small part of me is embarrassed to ask. Theoretically, I know I should. I've seen enough in the news and learned enough in my classes so far to know I should be able to ask. But something is keeping me silent.

I need to think about it more, maybe even talk to Sydney about it later and get her advice. She'd never be caught in a situation like I had found myself in. Mind made up, I spend the rest of the day in my cubicle or with Lindsay, not wanting to be caught alone—and off guard—by Kenneth again.

Counting down the hours until I can go home and shower.

CHAPTER 12

MURPHY

"O'Connell!" Captain Overton's voice echoes through the office as I walk through the door.

I speed up, not wanting to risk having to be called a second time. No one wants the second time. Not by Captain Overton.

Poking my head in her office, I find her where I expect her—fuming behind her desk.

"Captain?"

Her icy glare meets mine as she drums her fingers on a manila folder on her desk.

"I get you've already accepted another job, O'Connell, but do you think you could do a better job with the paperwork to close out your remaining cases?"

"I'm sorry?" I ask, stepping into her office and closing the door.

But not before catching looks—some sympathetic, some amused—by my soon-to-be-former peers.

"I just got my ass handed to me by the DA. They took your word for it that this case was an easy conviction. The fucking Deputy PD got the case thrown out because your report had errors in two major sections." She tosses the file on her desk, and I crane my neck to see the name.

V. Ellis.

"What? I triple-checked everything before I dropped it on your desk last week. This case was a slam dunk."

"Not according to Kenneth Scott. Or to the judge who threw out the charges this morning."

"Then Scott fucking tampered with it. Cap, I promise you, the report was fine when I put it on your desk," I say, lowering my voice when I realize I'm yelling now too. "What errors?"

Snatching up the folder, I scan through the contents until I find the sections where two of the numbers have been changed and so has Ellis's middle initial.

"What the fuck? I know Ellis's middle initial stands for Daniel. No way would I have put the B."

"But you did, otherwise, how did it happen? Nobody else touches the report from the time I get it until the DA goes to court."

"What about the electronic file?" I ask.

"I checked it while I was on the phone with the DA. It matches what's in here." She taps her finger on the envelope, and any hope I had deflates.

"Michelle," I say, using the captain's first name. "You've known me for over ten years. I don't make these kinds of errors."

Her expression loses some of the angry edges, verging on contemplative. The anger is still there, but less than it was a minute ago.

"Not normally, no. But I know with the move coming up and trying to clear your open cases—"

I shake my head, slashing a hand through the air to stop her.

"No. Even then. I know how important these are. Ellis needs to be off the street for good. This was going to be the way to keep him off them for a while." I groan and toss the file back onto her desk and drop into one of the chairs across from her.

"Well, he's free again. And soon to be somebody else's problem," she tells me, shaking her head.

"He should have been put away the last time after he assaulted his girlfriend," I manage to grit out through clenched teeth.

Fuck. There were times I hated being a first responder. Showing up at the run-down apartment complex of Ellis's girlfriend was one of them. The bruises on her body, the state of her apartment—it made me want to track Ellis down so I could teach him to pick on someone his own size. I had found him that night, right on his favorite bar stool in the dive bar he frequented. But it had been to arrest him with the promise he was going away for good.

Only my definition of good was different than the law's apparently. The bastard had been bonded out—by his girlfriend—the next day.

"Difficult to do when she recants and won't testify. The DA wasn't going to touch that one. You and I both know it despite wanting a different outcome." Her resignation is just salt in the open wound of Vinny Ellis walking free when he should be behind bars.

"This is bullshit and you know it," I grind out, the anger still bubbling through me.

"What do you want me to do, O'Connell? Go to the DA and tell him the report mysteriously changed? That you know Ellis's middle name is Daniel and your D looks like a B?" She snorts. "They'll laugh their asses off and never take me seriously again."

"Cap—"

"Just double-check your work. Make sure it's accurate, and hand shit directly to me from now until you leave. Then I'll review it before turning it in."

I haven't had my work reviewed at a detailed point in almost ten years, and the thought that it's happening now, just before I leave, grates on my last fucking nerve. But I know better than to argue with Captain Overton about this.

"Fine."

"Dismissed."

She nods toward the door and I open it, stepping out into the area and nearly running into one of the less experienced detectives. Spencer Aldridge is a brown-nosing punk who got put in our precinct because his dad is friends with the mayor. He is a smug little asshole and grates on my nerves, and he is one of the reasons I am glad to be leaving.

"Is she free?" he asks with a nod at Overton's office.

"Yeah. But, word of advice? You may want to give her some time to cool off."

He brushes past me, bumping me out of the way.

"Why would I take advice from you?" he mumbles.

"What was that?" The receding anger rises back to the surface.

"I'll take my chances," he sneers and steps into her office.

My knuckles crack as my hands clench, the tension in my skull radiating down my neck and shoulders. Now is not the time for paperwork.

Bypassing my desk, I head for our locker room and toss on my workout gear.

The big bag taking the brunt of my frustration has a hundred different faces. Today? It's Kenneth Scott and Vinny Ellis. And I don't stop until my arms throb and hang spent next to my body.

"Fuck." I blow out a breath, leaning my head against the bag that still swings faintly from my latest onslaught.

The job in DC can't start soon enough.

But when I leave Nashville, Scott and Ellis are still around. To do God knows what.

It's not your fight once you leave.

So why does leaving sound like they've won?

The neighborhood is just as quiet as every other time I've

been here, although the last time I was here was when Hannah Grace and Cole were still around. Fuck, that feels like a lifetime ago. More than one after this week.

Striding up the walkway to Leigh's, I make note of the surrounding houses while an ice cream truck's tinny soundtrack carries on the slight breeze. Ringing the doorbell, I wait, shifting my weight from foot to foot as I take in the quiet suburban neighborhood. The muffled sounds on the other side of the door stop, the solid wood opening after another pause.

The sight in front of me makes me forget how to breathe.

Her blonde hair is down, curled slightly, and my fingers itch with the urge to bury themselves in the silky waves. She's wearing a blue V-neck T-shirt, the color bringing out the deeper flecks of blue in her eyes, the fabric showing off her breasts in a way that has my mind going to a no-fly zone—one with more than friendly activities involved to occupy our time. She's paired the shirt with a pair of tight stone-washed denim jeans and boots. She's temptation in a tiny package, and I have to remind myself of that to keep my smile friendly. To keep from backing her inside the house and taking what I want.

"Hello," I manage to get out.

"Hi. Do you want to come in? I just need to grab my purse."

"Sure."

I'm not one hundred percent sure I trust myself despite the nod I give her. But I still follow her in, closing the door behind me. I step forward and she retreats, a coughing fit starting as she bends at the waist.

"You okay?" I ask.

"Wrong pipe," she manages to croak out.

She recovers and shoots me a smile before retreating to the kitchen. Christ, this is more awkward than my first date, and I second-guess my decision to keep our plans as my gaze strays to the frozen screen on TV.

"Is this *Searching for Love?*" I ask, pointing at the screen when she steps back into the room.

She groans.

"Sorry. I forgot to shut that off." She turns, finding the remote to point it at the screen until it goes dark.

"Compass ceremony, right?" I ask.

Instead of roses, the person searching for love hands out compasses to prospective contestants.

"Yeah..." She says the word slowly, not entirely sure about my line of questioning, and a smile twitches at my lips.

"Max's season?" I ask and her eyebrows shoot up.

"You watch *Searching for Love?*" Her question comes out as a squeak.

Heat travels to the tips of my ears and I duck my head.

"I—my sisters got me hooked a few years ago. We even created a dinner night around it. We had it at Quinn's house and called it dinner and drama."

"Awww, that sounds adorable. You never hosted?"

I shake my head.

"Nah. Quinn had my first niece and nephew already so it was easier to just watch at her place."

Now the level of noise would be too much to try to watch anything not involving animation with a seven-, five-, and two-year-old.

She locks up the house and I walk her to the passenger side of my SUV, opening her door and helping her in.

The heat of her body mingles with mine and I take a deep breath, instantly regretting it as the temptation of whatever perfume she wears teases my nostrils.

Once she's settled, I close the door softly behind her, using the momentary reprieve to remind myself what we're doing isn't a date. There's no kiss at the end of tonight. No invitation back to her place. But since my body and imagination don't get the memo, it's not long enough.

"How many nieces and nephews do you have?" she asks, turning that mesmerizing blue gaze on me until I feel like the center of her world.

I settle into the driver's seat, gripping the steering wheel to avoid reaching for her.

"Quinn has two girls now and my nephew and is pregnant with what I'm told is my last nephew from her."

The tension riding piggyback along my neck and shoulders after a hellacious week lessens, becoming more distant as I focus on our conversation, a welcome distraction from the work weighing me down.

"Sounds like a big family."

I nod, backing into the street.

"It is. And Riley hasn't even gotten started."

With a jolt that tightens my fingers on the steering wheel, I realize I won't know Riley's kids as well as Quinn's. I've always been there for Jasper, Erin, and Aisling. Holidays and birthdays, zoo trips, and even a sleepover once with Aisling last year.

"I hope Cole and Hannah Grace have kids soon," she says.

I glance her direction to find her face turned toward her window as she watches our surroundings.

"Looking forward to being an auntie?" I ask.

I wish I could focus solely on her, but the green light pulls my attention to split between her and traffic.

"Hell, yes. I'm going to spoil them rotten. I'm going to be cool Aunt Leigh and descend with presents and junk food as often as I can."

I can picture it. Her blonde hair pulled high as she holds a baby or sneaking ice cream before meals with small kids as all cool aunts and uncles do.

"Are you looking at relocating to California or something?"

Why does the thought of her moving away make me sad when I'll be leaving sooner rather than later?

She shrugs.

"Maybe. I've thought about it. Hannah Grace is there. And Sydney. She keeps trying to talk me into it. Mistletoe Creek is home, but there are more opportunities in California." Her face turns toward me, her lips turned down. There's wanderlust in her expression—I recognize it, having felt it myself—but sadness too.

Like she's not quite sure whether to stay or to go.

Join the club.

"What's with the frown?" The words are out of my mouth before I can stop them.

"Huh?"

"Your frown. Here." I run my index finger between her brows, taking advantage of the red light to reach out and glide my finger along her skin.

She lifts her own and mimics the motion, our fingers skimming and sending little electrical pulses through my body.

I drop my hand back to the steering wheel, the side of my finger where hers brushed against it still tingling with the memory.

"I didn't realize I was frowning."

"You went from excited to frowning in zero point five seconds."

Her smile is smaller than normal, still tinged with whatever thought created the frown.

"I…miss Hannah Grace."

I don't believe that's what she was going to say, but don't call her on it outright.

"Hmm," I say, accelerating with the traffic.

"What? You don't believe me?" Her mix of sass and sweet, serious and not, is pulling me deeper into her orbit by the minute.

Several other blocks pass by as I consider what she said.

"I do believe you miss your sister," I say at last.

"But?"

"How do you know there's a but at the end of that statement?"

"I just do. But what?"

"But I think there's something else." I feel it in my gut. There's something else on her mind. Something she hasn't shared. And it's up to her to tell me.

"Interesting observation, Detective." She turns her attention back out her window, and I want to groan.

I no sooner peel one layer and another presents itself. A rose barely opening, the beauty teasing me in its complexity.

We're almost downtown, the neon starting to flicker on. Bright lights tout open mics and concerts—some artists trying to get their start, or recognizable names doing a smaller show for one reason or another. I change the subject, hoping to have her gaze on me again.

You like it too fucking much. Having her eyes on you.

I don't bother to deny it.

"Do you like Max?" I ask.

Her head whips back around.

"From *Searching for Love*?" she asks.

"Yeah."

Her gaze softens, her mouth parting as a breath rushes out. The softness of her lips tugs at my attention, and I have to force myself to focus on the street, on finding the turn for the parking lot I need.

"I…I do. Although I wish he would have picked Kenzie. I don't think Tara was the right fit for him."

"Agreed. The two always seemed…fake." I pull into the public parking lot and find an open spot. "I probably should have asked, but are you okay with a little walk?"

She glances down, lifting her leg to reveal the block-heeled booties on her feet.

"Okay."

"You're sure?" I ask, remembering the last time I brought Quinn with me and she had some crazy heeled boots on.

We'd ended up with her riding piggyback the way she had when we were kids.

"Positive. If these were my stiletto heels, no go. But these are pretty comfortable."

I nod and grab the keys, getting out of the car where she meets me at the back. Fuck, I had wanted to get her door.

"What?" She runs her index finger between her brows.

The tightness between my own confirms she's asking why I'm frowning.

"I was going to get your door," I tell her.

She lifts a shoulder and her purse swings next to her until she shifts it to cross her body. It fills me with an unexplainable pride she does, aware downtown Nashville is not the same as her small hometown.

"I got it."

"Dad would have had my head. 'Women don't touch doors in the presence of a man,' he would tell me." His deep voice still sounds as clear in my mind as if I had just heard it yesterday, the slight tinge of his accent peeking through.

"He sounds very chivalrous." She falls into step beside me, the moment comfortable as we join the crowds beginning to form on the streets.

"He was. Mom didn't touch a door until after he died and even then it wasn't very often. I wanted to do that for her."

The words are wistful, far away, and much too serious for a Friday night.

"You're very sweet," she says, reaching over and squeezing my bicep. Her hand is small, her fingers cool, even through the thin fabric of my Henley. "Sydney thinks it's fake."

"Me?" I ask, glancing down, finding her gaze with mine.

Amusement lights up her face and she giggles.

"No. Sorry. The show. *Searching for Love*."

I stop, not caring that people stream around us as the neon continues to hum to life.

"It's not fake," I tell her.

A breeze kicks a strand of hair against her cheek, and I can't resist the urge to lift my hand to tuck it behind her ear.

"H-how do you know?" she asks, slicking her tongue along her lips, and the moisture glistens in the neon light.

"Because love exists." Maybe not for me. But I've seen it.

My parents. My sisters.

And I know someday, Leigh will fall in love.

That reality breaks the spell she has over me and I step back, clearing my throat, and we continue walking down the street. If she notices the momentary lapse in my sanity, she doesn't comment on it.

"I know. That it's real. Or mostly real. Some of it has to be staged. Otherwise how else do you explain the fight between Catherine and Julia on Peter's season?"

The better word for what she's describing is brawl, but I don't correct her.

"You've never met my sisters when they would get into fights as teenagers." I shudder dramatically, loving her giggle.

"Your sisters sound amazing."

"They are, but no one needs to tell them. Their heads are already big enough."

We stop in front of a stone façade building. The bricks may be old, but they are lovingly restored, and it's one of my favorite places to hang out on a Friday night.

"My lips are sealed," she says, miming zipping her lips and dragging my attention back to her very kissable mouth.

I have to force my gaze back toward the opaque door, tracing the lines of the giant CC on the center of the door until I can safely look over my shoulder at her. Country music blasts us as I open the door, her eyes widening at the level of sound reaching out toward us. But it's the curiosity in her expression that has me moving us forward and has my own excitement building.

"Welcome to Cue Craft, Leigh. My favorite pool hall and place to grab a beer in all of Nashville." I drop my hand to her lower back as I usher her inside, enjoying the slight body heat through her shirt and the tiny patch of skin above the waistband of her jeans.

The fact that as soon as we walk in we come face-to-face with Kenneth Scott?

My knuckles crack at my side as Leigh's body radiates tension.

What the fuck next?

CHAPTER 13

LEIGH

What are the odds?

The universe has a weird sense of humor. It has to. Because why else would I come face-to-face with my sleazeball of a boss as soon as I step into Murphy's favorite place?

Maybe I broke a mirror in a previous life. Or walked under a ladder. It couldn't possibly be the number of umbrellas I opened as a child playing beach in our living room.

I had hoped to forget about Kenneth. To enjoy my time with Murphy despite the fact I'd had to make sure the excess saliva in my mouth didn't puddle at my feet when I answered the door tonight. Tough to do when every seam of his Henley strained under the onslaught of firm muscles beneath it. Muscles I had felt when I put my hand on his bicep earlier. His sleeves were still tugged up, showing off one bare arm and the beginnings of his sleeve tattoo I've only seen peeks of at the wrist and collars of his dress shirts. Pair the seam-tested tee and the jeans molding to his thighs over scarred leather boots? I was a goner. Even if I was able to stuff the attraction down, it still simmered like a watched pot. I just couldn't let it boil over.

Murphy O'Connell is like some sort of Greek god come to life.

No, not Greek. Gaelic.

A Gaelic warrior who now stands at my back as I face a man who wants to haunt my nightmares. Kenneth's icy blue gaze shifts behind me briefly before capturing me again.

"Leigh, I didn't realize you decided to join us," he says, his attention roving from the top of my head to my feet, staying way longer on my chest than he needs to.

The urge to reach up, to tug my neckline higher, itches at my fingers but I fight the need.

I'm not wearing anything inappropriate, despite the way Kenneth's attention makes me feel. Three other people stand just behind him, and I recognize two of the women as other interns and the third as a junior associate. Is it a coincidence all three of the people with him are women?

Probably not.

Thank God for Murphy.

I clear my throat, aiming for a professional tone, since what I really want to do—tell this asshole off—would get me fired.

"Actually, it's a coincidence. I thought you guys would have been long gone by now." Especially seeing as how the four of them had left just after lunch, but I keep that to myself. "I'll see you guys on Monday. Have a great weekend."

Lacing my fingers through Murphy's, I yank him behind me. Ignoring the halfhearted goodbyes and Kenneth's sputtering behind us, I don't stop until we're standing at the bar. Untangling our fingers is harder than it should be, and I immediately miss the calloused strength of his hand wrapped around mine.

But this isn't a date.

"Sorry," I tell him, weaving my fingers together to curb the urge to reach for his hand again.

He shrugs, a smile playing on his lips.

"Doesn't bother me any. I'm not a big fan of Kenneth Scott."

"Me neither."

He opens his mouth to say something, his attention zeroing in on me in a way that has me convinced he can read my every thought.

"Can I get you something?" A bartender waits patiently next to us, interrupting whatever Murphy was about to say.

"Can I get a table and a bucket of your local beers?" He glances at me.

I nod before shifting my gaze to the muted blue room around us. Each table is lit up where players are, several of them in darkness, waiting for the rest of a crowd while country music croons through the speakers.

I blow out a breath, and a light flickers on above a table as Murphy nudges me.

"Table 5." He leans down, his breath tickling my ear to be heard over the music.

I fight a shiver and our eyes clash over my shoulder. His lips are close—too close for me to fight the temptation.

So I do the only thing I can.

And move as fast as my two feet will carry me to the rack of cues next to the fifth table.

Murphy is staring at me with an odd expression on his face as he moves at a more normal pace, putting the tray of balls down on the felt and the bucket of beers on the nearby table.

"You alright, Leigh?" he asks, reaching for the stick next to the one my fingers are wrapped around.

"F-fine," I squeak, pulling too hard on the cue and almost smacking both of us with it.

He reaches up, holding the cue steady before I can take control over it.

And myself.

What part of not a date do you not understand? Murphy is not a date, he's a friend. You've had guy friends before.

But none who looked like him.

Get a grip.

Rolling my eyes at myself, I prop the cue next to the chair and reach for a beer, twisting off the cap and enjoying the light flavor of blueberries as the drink fizzes on my tongue.

"You didn't have to walk away from them if you wanted to visit," he tells me, grabbing his own beer.

His swallow is visible as he tilts his head back, but his attention stays focused on me. Is that what he thinks my awkwardness is about? Maybe I'm doing a better job at hiding my attraction than I thought I was.

"I didn't. I meant what I said. Kenneth gives me the creeps." Gooseflesh ripples down my arms, and I rub at the spot where his hand had grabbed my leg earlier this week, trying to get rid of the creepy-crawly sensation.

"Did something happen?" he asks, his wolf-colored eyes dropping to where my fingers press against the thick denim of my pants.

Chewing on my lip, I debate what to tell him.

"I'm probably making more of it than there is," I start, taking another drink of my beer.

"Why don't you let me be the judge of that?" His gaze finds mine again.

I hesitate with the word judge. What if I tell him and he doesn't believe me? What if all I do is show how naïve I am and how I don't really belong in a big city? That I just reveal exactly what he's already cautioned me about—the age gap between us.

"Leigh?"

He moves closer, his warmth enveloping the two of us. His presence drowns out all the sounds of the bar and the loud questions in my brain. But it's the warmth radiating from him that unlocks the words where I've been holding them, and they tumble out.

The job offer, the way he touched me, the invitation to

tonight's happy hour. Murphy's golden eyes darken the more I share, shifting from amber to brown, like the light extinguishes behind them. His hands fist at his sides, the knuckles standing in relief when I get to the part about Kenneth grabbing my leg. Only when I draw a shaky breath at the end does his attention shift away from me, releasing the spell around us. He finishes off the bottle in his hand, the glass hitting the wood of the table with a hard thunk while my heart races in my chest.

The way his large hand gentles around the bottle, the restrained power in the movement, creates a different kind of warmth, a heat pulsing out from my core to my extremities.

Why is the simple gesture such a turn-on?

"You need to report him," he says.

It takes several beats for his words to penetrate through the fog of lust.

"To whom?"

"To whoever will listen." He reaches out, lacing his fingers through mine and tugging me into the mesmerizing sphere of his cologne. "As much as I want to go beat his ass right now, that won't do you any good. What about the attorney you work for? Lindsay? Can you tell her?"

"I…I don't know. What if she doesn't believe me?"

What if she thinks I did something to encourage the behavior? What if I get fired? What happens to my shot at getting on with Project Justice then?

"Then quit." He says the words like they're simple. The solution we've been looking for.

But again, it won't do me any good with my application at the end of the summer.

I tug my hand free and spin for the table.

"It's not that easy." I toss the words over my shoulder as I rack the balls, needing something to keep my hands busy as my mind skitters into a thousand different directions.

His hands come up, running up and down my arms, the gesture soothing, and my hands still on the cool, heavy spheres beneath my fingertips.

"He's a predator, Leigh. Anyone who looks at him recognizes that. What happens if he does it to someone else? What happens if he tries something more with you?" There's a banked anguish in his voice, like he couldn't stand to see something happen to me.

I turn in his arms and his hands drop to the table on either side of my hips. But being caged by him doesn't scare me. My growing attraction to him? That's scary. But in a completely different way.

"You're worried about me," I say, my pinkies teasing along the warm skin they can reach.

"You're damn right I am." A muscle tics in his jaw, reinforcing his words.

"What happens if I do and nothing happens?" I don't voice the question bothering me the most—what happens if I do and something bad happens?

"I'll be here for you. I can help." His words are comforting, a promise I'm not walking into this alone.

"You're moving," I remind him.

"It doesn't matter. Here or DC. I'll be here. Supporting you."

"So I have to report him." It's a borderline statement-question but he nods.

"You do. As soon as possible."

If he thinks there's enough there, maybe there is. Lindsay has been as much of a mentor as a boss over the last few weeks. Maybe I should trust her.

"O-okay."

"Okay?" His eyes lock with mine, imbuing me with some of his warrior energy.

"I will. Monday. First thing."

"Good girl."

My whole body flushes at the innocent use of those words, and he clears his throat, stepping back. Cool air, along with sanity, rushes across my overheated skin.

"Have you played before?" he asks.

I recognize the change of subject to less risky territory. We've been riding the line into something dangerous and more than friends.

"A couple of times," I tell him, biting back the smile that threatens.

He cocks his head to the side, studying me intently.

"You're not telling me something."

"You want to break?" I ask and reach for my beer to hide my warm cheeks.

"You don't?"

I shake my head. "I'm not that good at it."

It's a partial truth. Breaking is not my strong suit.

He nods and moves back to the table, lining the cue ball up and taking his shot. There's a satisfying clack of balls as they bounce and spin against each other, scattering across the table, but none drop into the pockets.

Excellent.

I study the table, finding a shot and leaning down to line my stick up. Glancing up, my gaze finds his, and Kenneth is forgotten for the moment. Instead, I focus on Murphy's face as I drive the stick forward, tapping the cue and forcing it toward the solid orange near the edge of one of the corner pockets. It sinks in and I can't hide my smile.

"A time or two, huh?" he asks, leaning against the stool near our table.

I lift a shoulder and let it drop as I walk around to line up my next shot.

"Would you believe beginner's luck?" I suck my lips against my teeth but know I'm failing to hide what I'm thinking entirely when he wags his finger at me.

"You need to work on your poker face, Stóirín."

My brain stumbles over the word and my brows furrow. "Starry?"

"You said you didn't like 'Little Bit.' Would you prefer pool shark?"

Laughter bubbles out. "I'm not that good."

"We'll see." The look he has creates heat traveling up my chest. "Don't think I'm going to take it easy on you."

Reaching over, I grab another bottle from the bucket on the table, holding it against my cheek before opening it and taking a drink. Setting the open bottle on our table, I brush past him, enjoying the swift intake of breath echoing in my ear from the brief contact.

"I never asked you to," I murmur before leaning over and taking my next shot that wins me the game.

We trade off games after that. He wins the second, and the third when I give him the eight ball after scratching. I win the fourth game and we decide to call it the best of five. The bucket of beers is long gone, our flirty banter growing the longer we play and the more beers we drink.

With the last game lined up and waiting, we switch to water. The attractive waitress continues to come and go, making eyes at Murphy every single time, but he ignores her, his attention staying focused on me.

It's heady having his golden eyes fixed on me every time our gazes connect.

It's confusing. Because I know nothing can come of the attraction, but it doesn't stop it from overwhelming me.

"Ready?" he asks.

I nod and line up my shot, wiggling my ass as I get into position.

"You're not fighting fair," he groans, closing his eyes.

"All's fair in winning at pool." I sink two stripes in succession, taking pleasure in the fact I'm already winning.

"Maybe we should call the game now," he teases.

I don't fight the smile stretching across my face.

"We could. Or we could make our tournament more interesting. We never did decide on a prize for the winner," I tell him.

"I thought bragging rights were the prize."

His voice comes just to the left of me, his breath whispering along my arm, and I miss my next shot, unfortunately lining up an amazing shot for Murphy who sinks three balls one right after another, shooting me a smirk as the third one glides in.

Fuck.

"What did you have in mind?" he asks as he lines up his next shot.

Leaning down across from him, I brace my arms on the table, knowing he can now see more of my cleavage and the lacy top of my bra. He closes his eyes, his lips moving, but no sound comes out.

A kiss.

The words almost come out, but I stop myself before they do, finding a safe, more friendly option that won't get me in any deeper than I already am.

"Loser provides the winner with dinner next weekend, and we have a *Searching for Love* marathon." I walk around the table as I speak, waiting for his reaction.

He doesn't disappoint.

Opening his eyes, he releases a breath, his gaze focused on the ball in front of him. His arm retracts slowly, gliding forward to tap the next ball into the pocket in one smooth motion.

"Deal. But why wait? I'm free tomorrow."

I wait until he's lined up for his next shot, dragging my nails along his nape just as he pulls back his cue.

"Deal."

His stick misses the white ball completely and he curses.

I make sure to line up next to him, my arm brushing his as I lean over the table and push my ass out. His fingers tighten on his cue, and the corners of my lips twitch with a smile.

"What are you doing?" he growls.

The vibrations have my nipples pebbling against my bra.

"Just taking my next shot." But the innocent words are belied by the breathy quality of my voice.

Play with fire, you're bound to get burned too.

"Not what I meant."

The way the words are more sensation than sound is firing up the attraction to an almost crazy level.

"Didn't I tell you?" I ask, running my fingers down my cue as I try to play it cool while my body feels like it's baking in a Phoenix summer. "I'm super competitive. I hate to lose."

"You know if we were dating, I'd have no problem smacking your ass where you have it sticking out now and then kissing the fuck out of you."

His hand lands on the wooden rail of the pool table, his fingertips brushing my hip. I miss the shot—precisely what he means for me to do—and turn my gaze back on him.

"Hey! That's not fair!"

Lifting his hand, his index finger taps my nose.

"Sweetheart, everything is fair when food is on the line."

"Is that so?" I ask, an idea coming to mind.

He lines up his next shot and I allow my body to lean against his, my front to his back.

He scratches and lifts up, eyes narrowing where they glare at me over his shoulder.

"You did that on purpose," he accuses.

"Did what?" I grab my cup and take a drink.

With the ability to line up my next shot, I finish off the balls on the table before taking aim for the eight ball.

"You really are a fucking shark. I'm glad we didn't bet money," he tells me, amusement lacing his voice as he shakes his head.

"No one will play with me anymore. Eight ball, side pocket." I gesture with the stick before following through.

"I can understand why," he mutters.

"I win. And I'll settle for pizza."

"Congratulations." He reaches his hand out, and I try to ignore the electricity that sparks as my hand slides against his. "And no pizza is needed. I can cook."

"We'll see about that, O'Connell."

CHAPTER 14

LEIGH

The headlights wash onto the pavement of my driveway, the front porch lighting up brighter with the added light before dimming back to the porchlight I left on earlier. The last game had been finished and I was getting dinner, but anticipation continued to build no matter how many times I tried to remind myself the flirting had been to win the game, not because it was a date.

"Thanks for tonight. I had fun," I tell him.

The hard planes of his face are dimly lit from the dash lights, but the attraction still buzzes back and forth between us like a live wire connecting him to me.

There's a flash of white with his teeth as he smiles.

"You had fun because you kicked my ass. I'll win next time."

Warmth sizzles through my blood at his words. Next time.

I shouldn't already be looking forward to it.

"We'll see. Maybe I took it easy on you," I tease.

His smile deepens, his eyes glowing with his amusement. Serious Murphy is dangerous enough to my sanity. But this Murphy? The smiling, amused, relaxed one?

Lethal.

"We'll see about that, Stóirín."

"You called me that earlier too and I thought you said starry. What does it mean?"

He leans back in his seat, one hand climbing up to rub at the back of his neck as he closes his eyes and blows out a breath.

"It's Gaelic," he says after a long pause.

"What does it mean?" I ask again, more hesitant than before since I'm not sure how I should react in light of his response.

"It means sweetheart." The words are quiet, rushed, like he doesn't want me to hear or understand them.

"Sweetheart?" I ask, trying to keep my voice level and not let it squeak in the mix of surprise and pleasure creating a swarm of butterflies in my stomach.

He glances at me, his gaze finding and connecting with mine as my heart flutters in my chest.

Only friends. Only friends. We're only friends.

But despite the numerous reminders, it does nothing to stop the way the word sweetheart circles in my brain, drawing the butterflies to it like a moth to a flame.

"I-I don't know how to respond to that," I admit.

It's the truth.

I know the safest thing for my sanity—and my heart—is to walk away. To forget he's been calling me the Gaelic word for sweetheart all night.

But my body stays frozen where it is, hanging on whatever it is he says next.

"It doesn't change anything," he says, even as his hand lifts to my jaw and his thumb skims my lower lip.

"I know." The words are a resigned whisper, but hope continues to glimmer since his thumb stays where it is.

"I'm trying to do the right thing here," he says, more to himself than to me.

"I know that too." My breath stalls in my lungs as I wait.

For what, I'm not sure. But the moment between us continues to stretch, anticipation building with every back-and-forth motion against my lip.

"Fuck it."

The words only have a heartbeat to register before he leans forward, his mouth claiming mine. But it's not an awkward first kiss—second kiss?—as his tongue glides along the seam of my lips. I open to his request, his tongue tangling with mine, as we settle against each other. It's as if we've been kissing for years instead of two kisses spaced almost two months apart. I moan, my fingers gripping where they can, finding his biceps as he masterfully controls the pace, both driving me crazy and satiating the ache as his lips lay siege.

I surrender.

There's a click of the seatbelt, and the fabric against my chest loosens. I shift closer, shrugging free of the confining strap to settle heart to heart against him. His hands delve into my hair, pulling my mouth from his for his lips to find my jaw and trace the line back to my ear with his tongue.

"We shouldn't do this," he murmurs, the vibration tickling the sensitive skin beneath my earlobe.

"You're probably right." I may say those words, but my fingers tighten against his biceps, a silent request not to stop. His teeth nip at my lobe and his own fingers tighten where they grip my hair.

He must not like the words either because his mouth claims mine again, silencing the words scattering like leaves on the wind in the wake of the chemistry between us.

Holy shit.

If the first kiss between us was explosive, this second creates a nuclear reaction. It would be easy to strip where I am, having my way with him where anyone could see us.

Invite him inside.

Rejection pricks through the fog of lust and desire, and I rip my lips away from his.

"What's changed?" I ask.

"What?" His eyes open slowly, his gaze unfocused as his lips glisten in the dim lights around us.

"What's changed? Why now?" My lips tingle, my body aching to forget talking, to use my mouth for a better occupation.

I swallow, trying to stem the lust and focus on his response.

"I…can't seem to resist you. Whatever this is between us"—his hand moves from him to me, resting against my thigh— "it's impossible to resist. It just keeps getting stronger."

My body wholeheartedly agrees, but I'll be damned if I allow myself to give in to the desire only to be rejected again.

"So the fact that I'm Cole's sister-in-law? That I'm younger than you are?"

A muscle tics in his jaw, his nostrils flaring with his breath.

"I don't care. I know I should," he confesses.

"But?" Anticipation builds in my stomach.

I'm at the beginning of a roller coaster, the climb taking me higher and higher as the butterflies take over my stomach.

"It's hard to remember why I should when your lips are still swollen with my kisses," he growls.

God, if my panties didn't incinerate at the words, they would from the desire burning in his gaze. But by some miracle, I still have a small bit of sanity with the sting of the rejection from the night we shared our first kiss. It's a good reminder to be sure.

For him to be certain.

I swallow, leaning back against my seat.

"I'm not saying no. But I want you to be sure, Murphy. I need to know you're not going to reject me the way you did before. If all this"—I mimic his gesture with my hand between us— "is a fling, fine. I can agree to that. But I won't agree just to have you change your mind. Not again. That's not fair to me."

He nods. "You're right."

"So which is it?" I ask, sounding a whole lot more confident than I feel in the moment.

The silence stretches between us, a song swirling through the car while I wait for his response. I lick my lips, trying to calm my racing heart, and run my hands along my pants.

"I…I need think about it. And doing any thinking when you're this close to me is proving impossible," he says, glancing down at his lap at the sizable erection still pressing against the denim of his jeans.

Oh. My. God.

My thighs clench together, the ache in my core anything but soothed, as a smile twitches at my lips with his self-deprecating words.

"I'll give you twenty-four hours. Tomorrow night. Dinner. And your decision."

He nods, reaching out a hand to lace his fingers with mine, squeezing gently.

"I can do that."

"Good night, Murphy." Leaning over, I brush my lips against the stubble of his cheek.

What would it feel like between my thighs?

That's a question not leaving anytime soon.

"Good night."

It takes almost everything in me to pull away, step out of the car, and walk to my front door on unsteady legs. The heat of his gaze between my shoulder blades is a safety I didn't realize I needed, but also makes it more difficult to walk away. He waits until I'm inside and the door is locked behind me before the headlights light up the room when he backs down the driveway.

"Your move, Detective."

Twelve hours later, I'm second-guessing leaving the ball in his court as I've spent every one of those hours wondering which choice he's going to make.

"I should have put my cards on the table," I tell Sydney, my cell on speakerphone as I clean up the kitchen.

Murphy had texted earlier and confirmed he would be bringing groceries over and to ask if I was allergic to anything. The texts were so innocuous given the attraction that had strung the moment tight between us last night.

I didn't know whether to laugh or cry because the texts gave me no insight into what Murphy was thinking.

Sydney yawns into the phone and I hear the crack of a can. In her defense, I had woken her up. In my defense, it was after two in the afternoon her time.

"Eh." She takes a slurp from whatever energy drink she's opened before continuing. "The way I see it, your whole date last night was foreplay."

"It wasn't a date. Wait. What? Foreplay?" I stop as the rest of her words register, the sponge I had been wiping the counter with skittering into the sink.

"Mmm. The push-pull of the pool games. Proud of you for kicking his ass by the way. The flirting—"

"That was just to win!"

"Was it?" she asks, sounding more awake than she had a few minutes ago.

"You're not helping," I mutter, retrieving the sponge and scrubbing at the already clean counter.

"Just because you don't like what I'm saying doesn't mean I'm not helping. I already told you before that the chemistry between you two at the wedding was H-O-T. It's about time the two of you acted on it." Her words are accompanied by a door opening and closing. "Hey, Jess."

"Hi, Jess," I echo through the phone, saying hi to Sydney's roommate.

"She said hi back before disappearing into her room. Looks like she's been crying. Her fucking boyfriend is a royal dick. Bowie. What kind of fucking name is Bowie?"

I open my mouth to respond when a text pops up on my phone.

MURPHY: Dinner in an hour?

"Fuck."

"What?" I had forgotten Sydney was on speakerphone.

"He's going to be here in an hour." I glance down at my athletic shorts and tank. "I need to get ready. I still have to shower."

The nerves and anticipation I've channeled into cleaning the house all day morph into kamikaze butterflies swirling in my stomach.

"Well, you could always answer the door in your towel. That'll definitely get you your answer sooner rather than later," she jokes.

Heat travels through my body, picturing Murphy responding to me answering the door in just my towel. His jaw would clench, the muscle ticking as his golden eyes darken and the flames roar to life like they did last night. He'd storm into the house, slamming the door behind him as he lifts me against the wall and—

"Leigh! Earth to Leigh!" Sydney's voice finally registers.

Holy shit. Blinking, I toss the sponge into the sink on purpose this time and head for my room and bathroom. If my imagination has me all hot and bothered, what would the real thing be like?

And will I have the chance to experience it?

"Sorry. Distracted," I mumble, kicking off my shorts and leaning over to crank the water on in the shower.

"You got this. Whatever his answer, it's going to be fine. At least tonight you'll know once and for all."

"True."

I had told him tonight we were done playing tug-of-war with my libido in the mix. I want an answer. I want *the* answer, but am going to settle for one regardless of what it is.

At least, that's what I keep telling myself.

"What are you going to wear? Because I doubt you're taking my advice and wearing nothing at all." The beep of a microwave on her end accompanies her comment.

That was the debate waking me up this morning. Do I dress it up? Play it casual?

"I'm just going to wear jean shorts and a tank top. It's freaking roasting outside."

"Mmm. What's he making for dinner?" she asks, her question muffled by whatever she's just put into her mouth.

"He said it was a surprise. What are you eating?"

"Leftover Chinese. Jessie and I grabbed it on the way back from the bar last night."

"Did you break your self-imposed sex-ile?" I hadn't heard anything from her yet today, so have no idea if she'd had any luck when she and Jessie went out or not.

"Nope, so my plan is to live vicariously through you, so either you need to get some—and share some details—or I'm going to have to go out again in the next few days. My vibrator isn't cutting it anymore."

"What if he—"

"No, no what-ifs. Jesus, I can see your anxiety from here and we're not even on FaceTime. You're good with either decision, right? Just friends? Rocking each other's worlds?"

Am I?

"Well, yeah. I think so," I tell her.

Because if he says just friends?

I can respect that.

I may not like it. But I can at least understand it. I can ignore my libido until he moves.

"And you're covered protection-wise?"

"Yeah. I bought some condoms before I left Knoxville. Right after we decided on our hot girl summer."

Back when I had sworn to avoid Murphy O'Connell like the plague once I got to Nashville.

Look how well that turned out.

"Then you're all set. Text me. I want details."

"What if there aren't any?"

She laughs.

"Oh, I'm sure there will be. Just text me."

She hangs up sounding way more confident than I feel, but I don't have time to spiral.

I take the fastest shower in history, taking a few extra minutes to make sure my legs are smooth and hair-free before jumping out. Rushing from the bathroom back into the bedroom, I dig through my drawer until I find the ice blue matching bra and panties I bought when I first got to Nashville—just in case—before throwing on my frayed denim shorts and a light blue tank top.

I don't bother with much makeup, just adding gloss to my lips before I blow dry my hair into waves I leave down. After nearly tripping over the towels, I lean down, picking them up to hang them on the rack before giving myself one last glance in the bathroom mirror.

"I guess we'll see what happens," I tell my reflection before turning off the light.

The doorbell rings as I'm dabbing on perfume, and my stomach somersaults as the butterflies begin a wild tango.

"Now or never," I mumble, trying to ignore the light tremor of my hand as I set the perfume bottle down on the dresser.

As much as I want to run at the door, I keep my pace steady, checking the peephole to find Murphy waiting on the stoop, a Gaelic warrior come to life with his thick, corded, inked muscles. A pair of aviators hides his eyes, and I wish he would take them off. Something the universe grants as I open the door and he tucks them into the collar of his tan short-sleeve shirt.

It's the first time I've ever had more than a peek at his arm sleeve, and the urge to lift my hand, to trace all the dark symbols up his arm where they curl at the base of his neck is almost overwhelming. He's more inked than I first thought, his shorts showing off the tattoos on the opposite leg.

Where does the ink cross?

I drop my attention to his waist before I force my focus back to his face.

"Hi." His lips twitch before blooming into a smile, and my own stretches in response.

"Hi."

"Can I come in?"

I step to the side to invite him in, and he reaches down and grabs several bags I've just noticed by his feet.

The choreography is a mix of polite strangers and something more, but the sexual tension stifles us in an awkward silence I haven't experienced with him before.

"Kitchen?" he asks, lifting both hands.

I point to the doorway behind the living room and trail him as he carries the bags and sets them on the counter.

"Have you ever had Shepherd's Pie and soda bread?" he asks, turning toward me.

"Do you have a decision for me?" I ask as soon as his gaze meets mine.

"I asked you first." He takes a step toward me and I retreat, overwhelmed by his presence.

"What was the question?" Because if I heard it the first time, I've already forgotten it.

"Shepherd's Pie. Soda Bread. Sound good for dinner? They're my mom's recipes." He smirks, taking another step forward.

I step back and bump into the wall, unaware of how close it was while trying not to melt into a puddle of goo on the floor.

But I'm not sure if it's the way his laser focus heats me up from the core outward or him making his mom's recipes for me that has my heart melting.

"You're making your mom's recipes for me?"

"If that's okay," he murmurs. "You still haven't told me if it sounds good or not."

He closes the distance between us, his chest teasing my breasts, and I fight the urge to drag him closer while the butterflies swarm in my stomach.

I nod.

"It sounds delicious." The words come out breathy and his nose drops to my jaw, dragging it down my throat.

"You asked me a question too," he reminds me, continuing the torturous glide of skin against skin.

"Mm-hmm." I tilt my head to give him better access, but he doesn't take it, and I want to groan in frustration.

"What was your question?" he prompts.

"Do you have a decision for me?" I somehow manage to get the words out despite the fact that my entire body feels like it's about to combust at any moment.

It's as if every interaction with Murphy has been leading here, to this point, this electrical charge that continues to consume me as he hovers above me, around me. Each heartbeat is a torturous delay, a stretching of the anticipation building since we first met.

He makes a sound, his chest vibrating with it, before he speaks.

"I want you, Leigh. More than any other woman in a long time. Maybe ever, as terrifying as that is for me to admit. And while I think you deserve so much more than me, I'm just selfish enough to stop fighting this magnetic pull you have on me. So if you tell me you want me right now, you better be prepared, Stóirín. Because once I have a taste of you, there's no turning back. Not for me. Not tonight."

My knees buckle with his barely leashed growl, my senses overwhelmed by citrus and bergamot as his cologne wraps around the two of us. But still he stands there frozen, poised, waiting for me. And I have zero doubt if I told him I had changed my mind, he would back off.

But everything in me—mind, body, and soul—is crying out for more, and I lift my hands, scratching my nails along his nape, the short hairs tickling my fingertips.

"I meant what I said last night. I want you. This. Whatever this is that's between us. It's burning me alive, and all I can think about is the way I feel when you kiss me."

"Is that what you want?"

"Kiss me, Murphy. Please."

CHAPTER 15

MURPHY

I'm done fighting this crazy attraction to the woman in front of me. But I still savor the electric explosion arcing between us in the instant before my mouth claims hers.

Holy fuck.

Every other thought leaves my brain at the taste of her again. She has the ability to obliterate every other piece of the world except her. With every brush of her lips against mine, it's cementing the decision I made.

I want her.

She wants me.

And I'm fucking exhausted from trying to fight it.

Lifting my hands to bracket her hips, I squeeze and knead the denim against the warmth of her skin, and she mewls before tangling her tongue with mine, pressing closer. The weight of her breasts presses against my chest, and I fight the urge to lift her in my arms and feel the warmth of her legs around my waist.

Her fingers scrape through my hair, her moan captured between us, and my hands drop to her ass, aligning our lower bodies. Another thread on my control severs, and it takes everything I have to keep her feet on the ground.

Fuck. Had I known it would be like this when I finally gave in, I would have given in to temptation a whole lot earlier than last night.

I crowd her against the wall, ripping my mouth from hers to brand a trail of open-mouthed kisses down her neck, reveling in whatever perfume teases my nostrils with the scents of vanilla and sandalwood. Her leg lifts to curve around my hip and I reach down to boost her higher, groaning as the heat of her pussy teases me through the denim seam of her shorts. My fingers tease beneath the hem, desperate to find her beneath the fabric.

She cries out and I stop, lifting my head.

"What's wrong?"

"Nothing," she murmurs. "Don't stop."

"You beg so sweetly," I tell her, teasing her swollen lips with a chaste kiss. "What about dinner?"

"Later," she murmurs, scratching her nails along my nape, and my hand tightens on her thigh.

"Not hungry?" I drop my lips back to the spot where her neck and shoulder connect, nipping at the tendon there.

"Not for food."

My dick kicks against my zipper and my fingers stretch, trying to find the edge of her panties beneath the denim of her shorts.

"I don't intend to stop, sweetheart. Not unless you tell me to."

"Don't plan on that happening," she says.

A smile curves my lips. Fuck, her sass is just as intoxicating as her body.

"Kiss me," she demands, confidence ringing through her voice.

I slam my lips back to hers, devouring the demand while her fingers wrap into my shirt. She tugs at the cotton, yanking at it as she tries to pull it off. I oblige, breaking the kiss long enough to reach behind me and grab the neck. Pulling it over my head, I let it fall to the kitchen floor at our feet.

She lifts her hands and my whole body stills, despite my heart thrumming a staccato beat in my chest where her hand presses, drawing up and down, her fingers tracing the ink on my chest.

"What does it mean?" she whispers and drags her fingers over the tattoo covering my right pec, brushing my nipple.

I groan, wanting her to repeat the caress, which she does.

This woman is fucking perfect for me.

I reach out, my fingers playing with the hem of her tank while I let her explore her fill. Her eyes lock with mine and she nods, granting me permission to my unspoken question.

"Someday I'll explain every one to you, Stóirín. But right now, I'm a little preoccupied," I murmur, using my hands to push the tank up and over her breasts. I skim my fingers over the silky fabric of the pale blue bra as I continue to push her top up. She grips the fabric, tugging it the rest of the way off, and stands before me in her bra and shorts.

Her breasts swell above the shimmery fabric and I drop my head, tasting the sweet skin of one swell while her nipples pebble, pulling my attention to them.

Soon.

But first I'm determined to commit every piece of her to memory. The swell of her breasts as I trace them one direction to the other. I flatten my tongue, licking along the cleavage, smiling at the way she pushes against me, mewling. Ready for more.

I tunnel my fingers between her back and the wall, finding the clasp to flick the bra open, and the blue fabric loosens. I slide my hands to her shoulders, intent on divesting her of the straps, when she shrugs the garment free and it flutters to the floor next to my shirt and hers.

Her nipples tighten even more in the rush of cool air, and I slide my tongue along my lips, dying for a taste. But I hold on to the frayed tether of my control while tracing hot, open-mouthed kisses along her collarbone while my hands settle at her hips, gripping them with a desperation while itching to trace the tight peaks of each breast.

"You taste like heaven," I murmur against her skin.

It's a mix of my favorite dessert—strawberry shortcake—and something more. Something sweeter. Hotter. Something uniquely Leigh.

She squirms against the wall as I stretch my fingers up, running along the hem of her shorts and hooking my pinkies in the waistband.

"More," she tells me, bumping her pelvis against mine.

I see fucking stars and my control snarls for release. Clenching my jaw, I fight for control, wresting it back.

"Slowly." I sink my teeth into the tendon between her neck and shoulder before laving the bite with my tongue. "I intend to savor you like the delicacy you are. And that takes time I'm not willing to give up."

I tease a kiss against her pouty lips, and she tries to hold me in place.

"I'm dying here," she whines.

My eyes find hers and one side of my mouth curves into a smile.

"No, sweetheart. But you'll absolutely see heaven before I'm through," I promise before allowing my lips to claim hers again.

This kiss is more forceful than before, my own control unraveling more by the minute. Her breasts crush against my chest and she moans into the kiss, her fingernails pricking into the skin of my shoulders.

My fingers find the snap of her shorts, and I drop them to her feet and open my eyes.

The thin, lacy panties are delicate, highlighting the curve of her hip as her arousal teases my nostrils. My hands shake faintly as I reach out, hooking them into the waist and dragging my index finger along the smooth skin of her abdomen.

"More," she tells me.

I toy with the waistband, tracing it all the way back and around to where I started, lifting my other hand so both hands now bracket her hips. My libido may be raging at me to rip her panties off, but I take my time, unwrapping her like a long-awaited present, holding the moment between us as I slide them down her legs until she shimmies them off the rest of the way.

"You're fucking gorgeous," I tell her, my hands finding her ass to yank her lower body back against mine.

I swallow her gasp, tangling my tongue with hers while my hands cup and knead the tender flesh, boosting her until she can wrap her legs around me. The heat of her pussy connects with my stomach and I'm fucking done for.

Ripping my mouth away from hers, I wait until her blue eyes open, dazed, lust filled. Light slants into the kitchen, highlighting her swollen lips, and it takes everything I have not to dive in for another taste. But not yet.

"I've dreamed of you, Stóirín. What you tasted like, what your skin would feel like beneath my fingers, of the sounds you would make if I did this." I brush my fingertips through her folds, and my name is a moan on her lips.

"Fuck. Again."

I repeat the caress, finding her clit and circling the hard bundle of nerves. My dick is an iron rod in my shorts, my body screaming at me to take things further.

"But my dreams pale in comparison to reality. There are not enough words to describe how exquisite you taste. How soft your skin is beneath my fingertips. No words can describe the sounds you make when I bring you pleasure."

Dropping my mouth to hers again, I swirl my finger around her clit. Her legs shake, and she nearly comes undone as I press her back against the wall, letting it hold more of her weight as I alternate pressure with every swipe of my finger against the hard bundle.

Her head falls back against the wall and my lips find her jaw, licking the salty sheen of sweat from her skin as she mewls.

"I-I-I'm going to come," she pants, her breathing ragged.

But I don't stop, doubling down on my efforts as my lips find her ear.

"Come for me, Leigh," I growl and tap her clit once, twice, until her entire body locks around me, her orgasm leaving only my name on her lips. A prayer. An incantation. A spell that pulls us both under.

CHAPTER 16

LEIGH

Thousands of stars envelop me as my orgasm crests in a curtain of bright light and pleasure unlike anything I've ever experienced before.

"That's my girl." Murphy's words push me even higher to a place where the stars now fall below me.

His finger stills against my clit, but he doesn't move away, and heat continues to pulse through me in rippling aftershocks.

"Better than I imagined," he murmurs, his lips finding mine in a kiss over far too soon for my liking.

Blinking my eyes open, I find him watching me, studying my reaction.

"So are you."

He barks out a laugh and I giggle, the move causing his fingers to brush my still-sensitive clit. I moan, my inhalation swift as lust sucks me back under. The amusement fades from his expression and it leaves only a heat behind it, threatening to consume us both. He lifts his hand, sucking his finger into his mouth and moaning his enjoyment.

My legs spasm around him as my core throbs with need.

More.

Again.

Now.

"Murphy—"

"Better than I imagined," he repeats, the words taking on new meaning.

I whimper at the onslaught of desire rushing through me in dizzying waves.

"I haven't had enough of you," he says.

I reach for the waistband of his shorts, ready to move us to the next step, but he shakes his head and bends backward away from my seeking fingers.

"Not yet."

How the hell can he be so calm and collected when I'm ready to combust on the spot…again.

"But—"

He moves so fast I don't track it until I'm slung over his shoulder in a fireman's carry with my bare ass right next to his face. I squirm, whimpering as my pussy rubs against his shoulder.

"Don't lose that thought, sweetheart."

Not freaking likely. Especially when one of his palms settles against my ass, his pinky teasing my folds as he leaves the kitchen to find the stairs. He moves swiftly, not lowering me to my feet until we're in my bedroom.

"Thank God I picked the right room," he tells me, a small smile curving his lips.

"Thank God indeed," I tell him, reaching for the waistband of his shorts.

He lets my fingers connect to the fly and I unsnap it, pushing his boxers and shorts down in one fell swoop. His dick springs free, bobbing with the movement, and my core throbs back to life, my mouth begging for a taste.

He's the one who closes the distance first though, his fingers tangling in my hair, tugging my head back until his lips tease mine.

I've never experienced this level of need before. This steadfast ache that only stops when he kisses me, and only for a second before it burns hotter than before. In this moment, it doesn't feel like I just came on his fingers downstairs.

I need him.

Right now.

With a desperation I can't explain.

"Are you ready for more?" He whispers the words against my lips.

If I were any more ready I would be a pile of ashes on the ground. My entire body—my entire being—is on fire for him. For his touch. For the pleasure he can bring me.

"Yes," I moan and lift to my tiptoes for a kiss.

It doesn't come.

Instead, he spins me in his arms, his dick pressing against my ass while his hands lift to my breasts and his lips tease the tendon where my neck and shoulder meet. Lifting my arms back and over my head, I weave my fingers through the short strands of his hair, and my breasts press more firmly into his palms.

"Do you like it when I touch you like this?" The question is more vibration than sound against my ear.

He pinches both nipples, and lightning arcs in a direct line of communication with my pussy.

Like is such a small word for the amount of bliss I'm experiencing in his arms.

"*Yes.*" I rub my ass against his dick and his fingers tighten, rolling my nipple between thumb and forefinger while the other hand drops, trailing down my stomach until he sinks a finger knuckle deep inside me.

My pussy spasms around the digit, the orgasm already building.

"Mmm." I moan the word, sinking my teeth into my lower lip to keep from begging for more.

He pinches my nipple hard enough I release my lip, crying out and panting.

"Yes, sweetheart. That's it. Let me hear your pleasure. Don't hide it from me. I crave it. Feel what you do to me." He taps his hard dick against my ass and I mewl.

"Please. I want more. I need it. Please."

His finger runs back and forth over my opening, avoiding my clit while the pleasure continues to drive higher.

"What about my tongue?" he asks, rimming my ear with his tongue. "Would you like that here?" He drags a palm over my distended nipple.

"Fuck, yes."

"I love when your sweet little mouth uses those dirty words. What about here? Do you want my tongue here?" His finger presses back inside and my knees buckle.

I'm only upright because of the way one of his arms bands around my waist, holding me to him.

I moan, nodding furiously, the orgasm already at its tipping point when all he's done is barely touch me.

"Tell me. Use those words," he grits out, sending vibrations of pleasure along my skin.

Spinning in his arms, I dislodge his hand—immediately missing the gentle pressure—while I tug him back toward the bed.

"I want your tongue, Murphy. No more teasing. I want you to fuck me with your mouth before you use your dick. And I want it right the fuck now." I have no idea where the words come from other than they're exactly what I need from him in this moment.

I tumble backward, yanking him with me until he rests in the cradle of my thighs, bracing himself up with a hand pressed on either side of my head. His hard dick drags through my folds and I moan, lifting my hips.

"I love hearing you tell me what you want, Stóirín. Tell me. Whatever you want, whatever is in my power to give you, it's yours."

He leans down, nuzzling my neck and pressing kisses along my collarbone until his mouth hovers over one breast. He glances up, his gaze meeting mine as he slowly lowers until he pulls the nipple into his mouth. My eyelids fall shut as pure pleasure radiates out from the connection, directly tethered to my core, aching with need. Lifting my hands, I thread my fingers through the short hair at his nape, attempting to hold him in place while his tongue spars with the stiff peak of my breast.

My breath comes in embarrassingly loud pants, his name keening from my lips as he nips at the distended tip, tugging sharply. My legs jolt while my back curves upward, pressing me harder to his mouth.

He repeats the caress on my opposite breast, the hard jolt followed by the warmth of his mouth as he soothes the ache. The orgasm pulses at the edges, threatening to drag me under.

"I-I feel like I'm going to come," I grit out, trying to stave off the orgasm, enjoying the way it builds hotter and hotter.

"As much as I would love to see you come just from me playing with your breasts, I'll keep that in mind for next time. Something else is calling my name."

Next time.

I'm still focused on this time. This moment. Every touch is its own unique moment and he's already planning a next time.

Holy shit.

I'm so focused, I barely register the way his kisses trail lower until my legs are on his shoulders, his hands pushing my legs up and back, exposing me to his heated gaze.

"Such a pretty pussy. And I already know you taste delicious from my little sample earlier. But what about now? Will you taste the same on my tongue as you did on my fingers?"

His gaze flicks up to mine briefly before he refocuses his

attention on my exposed pussy. My body ratchets up in temperature under the inferno raging in his hazel-colored eyes. The hunger on his face is like a starving man finding food after too long without.

But still he makes me wait.

Turning his head to the side, he places an open-mouthed kiss on the inside of one thigh, sucking the tender skin into the heat of his mouth, nipping at the flesh, before turning and doing the same on the other side.

Marking me.

As his.

Why is that so hot?

I squirm, wiggling my hips against the cool sheets on the bed while fire consumes me. His grip tightens, halting my movement, and I whimper. Only when I'm still does he move again, dragging his tongue up my slit in one long, slow stroke, before he curls it when he reaches my clit.

"Oh, fuck." My hands flutter, looking for purchase before tangling in his hair.

"Mmm." The sound is a vibration against my sensitive flesh, and my hips buck against his hold.

He repeats the caress, a finger joining his tongue as it presses inside. It's not enough, yet it's too much, as his tongue begins to circle the hard bundle of nerves. Every time I think I'm used to the pressure or the movement, ready to ride the wave to ecstasy, he changes it up and I can't find the rhythm before he's changing it again.

"*Murphy*."

Another finger joins the first, his tongue tapping against my clit before he flattens it and drags it along the top. While his grip has relaxed enough I can shift my hips more, he sits up. Lifting my lower half off the bed, a third finger finds the pucker of my asshole and presses forward gently.

"Oh my God." The sensation is foreign, but it feels too good to ask him to stop.

I want more.

He lifts his mouth from my body momentarily, all three of his fingers still working me.

"That's it, sweetheart. Ride my hand. Find your pleasure. I'm not stopping until you come. You taste so fucking good."

The last part is growled against my pussy as his mouth finds it again, his tongue starting up its rhythm again, and the orgasm pulses harder around, taking over more of my vision. It's the beginning of a roller coaster, the car moving to the top, the promise of pleasure within reach.

Lifting my hands to my breasts, I tug the sensitive flesh. Between that and a mix of his fingers and mouth, I reach the top. Suspended in time for a heartbeat, then two, before I catapult forward, tethered to the earth only by the man between my legs.

His name rips from my throat on a scream, my body locking as the orgasm shatters through me. Shatters *me*. Around me, over me. It drowns me in sensation. In a pleasure reminding me of a phoenix—death and rebirth all in one breath-stealing moment. His tongue continues to work, his fingers slowing down until I'm spent beneath him.

Only then do his lips retrace their path from earlier, climbing my body as he shifts on top of me.

"More." My lips feel foreign wrapped around the word, and amusement joins the fire in his eyes.

"Greedy girl," he says, dropping a kiss to my nose.

I wrap my legs around his waist, hissing a breath as my sensitive skin brushes his.

"I want to feel you. Inside me."

His eyes search mine, the silence stretching between us until he nods.

"I have something. In my drawer. Protection." I point to the nightstand and he opens the drawer, pulling out the box of condoms and tossing one of the foil packets on the bed.

My hand wraps around him and he moans, nearly falling on top of me.

"Fuck," he grits out.

Falling on his back on the bed, he tugs me with him until I straddle him.

"You're no fun." I pout, my fingers having lost their purchase in the process.

He chuckles, sitting up to catch my lips with his.

"I think the two orgasms you've had so far show you how much 'fun' I am." He waggles his brows.

My giggle is strangled by the need overwhelming my entire body.

"So far?" My core clenches and I squeeze my thighs around his hips as desire continue to build.

His hand comes up, swatting my ass and catching me off guard. The moan I let out is loud, my ass already pressing out, wanting another touch.

"You're so fucking responsive," he murmurs as his hands flex on my thighs.

"Not usually. This is...different." I have never been this way with any other man I've slept with.

"Different? Different how? You're not a—"

"I'm not a virgin. But I don't typically laugh the way I do with you when I'm this turned on."

His eyes darken, his grip tightening on my hips.

"How turned on are you, Stóirín?" He shifts, his finger sliding through my folds until he finds my clit.

I moan at the touch, my eyes fluttering shut. It wouldn't take much more to set me off again, and I squirm against his hips.

"Grab the condom," he grits out.

When I open my eyes, a muscle tics rapidly in his jaw, his hands an iron vise at my hips. Reaching over, I snag the foil packet and open it to pull out the rubber. My nipples rub along his chest as I bend and shift, the friction setting off sparks like fireworks behind my eyelids.

"Can you put it on?" he asks.

I nod, opening my eyes while his hand shifts back between my legs. Biting my lip, I try to hold off the orgasm until the condom is in place. He moves his hands back to my waist, and I'm not sure if I want to beg him for more or tell him not to stop as he lifts me enough to poise me above him, lowering me slowly until his pelvis taps mine.

"*Fuck.*" His eyes are closed, head thrown back, and every muscle and tendon in his neck stand at attention. "You feel so fucking good. Your pussy was made for my cock. I'm so fucking close."

"How close?" I pant, desire blurring the edges.

"Closer than I want to be. I'm about to fucking embarrass myself," he growls.

The orgasm continues to build and I'm balanced on the edge, ready to tip over with the slightest breath.

"I'm so close," I whimper and shift my hips, rocking against him as stars pop in my vision.

"Stóirín. Look at me."

I open my eyes as he threads his fingers through mine and squeezes.

"There's no going back from this. Are you ready?"

There was no going back from the first time I kissed him. Even if I didn't want to admit it then.

I nod.

"Words, sweetheart," he says.

"*Please.*" The orgasm is just out of reach. And I'm practically vibrating with the need to come.

"Please what?"

"I need you," I tell him.

It's past want at this point. If he doesn't start to move soon,

I'm going to go up in the flames continuing to lick along my skin. But the words must be the answer he's looking for.

He nods.

"Hold on to me, sweetheart."

And I do.

All the way to heaven and back again, eventually falling asleep in his arms with the steady thud of his heartbeat in my ear.

CHAPTER 17

MURPHY

"O'Connell!"

Fuck. My name ringing from the captain's office first thing Monday morning can't be good.

My stomach knots, rebelling at the thought of coffee that sounded so appealing walking through the door.

Captain Overton stands in her office doorway, finger crooked, as she glares at me.

The leftover high from spending the weekend with Leigh fades, and walking toward the captain feels more like I'm walking to my death via public execution than to her office. The heat of everyone's attention is focused between my shoulder blades, and my ears grow warmer with every five-hundred-pound step. When I make it to her office, she follows me in, all but slamming the door behind the two of us.

Fuck.

I'm not sure what the hell happened between Friday and today, but whatever it is, she's pissed to a point I've rarely seen. And it's never been hurled in my direction before.

My muscles tense, my heart pounding, as I wait for her to take her seat. But when I start to lower to the chair in front of her desk, her look freezes me in place.

"This won't take long, so you don't have to worry about sitting down," she clips out.

I go from somewhat crouched to ramrod straight. The last time that happened was my first day as a brand-new boot.

"You want to explain this to me?" The words are a snarl as she reaches for the stack in her inbox, yanking out two folders and slamming them on the scarred wood in front of her.

Maybe if I were still that same day-one rookie, I would jump. Instead, I crane my neck, reading the names on the folders.

What the hell? I had submitted both of those reports last week after she and I talked about Ellis's case.

"Cap?" I ask.

"O'Connell, can you explain why when I asked you to double-check your work you ignored my order?"

I had done what she asked.

"Cap, I not only double-checked. I triple-checked." Because I didn't want another career criminal like Ellis getting off on a technicality.

"Is that what you want me to tell IA?"

Fuck. Internal affairs.

"What the hell? Why are they involved?"

But I already know the answer to my question.

"Three cases in a week. Both of these have errors in the incident section. The charges we arrested them on were not the ones listed on the report."

"What?" Grabbing one of the reports, I skim through, recognizing what she just said before reviewing the second and finding the same issue. Plus more issues not as easy to spot. "I didn't write these."

"Your name is on the reports."

Glancing up from the one still in my hand, I step closer to her desk, and drop my voice as a feeling grows in my gut. I'm being set up and I don't know by who or why.

"Michelle, I didn't make these mistakes. I know this case"—I lift the manila folder still in my hand— "had three witnesses. I listed all three of them on my report. It's on my computer."

"Show me."

It takes a minute to boot it up after grabbing it from my bag, but once it's up, I open the file on my desktop I saved as a precaution.

I've never been so glad I'm obsessive over saving documents as I am right now.

"Here." Spinning the laptop, I point to the section still listing the three witness names and contact information.

She's silent for a moment, skimming through the rest of the report before her attention shifts back to me.

"Is this an earlier report?" She gestures to the manila folder.

"No. I don't print reports until I file them in the system too."

She spins back to her computer, pulling up the report in our electronic filing system.

"This matches the report you turned in. There aren't any witness names."

"Then someone changed it. I swear to God, I swear on my mother, when I turned it in, this report"—I grab my laptop—"matched what I submitted." My molars click together, my mind whirring a thousand miles an hour.

Someone wants my cases to be dismissed.

But who? I'm leaving. Everybody knows about my new job in DC. Why make me look bad now? And if someone wanted to undermine me, why are they doing it in a way that's putting perps back on the street? Suddenly the focus I felt on me earlier takes on a whole new meaning. Any one of my peers could be changing my reports—both electronically and the hard copy file.

But I still don't have an answer as to why.

"What about the other report?" she asks, nodding toward my laptop.

I pull up the second file and show her the date and time stamp on the saved file before opening it too.

"Son of a bitch," she murmurs, her fingers moving on the trackpad as she processes what's happening.

"Can we tell who accessed my reports in the database? These two and Ellis?" I ask.

She hands me back the laptop and I stuff it back in my bag.

"I'll have to check with IT. Last I heard the only ones who could authorize something like that was IA."

"And since they're already involved..."

"They've probably already put in the request."

"How many cases do you think they're looking at?" The rock sitting in my stomach grows to boulder size.

"You already know the answer. They're going to be going through everything."

I flop into the chair in front of her desk, running my hands through my hair.

"I leave in a month, Michelle. I really don't want IA up my ass for the next three weeks."

You don't have anything to hide.

No, but I also don't have the time it takes to deal with them either. I still have a mountain of cases to get through, and having them comb through every one as I close it is not something I have the energy for.

"I'll see what I can do. But no promises. I'm taking enough shit from the DA, and I may not have a leg to stand on," she says.

"Understood."

She sighs. "You're a good cop, Murphy. And a hell of a detective. Which is the only reason why I asked IA if I could meet with you first. These mistakes *aren't* like you. But if enough questions get asked, if there are any more errors in your files—and only yours—it'll look like you're slipping. Or something worse."

Her words coat my tongue in a bitterness I can't shake despite my attempts to swallow.

"I'm not," I grit out, hating the implications all of this has.

"And we're going to have to prove it. Because right now? What's on your laptop isn't strong enough to convince anyone otherwise. We need more. I'll see what I can do. But for now, you need to act like everything is fine. Keep this close to the vest," she says, freezing me with a look.

I nod.

"I won't tell anyone."

"Good. Dismissed." She shoves the two folders under a different pile on her desk and nods toward the door.

It takes a lot for me to close it calmly behind me when I want to storm into the general office area and start barking questions. I shift my attention around the room, meeting gazes of those present before they break eye contact.

Guilty at being caught eavesdropping? Or guilty of setting me up?

But who would do it?

Bryan? No, he was out all of last week so he couldn't have changed the reports.

Smith? Henderson? Martinez? Jenkins?

Fuck. I have no idea. And the sensation of something crawling on my skin as I try to focus is making it impossible. With a sigh, I walk to my desk, unpacking my laptop and grabbing the first file on the top of what I had left.

But it's impossible to focus as the sensation of being watched continues to heat between my shoulder blades. And every time I glance up, no one is looking at me. It's fucking unnerving. Sliding my chair back, I lock my computer and walk to the break room for some coffee.

My phone vibrates as I walk and I wait until I'm in the break room, cup of coffee in hand before I pull the phone from my pocket and see a text from Leigh.

LEIGH

Good morning.

What time did you leave?

For the first time since I walked into work this morning, the knot in my stomach relaxes and the tension in my skull eases.

Leaving the warm bed with her naked form pressed against mine had been one of the hardest things I've had to do in a long time. But the weekend was over, and I had to go home to get ready for work. I'd walked out to my car before the sun was up just so I could get to my apartment to shower and change before tackling the traffic downtown. Now I wish I hadn't left.

It was early.

LEIGH

You could have woken me up.

I can imagine waking her up how I had over the weekend—with my face between her thighs. But I doubt that's what she meant and I need to concentrate to avoid embarrassing myself at work.

You didn't need to get up when I did.

It's not like we got a lot of sleep this weekend.

I lean against the counter, crossing my feet at the ankles as I wait for her response.

LEIGH

I'm okay with that.

I'm even okay with the fact you told me you would cook and we ended up ordering pizza instead.

It's not MY fault you distracted me.

Every time we headed for the kitchen, my need for Leigh would erase any plans I had of making her dinner. Considering I had delivered her first orgasm in her kitchen, I could easily understand why.

I may need to rethink making her dinner at my place.

Location isn't going to matter. Not with a woman like Leigh.

LEIGH

Maybe you're just easily distractible.

Only by you.

It was a true statement. Never in my life had I experienced what I had this weekend—no matter how many times we had sex, it only increased my need for her. What had started out as a fling, as a scratch to an itch, wasn't feeling very casual anymore. My plans to leave on Saturday night had died a fiery death in the wake of her lips around my cock. Sunday morning, she had wiggled her ass against me while she slept and I was a goner. Which was why I ended up awake before the ass-crack of dawn. Because the only thing that could pull me from her side was a job I had dedicated my life to.

I still owe you dinner.

LEIGH

You could come over tonight to cook.

Is that what the kids are calling it these days? 😉

LEIGH

I meant, actually make dinner. We'll stay in the kitchen the whole time.

You and I both know how good I am in the kitchen, sweetheart.

My dick twitches to life at the memory of the way the

sunlight from the kitchen windows hugged her curves on Saturday.

LEIGH

Murphy!

Now I can't wait for work to be over.

That makes two of us.

Closing my eyes, I lift one hand up to pinch the bridge of my nose before adding to my text.

I'll need to let you know about dinner tonight though. I may have to work late.

Especially if I am going to try to figure out who is sabotaging my reports.

LEIGH

Okay.

Just let me know.

I will. I'll call you later.

Have a good day! 😊

I can picture her smile with those words, the one I learned intimately over the weekend. The one that plays on her lips when she isn't even aware of it. Fuck. My whole body burns with the need to see her again. To be with her.

You too, sweetheart.

The term of endearment comes way too easy when it comes to her.

But I'm not minding it as much as I should have.

My phone is nearly in my pocket when it rings. I half expect it to be Leigh, so am surprised to find the DC number of Rachel Park, the special agent in charge of the task force and my new boss.

"O'Connell."

"Murphy. How are you?"

"I'm good. Looking forward to starting with the bureau in a few weeks," I tell her, but the words aren't as true as they were a month ago.

I'm still excited about the job. But the thought of leaving Leigh is a dark spot in an otherwise amazing opportunity.

"That's what I wanted to call you about." She sighs.

The coffee I've been drinking curdles in my stomach.

"What about it? The job is still available, right?" I ask, the loosening knot reforming in granite.

"It is. But my leadership is concerned. We received a phone call this morning. About you."

"Me? From whom?" I ask, even though I already know where this is heading.

"I'm not at liberty to share. But what I can say is my leadership is concerned. I'm concerned. We've been told about several discrepancies with your work which resulted in at least one case being thrown out. I don't have to tell you how important attention to detail is in the bureau."

Overton had asked me to keep the fact that I was being sabotaged confidential. I trusted her decision, but it still stings to not immediately jump to my defense and my jaw clenches.

"I understand."

"I wanted to get your side of things so I could better identify what's going on."

Glancing around, I don't see anyone, but still stand and move into the empty room next to Overton's office. As much as I'd love to share what's going on, I can't. Not yet.

"Ma'am, I'm in the process of trying to understand that myself."

"Are you saying the information we received is false?"

Anger boils under the surface, the need to explain myself crowding my tongue.

"I've been asked not to discuss it for the time being, but I will absolutely let you know as soon as I know more."

"Do you have anything I can pass to leadership?" she asks.

"Nothing concrete. At least nothing yet." I pace to the window, staring out into the brilliant blue of the summer sky.

"Keep me posted. Leadership is now aware of what's going on and want me to monitor the situation. If anything else happens, I will have to rescind the offer. It's not something I want to do, but my hands will be tied."

Fuck. Fuck. Fuck.

That's what I've been afraid of since my conversation with Overton this morning.

"Understood."

"Good luck, Murphy. I'll be in touch."

"Thank you, ma'am."

The phone beeps in my ear, and exhaustion hangs heavy around my neck.

I'm barely hanging on to a job offer I've wanted since I was in college.

I'm being sabotaged at the job I've already given up.

I've never relied on luck before. I've never needed it.

But maybe my luck is running out.

CHAPTER 18

LEIGH

Waking up alone in my bed, reaching for Murphy, had only been the start to my Monday. Texting him had been a whim, the disappointment setting in when he told me he might have to work late.

Was he trying to distance himself? Or did he really have to work late? A notification buzzes on my phone, bringing me out of an internal debate, and my eyes drift to the clock in the bedroom.

"Shit!"

It's later than I realize and I rush through getting ready for work, making it out the door thirty minutes later than normal.

"Sorry, running late. Be there as soon as I can." I send the voice text to Lindsay, throwing my phone in the cupholder and trying to maintain the speed limit through the neighborhood at least.

But the main roads are a slow crawl after two accidents, and it's almost an hour past my normal start time when I rush into my cubicle to find my phone ringing.

"Hello?" I try to catch my breath quietly, my nerves a wreck between rushing out the door and the traffic.

"Leigh? It's JoAnna. Kenneth would like to see you."

Fuck. Am I in trouble for being late? I never heard back from Lindsay and her office is dark. Did I miss a court appearance?

"Now?" I ask.

"Yes. He's waiting for you."

"I'll be right there."

Dropping my bag on my desk, I spin on my heel and walk quickly to Kenneth's office. The stiffness in my muscles reminds me what I've been doing all weekend.

Focus. Now isn't the time to relive your steamy weekend.

JoAnna isn't at her desk, so I knock on the partially open door behind it.

"Come in." Kenneth's tone is more clipped than normal.

Wiping my sweaty palms on the back of my skirt, I swallow, taking a deep breath before opening the door.

"You wanted to see me?"

His head shoots up at the sound of my voice, his eyes lighting up while his mouth compresses to a line. This Kenneth is not one I've experienced before, and the fine hair on my arms stands in warning.

"Ms. Whittaker. Please close the door."

Ms. Whittaker. Not Leigh.

I should listen to the way my body screams at me to leave, but I don't. I need this job for the experience on my application. So, instead, I do as I'm told, suddenly wishing JoAnna were at her desk.

When I turn back around, Kenneth is standing, still behind his desk, and I take a small step into the office.

"Have a seat," he says, and motions to one of the two chairs in front of his desk.

I move forward on leaden legs until I'm able to take a seat, smoothing my skirt as I sit in the hard chair.

"Ms. Whittaker, what time do we start work every day?" He

clasps his arms behind his back and moves casually from behind the desk to stand in front of it.

But the question is anything but casual. His tone of voice, the sharp way he moves, reminds me of the principal at Mistletoe Creek High School. But even when I was in the office, I was never in trouble, and this very much feels like a lecture in the making.

"Ms. Whittaker. Do I need to repeat my question?" Kenneth sneers.

Startled, I look up and find him hovering next to me.

"No, sir." I squeeze against the opposite edge of my chair.

"What time?" he asks.

"8:30," I say quietly, dropping my gaze back to the floor at my feet.

Kenneth leans against the desk directly in front of me, his fingers gripping the wood so tightly his knuckles are white from the effort.

"What time is it now?"

Fuck.

"A-almost 9:45. I texted Lindsay I was running late and then there were two accidents and—"

"If I wanted your excuses, Ms. Whittaker, I would have asked for them. I don't know what Ms. Carter allows, but I will not tolerate tardiness from an intern," he snaps and the words of my explanation die on my lips.

No matter any trouble I've managed to get myself into, I've never been spoken to with the amount of derision Kenneth exhibits right now. Tears burn the back of my nose, and I blink rapidly, trying to clear the moisture in my eyes before it can fall.

"I…I'm sorry."

"It's hard to believe a week ago I was thinking how much promise you had. Do you think I'm an idiot? That you could take advantage of me? Now I'm wondering if we shouldn't end your internship early."

"You're firing me?" I ask, glancing up at him, wishing I hadn't.

His expression morphs from anger to a leer and my stomach nose-dives.

Suddenly, I understand what this is about.

I declined his advances last week, then showed up at the same place the happy hour was with Murphy. This isn't about me. It's about my rejection of him.

"That depends entirely on you," he says and confirms my suspicion. His voice drops to a murmur and he takes a step, caging me into the chair by placing a hand on either side of me.

But regardless of knowing what his behavior is about, it doesn't change the fact that I need him. Or at least the experience on my resume when I apply for Project Justice in September.

Who cares about the experience? Get the fuck out of here!

The voice sounds suspiciously like Sydney.

Is that what she would do?

Probably, but only after kneeing Kenneth in the groin first. But before either of us can do anything, there's a knock on the office door and Chief Bailey pokes his head inside.

"Ah, Kenneth, sorry to interrupt. JoAnna said you were free, and I wanted to talk to you about the Oliver case."

Kenneth straightens, dropping his arms. I stand as well and shift as far away from him as possible without drawing attention to myself.

"William, have you met Leigh Whittaker? She's one of our interns for the summer," Kenneth says, catching my eye—the *for now* is a silent part of his statement meant only for me.

William smiles and extends a hand as he gets closer to Kenneth.

"Ms. Whittaker, a pleasure. I hear great things about you from Lindsay."

"Sir." I shake his hand and head toward the door, my escape route clear. "It's nice to meet you as well. I'll…umm…I'll let the two of you talk."

Chief Bailey turns back to Kenneth while Kenneth's gaze continues to burn a hole between my shoulder blades until I close the door behind me. JoAnna, back in her seat, looks at me. Her bright blue eyes hold a sympathy and the burn of tears returns.

"Are you okay, Leigh?" JoAnna asks, her voice kind.

But it's the expression on her face—a mix of understanding and determination—that makes me do a double take. Did she have anything to do with Chief Bailey coming in when he did?

I nod. "I'm fine. Thank you."

The last words are meant for more than just her question. Without her, who knows what Kenneth would have done.

Would you have let him?

It's the fact I don't know that has me questioning what I'm willing to do for an opportunity with Project Justice.

"I'm sure you'll want to get back to your desk. I heard that Ms. Carter is out sick today, so Kenneth said he'll be reviewing your work during her absence."

Her absence?

"Will she be out for longer than today?"

"I don't think so."

Thank God I only have to work with him today. But even that horror must show more than I think it does because she makes a compassionate noise.

"It's okay, hon. Just email me whatever you're working on. I'll get it to him."

Sighing with relief, I offer JoAnna a shaky smile.

"Thank you, JoAnna."

"Call me Jo. And you're welcome. Anytime."

My legs feel wobbly as I make my way back to my desk, the adrenaline flagging from my body as I boot up my computer. Sure enough, Lindsay is out sick for the day and sent me an email early this morning. But her email says she'll review everything when she gets back. There are no directions to work with Kenneth.

With a sigh, I respond back, hoping she feels better. At the tail end, I ask to set up a time for the two of us to talk when she's back. I had promised Murphy I was going to report Kenneth, and while I haven't had the chance yet, I don't like that I questioned what I would do simply because I need the experience this job will give me. What would I be willing to do next? I'm not going to find out. If I get fired for reporting Kenneth, I will figure it out.

Email response sent, I start to tackle the list of tasks she sent me. There are several case files to organize for her and two memos she wants me to draft for her review. She's also asked me to start reviewing potential cases where we can apply funding for the Wrongful Conviction Fund but no clear indications on whether I'll be working on it full-time or not.

I'm nearly ready to start looking through potential cases when my phone rings again.

"Public Defender's Office, this is Leigh. How may I help you?"

"I'm emailing you notes on memos I need drafted. I want it done in two hours," Kenneth says into the phone before the click tells me he's hung up.

My inbox pings and there are ten different attachments of lackluster notes not at all helpful for crafting the documents he's asked for in the email. I spend the next two hours working through three of the cases—doing the majority of the research myself—when my phone rings.

I eye it cautiously and pick it up, dreading what's on the other end of the call this time.

"Leigh Whittaker. How may I help you?"

"Leigh?" The voice is familiar, but not one I can pinpoint exactly.

"Yes?"

"It's Charlie. Vanderweel."

Some of the nerves in my stomach relax, and the knot of tension between my shoulder blades releases.

"Hey, Charlie. How can I help you? Did you need Lindsay? She's out of the office today."

"No, actually, I was calling to talk to you. I didn't have your personal cell, so figured I could call you here."

"What can I do for you?"

"Would you be my date for a charity event my dad is hosting on Saturday?" He rushes the request out.

How would Murphy feel about this?

The fact that that's my first question shows me how much Murphy has come to mean to me in a short time.

I already know he wouldn't like it. He's made his feelings about Charlie clear.

But how do you *feel about the invitation?*

It's coming out of the blue since he told me the other day he doesn't have feelings for me. And while I might have entertained it before Murphy, it's different now.

"I... Charlie, I'm sorry, but I'm kind of seeing someone right now," I tell him.

Ugh. This is awkward.

"Oh. No. Sorry. Just as friends. My dad is bugging me to bring a date, and normally I take my cousin Lacey, but she's out of town this weekend and can't go with me. If I show up alone, my dad will go ballistic because I have to 'keep up appearances.'"

"I...just friends?"

Does that change things?

How would you feel if Murphy were going somewhere as "just friends" with someone?

The jealousy firing through my blood gives me an answer.

Hell, no.

"Absolutely platonic. Better than platonic. My dad is announcing the donation and establishment of the Wrongful Conviction Fund and he's invited several of the bigwigs from Project Justice to sit at our table. I thought it would be a good chance for you to network and I get a buffer from my dad. It's a win-win. I'll even cover the cost of your dress."

A chance to interact with senior executives with Project Justice? Who might even be part of the selection committee? I wouldn't have to rely on Kenneth—or a recommendation from this job—for my application. How can I say no?

Surely Murphy is going to understand. In his hierarchy of hatred toward Kenneth and Charlie, I'm pretty sure he'd much rather I not have to rely on Kenneth.

"That's okay. I'm sure I can find something," I say, mentally going through my closet.

"So you'll do it? You'll come?" he asks.

"Um...maybe? I need to check with M—the person I'm seeing." I almost say Murphy's name, but I'm not sure how Murphy—or Charlie—would feel about me sharing, so I keep that to myself.

I just need to figure out a way to explain this to Murphy.

He's been crystal clear about wanting me to steer clear of Charlie. But the benefit of meeting with Project Justice is too much to overlook. I have to convince him.

He'll have to trust my judgment.

Right?

"Understandable. I can check with you later this week, if that works?"

"It does. I'll get you an answer as soon as possible."

"I'll text you the details so you have them. I just need your number."

I rattle off the number and hang up the phone.

"What part of two hours do you not understand?" Kenneth hisses.

Jumping, I swing around in my desk chair to find him leaning over the top of me, his eyes full of hatred as he stares me down.

Shit.

"I—"

"Obviously you had time to set up a date on company time, but you can't get simple memos done?"

"I got three of them finished. I'm sorry, I—"

"If I don't get *all* the memos I requested in my inbox by the end of today, you're going to be more sorry than you are right now."

I glance around, looking for anyone who might be witnessing Kenneth's threat toward me.

But there's no one. I'm on my own.

"There's no one to do your work for you, Ms. Whittaker. Do you understand? Everything done, 5 p.m. No excuses. Otherwise, don't bother coming in tomorrow."

He leaves as quickly as he showed up, and I strongly debate just leaving. I don't need this job. I don't need the recommendation.

Are you sure?

All Saturday is going to do is give me the chance to meet them. It doesn't guarantee me anything.

And I don't want to leave Lindsay in a lurch. I want to give her the chance to do something about Kenneth's behavior. Other than him, this job has been amazing.

Shaking my head, I shelve my debate for later and dive back into research, using every spare minute to finish all the memos, as requested. Luckily, not all the cases are as in-depth as the first few were, and I send the final files before checking the time on my computer.

4:47 p.m.

"Take that, you jerk," I mutter to myself.

My phone rings again and I consider letting it go to voicemail, wishing it had some sort of caller ID on it. With a sigh, I lift the receiver, bracing myself for whatever comes next.

"Public Defender's Office, this is Leigh. How can I help you?"

"Leigh, it's Jo."

My body deflates, a headache building at the base of my skull.

"I see the memos in Kenneth's inbox. I don't think he expected you to get them all done today. Some of them aren't even on his calendar for weeks."

By five o'clock, my ass.

I swallow the smart-ass retort.

"Oh. I just figured I would get them done."

Especially if it meant not having to work with him anymore.

"Why don't you take off a few minutes early? It's almost 5:00 anyway."

"I was late—"

"Don't worry about it. Everyone is occasionally. I'm guessing you didn't take a lunch either, so let's call it even."

"But Kenneth—"

"Kenneth left an hour ago."

I'm done questioning, ready to go home and forget today even happened.

"Okay, thanks, Jo. Good night."

"Have a good night, Leigh. We'll see you tomorrow."

I hope not. As much as I like Jo, her proximity to Kenneth is enough for me to keep my distance. How does she stand working with him?

Not worth my time or energy right now. Hanging up, I pack up as quickly as I can, making my way out into our parking lot in under five minutes. My keys are in the bottom of my purse, and I dig for them while walking to my car. Keys in hand, I look up, gasping when I come face-to-face with the grizzled appearance of the man I saw in the lobby a couple of weeks ago.

"H-hi."

"Kenny around?" he asks, the stale smell of sour alcohol burning my nostrils.

I try to hold my breath, my heart racing in my chest as I take a few steps back.

"Kenneth?" I ask.

"S'what I said," he slurs.

"Um, he already left for the day, Mr…?" I trail off, hoping he'll provide his name.

"You're pretty." His glazed eyes focus on me for a terrifying heartbeat, and he reaches out a dirty hand.

I shrink back, wishing I was closer to the door to get back inside. But my badge is in the bottom of my purse—right next to where my keys were—and I don't want to turn my back on the man in front of me.

No one else is around, the entrance into the building far enough from the busy street it's not like anybody is just going to happen by.

"Can I take a message for Kenneth?" Dammit, I wish I had pockets in this skirt I could stash my pepper spray in. Or that I had connected the key ring it's on to my keys sitting useless in my hand.

His gaze sharpens as he studies me and he takes a step forward. I take another step back, but it's not like I have anywhere to retreat.

"You were with that fucking pig the last time I was here." He reaches over and I shrink back so his fingers grasp only the fabric of my sleeve versus my arm.

"I'll tell Kenneth you stopped by," I tell him, trying to step back again, but his grip on the fabric is enough purchase that he can grab my arm.

I try to twist out of his grip, but it tightens, frissons of pain sparking through my body.

"Let go," I tell him, trying to remember the self-defense the sorority sisters had gone through right before I graduated.

But my heart pounding and the building headache make concentrating difficult.

"I'm not done talking to you, bitch. I have a message for the pig I saw you with."

The door behind me opens, the clang of the metal door against the brick facade a welcome reprieve.

Relief floods my body, and I spin as much as his grip will allow me, taking my eyes off him, to face the two employees who both seem surprised to see me. Or maybe it's the man with me who surprises them.

Something hard strikes the back of my head, stars whirling in my dimming vision. I fall to my knees, finally free of the grip as I struggle to form words.

"Leigh?" Jo's voice sounds like it's coming from a distance but she's right next to me, gently shaking me. "Leigh? Are you okay?"

Words still aren't possible, Jo's image fading quickly.

"Leigh!"

It's the last thing I hear before I fall forward.

Funny, I expected pavement to be hard.

It's the last thought I have as darkness falls.

CHAPTER 19

MURPHY

I'm on my way to Leigh's when the police radio goes off in my car.

Since I'm technically off-shift, I move to turn it down when the call catches my attention.

"Unit 217, Unit 122, Code 3. 1822 W. Kennedy Avenue. Woman attacked in parking lot. EMS en route. Victim is unconscious but breathing. No other information known."

"Unit 122, 10-4. Show us attached and we are en route."

1822 W. Kennedy is the address of the public defender's office. I've been there often enough I know the address—it has nothing to do with Leigh.

Denial. Not just a river in Egypt.

I was already almost to Leigh's house when the call came in and I don't hesitate to flip a U-turn in the middle of the residential street, going as fast as I can back in the direction of her building.

I turn up the radio, hearing a second unit attach.

Fuck.

Don't be Leigh. Don't be Leigh.

But there's a pit in my stomach as I reach for my phone,

finding her contact while still trying to keep my attention on the road. The phone starts to ring and I hold my breath, several agonizingly slow heartbeats thudding against my chest before it goes to voicemail.

"Hi, you've reached Leigh..."

I hang up, tossing the phone back into the console and pressing my foot against the accelerator. The car lurches forward and my fingers tighten on the steering wheel as I race back through town. Horns honk around me as I weave in and out of traffic, and I catch a finger or two raised in my direction.

Oh fucking well.

A light shifts from yellow to red and I blow through it, the sound of horns echoing behind me.

A drive that should take me forty minutes or more at this time of day takes me fifteen minutes. There's a unit parked in the street, an officer standing in the driveway who I wave my badge at before he lets me turn into the parking lot on the side of the building. Finding the closest open spot, I throw my car into park and notice the ambulance lights near the back of the lot, the doors wide open, with another police car next to it.

The pit in my stomach has only grown with the presence of the red and blue lights. A part of me had hoped I heard the address wrong. That Leigh would call me back and ask if I was still coming for dinner.

But my phone had stayed frustratingly silent.

I attempt to take a deep breath to calm my racing heart, and all I can do is remember Mom answering the door to the two officers. One of them Dad's best friend. The way she had crumpled to the ground, her fingers still gripping the door frame.

My stomach rolls with the urge to get sick, but I catch my own gaze in my rearview mirror, repeating what I had heard on the radio.

"Unconscious but breathing," I whisper.

It's not the same.

But I still have no idea what I'm going to find.

I run my hand over my stomach, pushing down the urge to puke. This is the feeling I'd been avoiding by not getting close to her.

You did such a good job at that.

It was impossible. There was something about her I couldn't resist. I didn't want to. All I wanted was for her to be okay.

Please.

Repeating the word like a prayer, I rush from the car with my badge in hand. I don't run, not wanting to incite panic, but I move quickly, eating up the distance from my car to the lights and flashing my badge at the uniformed officer attempting to corral people back to allow the paramedics to do their jobs.

Please.

My heart is in my throat as I try to swallow.

The gurney is already out, resting against the ambulance. Her blonde hair comes into focus first, and a combination of rage and anxiety hits my body like a one-two punch.

Fuck.

I should have been here sooner.

She shouldn't be lying there.

And I shouldn't be falling for her.

My feet screech to a stop as the realization hits me.

I'm not sure when it happened, but I am.

And that scares the shit out of me.

Taking a deep breath, I push it out, refocusing on the moment and not my own internal battle. Her face is pale, her eyes closed, and my hands fist by my side. But they must have only been closed for the moment, her eyelashes fluttering against her cheek before they open to reveal her bright blue eyes that remind me of the Caribbean ocean dimmed like a storm has rolled in. But they're open.

I relax my hands, my legs moving with a mind of their own. Bringing me closer to her.

She's awake.

Thank fucking Christ.

"Leigh…" I say her name and her gaze jumps to mine, the relief in them hitting me squarely in the solar plexus, stealing my breath as easily as she steals another piece of my heart.

She lifts a hand and I close the distance, interlacing our fingers before she can even say my name.

"Baby, what happened?" I ask, searching her for obvious injuries, but aside from two angry red marks on each of her knees and dirt on her cheek, there are no obvious signs of trauma.

The knot between my shoulder blades releases a fraction. It could already have been so much worse.

She could have been—

I don't allow myself to finish the thought, looking to the first responder checking her vitals before her cool hand squeezes mine and brings my attention back to her.

"I-I was leaving work and there was a guy in the parking lot. I didn't see him until he was right here. He was looking for Kenneth."

I can only imagine what scumbag was looking for Kenneth when he found Leigh.

"What did he look like, ma'am?" The uniformed officer is scribbling quickly in a notebook.

I want to bark at him to let her rest, but I know he's only doing his job. I've been in his shoes more than once. So I bite back the lecture, swallowing the overwhelming urge to sweep her up off the gurney and take her somewhere safe. I console myself by running my thumb against the soft skin of her hand, finding the pulse point beating steadily in her wrist.

Its reassurance helps calm the beast in me. Until her eyes widen.

"What is it?" I murmur.

"He recognized me. He said he saw me with you before. In the lobby."

Ellis.

Fuck me.

The man should be behind bars, and instead he's attacked Leigh in broad fucking daylight.

Goddammit.

Why, though? Why is Ellis coming after Leigh?

I can't focus on that. The fury is like a tidal wave, hazing my vision in red. Anger at Ellis. And frustration because the report was changed. It allowed Ellis to get off on the technicality he needed to be free.

Because of fucking Kenneth Scott.

Ellis had been looking for him. And Leigh had been caught in the crosshairs.

But was she another of Ellis's victims because of Kenneth? Or because of me?

I start to disentangle my fingers from Leigh, needing to do something—anything—to tamp down my anger, but Leigh's grip tightens.

"Don't leave," she whispers.

The words are a whisper, but the effect is like an unbreakable chain.

"I'm not going anywhere, Stóirín." I keep my voice low, leaning down to brush my lips against her forehead before I turn to the officer still next to the gurney. "His name is Ellis. Vinny Ellis. I've run into him here before, and last time he and I had some words."

The responding officer continues to take notes.

"Grab whatever witness statements you can. I don't want him to get away with this," I tell him.

Maybe I'm overstepping my bounds, but I don't fucking care.

Someone attacked Leigh which leaves those boundaries more flexible than before.

He nods. "I'm familiar with Ellis, sir. Picked him up last year on a drug charge."

"There's security footage." The middle-aged woman with shocking red hair speaks up from where she stands next to Leigh. "You'll need a warrant."

"Who are you, ma'am?"

"JoAnna. JoAnna Kirby. I work here with Leigh."

The paramedic finishes his exam of Leigh, and she struggles to sit up.

"And just where do you think you're going?" I ask her.

"I want to go home," she says with a determination that worries me.

"The only place you're going is the fucking hospital."

That's the wrong thing to say based on the thin line her lips form.

"Not in that, I'm not. I've had enough of ambulances to last a lifetime." She shudders, and the memory of the night Cole and I rescued Hannah Grace and Leigh swims to the surface. "He says I can drive myself. That I'm okay—" She gestures to the EMT, who steps in.

"I said I think everything appears okay based on the exam I was able to do. But I didn't say anything about you driving yourself. You need a head CT and a licensed doctor to confirm you don't have a head injury."

"Head CT? You hit your head?" I ask, the rush of moving from caveman ready to fight to concern for her a dizzying rush of emotion.

"He hit her. In the back of the head," JoAnna speaks up from behind me.

My attention stays focused on Leigh, who bites her lip to stop it from trembling, but she can't hide the sheen of moisture building in her eyes.

"I-I didn't see it…I just remember a sharp pain and then falling on the asphalt."

"And then she passed out," JoAnna adds from behind her.

"You're going to get checked out," I tell her.

"And I will. But not in that." She points to the ambulance before crossing her arms and setting her jaw. Fuck. I'm not sure if I should carry her to the ambulance or kiss her.

"Ma'am, I highly recommend it. You can refuse transport, but if you were my girlfriend, I wouldn't want you driving," the paramedic says.

A possessiveness unlike anything I've ever experienced overrides every other emotion. She's not his. She's mine.

Mine.

"I'm fine. I just have a headache." She says the words, but I can see the stubborn mask slipping.

Her bravado is crumbling.

"Stóirín," I murmur, lifting my hands to her jaw and cupping her face gently. "Please. You don't have to go in the ambulance if you don't want to. But I do want them to tell you you're okay. It will give me some peace of mind." Because I can't imagine if something did happen to her.

"I—" She's gearing up for another battle by the way she squares her shoulders.

My little warrior.

But she doesn't have to be so brave.

And I, for one, would feel a whole lot better verifying she really is okay.

"I'll drive you there myself. You won't have to go in the ambulance. And I'll stay with you the whole time. You don't have to go alone," I promise.

I don't blame her for not wanting to ride in another ambulance. The last one—the night when we met—was a traumatic enough event for her. She doesn't need to add more stress to a potential injury.

"She really should go in the ambulance. But she wouldn't let us put the stabilizer on," the paramedic grumbles, referencing the neck brace I've seen used a few times when I responded to traffic accidents.

I fight the smile twitching at the corner of my lips while I point at the medical professional.

The sassiness is a welcome sign—she is the same woman who draws me to her like a moth to a flame. But I still want reassurance.

"Please, Stóirín," I whisper. "I'm sure you're right and you are okay, but…"

I'm not able to finish the sentence, thoughts of my parents crowding out the words.

Whatever she's able to see must convince her. Her jaw relaxes and she lifts her hands to lightly grip my wrist.

"You'll drive me?" she asks, hints of vulnerability becoming more apparent.

Relief is a welcome rush through my blood.

I nod. "I will."

"And stay with me?" she asks.

"Nothing will stop me," I promise.

CHAPTER 20

MURPHY

"I told you I was fine," Leigh says around a yawn as we settle into my bed hours later.

After an eight-hour stay in the emergency room—where the doctor had in fact confirmed she was fine—I had convinced her to come to my place since it was a ten-minute drive versus a thirty-minute one to her place.

"And I'm glad the doctor told us so," I murmur, brushing my lips against her forehead.

After a head CT had been ordered.

After they had checked for signs of a concussion.

After they had bandaged her knees and given her a prescription for extra strength ibuprofen if she needed it.

After I had drilled the doctor about signs or symptoms we should be watching for since she didn't present with anything at the moment.

Finally, two pills and one shared shower later, she is lying in my arms, dressed in one of my T-shirts.

Shifting, she moves until her head lies against my chest, her damp hair creating gooseflesh along my skin, while her fingers absentmindedly drag against the skin of my right pec, tracing my tattoos. Lifting my head, I glance at the alarm clock across the room.

"It's late. You already let Lindsay know you won't be at work tomorrow?" I ask, tightening my hold around her.

She nods and her damp hair tickles my skin.

"Are you sure you're going to stay home tomorrow too? I don't want you to get in trouble."

The doctor had given Leigh a note for two days off from work. As we left the hospital, I'd texted Captain Overton to let her know I wouldn't be in either.

"It's absolutely fine. I have sick time and someone needs to keep an eye on you. Make sure you're actually taking it easy," I tease her.

Her breath blows out in a warm gust.

"The headache is already gone," she grumbles.

"The doctor said—"

Her head shoots up.

"I was there. I heard what the doctor said. And I will take it easy. Even if you're not there to babysit me."

"I was teasing you, sweetheart. Apparently not well, but I know I don't have to babysit you." I run my hands up and down her back, and a sheepish expression covers her face before she drops her forehead back to my chest.

"Sorry. Shit. I'm sorry."

"It's okay. We're both tired. We should get some sleep."

She rests her head back against my chest, her breath moving in even patterns while her fingers resume their circles after a few more heartbeats.

"I'm still sorry," she murmurs.

"There is absolutely nothing to be sorry about. Forget about it."

"I need something to distract me. I'm a dweller. I dwell."

Another fact to file away.

"So I'm noticing."

"Can you distract me?"

My dick knows of one way to distract her.

Is that the only thing you think about?

No, but when it comes to her, it's never far off.

"Distract you how?" I ask.

She lifts her head again, her eyes blazing a different type of fire than earlier.

"You could kiss me," she says, slicking her tongue along her lips.

Fuck.

A woman after my own heart.

I don't think that's your heart.

I groan, my hands fisting in the material along her back as my dick hardens in a rush.

"Doing that would definitely not be 'taking it easy,'" I tell her, fighting the need to say fuck what the doctor says and kiss her the way she's asked me to.

She pouts her lower lip, leaning her head on her hand.

"Do you always follow the rules?" she asks.

"This one, I fully intend to," I counter.

"But you flirt with the line."

I nod. "I do."

"Like with your tattoos." Her gaze drops to trace along my tattoo, her fingers following her gaze.

It feels like a lifetime ago since I told her how they pushed the boundaries of what the department would allow.

"Yes," I tell her.

"You've never told me about them. Your tattoos," she says, her hand splaying over the one on my right shoulder.

"You really want to know? Now?" I ask.

"I asked to be distracted. It's either that or the amount of bubble bath you have on your bathtub. Most men don't have three different types."

A corner of my lips twitches with a smile.

"My sisters are to blame for that."

"Something tells me I'd really like your sisters," she says and lays her head back down against my chest.

It fills with warmth at the thought of her interacting with Quinn and Riley. Of her meeting Mom and my nieces and nephew. It's so vivid, so real, I have to blink to realize it's only in my mind.

"They'd love you." Guaranteed. They'd want to know when Leigh was going to make an honest man out of me. They'd be halfway planned to a wedding within the first day.

"They got you the bubble bath?"

"The first bottle they got me was a gag gift. It was the season of *Searching for Love* with Jake and Meggie. When they shared that bubble bath. They started talking about their own experiences in bubble baths—not something their older brother needed to hear, by the way—and I said I hadn't taken a bath since I was a kid with the cartoon bubbles."

"Awww." The sound is more a vibration against my chest than anything else.

"But the joke was on them. I did use it. The whole bottle. Then I bought another one. And they started buying me bottles of bubble bath for my birthday and Christmas. There are absolutely times when I enjoy relaxing in my tub—it's why I found a condo with a tub I could fit in."

"It's big enough for two. Maybe we could try that sometime," she muses and my dick jumps against her.

She squirms, wriggling her hips against me, and it takes everything I have to cage her hips with my hands and hold her still.

"You're going to be the death of me, Stóirín," I clench out through gritted teeth, trying to recite police regulations in my head until the urge to roll her beneath me fades..

Her teeth flash white in the darkness.

"I never promised to take it easy on you."

Everything she says only makes me like her more. I'm in dangerous territory here. I've never been as turned on by a woman's wit as I am her body.

But for Leigh?

She's the full package, and after the day full of roller-coastering emotions, I need time to process everything.

"We need to get some sleep," I tell her.

Although with all the thoughts running rampant in my head, I doubt sleep is going to be possible for me just yet.

"Will you tell me about your tattoos now?" she asks.

"Are you going to go to sleep if I do?" I tease, finally able to relax my hands as I trace them back up the soft cotton of my T-shirt she's wrapped in.

"Consider it my bedtime story." She lays her head back to my chest, a sigh gusting out of her as she settles against me. "I'm ready."

Her touch is almost ticklish where it drags along the sole tattoo above my heart. The date emblazoned there was only the beginning.

"That's my first," I say, still clearly remembering the initial feel of the needle as it vibrated against my skin. The hum of it was a comforting sound. One I have grown addicted to. But despite the intricacies of the rest of my tattoos, the first remains pure. Simple.

"What is it?"

Grief clogs my throat and I swallow around the lump.

"It's a date with a police shield. August 15."

"Is that…?"

"Yeah, the day my dad died," I whisper into the darkness.

Her arms wrap around me, squeezing as hard as she can, and the darkness doesn't feel as lonely as it did a moment ago.

"I'm so sorry."

I can't tell her it's okay—it probably never will be. But the pain recedes a little more every passing year. I sigh, spanning my hands along her back.

"It was a long time ago. But I remember how badly I didn't want to forget him. Nothing about him. The sound of his voice, the way he laughed. The memories are still there, but they're fuzzier than they used to be. When I turned eighteen, I thought adding the date to my body would link him to me permanently."

"You already are. In here." Her palm rests against my chest and my heart beats against it.

"I didn't really understand that at eighteen. So I thought, why not get a tattoo?"

"How did one turn into everything else?"

"The most amount of clarity I had in my life was when the needle vibrated against my skin. It's like the sensation focused me in a way nothing else ever has. By the time I joined the force, I already had most of my chest and shoulder done and was working on my leg. It wasn't until after I made detective I started on my sleeve since I was able to cover it. You'd be surprised how people feel about a policeman with tattoos."

"Whether you have them or not doesn't change the kind of person you are," she murmurs, resuming the gentle glide of her fingers against my chest.

"Not everyone thinks like you do, Stóirín."

"Well, that's dumb," she grumbles.

I bark out a laugh, wrapping my arms around her to hold her to my chest.

"What about you?" I ask her.

"What about me? Tattoos?" she asks.

"Mm-hmm. Have you ever wanted one?"

"How do you know I don't already have one?"

"I've explored every inch of your body at length, sweetheart. I've never seen a drop of ink against your perfect skin."

"Perfect?" Her fingers still and she lifts her head to lock gazes with me.

"Yes," I tell her, letting the truth shine in the way I keep my focus locked on her.

Her next breath is an audible intake of air, the moment stretching between us until she lowers her head again and resumes the drag of her fingertips as they trace patterns on my tattoos.

"I've thought about it. A few of my sorority sisters had them. But I didn't want to get something I didn't want on my skin permanently."

"That's a wise decision," I tell her.

"I still might. If I ever figure out what I want. Maybe then I can get the name of who did yours."

"Of course."

Neither one of us mentions the looming date of me relocating to DC. It doesn't belong between us right now.

My thumb rubs back and forth against the skin of her shoulder, the silence comfortable in the darkness while she continues to draw nonsensical patterns on my chest. Her breathing grows deeper, evening out, and her fingers pause, resting where they lie.

But the damage is done.

Every pass of her fingers against my skin is another tether between us. Another link.

"You're not supposed to be the one," I whisper.

She murmurs in her sleep, her legs scissoring, and I brush my lips against the top of her head.

"Sleep well, sweetheart."

At least one of us should.

CHAPTER 21

LEIGH

"What are you doing? Why are you picking Sarah? She's a fucking drama-loving psycho," Murphy mutters in my ear as the two of us watch a season of *Searching for Love*.

One arm tightens around me while he reaches with his other hand for the popcorn balanced in my lap.

A smile stretches my cheeks. He's been like that most of the season we're bingeing on our day off. Making comments at the TV, debating when he and I disagreed between two of the men who were fighting for Sophie during her season.

"You're very...passionate," I tease, reaching for a handful of popcorn for myself.

"It's so obvious," he says around the mouthful he's just eaten.

"Tell me how you really feel."

"I'll do you one better and show you instead." His fingers dance along my ribcage and I squirm against him, popcorn going everywhere as I try to evade the ticklish sensation while laughing.

"Okay, okay, I give. Make all the comments you want." I manage to pant the words.

Watching *Searching for Love* with Murphy has been a journey in entertainment.

"Thank you," he says before tugging me back into position against him.

My phone chimes with a text, and I reach over with my free hand, grabbing it from the table while he picks up spilled popcorn off the couch and me and puts it back into the bowl.

CHARLIE

Here are the details I mentioned yesterday.

Crap. My body flushes hot and cold as I read through the texts.

I had forgotten.

Several other texts come through with the location, time, and offers to pick me up as well as the second offer to pay for my dress. I'm not sure whether to drop my phone like a hot potato or ignore it. It's not like I've done anything wrong.

Except you didn't tell him about the invitation.

I was going to. But after everything yesterday, I had forgotten. And now my time is up. The sound on the TV stops as Murphy pauses it.

"Everything okay?" he asks from behind me.

Not quite looking over my shoulder, but is he close enough to see what's on my phone?

Double crap.

Had he read my texts?

"Umm…"

His hands move to my shoulders, his thumbs dragging along the tension on either side of my spine.

"Your headache is going to come back. Your shoulders just went up around your ears. Is it work?"

Aside from an email earlier this morning from Lindsay acknowledging mine, I hadn't heard from anyone at work.

"No." Anxiety rolls through my stomach, and I set the popcorn bowl on the table.

"What's the matter?" he asks.

"I...I need to tell you something," I say and turn around until I can face him.

What is he going to say? How is he going to respond when I tell him about the invitation? I still haven't accepted it—a small saving grace—but I intend to. The opportunity to meet the executives with Project Justice is too good to pass up.

But what does that mean for us?

"Okay." But he says the word slowly, hesitant, and I have zero doubt his response is based on my own behavior.

Because you are being weird about it.

"I forgot with everything that happened yesterday. I got a phone call at work. There's a charity event on Saturday night and I got an invitation. It's to announce Nashville's Wrongful Conviction Fund, and several individuals from Project Justice are going to be there too." I'm leaving out some information—namely a critical piece of information as to who invited me.

I should know better given his job.

"I take it the invitation wasn't from your office," he says, starting to connect the dots.

"What makes you say that?"

Quit stalling. Rip it off, like a Band-Aid.

"You won't stop messing with your cuticle and you won't look up from what you're doing."

Sure enough, I am picking at a cuticle, my attention focused on my finger.

But I'm not a kid asking a parent's permission.

I'm a woman doing something for my career.

By telling her boyfriend she's going on a date with another man.

Murphy isn't my boyfriend though.

Lifting my gaze, I find his steady one waiting for me.

I shift my fingers from my abused cuticle and take a deep breath, releasing it as my hands rest against my legs.

"You're right. I didn't get the invitation from work. It…it came from Charlie Vanderweel."

A muscle tics in his jaw, his expression moving from curious and concerned to anger.

At me?

Would you be angry at him if the roles were reversed?

"Leigh—"

"I know you don't like him," I rush to say.

"It's more than that. It doesn't matter whether I like him or not. He's dangerous. You and I have both had enough excitement for the week." He's not telling me no, so I can't use the response I already have cued up for an outright no.

"He's not dangerous," I say, focusing on the other piece he's shared.

I know that as much as I know that about Murphy. Neither man presents a danger.

Except to my heart. And Murphy is the most dangerous to that.

"Then how come he was the one we arrested for his fiancée's murder?" he asks.

"The conviction was overturned," I point out.

"Fuck," he mumbles.

Standing from the couch, he paces the room.

"We agreed to disagree before. About Charlie," I remind him, thinking back to the last time we had debated Charlie's innocence. "And I'm not really asking. I'm informing. My plan is to attend the charity event on Saturday. I figured as the man I'm…involved with…I should tell you. This is a really good opportunity for me. One that means I don't have to rely on Creepy Kenneth for a recommendation at the end of the summer."

He stops, his eyes closing while his lips move without sound for several heartbeats. When he opens his eyes again, his jaw relaxes.

"Is there anything I can say to convince you not to go?" he asks as he walks back toward the couch and drops to his haunches in front of me.

"Why don't you want me to go?" I ask.

Studying him this close, concern still furrows a line between his brows. But there's something else too. A softening of the fire there. One tugging on my heart.

"I already said why. He's dangerous."

"He's not. Even if you don't want to trust that, trust me. But that's not it. Or at least not totally."

Will he put a name to the emotion that's barely discernible?

My breath backs up in my lungs, a tingle forming on my skin. It's like the moment in a storm just before a close lightning strike. Waiting for him.

"Why don't you want me to go?" I repeat my earlier question after the moment stretches between us.

"I… yesterday was the second hardest day of my life, Stóirín. Hearing that call on the radio, I got this feeling. Here"—his hand drops to his stomach—"and I just knew. It fucking scared the shit out of me. Not knowing how badly you were hurt. Not able to get to you right away. That feeling came only second to the day I watched my mother crumple at the door when my dad's best friend came to tell her he had passed away."

My heart melts—a combination of grief for the young man who lost his dad too young and euphoria at his confession. I shift to the edge of the couch, and his hands drop to my knees.

"I'm so sorry, Murphy," I tell him, covering his hands with mine.

"It's why I promised myself I would never get married. I didn't want anyone to go through that pain because of me. But no one warned me how it would feel knowing something happened to you. Scared shitless if something worse were to happen," he whispers and worry fills his eyes, turning the light in them soft and golden.

Warmth flows through my body.

"I'm catching feelings for you, Leigh. I didn't plan on it. In fact, I planned the exact opposite. But it's impossible to fight. And there may be a thousand reasons for us not to be together, but none of them change how badly I want you. How fiercely I need you."

Holy shit.

The bliss that lands on my skin at his words like a butterfly's wings is reality. And overwhelming.

A few weeks ago, this was the man who could only promise a few weeks of fiery sheets and wasn't even willing to give me that. But maybe whatever is happening between us did impact him like it has me. I can't imagine my life without him.

Leaning over, I thread my fingers through his hair as my lips find his. He takes possession of the kiss and slides his hands along my thighs until he can grip my hips, tugging me off the couch and closer to him.

Maybe I should feel powerless in light of all his strength, but the careful way he holds me, the leashed control, makes me feel powerful.

"Is this… are you okay?" He rips his mouth away from mine to ask.

Eyes the color of honey study me, filled with an emotion neither of us has put a name to. If I wasn't falling before, I damn sure am now.

I nod.

"I'm good. Better than good."

Leaning up, I capture his mouth with mine again, moaning as his tongue tangles with mine, and he leans back, lying on the floor while I straddle him.

The sweatpants he lent me provide no barrier, and his hands slide under the waistband, palming my ass and rubbing me back and forth against him. My nipples pebble against the shirt, teased through the layers of cotton between him and me. I whimper, fireworks building behind my eyes with every pass.

"Not here," he growls against my lips.

I'm confused but only for a moment before he stands, still holding me to him to head for his bedroom. The bed is unmade, the dark blue sheets beckoning. He releases me slowly to slide down his body and pushes the too-big sweats to fall to the floor. His T-shirt may as well be a dress since it comes down almost to my knees. He reaches for it and I shake my head.

"You first."

A corner of his lips lifts in a smirk as he grabs the material at the nape and tugs it up and off, tossing it to the floor. My mouth waters with all the beautifully inked skin on display. A light dusting of hair trails down, disappearing into his pants. I close the distance, lifting my hands to the top of his chest and tracing the hair line down to the waist of his sweats. His abs ripple under my exploration and my fingers itch to keep going. To make him lose control. Hooking a finger in the waistband, I run it along the hot skin, and he bumps his pelvis forward.

My cheeks stretch with my smile, my teeth sinking into my lower lip while I consider my next move. Raising my other hand, I grip either side of his waistband, pushing his sweats free. I wrap my hand around his hard length, running my thumb over the moisture at the head.

"Fuck."

His tendons stand in relief at his neck as he holds himself still, allowing me to explore with my hand before I sink to my knees in front of him.

"Stóirín." His nickname for me is a harsh groan with a direct line to my core that throbs in response.

I don't think I'll ever get tired of hearing him call me that. The partial groan only adds to it, speaking to me on a level of body and soul connected. I squeeze my thighs together to curb the ache and raise both hands. Bracing one on his hip, I wrap my fingers around him and shift until my lips barely brush the head.

I wait until his gaze finds mine before I lean forward and lick the underside of his dick from root to tip.

"Fuck me," he grits out and his fingers thread through my hair.

With a hum, I pull him into my mouth until he bumps the back of my throat. An intense power mixes with pleasure as I make this powerful man's knees buckle with my mouth.

My panties are absolutely soaked, my breasts heavy against the cotton of his T-shirt as I roll my tongue around him, loving the way he can barely string together a sentence.

"That's—sweetheart, fuck, right there. Your mouth. So fucking good. *Fuck.*" Words escape him, his jaw locking as a muscle tics in a steady rhythm.

It's a heady sensation, and I'm drunk on the power I wield. His hands fist in my hair, his hips pulsing gently against me, driving him to the back of my throat over and over again. Swallowing, I take him a little deeper, my cheeks hollowing out by the amount of suction I use.

I've never been this turned on by giving someone else pleasure. Never felt the connection as I do right now.

Because it's different. He's different.

And I'm different because of him.

I roll my tongue around him, finding a spot on the underside near the crown that has his fingers yanking through my hair and his cock jumping against the roof of my mouth.

"Fuck. Leigh, sweetheart, I'm going to come." He manages to get the words out, his hips pulsing more rhythmically.

I run my tongue on the same spot, ready for him to come.

"Fuck."

The word is barely out before he reaches down, lifting me off his dick and slamming his lips to mine while I wrap my legs around his waist.

"You taste like me," he says against my lips and takes the few steps it takes to get us to the bed where he lowers me down.

And I love the taste of him.

I want more.

But when I reach for him again, he shakes his head.

"I'm too close. You're really fucking good at that."

His hand delves under the hem of his T-shirt I'm wearing, yanking it up so his fingers can drag against the center of my panties.

"You're fucking soaked. That turned you on, didn't it?" he asks.

I nod, unashamed of how much I liked it. How much I want to do it again.

"I liked seeing you that way. Almost out of control." I gasp as his finger presses through the fabric against my clit.

"You definitely had me on the brink, Stóirín. Too close to the edge for my comfort." He leans down and presses a chaste kiss against my lips.

"I liked it," I tell him, trying to hold him to me.

"And I like watching you fall apart for me," he murmurs, pulling away.

As he shifts up, he pulls my T-shirt with him. My nipples pebble under his scrutiny, his tongue peeking out to lick a trail of moisture along his lower lip before he pulls it into his mouth.

An electric charge builds between us the longer he stares, the fire burning bright in his eyes. His hands reach out and I jolt, nearly combusting as he drags my panties down my legs, leaving me fully exposed. But he still stands there, studying me, trailing heat wherever his gaze pauses until it feels like my entire body is engulfed in flames.

"What are you waiting for?" I ask, my voice rough around the desire filling me.

"I'm trying to decide." He says the words absentmindedly, still dragging his gaze down my body.

"Decide what?" I lift my hands to my breasts, dragging my palms against my nipples, and squirm against the bed.

His gaze sharpens and his muscles lock.

"Where to start." His eyes darken, the fire eclipsing everything else.

"Start?" I ask, gasping as I pinch one of my nipples between my forefinger and thumb.

"Do I use my fingers, my tongue, or my cock to make you come?" He arches an eyebrow with his question.

"Why not all three?" I ask and shift a hand between my legs.

That must be the starting gun because he drops down, pushing my hand out of the way as his mouth latches onto a distended nipple, his hand replacing mine between my legs.

"You're a greedy girl," he says.

I moan my agreement, my fingers tunneling through his hair as his fingers glide through my folds to find my clit. His finger rotates around the hard nub, his thumb alternating pressure against it until I cry out, the orgasm poised, ready to let loose. My toes curl and my nails scratch against his scalp.

"Are you ready to come?" he murmurs, nipping at my breast.

I whimper, squirming between the bed and his finger. I'm not sure if I'm trying to get closer to the orgasm or further away. It's an overwhelming sensation, balanced on the edge like this.

"I—" Whatever I was going to say, I forget it.

He presses a finger in, finding a spot to release the orgasm the way an ocean releases a tidal wave. From one breath where I'm ready to answer a question to the next where the only thing I know—that I've ever known—is the white-hot pleasure streaking through me.

I'm not even fully recovered from it when he drags his tongue along my pussy, flattening against my clit to start the build toward the next orgasm.

"*M-m-m...*" I'm trying to say his name, but the word is lost as my breath comes in embarrassing loud pants.

This orgasm is more intense than before, bordering on explosive as my entire universe centers to what he's doing between my thighs.

"You're mine, Stóirín," he growls before dropping his mouth back to my clit.

His. God, I like the sound of that. No. I love the sound of that.

"Mmmm." My back bows off the bed, chasing the orgasm he teases.

"Tell me," he demands, nipping at the inside of my thigh.

I jolt and it takes several heartbeats for me to understand.

"Tell me," he says again, blowing lightly on my clit.

"Yours."

The word ratchets the fire higher, another flame catching hold, threatening to burn us both to the ground.

I am his.

Is that why it's so intense between us? Because of how fully I have given myself? The questions scatter at another drag of his tongue against me.

"More." His tongue traces my clit and my knees shake.

"I'm yours," I wail.

The words are the truest I've ever spoken. It's like I've given my heart as they echo through the room.

"That's right. You're mine. Just like I'm yours. All of me for all of you, Stóirín. An even trade." His tongue finds my clit, his finger pressing against the pucker of my asshole, and the orgasm explodes.

Stars fall around us, the light blinding and binding in the same instant. I float back to earth, blinking my eyes open to find him watching, waiting for me as he hovers at my entrance, condom in place.

He eases forward, going at an almost glacial pace, as he fills me. He keeps his eyes locked on mine the whole time, letting the fire consume us, more intense as he releases the emotions simmering between us since Cole and Hannah Grace's wedding.

My eyelids flutter shut as the pleasure sharpens and builds, sweat slicking along our skin.

"Eyes on me, Stóirín," he murmurs, brushing a kiss against my forehead.

I open them as his pelvis bumps mine. Bowing up, I try to adjust to all the sensations swamping my body.

Lust. Desire.

Pleasure.

Love.

In that moment with his heart beating against mine, our gazes locked with each other, the realization hits me with the fiercest wave yet. I desperately need him to move, to dissolve the emotions burning through my body in the fire of lust. It's terrifying. It's exhilarating. And I'm not sure what comes next.

"Murphy." It's only his name.

But it's so much more.

He nods like he understands. Maybe he does.

"I'm here, sweetheart." He retreats, weaving his fingers with mine before squeezing.

I need him to move, but even the slow movement of his hips focuses on the emotion building between us. On the moment stretching around us like we're the only two that exist in the world. Or maybe it's that he is my world in this heartbeat.

Almost fully out, he pauses, studying me for a heartbeat. Then another.

This time as he presses forward, his lips find mine. But it's less frenetic than before. It's an ease of our tongues coming together. It's like we were made for each other, my body relaxing against his in a sigh of coming home all while he continues to piston his hips in a steady rhythm. The orgasm shimmers in the distance, the gentle lapping of a wave versus the earlier storm.

I always thought passion came with a quick pace. But I've never felt it stronger than right now, in this unhurried moment.

He releases one hand, dragging it down my body to tease

along my breast before he finds my clit between us. My eyes refuse to close, still locked with his. Sheer bliss is the way he moves with me, the feel of his hands on me, the vibration of his heart against mine.

I whimper, on the edge without really knowing how I got here.

"That's it, sweetheart. Give me one more. Give me everything you've got."

"Come with me," I beg, my fingers flexing against his biceps.

He nods. "I'm right here."

His hips speed up at the same time his fingers reach a crescendo on my clit, and I tumble over, my body flying as it stays tethered to his, his own release moaned into my ear as he comes with me.

As we soar to heaven together.

CHAPTER 22

LEIGH

My stomach is on the worst roller coaster ride ever as I stand to the side of Lindsay's open office door bright and early Thursday morning. For once, I'm glad she's one of the earliest in the office because no one is there to witness my nerves as I wipe my hands on the back of my black pants before taking the giant step that is, in reality, only the span of one step.

I clear my throat and Lindsay looks up from her laptop, her face a mix of concern and happiness.

"Leigh, good morning. How are you feeling? Come in. Come in." Lindsay waves me forward.

I step inside, taking a pause to ensure the door closes behind me before moving closer to her desk. My palms grow clammy again, my heart racing as I take a seat.

A lump sits in my throat and I swallow, hoping to get rid of the sensation.

Lindsay isn't Kenneth.

I've never had the issues with Lindsay I had with Kenneth, but was Kenneth's behavior an indication of what everyone thought of me in the office?

No.

Kenneth and Lindsay couldn't be more opposite. It is mind-boggling how they are both deputy public defenders hired by the same person.

"I'm…okay." I start slowly, not sure how to answer her question.

Okay is the closest word to describe it. Physically, I am. Minus a bump on the head and a scrape on my right knee. But when Murphy dropped me off, my eyes jumped to the spot where the ambulance had been. To the spot where I fell. It hadn't helped walking toward the door either. What reception would I get when I walked through it?

Kenneth had made it clear what he thinks of me.

But I am more and more convinced it is my relationship with Murphy—or whatever his perception of what our relationship is—influencing his opinion. Little does he know even without Murphy I wouldn't entertain any situation where he touched me. The warmth between my shoulders with Murphy's eyes on me when I walked into the office this morning had been the only reason I kept walking—I have his support. Regardless of what happens.

"I'm so sorry I wasn't here on Monday. I had a lengthy conversation with William yesterday and we're fully cooperating with the police. We're also looking at additional security measures for our parking lot. We can't believe this happened."

That provides a level of relief, but what I have to say still sits like a rock in the pit of my stomach.

"He was here to see Kenneth."

Her brow furrows as she processes my words.

"Kenneth?" The shock is clear in her voice.

I nod. "He was looking for Kenneth and then he recognized me from the lobby when I was talking to Murphy."

A shudder racks my body at the memory. The momentary clarity in his eyes when he had recognized me. Chilled, I run my hands up and down my arms.

"I appreciate you telling me," she says vaguely.

I know she can't tell me if she and Chief Bailey already knew. And Lindsay is nothing if not a good attorney—able to keep confidences close.

"I, um, I need to tell you something else." I stumble over the words, slicking my tongue over my suddenly dry lips.

"Okay?" Lindsay leans forward, hands clasped on the desk.

She tilts her head, studying me with an astuteness I've come to expect from her.

"It's about Kenneth," I start.

Will Lindsay believe me? Will I still have a job when I tell her everything? The risk curdles in my stomach, but I can't back down now.

Something flashes across her face—regret, concern—but it's too fast to make out before it's gone.

Here goes nothing.

I take a deep breath, let it out, and interweave my fingers as I try to put my thoughts into coherent form.

"Last week, he called me into his office. I thought it was to talk and, at first, it was. But he"—another shuddering breath and I rush on—"he touched my leg. And I got this weird vibe from him. Like he was coming on to me—"

"Fraternization among the office is strictly prohibited. Especially as one of the deputy chiefs," Lindsay says.

"There's no interest there on my part. He…well, for lack of a better way to say it, he gives me the ick, Lindsay. Like a frat boy who won't take no for an answer."

This time the regret stays long enough in her expression for me to identify it.

No, not regret. A similar emotion.

Shame.

I open my mouth to ask her about it, but don't get the chance.

"Did anything else happen?" she asks.

"He invited me to the happy hour that happens every Friday."

A frown drags a line between her eyebrows.

"Those are not office sanctioned events."

"I know. I declined. I already had plans but even if I didn't... no thanks. But it turns out, we ran into Kenneth at Cue Craft."

"We?"

By this point Lindsay has grabbed a pen and is taking a few notes as she maintains eye contact.

I squirm, not sure how my relationship with Murphy will be taken.

"Murphy O'Connell and me. We're seeing each other," I say.

If she has any thoughts on my dating the older detective or a detective period, she keeps them to herself.

"Anything else?"

"I-I don't think he liked it. When you were out on Monday, he called me into his office." I go on to explain the physical crowding and the innuendo before he was interrupted by Mr. Bailey. The almost Dr. Jekyll and Mr. Hyde personality switch followed by the demand for me to work on memos and the looming deadline with the implied threat I would be fired if I didn't meet it.

When I finish, she releases a breath, setting her pen down carefully on the notebook.

"Leigh, I'm so sorry this has been your experience. Please know that the kind of behavior you're describing is not one William would condone. I need to speak with him on next steps, but I appreciate you bringing your concerns forward. I wouldn't be surprised if you were also going to resign after your experience, but I hope you give me the time I need to look into this further."

Relief hits me in the stomach, blasting the rock sitting there since I stepped foot into work this morning.

She believes me.

"I don't want to leave. I've enjoyed the rest of my experience here. And I think it will make for really good experience when I apply for Project Justice at the end of the summer," I tell her.

She tilts her head as she pauses for a breath.

Did I say something wrong?

"Is this really what you want, Leigh? Working as a defense attorney? Working with people who are guilty of some really graphic crimes?"

What prompted her questions? Anxiety zips along my skin, and I want to respond right away, to defend myself and my decisions.

It's not the first time I've had to.

"I—"

She holds up a hand.

"I don't need you to answer right now. Or even today. But by the end of your internship, I'd love to hear your thoughts."

I snap my mouth shut, the nervous energy of defensiveness stuck without the outlet.

"Okay." I can at least give it the thought she's asked for.

But I know what I want.

"As for Kenneth, I want you to keep your distance. As my intern, there is absolutely zero reason you would need to interact with him. For anything." Her words are firm and exactly what I was hoping to hear.

Tears burn my nose and I blink several times, unsure why they're there, except for how grateful I am to have Lindsay respond like she has.

"Thank you," I tell her.

"Thank you for trusting me enough to bring this information forward. I'm going to go see if William has some time right now."

"Do you have anything you want me to focus on today?" I ask, slipping back into our daily routine.

"I emailed a few files I need some summaries on, and I'd like you to cull through some of our previous cases for potential recipients of the Wrongful Conviction Fund."

"Isn't Kenneth running that project?" I ask, remembering how he'd made it sound during the conversation last week in his office.

She smirks.

"He tried to take over."

It's what she doesn't say that has a giddiness taking over the anxiety.

But I try to copy Lindsay's poker face instead.

"Are you sure you should be back to work already?" Lindsay asks when we're both at the door to her office.

"I feel fine. Better than fine," I tell her.

I have a job I really like and a sexy-as-hell man I'm falling for.

And I'll get the chance to meet several people from Project Justice in just a couple of days.

❦❦❦

"Pinch me," I tell Sydney later that night as I lie on the couch in my living room, a glass of wine within reach.

"Kind of hard to do from two thousand miles away," she says, slurping on a drink on her end of the phone.

"That's the only bad thing about my life. You live too far away."

"I take it your dinner with Murphy went well?" she asks.

I jolt upright.

"I didn't tell you?"

"Girl, it has been radio silence on your end for four days. I wasn't worried because, one, Detective McHottie. And two, I have tracking capabilities on your phone."

Warmth travels to my cheeks and I lie back, sighing happily.

"You could say it went well."

"Five-alarm fire well?"

"Burn the bed to ashes well." Even the memory is enough to have me hot and bothered.

"I fucking knew it, you lucky bitch. Tell me everything."

"We never even made it to dinner. He had a decision for me as an appetizer."

"Kitchen sex is hot," she says and takes a drink.

"We didn't have sex in the kitchen. Not exactly."

"Bitch. Quit skimping on the details. I already told you I was living vicariously through you. Dish those deets."

"We lost clothing in the kitchen," I tell her.

"And…?"

"And I've never had an orgasm in a kitchen before," I admit.

Her hoot on the other end of the phone screeches in my ear.

"They're better there," she tells me. "Although don't tell Jessie I said that. Shit!"

"I'm done with Bowie this time. I swear I'm done!" Jessie screams and the door slamming echoes through the phone.

"Jess? Fuck, what happened?" Another door bangs shut and Sydney knocks on the door. "Jess?"

"What's going on?" I ask, sitting up, my stomach aching for the pain so clear in Jessie's voice.

"I'm not sure. She walked in screaming but crying too. Like, mascara running down her neck crying. Jess?" More knocking.

There's a muffled sound followed by Sydney's sigh.

"I'm going to murder that jackass," she mumbles into the phone.

"I'll let you go so you can talk to Jessie. Give her a hug from me." I had planned on telling Sydney about the attack now that she is caught up about Murphy, but it sounds like Jessie needs her more.

"I will. I still want details, but later. First, Jessie. Then I'm going to deal with that asshole once and for all."

"Don't do anything you're going to need bail money for."

"Sawyer and Cole already have me covered."

"Here if you need me."

"Thanks. I'll call you later."

The phone beeps in my ear and I drop it next to me, chewing on my lip.

I've been Jessie before. Dumped.

Hurt.

Angry tears.

Is that the outcome with Murphy?

I don't think so.

But I guess I really don't know, do I? He's moving to DC in less than a month, and I'm heading back to law school. Yes, I may be falling for him and he may have feelings for me, but what does that mean in the long run?

My phone buzzes on the table and I pick it back up, still somewhat distracted by what my future with Murphy holds.

MURPHY

What are you doing?

Just hanging out.

Was talking to Sydney.

You?

MURPHY

Hoping to visit my favorite girl.

Fuck, this man not only melts my panties, but my heart too. But I can't help but give him shit too.

Your favorite girl, huh?

Exactly how many girls are there?

MURPHY

One.

There's only one I want.

Swoon.

You say the sweetest things.

MURPHY

Easy where you're concerned.

You still want to come see me?

MURPHY

Yes.

When will you be here?

MURPHY

Open your door and find out.

Squealing, I toss my phone on the couch and run to the door, throwing it open to find him standing there in a forest green T-shirt and khaki shorts with a duffel bag slung over his shoulder.

"Hey, sweetheart."

I don't respond. Not with words. Instead I yank him inside and cup the back of his neck, pulling his lips to mine.

I'm not ready to think about what happens a month from now.

I just want to live in this moment. In his arms.

CHAPTER 23

MURPHY

"O'Connell! My office."

Fuck.

I'm really beginning to hate starting work like this. But the captain sounds like she's ready to go on a rampage, so I drop my bag before heading for her office, passing Aldridge with a giant smirk on his face.

"You must not have much ass left the way Cap is chewing on it, O'Connell," the asshole dares to say, and several intakes of breath follow it.

Good, I'm not the only one who thinks he shouldn't have said it.

I stop, turning to freeze him with a glare.

"At least she bothers to speak to me, Aldridge. You're not even worth her time."

The smirk dies on his face, hatred replacing it.

"You're lucky you're on your way out, O'Connell."

"Why? You think you can do the job better? The only way you'll be better than me is once I'm gone."

He stands, his chair clanging backward against a file cabinet.

I have to fight a smile. Cowards always rise to a challenge and Aldridge is no different.

"You want to make something of it?" he snarls, puffing out his chest.

Fucking peacock.

"You're not worth my time."

"The two of you quit it. If I wanted a pissing contest I would have asked for one. O'Connell, my office. Now. Aldridge, don't you have a court date to get to?" Captain Overton steps out of her office, arms crossed as she levels both of us with a look that screams to fuck around and find out.

No, thanks.

I move more quickly than before, ignoring the heat of everyone's attention where it burns a hole between my shoulder blades.

It takes the captain a few minutes to join me, and something tells me Aldridge and I weren't the only two to get the look.

"What the hell is wrong with you?" she asks, stepping into her office and slamming the door.

"Me? You didn't hear what he said. He—"

"He's a half-assed detective who couldn't find his ass from his elbow. He's never bothered you before. Why now?"

Because I've never been this torn before.

I want the job in DC, but for every hour I spend with Leigh, I want it less and less. And it is fucking confusing.

I've been with other women before for a few weeks or even a few months. But none made me want to fall for them the way I am with her.

I doubt Captain Overton wants to hear any of that.

"He just gets under my skin," I say and drop into the chair in front of her desk.

"Well, quit letting him. He loves your reaction. But he'll leave you alone if you quit reacting."

She's right and we both know it, so I change the subject from

Aldridge since he really isn't worth any more of my time or effort.

"I'm sure you didn't ask me to come in here because of Aldridge," I say.

Maybe she's heard something from IA.

"I have two things I want to talk to you about." She takes a seat at her desk, pulling an envelope from her drawer.

An envelope.

Not a file.

I'm not sure whether that's a good sign.

"About my cases?" I ask.

She takes a breath, releasing it before she answers.

"IA has found something. They're being pretty tight-lipped, and I can't share anything more than they may have found something that clears you of any wrongdoing."

Halle-fucking-lujah.

Even if it does irritate the shit out of me that she can't share any more, I have to be thankful for this small lead.

"What can I do to help?"

I need to do something with this surge of energy.

"Nothing."

Record scratch.

What?

"Nothing?" I repeat.

She nods and my entire body deflates.

Fuck.

"IA is in charge of the investigation. If you come in, anything they're doing could be tainted. You need to stay well clear of what they're doing. I mean it," she says when I open my mouth to argue.

Dammit.

I hate this helpless feeling locking my limbs and mind when I know I can help.

"I'm a good detective," I tell her.

"The best I have," she agrees.

She and I had been peers at one point in time, partnered together occasionally, but her words still come as a surprise.

"Which is why I have a favor to ask," she says, lifting the envelope.

I should have known there was an ulterior motive to her words.

"What kind of favor?" I ask. The envelope could hold anything knowing Captain Overton. It could even be empty and she's using it as a prop.

"I was notified this morning of a charity event brass wants all captains to be present at. And one I can't attend."

This is probably one of the reasons I never would have made captain. I hate the politics I've witnessed from my vantage point. And charity events are a big part of their life.

"What kind of charity event?" I ask, wanting to groan while at the same time wondering if I can take Leigh as my date.

"It's Saturday."

"Saturday? As in tomorrow?"

Fuck. Not only does that stop me from inviting Leigh, but I won't be able to keep my eye on her like I was planning to. I might have said I was okay with her going with Charlie Vanderweel, but it didn't mean I wasn't going to be close by.

Or that was my plan before now.

"You have to love the speed of communication from our public affairs group." She rolls her eyes.

"You can't find anyone else?" I ask.

"Would you rather I send Aldridge?" She arches an eyebrow to make her point.

Fuck.

With a sigh, I reach for the envelope she hands me where a ticket is nested inside.

"What's this event for anyway?" I ask.

"It's an announcement of a charity called"—she looks at a

Post-it note on her desk—"Shield 615. It's aimed at providing protective equipment to police officers."

At least it's a cause I can get behind. I glance down at the ticket, the calligraphed name jumping off the cream card stock.

"Vanderweel?" Isn't this weekend when they are announcing the Wrongful Conviction fund?

"Charles Vanderweel. It's apparently one of two new charities he's announcing tomorrow night. The other is, I'm sorry to say, a fund for individuals to fight their convictions."

"Some people who are convicted are innocent." The words are out of my mouth before I can stop them, so much a reflection of Leigh I'm surprised to hear them in my voice.

But she's not wrong.

And maybe that was the connection I needed all along.

Captain Overton's eyebrows lift, equally surprised.

"I never thought I'd hear those words come from you," she says.

I shrug.

"I'm not saying every person convicted is innocent. But some." I had told Leigh in the courthouse that I could agree with her. The legal system makes mistakes.

I still believe some people are wrongfully convicted.

I'm not so sure some people include Charlie Vanderweel.

Besides, I'm not going to focus on that. Or even the protective equipment for police officers like I should.

Instead, I'll get to keep a much closer eye on Leigh. And Charlie Vanderweel.

Fuck, yes! The relief cooling my body is like the first cool fall breeze after a blistering summer. Nothing can happen to Leigh if I'm there.

A grin twitches my lips and I suck them in, trying to keep my elation from the captain who eyes me curiously.

"You going to be alright, O'Connell?"

"Of course. How come you're not able to attend?" And will she tell me at the last minute that she can?

"I'm heading out of town tonight for my already delayed anniversary trip. If I try to reschedule these plane tickets, I'll lose money and more than likely no longer need to celebrate anything since I'm sure Jack will try to file for divorce if I ask him to postpone one more time."

"I've got you, Cap. You and Jack go enjoy your trip. Don't worry about a thing here."

"I fully intend to be on a beach by tomorrow morning with a mai tai in hand."

And I intend to keep an eye on my girl. With the captain gone, there won't be any last-minute change of plans.

"Have one for me while you're at it," I tell her.

"You seem significantly happier about this event than I thought you would be. I know you've done them once or twice before. But usually it takes a lot more persuasion to get you to go."

I have all the persuasion I need with Leigh there. Not something I am going to share with the captain though.

Keeping a lot of things from the captain lately.

I attempt to ignore the barb from my conscience and shrug one shoulder.

"These things normally have decent food. Open bar. I can get behind both of those things…" I can also get behind being in the same place as Leigh. "I'm not going to lie though. I'm not excited about breaking out my tux."

Fucking black tie.

I hate wearing it, but after the last few years of events and weddings, I had gotten tired of renting and spent the money on a custom-tailored suit. It's probably some sort of sign I haven't packed it away yet.

I haven't packed much of anything.

And my lease is going to be up in just a few weeks.

I've been busy.

Busy? Or busy?

Jesus Christ. I've been trying to figure out who the hell is trying to sabotage me and keeping an eye on Leigh.

And other body parts.

"Any questions?" Captain Overton asks, interrupting my internal debate.

"No, no questions."

At least not for her.

I have plenty of them for myself.

But one thing I'm not questioning is my luck. Not with this news.

The saying is don't look a gift horse in the mouth.

Well, this is my horse and I'm not looking anywhere.

I leave the captain's office, waiting until I'm at my desk to send a text to Leigh.

Looks like you're going to have company tomorrow night.

CHAPTER 24

MURPHY

Leigh's initial reaction to my coming tonight was an equal mix of resistance and excitement.

She didn't want me to babysit her.

This wasn't for her; it was for my own peace of mind when it came to her.

She was excited to see me in my tux. But this wasn't an event we were attending together. She was attending with Vanderweel and I was attending solo.

But I still had several stipulations. First, Vanderweel didn't need to know where she lived and I didn't need tonight to feel any more like a date than it already did. She could meet him at the venue. I would be the one picking her up. I would be the one bringing her home.

Because Leigh Whittaker isn't Vanderweel's.

She is mine.

If she had a problem with it, she didn't say anything. And something tells me she isn't shy about sharing her opinion.

Fidgeting with the too-tight necktie of the tux, I stand on Leigh's front porch, more than ready to see her in her dress. Her bridesmaid's dress had been temptation wrapped in pink silk. I'd had to resist then. Or, at least, I told myself I had to at the time.

I no longer have that problem.

Which is going to create its own version of hell tonight.

I reach forward, pressing the doorbell, and wait for her to open the door, nearly swallowing my tongue at the vision she creates in front of me.

To say she looks amazing is an understatement. Stunning would be a better word. Ethereal also comes to mind. But if she's angelic, her halo is a bit tilted by the way the black dress hugs her curves like every manner of sin I want to commit. The swells of her breasts tip over the edge, the long slit playing peekaboo with her toned leg and tan thigh.

Her blonde hair is pulled up, loose tendrils floating in the breeze, teasing the jasmine and lemon scent of her perfume that pulls me to her like a siren's call. She returns my kiss, stepping back when I'm ready to back her into the room and forget all about the reason we got so dressed up in the first place.

"Mmm," she hums, rubbing her lips together, her lip color still in place despite the less-than-chaste kiss we just shared.

"Agreed. Are you sure we have to go tonight?" I ask.

If she's willing to play hooky, I will too. Damn the consequences.

She nods, her impish smile transforming her face.

"We do. But if you're a good boy while we're out, you get a treat when we get home."

Her eyes widen, the deep blue showing her shock at the slip-up.

Home.

With her.

There are worse things I can think of.

I drop my lips to the tip of her nose in reassurance.

"I'm going to hold you to that," I murmur.

Her pupils dilate, eclipsing the blue, and I very much want to forget all about everything else and drag her inside. So I do the only sane thing I can and step back. She locks the door and I walk her to the passenger seat, loving the way her breath catches when I hold her waist a heartbeat longer than necessary to help her into the higher car.

Her blue eyes catch mine as she settles into the seat.

"I could have gotten in okay myself. This dress has some room." She sticks her leg out of the slit as if to prove her point.

I glide my hand up the backside of her leg, brushing my fingers behind her knee.

"Maybe I like my hands on you, Stóirín," I whisper to her and slide my fingers along the inside of her thigh.

She gasps, her fingers wrapping around my wrist. Not to stop me, but to hold me in place when I try to pull away.

"Maybe my body likes your hands on it too," she tells me.

I groan.

"If we don't go, sweetheart, I'm going to yank you out of this car and carry you back into the house."

"Promises, promises," she teases, but releases my hand.

I muster the little self-control still intact and close the door, taking several deep breaths at the back to cool my libido before getting into the driver's seat that now smells like jasmine and lemon.

"You have learned what they say about playing with fire, right, sweetheart?" I ask her, backing down her driveway.

"I'm well aware. And looking forward to it." Her hand lands on my thigh, her fingers brushing my hardening cock until I have to weave my fingers with hers to focus on the road.

"You look beautiful," I tell her, keeping my attention on the road but lifting her hand and pressing a kiss to the back of it.

"Thank you. You look nice as well. That tux looks like you were made to wear it."

"Reverse it and you have it right. For a while, so many friends were getting married I thought it would be better to have something custom done versus continuing to rent. At least this way, it doesn't have any weird quirks."

She laughs.

"I'll take your word for it."

"What about you? You just happen to bring a dress like that to Nashville?"

"No way. I don't own anything like this. All my deb dresses and sorority formals are hidden in my closet at my parents' house. This is one of Hannah Grace's from when she was Miss Tennessee. It's a good thing she and I are close to the same size. It's a little tight, but not bad."

I glance at her, and the way her dress is stretched tight across her chest has me almost regretting the decision. I want to groan as the image sears itself in my brain.

"Not bad at all," I growl out, squeezing her hand.

"Have you been to the place where we're going before? The Bell Tower?"

I nod.

"Yeah. For a friend's wedding. It's in downtown Nashville and is an old, converted church that's an upscale wedding spot."

"A church? Dammit, I wish I had my camera. I bet it photographs beautifully."

She's shown me a lot of her pictures of Nashville and has a few prints hung around her house. She's really fucking good and I've told her so.

"I'll bring you back another time. Just to take pictures," I promise her.

But my stomach rolls. Because when?

The rest of the ride is spent in silence, but she holds back when we're both at the back of my car.

"I...I should probably head up separately. Because, you know..."

Only I'm not ready to let her go. Not just yet.

"How about this?" I ask, reeling her into my arms. "I'll give you the goodbye kiss now and promise not to touch you between now and later, but I want to walk near you when we go in."

"I'll be fine," she promises.

"I know you will be. You told me you packed your pepper spray in your bag and—"

"And I do know self-defense," she adds.

"Humor me." There's something in my gut telling me this is wrong. I'm not meant to let her walk away.

It's served me well since I was sixteen. When I'd had to start relying on it more than my dad. Everything about her in my arms feels right. Like this is where she is meant to be.

We stay locked together for several heartbeats, the heat building and stretching between us before she nods.

"Okay."

The word is still on her lips when I claim them, laying siege to them as I plunder and find her tongue. Fuck, each time is better. Hotter. Not enough.

But it has to be.

For now.

I capture her moan between us before I slowly gentle the kiss, taking my time to let us both come back to the real world where I have to let her go for the time being.

"That was quite the good night kiss," she says, her expression dazed, lips swollen from my kiss.

"You ain't seen nothin' yet," I tell her, squeezing her to me for another heartbeat before I have to let go.

Stepping back, I wait for her to walk away but she doesn't. Instead she stands there, studying me, and my breath backs up in my lungs.

"Are you okay?" I ask her.

"I…I am." Only she doesn't sound like it.

She opens her mouth to say something else, but her phone buzzes in her purse.

Spell broken, she pulls the phone from her small evening bag and reads the screen.

"It's Charlie. We're meeting at the front," she tells me.

"You should probably go then. Meet me at the front to leave at ten?" I ask her.

She nods and closes the distance, pressing a quick kiss against my lips.

"I'll see you in there," she says and runs her thumb along my lips, no doubt wiping evidence of our kiss away.

"Not if I see you first."

She smiles like I intended, and I watch her walk away and turn the corner before I take a deep breath and drop my head back to stare at the sky.

Fuck. Why is this so hard?

But if I thought watching her walk away was hard, it's nothing compared to watching her inside the event. In a room of glittering jewels and expensive fabric, she stands out, capturing not only my attention but the gazes of several other men as well.

She is everything centered in this room right now. And Charlie Vanderweel gets to enjoy her laugh and her smiles while I'm stuck sweeping the room and playing politics with other captains and prominent citizens the Vanderweels have invited.

It's as if she was made for this world though. The way she glides from group to group and the way she interacts with Vanderweel Senior and his cronies. The only one I see her shy away from is Kenneth, and after she speaks to Charlie, he steers them clear.

Good.

Means I don't have to go deck the doll look-alike for salivating over Leigh's breasts.

Charlie's taking care of her.

That's my fucking job.

Only it's not. Not tonight.

Like hell.

It's still my job. But one I'm doing at a distance.

A glance at my watch reflects time has slowed to a glacial setting. Either that or my watch is broken.

It's five minutes later than the last time you looked.

So it's not broken then. Fine.

But suddenly, waiting for the event to end feels like it's going to take forever. Ordinarily, I wouldn't wait for the end. I'd make my rounds and look for the quickest exit. But not tonight. Not until I watch Leigh leave and meet her at the entrance.

"Detective, are you enjoying your evening?" Charles Vanderweel Senior walks up, hand outstretched as he greets me.

We've met a time or two at these types of events, but it still surprises me he knows who I am.

"Yes, sir," I say. The polite smile I ordinarily struggle to paste on comes easier than normal.

Charles Vanderweel has done a lot for the police department and is down-to-earth as well. In one of the few times he and I have run into each other, I found out he's a Nashville football fan, just like me.

He chuckles.

"You're not quite as convincing as your captain. Something tells me you'd much prefer a cold beer and a football game to this monkey-suited party."

His response surprises a laugh from me.

"I'm not going to lie, that does sound like heaven compared to this. But I have to tell you I appreciate how much you give back to Nashville PD. I know this charity will put a lot of minds and hearts at ease given what our officers in the field deal with more and more frequently."

The protective equipment furnished by Shield 615 will

provide officers with something my dad could have used. I swallow around the lump in my throat and take a drink of the sparkling water in my glass. I didn't trust myself with alcohol tonight.

"I've been fortunate enough in life I can give back to the city that has given so much to me and my family. Although if I had my way, this party wouldn't look like this," Vanderweel Senior says.

"Then why…" I gesture to the elegance around us.

He smiles wryly.

"Sometimes the decisions are not always in my hands. Besides, it gave my son the chance to introduce everyone to his new girlfriend. She works for the public defender's office. Have you had the chance to meet her?"

Girlfriend? What the fuck?

Is that what Charlie Vanderweel is telling everyone?

A red cloud hazes my vision, and I tighten my grip around the glass in my hand. But the man in front of me with silver in his temples doesn't seem to realize the impact his statement has on me. Taking a deep breath, I count silently to three before opening my mouth to respond. The tinkle of silverware against crystal distracts me from my response, and Vanderweel shifts his attention to where the sound is coming from.

"Ladies and gentlemen, if you'll please find your tables, dinner is now served." The master of ceremonies for the night gestures toward the dining area on one side of the room.

"Detective, it's been a pleasure, as always. If you'll excuse me?"

He leaves without waiting for a response, and I wait while everyone rushes for their tables. Leigh is easy enough to spot, and I watch her make her way to her table with Charlie.

Does she know he's introducing her as his girlfriend?

The question weasels its way into my brain, and I set my now-empty glass on the cocktail table. Only a few tables have empty seats, and I find mine with the other captains, tuning out their conversation to focus on Leigh. She's not Charlie's.

She's mine.

And I'm not giving her up.

New job be damned.

The din of the conversation quiets, a hush falling over the crowd as everyone's attention shifts to the microphone in the front of the room. Vanderweel Senior is at the mic, and I fidget in my chair, trying to focus on what he's saying in respect to him.

A screen drops down as he begins to speak, and I recognize many of the fallen officers throughout the years, jolting when my dad's service picture comes up before shifting to the next.

Fuck.

Lifting a hand, I rub it along my breastbone, trying to breathe. One of the other captains, Captain Pryce, who was seated on my right, squeezes a shoulder.

"Good man," he says.

He was the best. And gone far too fucking soon.

"Ladies and gentlemen, I want to thank you all so much for coming to the inauguration event of Shield 615. This charity is being founded to help protect so many men and women who defend us every day. I'm sure many of you might be surprised at how big a proponent I am of our police force after everything that happened with my son several years ago. But I'd like to make it clear—I am. It was their hard work and dedication that captured the real killer of my son's beloved fiancée. And because of that, I want to give back to them, the men and women who put their lives on the line every day for our city."

My gaze flicks to Leigh who appears to be speaking quietly to Charlie who looks close to tears.

Senior continues speaking, and I shift my gaze back to him.

"I intend to make this event an annual one and I'm asking you, my friends, to support this cause just like I have. To provide equipment for those at the front line. To put hearts of loved ones at ease when we can. If you would like to donate this evening, please see Monica—there she is"—he points to someone who waves from the side of the stage—"who is available to discuss any contributions you would like to make tonight. Thank you."

There's a round of applause as he moves back to his table, his path taking him just past the table where Leigh and Charlie are sitting. Vanderweel stops, saying something to the two of them that makes Charlie smile and Leigh look uncomfortably between the two of them. When Senior leaves, Leigh excuses herself, exiting the room, and I'm on my feet before I realize it.

"Excuse me."

Leigh is not in the vestibule outside the room when I make my way through the exit, but I have a good guess as to where she is and post myself outside the bathroom to wait. It's not long before she steps back through the door, her eyes widening in surprise when she sees me.

"What did they say to you?" I ask, lifting my hands to wrap them around her bare biceps.

My heart rate slows with her back in my arms, but it still doesn't ease the knot in my gut.

"Who?"

"Vanderweel and his dad. I saw him say something to you that made a line form here." I trace a finger between her brows and she rolls her eyes.

"Oh my God, you won't believe this. Mr. Vanderweel somehow thinks I'm Charlie's girlfriend. Even though Charlie introduced me tonight as his friend. His dad seems to get the impression we 'look good together.'"

"Charlie hasn't introduced you as his girlfriend?" I ask.

She laughs.

"No, of course not. I would have corrected him right away. I'm here as his friend. Only his friend. The only person whose girlfriend I want to be is..."

She trails off and I hold my breath, waiting for her to finish.

"Is who?" I prompt.

She swallows and meets my gaze with a confidence I only wish I had at her age.

"Yours."

My mouth slams against hers as I yank her to me, tasting the word on her lips.

Mine.

CHAPTER 25

LEIGH

Murphy backs us against the wall, darker in the shadows of the hallway to the bathroom, as he masters the kiss just like he's mastered my heart.

I hadn't meant to let that part slip out.

I was going to tell him about what Mr. Vanderweel had said. Charlie had looked just as shocked as I was, so I know it was Mr. Vanderweel and not his son who created that truth. But what had started as just a conversation had shifted.

It was true.

The only man whose girlfriend I want to be is kissing me boneless against the wall in a very public venue. And I want more. His lips trail down to my jaw, tracing the line back to my ear while his hand grips my hip, holding the leg up I've wrapped around him.

"Mine," he growls against the skin, nipping at the column of my throat before pressing his lips to the pulse jumping wildly beneath my skin.

Gooseflesh ripples through my body, leaving desire in an aching wake.

I tug at the starched shirt tucked into his pants, my hands finding the warm skin of his back as I hold him close to me.

"Yours," I murmur.

His mouth claims mine again, his hand finding the opening of the slit, squeezing my ass since the thong I've worn with the dress provides no barrier. I gasp and he takes it, just like he takes everything else I have to give.

My fingers dig into skin and he yanks his mouth from me, eyes on fire as breath saws in and out of his lungs, crushing his chest against my breasts.

"You make me forget where we are, Stóirín," he says, leaning his forehead against mine.

"You have the same impact on me. It wasn't me who kissed you brainless against a bathroom wall," I retort and slide my leg back down his before tugging my dress back into place.

He cracks a smile, his hands landing on my hips.

"Do you have to go back in there?" he asks.

I want to say no. Every part of me would prefer to leave with Murphy right now, to go find somewhere private where we can get horizontal—or vertical, I'm not picky. But Charlie has told me numerous times tonight how I'm making this event bearable for him. And on the selfish side of things, I've had an amazing conversation with Gavin Ellery, the CEO of Project Justice.

"Yes, and so do you," I say as he groans and tugs at the bow tie around his neck.

"I'd rather go home. Just you and me."

The fire banked in his eyes heats up for a heartbeat and my core throbs.

"I'm looking forward to that too. But for right now, we both have a job to do. Then we can go home where I can have my way with you," I tease, palming him through the front of his pants.

He locks his fingers around my wrist and yanks my hand up to his mouth to burn a kiss into my palm.

"You're the fucking devil," he growls, nipping at the skin at the base of my thumb.

"Me? You're the reason I'm walking back in there with drenched panties," I whisper, drilling his chest with my finger.

The smirk he gives me is one set to incinerate said panties.

"I can't help what you do to me, Stóirín."

I feel the vibration of his words more than I hear them. Yep, my body is officially on fire, and my heart melted somewhere along the way.

"Murphy! When you say things like that..."

How do I put into words how he makes me feel? Like I'm flying and falling at once. Like I'm myself, but more than I ever thought I could be. Because of all these emotions bubbling inside, overwhelming any ability at rational thought.

"When I say things like that...what?" he asks when I don't continue.

"That you can't help what I do to you. What about what you do to me?" I say, breathless.

"What do I do to you, sweetheart?" It's practically a growl that has me melting against the wall.

He's already told me how he feels, so I guess it's my turn. Not like the words would be held back even if I wanted to. But I'm tired of fighting them. Of holding them in.

"I...I'm falling for you. And I know our situation is temporary. I *know* you're moving to DC soon. But I can't seem to help it, especially when you say things like that. They're a turn-on but something more."

He nods, his gaze softening as the heat simmers between us.

"I understand. And, yes, I may be moving in a few weeks, but I meant what I said, sweetheart. In every way I can mean it."

Holy crap!

That's a big admission from someone who was convinced we didn't belong together. He reaches out, gliding his index finger along my jawline and I shiver, trying to process what he's telling me without saying the words.

Not like you're using them either.

No. Because it's too soon.

Standing on my tiptoes, I brush a kiss on his lips before wiping my thumb across them.

"We're not done talking about this, but we need to get back. And you don't need to be wearing my lipstick when you do," I tell him.

He smiles.

"I wouldn't mind."

"It's not really your color."

He barks out a laugh and reaches behind him, his dress shirt stretching as he tucks it back in.

Done wiping the lipstick from his mouth, I step back, admiring my tattooed, well-dressed warrior.

"Ready to head back in?" he asks.

"I need to…" I gesture to the bathroom and he nods.

"I'll wait."

Swoon.

The mirror in the bathroom shows a small mess of my updo, and I try to fix it as best I can before I reapply my lipstick. With a nod, I step back out and he grabs my hand, weaving our fingers together as we walk toward the main room again.

At the closed door, I reluctantly release his hand.

"I'll see you later?" I ask, closing my fingers against my palm to curb the need to reach for him again.

"Count on it," he whispers and steps back, allowing me to step through the door first.

My bag is in my hand, but I can't shake the feeling I've left something behind as I move back to the table where Charlie is waiting.

But I have.

My heart.

It's with the man making his way to a back table while his eyes stay glued to me.

I can't turn around to confirm it.

But I know it the same way I know I've fallen.

Completely.

Irrevocably.

Head over heels in love with Murphy O'Connell.

CHAPTER 26

MURPHY

"So I've been thinking…" Leigh says from the cocoon of my arms.

Candlelight flickers off the floral- and vanilla-scented bubbles surrounding us. Some of the tension that had ebbed after spending the rest of the charity event watching Leigh smile next to Charlie comes back as Leigh's shoulders tighten.

I can deal with another hellacious week of two other cases being questioned and a report of police brutality, but her tension hits me differently.

Yeah, because you're in love with her, dumbass.

"About what?" I ask cautiously, lifting my hands to run my fingers along her shoulders.

I find a particularly large knot at the base of her neck and spend several heartbeats kneading it loose.

She moans, leaning her head back against me.

"That feels amazing," she whispers.

"I thought we agreed we weren't going to think any more tonight," I tell her, pressing my lips to her shoulder.

That was my plan. Shedding our black-tie clothes to enjoy a hot bath with the gorgeous woman in my arms. The only thing I wish I had thought of was to bring a couple of beers up when I suggested the idea.

"And we're not. This was a thought from earlier."

"What kind of thought from earlier?" I ask, still working my way from her neck to her outer shoulders.

She turns her head, meeting my gaze over her shoulder, and my hands still. Her ocean-like eyes are filled with a variety of emotions that tug at the heart strings in my chest I never realized existed before her.

Love.

We may not have said the words, but the overwhelming feeling that had been building since that first night is impossible to deny any longer.

Longing.

I may not be able to get enough of her—case in point, it was my idea for the bath together tonight—but I recognize the same need in her that constantly hums through my blood.

Hope.

The emotion that makes my heart pound harder against my chest. A future that exists when I let myself imagine.

"Is it crazy that I googled law schools near the DC area today?" she asks.

Holy shit, yes. I would love to have her there with me. Then I get the job I want and the woman I can admit I've caught feelings for.

Her brow furrows, like she's ready for me to call her seven types of crazy. Meanwhile, I'm glad she did. Because it means I'm not crazy either. Or maybe we are, but together.

"Not any crazier than me looking at apartments a commutable distance from law schools." Because I had. I figured I could always bring the idea up with her when I found one.

She beat me to the punch.

Her face brightens, the candlelight in the room reflecting in her eyes.

"You did?"

I nod, lifting a finger to drag it in an X over my heart.

"Swear to God."

Water swirls as she shifts to face me, her legs landing on either side of my thighs. Her warm pussy beckons, and my cock stands at attention at the sight of her breasts peeking above the water.

I grit my teeth against the sharp stab of need and keep my hands gentle on her shoulders, despite the urge to yank her to me.

"So this…thing between us—"

"We're more than a 'thing,' Stóirín," I tell her.

I lock my eyes with hers, letting her in. Letting her see everything she makes me feel. Her intake of breath, the way her nipples now kiss the water, tells me she sees what I want her to.

"W-what are we?" she whispers then holds her breath.

Waiting.

"You are my chompánach anam," I say, using the phrase I've heard Mom use all my life when she referred to Dad.

It's like a vow, weaving the last bit of thread between her heart and mine. Creating one whole from two halves. It calms the nerves jangling in my gut, silencing the last moment of hesitation preventing me from spilling all my secrets.

"Your what?" Her pulse flutters visibly in her throat, and I place my fingers there, feeling the trill beneath their tips.

"Soulmate. You are my soulmate, Leigh, and I…I've fallen in love with you. There's no denying it. There's no running from it. You are the woman who owns me—body, heart, and soul."

The words are both foreign in my mouth and the truest ones I've ever spoken. Her entire face lights up, her hands coming up to cradle my face as she brings hers closer.

"I love you, Murphy," she murmurs, just before she captures my lips with hers.

Each word is another shape to my universe. Another breath, another heartbeat that now entirely belongs to her.

This glide of her flesh on my flesh, her lips on mine, is different than it's ever been. More powerful than Superman, more potent than any drug. She is my addiction. With one hand, I find the back of her neck, tilting her head to deepen the kiss while my other hand splays on her ass, aligning our lower halves. Her hips squirm against mine and a whimper escapes her mouth, staying trapped in the fusion where we connect.

I could kiss her forever.

And the thought doesn't scare me the way it used to. Instead, a warm contentment filters along my extremities, basking me in a light unlike any I have ever known before.

I break our kiss, dragging my lips to her neck and sucking on the slick, heated skin before I nip at the tendon between her neck and shoulder.

She jolts, more water swirling around us, and her nipples rub against my chest in a delicious torture of friction, making my mouth water for a taste. Boosting her, I find one with my tongue, sparring with the hard bud until I pull it into my mouth. She tastes like roses, jasmine, and vanilla—the bubble bath—and something unique to her. Something that makes me come back again and again until she mewls, pushing herself upright until her breast pops free.

My dick slides through her folds, pausing at the entrance before I shift my hips away from the temptation sliding into her with nothing between us brings. Her hips follow mine, creating a figure eight until I have to hold her still in my lap.

Closing my eyes, I grip her hips more firmly when they try to move. Her breath rushes across my chest, a cool counterpart to the warm water at my back. I glance up, and the vision she makes above me bathed in candlelight burns itself into my brain in an instant. Her blonde hair has come partially loose from the bun she put it in as we climbed into the tub, and tendrils tease her lips, swollen and dark from my kisses.

Shadows and light play peekaboo with her breasts, highlighting the swell of one breast and the plump tip of the other. I groan, wanting to touch her but not trusting myself to let go of the grasp I have on her hips where they push against me.

"We should get out. I need to get—"

She shakes her head.

"I'm good right here," she teases.

I'm not one to argue. But my control unravels with every small shift of her hips against mine.

It's maddening.

"Stóirín."

She leans forward, her breasts dragging across my chest. Her lips tease my earlobe and gooseflesh dots my skin, and I press my feet against the porcelain edge of the tub, trying to maintain my grip on her slick flesh.

"I want you inside me, Murphy. Right now. Nothing between us. I'm on birth control and I got checked ou-oooohhhhh."

Her words turn into a moan of pleasure as I shift, pistoning my hips up at the same time I drag her down. Water teases the edge of the tub as I fill her in one thrust, but all I can focus on is the overwhelming pleasure at the way her pussy grips my cock like a damn vise.

"Holy shit," I grit out, managing to pull her mouth to mine to plunder her lips with my tongue while my body mimics the movement with my hips.

I hold on to the kiss as long as I can, breaking it only when my lungs burn for new oxygen and I suck in a breath against her jaw, breathing in the remnants of the bubble bath as her hips continue to meet mine thrust for thrust.

Water laps at our chests, smoothing the slide of skin against skin, and my hands lose purchase on her hips. I slide them back, gripping her ass as she continues to lift up and down. Her head is thrown back, her hair a curtain and the ends teasing my legs along the bath's surface.

I struggle for control, desperately grasping for it as it tries to break free. Planting one hand on her back, I bring her breasts back to mouth level, sucking a nipple into my mouth and teasing the hard point with my tongue and teeth. Her pussy ripples around me and I repeat the caress, harder this time.

"Oh, fuck," she pants, pressing her breast more fully into my mouth.

I repeat the nip a third time before shifting to her other breast and repeating the touches.

"I'm going to come," she moans, the words spilling out on one long breath.

Mouth occupied, I slide my hand beneath the water, finding the hard nub of her clit with my thumb.

"Murphy."

I'm right there with her, ready to explode as soon as she does. I run my thumb across her clit, nipping her breast at the same time, and her entire body locks against mine, yanking my orgasm from my control to slingshot us both into the universe together.

The stars couldn't be any brighter as they flicker behind my eyelids, pleasure coming in white-hot waves as we continue to move until we're both spent. She collapses against my chest, and her labored breaths create goose bumps in the cooling water. Her fingers trace the texture, resting against my heart.

"Well, that was an experience," she murmurs.

I bark out a laugh, squeezing her to me and groaning when her laughter tightens her around my cock once again.

"A first for me too," I admit.

"You've never had sex in a tub before?" she asks.

"I've never made love in a bath before," I correct and she nestles against my chest.

Because it may have been hotter than the hinges of Hades, but that's what it was.

Sex stopped existing for us. What we had was better.

"I love you, Stóirín." The second time I've said those words tonight and they still hit me in the solar plexus, stealing my breath for a heartbeat.

"I love you," she whispers and presses a soft kiss against my heart.

Fuck.

I'm never going to get tired of hearing her say those words.

Because every time she does, I fall a little more under her spell, and forever is no longer long enough.

CHAPTER 27

MURPHY

I'm staring at a half dozen files on my desk, switching from one to the next as I try to identify common errors. Captain Overton may have told me not to get in the way of IA's investigation, but that doesn't mean I can't try and piece together my own pattern. If I find anything, I am going to take it to Overton for her to turn over to IA.

But there's no commonality besides the fact that all of the errors in each report were changed after I saved them to my computer and submitted them. The paper copies match the electronic system. Only my compulsive need to document everything on my laptop has saved me from suspension.

Otherwise, the errors are small. Almost unnoticeable. But enough for the attorney who represents the defendant to be able to get them off on a technicality. It's a mix of private attorneys and attorneys from the public defender's office with Kenneth only on one report—Vinny Ellis.

Balling my hand into a fist, I tap it against the papers fanned out along my desk and reach for my coffee with the other.

"Fuck," I say as the cold coffee registers, resembling more motor oil than life-giving nectar.

I push back from my desk, stretching out the kink in my lower back before walking to the break area for a fresh cup.

"What am I missing?" I murmur.

Missing anything isn't like me.

Might help if you were able to focus and not think of Leigh for more than ten minutes.

Frowning, I take a sip of the scalding hot coffee.

"What'd that coffee do to you, O'Connell?" Eli Warren asks.

Warren is a recent transfer from Georgia and I don't know him well, but he seems okay. Better than Aldridge.

"Just got a lot on my mind." I'm not willing to get into details since I don't have many to share.

"Well, if I can help, let me know," he says, lifting his now full cup in a salute before heading back to his desk.

It used to be Natalie Colburn's. She retired last year, and it sat vacant until recently when Warren transferred in.

"Hey, Warren?" I ask.

"Yeah?"

"You settling in okay? You've been here what? Two months or so?" I deliberately get the timeline wrong, wanting him to confirm he transferred in just before my reports started showing up with errors.

"Not quite. A little over a month. It's a good team. And Overton seems like a good captain."

I nod. "One of the best."

I head back to my desk, my mind in overdrive.

Is it a coincidence Warren transferred around the same time my reports started showing up with errors? He said he transferred from Georgia, but is that true? Why did he transfer?

Warren turns back to his computer and I refocus on my files, trying to make heads or tails of the mistakes.

When my phone rings, I lean back, welcoming the reprieve.

"Hello?"

"Detective O'Connell?" The woman's voice is a whisper, my

name a rush of breath. "This is Sara Connor—" There's a commotion on her end of the phone, a pounding followed by a man yelling and she whimpers. "You…um…you gave me your card when we talked before about Vinny."

Vinny.

Ellis.

This is his girlfriend.

I tune more into the phone call, forgetting everything else.

"Are you okay?"

"You told me to call if I needed help. And Vinny's here. He's drunk and—oh God." There's a sound of splintering wood.

I'm already standing, shoving all the files in a pile and into my desk drawer before I'm rushing for the door.

"I'm locked in the bathroom, but the door is breaking. I'm scared." The tears are audible in her voice.

Her fear elicits an equal adrenaline rush for me and I pick up my pace.

"Where are you?"

I'm racking my brain for an address but only the general area is coming to mind.

"The Heritage Arms Apartments. Unit 3B. Please hurry."

"I'm already on my way. Call 911."

More splintering and Ellis's voice is clear.

"Who the fuck are you talking to, bitch?" he bellows.

There's a thud and the phone beeps in my ear.

I'm at my car and slide into the driver's seat, immediately radioing dispatch to let them know to dispatch units closer to the apartment complex.

Call made, I drop the radio, concentrating on where to go, and I pull up to the dilapidated apartment complex as the first car does as well. Fuck. It's been fifteen minutes. What the hell are we walking into?

It takes an agonizing few more minutes for me to brief the responding officers.

"3B," I say and lead the way into the main entrance hanging on by a single hinge.

The dirty hallway smells like a combination of body odor, rotten food, and piss. A lone lightbulb flickers over spray painted mailboxes and the stairs are dark. My gut rolls, my hands gripping my gun as I make eye contact with the other officer. He looks just as disgusted as I am but points to the stairs and I nod.

The second-floor landing brings the smell of cooking food and a baby crying down the hall. The wallpaper has deep gouges in it, the carpet duct taped in spots.

"One more," I whisper.

He nods and we take the stairs as quietly as possible, despite the deep groans of the wood under every footfall.

The third floor is identical, the window at the end of the hall boarded up, making it darker than the other two so far. I point at 3B, not wanting to talk and give our presence away. Not until we're ready.

I take a deep breath and hold it, listening at the door for any sounds coming from the apartment.

"I'll teach you to cheat on me, you fucking bitch!" Ellis's voice is as clear as if we were in the same room.

Rage hazes my vision and I have to take several breaths for the red to clear before lifting my hand to knock firmly on the door three times.

"Nashville PD. We need to speak with Sara Connor. Open the door."

There's a grunt, but no other response, and the next minute we're required to wait feels like an eternity.

I knock again.

"Vinny Ellis, we have a warrant for your arrest. Open the door."

Thirty seconds.

At twenty-five the other officer and I back up. The final

seconds tick down and I lift my leg, kicking the door free of the lock. It shatters inside and the other officer and I enter the room.

Furniture is overturned, some sort of liquid running down the wall behind the TV with a starburst of pixels around a hole the size of a fist.

But no sign of Ellis. Or Sara.

I turn the corner to the hallway, and Ellis is visible through the splintered bathroom door. He's got his pants halfway down his ass, and it takes me another moment to realize two legs peek between his.

"Freeze," I yell, moving closer, gun raised.

When I get to the bathroom, I don't know whether I want to throw up or kill Ellis.

I can't even call him a man. No man does what he does.

Sara's face is a bloody mess, one eye already swollen shut, a deep gash in one of her cheeks.

But it's the facts that her shirt has been ripped open, her pants are down, and Ellis's dick is in his hand that create a fury I have never known before.

I don't even trust myself to yank him off her, waiting for the other officer to yank him up, slapping him into cuffs while I step in the bathroom. Reaching for a towel, I cover her up, kneeling down and feeling for a pulse.

It's weak, but there.

Thank fucking Christ.

I'm not sure what I would have done if it wasn't there.

Reaching for my radio, I request an ambulance.

She moans and Ellis struggles against the cuffs for the first time.

"I'll fucking kill you, you bitch," he snarls.

She whimpers, the one eye not swollen shut wide with fear as a tear leaks from the corner.

"Get him out of here," I tell the other officer.

They lead him out and I look back at Sara.

"It's okay. You're safe. I've called for an ambulance."

She tries to open her mouth, struggling as more tears track down the blood across her face.

Fuck. What the hell did he do to her?

Suddenly it's not Sara lying on the bathroom floor.

It's Leigh, lying on the asphalt of her parking lot.

Pure, unadulterated terror hits me like a freight train, and I have to take several breaths with my eyes closed to clear some of the fear. Opening my eyes, I find Sara watching me and I focus on her.

"Is there anywhere else that hurts?"

She lifts a shaky arm, pointing at her mouth.

Bruises are blooming on her neck, deep purple in the shape of fingerprints.

"I'm sorry I wasn't here sooner," I tell her, overwhelmed by regret.

I got here as fast as I could.

But it wasn't fast enough.

You prevented her from being sexually assaulted.

I don't want to think about what would have happened had I been a few minutes later.

CHAPTER 28

LEIGH

Friday night. In the last five days I've gone from confused to concerned to downright pissed.

"He won't respond to my texts anymore. At least Monday he told me he wasn't coming over. Something had 'come up,'" I tell Sydney and reach my spoon back into the nearly empty half gallon of salted caramel ice cream I pulled from the freezer for tonight's dinner.

Because why the fuck not?

I am feeding my feelings. The concern wanted salty, the anger wanted sweet, and the confusion decided ice cream would fix the problem.

"He told you he loved you, right? I'm not imagining that part?" Sydney asks.

I snort, nearly creating brain freeze. "I wish."

"So he tells you he loves you, you tell it to him back, and he just what? Fucking ghosts you?"

I've just spent the last thirty minutes catching Sydney up on the Murphy situation—to include our bathtub confessional—and venting about him ignoring me for the better part of the week.

"Unless you count the two texts he sent me." So not completely ghosted.

But close enough to count.

She huffs.

"No. So why don't you go show up at his door? He can't ghost you if you're at his house."

"I don't want to be some creepy stalker. I swore I would never just show up at a guy's house like that." I take a deep breath and reach for another spoonful of ice cream. "Besides, I drove by after work a few days ago and he wasn't there."

And that galled.

I had finally bitten the bullet and swallowed my pride to show up at his house. I was going to ask him in person what the fuck was going on. Only to not see his car parked in front of his condo, and when I did knock on the door, there wasn't an answer and there were no lights on.

"Want me to work my magic? I can tell you exactly where he is and you could show up," she offers.

I shake my head. I am done with being that girl.

"No. If he reaches out, I'll decide if I want to talk to him then. I tried to be understanding but now I'm pissed. At first, I do think something really came up. I know he's been working hard to try to figure out the errors in some of his reports popping up recently." At least, I had wanted to think there was a reason other than him getting cold feet after calling me his soulmate.

But the more time passes and he doesn't reach out, the more I am starting to think I am right.

He regrets telling me he loves me.

And shit, that hurts. Whoever coined the term heartache definitely figured out the best way to describe the constant hum of pain in my chest. But mixed in with the hurt is a building anger.

If and when Murphy O'Connell decides to reach out, he has a massive apology to issue.

"Errors?" Her voice perks up.

Leave it to Sydney to pick up on that one word. But at least I'm smiling for the first time in a week.

"Yeah. Several of his reports. After he submits them, these random errors show up meaning his arrests are getting off on technicalities. And so far it's just his cases. Nobody else's."

The crack of her knuckles is audible through the phone.

"You know, I could do some digging..."

Sydney is the best hacker I know—she's the only hacker I know, but even if I knew more, I know she'd still be the best.

"I'd make that offer, but he's not really responding to any of my texts."

And while I understand the drive to clear his name before leaving, I don't understand the radio silence from him. He isn't letting me in and I have zero clue as to why. It's like we are back to square one which has created a knot of frustration between my shoulder blades as the week has progressed.

"So you think he's just focused on these cases?" she asks.

I shake my head even though she can't see me. "No. At least I don't think that was it on Monday. A police officer was killed in the line of duty. Kind of like his dad was. So I texted him as soon as I found out. Well, first I tried to call him but when he didn't answer, I texted. I figured there would probably be some sort of emotions since his dad was killed when he was sixteen. I wanted to let him know I was here for him."

"You love the idiot," she adds.

"Exactly!" Blowing out a breath, I reach for another scoop of ice cream. "But how do I tell him that?"

The fact she can understand me around the mouthful of sweet, salty, cold goodness is impressive.

"I'm sure you've already tried."

"Mm-hmm," I hum, mouth too full to respond.

Because I had.

When he hadn't answered his phone, when he hadn't responded to the original texts or the one just asking for him to respond, I typed out a long text. One where I told him how I understood why he wasn't answering, but I was there whenever he was ready to talk.

That was Wednesday.

His response?

"He did send a response to that one. A whopping two words. Thank you. *Thank you*? I fucking pour my heart out to you in a damn book of a text message and I get two words back? Are you fucking kidding me? Thank you. Thank you. Ugh." I stuff another spoonful of ice cream into my mouth to stop the rant.

Because I am done ranting.

And if I didn't love him as much as I do, I wouldn't be this upset.

And all of it is creating a massive stomachache that has nothing to do with the massive amount of ice cream I've just eaten.

"What can I say? Most men are only good for one thing. And they can be substituted by the much better battery-operated version."

I snort with a laugh, inhaling some ice cream and coughing.

"What? It's what I tell Jessie too," she says as I wheeze for several more breaths until the burning sensation fades.

"Did she really break up with her boyfriend?" I ask, hoping by focusing on someone else's lackluster love life it will help me avoid the train wreck of mine.

"I wish she had broken up with him. That would mean she actually saw the problem. But no. He broke up with her. With his dick hanging out and some groupie on her knees in front of him. Jessie walked in on them."

Disgust is a bitter flavor and I reach for another spoonful, drowning out the taste.

At least that hadn't been me.

"Poor Jessie," I say.

"He was only using her to get to her brother. Bowie only

wanted a record deal and thought dating Jessie would be his golden ticket to get signed by Jax's label," she mutters.

Jax Bryant.

Famous musician.

Label co-owner of Arrhythmic Records.

"What a creep," I spit the words.

Maybe Sydney is right and battery operated is the only way to go.

"I kept trying to tell Jessie. Especially after he hit on me when she was asleep the last time he was over. It's the exact reason I vetoed his presence in our apartment. Asshole. I can't believe she's been dragging around here for the last few weeks because of him. But no more. Nice Sydney is gone. Naughty Sydney is coming out to play. Tonight, I'm taking her out. The goal is to get her laid, to show her there are plenty more fish in the sea. Nicer fish. Hotter fish. Any fish not a fucking musician."

"Tell me how you really feel," I tease.

She barks out a laugh.

"Jessie has sworn off musicians. Forever. Fine by me. I don't think highly of them myself. The only thing that would make tonight better is if you were with us. I know you were looking at transferring to DC, but come here. We can find a bigger apartment. It'll be the three of us against LA. This city will never be the same!"

I laugh, but there's an undercurrent of sadness too. The combination of feeling like an idiot because I had actually been considering transferring to a law school in DC and because the thought of walking away from Murphy—even if he has decided to walk away from me first—creates an ache that makes me feel like I'm missing part of myself.

And I guess I am.

My heart.

"I'll think about it," I tell her.

But she and I both know I won't. At least not right now.

Done with the ice cream, I put the carton back in the freezer and drop the spoon into the sink before heading into the living room to flop on the couch. But while normally I would put on *Searching for Love*, my finger hesitates to scroll to the recorded shows.

I just can't.

Instead, I scroll the guide mindlessly, not interested in watching someone else's happily ever after. The movies have it wrong.

And I don't want to pretend tonight.

I'm too pissed. My happily ever after is falling apart.

"If you don't want to transfer, you could always come out for a weekend? You could see Hannah Grace and we could team up against Cole and give him a bunch of shit," Sydney offers.

Scrolling forgotten, I sit up. The idea has some merit. It's not running away, it's…taking a break. Recharging my batteries.

"My internship ends two weeks before school starts back up. What if I come out there for a whole week before I head back to Knoxville for school? You could show me around the city." The words start slowly, picking up steam the more detail I add.

Hopefully the last weeks of my internship will go just as well as this week had. Because the best part about this week? There was no sign of Kenneth Scott.

Hanging out with Sydney? And Jessie? The three of us together? And add in seeing my sister and Cole?

All of which sounds amazing.

"Can we hit up a beach?" I ask, already feeling the warm beat of sun against my skin.

"Duh."

"I'll start looking at flights and let you know for sure once I get a ticket bought," I tell her, getting more excited about this idea.

Sun. Sand. And Sydney.

Every S I need.

"Okay, babes. I gotta go. Sawyer and Cole scheduled a meeting and I need to log on."

"Yuck? On Friday night?"

"It's still working hours here, and you know me."

I do. Her working hours are whenever she's at her computer.

"Okay."

"Try not to stress over Murphy. If he's going to ghost you, he's not the man I thought he was."

"I'm not stressed; I'm pissed," I correct.

But am I pissed enough to give up? Or am I only regrouping?

Only time is going to tell.

"Yeah, yeah. Tell it to somebody who doesn't know you as well. Maybe they'll believe you."

"I am pissed."

"Well, whatever you are, don't be that way because of a boy. They're not worth it."

I would love to have Sydney's blasé attitude about guys.

Instead you fell head over heels for an emotionally unavailable, smoking hot, tattooed detective.

Just my luck.

"Turn on some terrible horror movie and veg out on the couch tonight. No rom-coms allowed. And no texting Murphy either. Let him stew in being ignored," she says.

I stick my tongue out even though she can't see me.

"That's what I'm already doing. The movie. But not horror. Something with explosions. I don't want nightmares for the night."

And I'm a big fat chicken when it comes to being scared.

"Okay, action it is. Love you! Bye!"

"Have fun tonight with Jessie!"

My phone beeps and I drop it on the couch and continue my scroll until I find an action movie almost entirely made up of explosions. No love story in sight.

"Perfect."

Getting comfortable on the couch, I tug the soft blanket up to my chin, my eyes drifting shut during a commercial for some medication.

Waking up hours later, I confuse the phone ringing on the TV with mine, and reach for my phone.

All it does is show me two things I don't want to see.

It's not even six in the morning on a weekend.

And there's still nothing from Murphy.

"Stop wishing there would be. Face the facts. Your time has come to an end," I tell the TV.

I'm resigned to the fact, but there's an itch under my skin I can't scratch. An unsettled, restless feeling. It drives me to stand and I pace the small living room, running my hands up and down my arms.

But I'm not cold.

It's like there's an electrical charge buzzing next to my skin, like the way lightning feels before a storm.

As if on cue, thunder rolls through the house.

Summer storms are my favorite.

But this one matches the one on the inside. I just hope the sun comes out soon in more ways than one.

CHAPTER 29

MURPHY

I should have let someone else do this. Anyone else.

It's not the day I need to be in the office—or at work.

But the day crept up on me before I knew it.

The twentieth anniversary of my father's passing.

And instead of being at home, or with my mom and sisters—or even apologizing and groveling to Leigh for ignoring her for the better part of a week—my shoes echo along the linoleum lined beige-gray walls of Grand River Hospital. Ironic, considering it was the same hospital I had brought Leigh to last week.

Two women sent to the same hospital by the same man. And it's my fault.

If Ellis wouldn't have seen Leigh with me, she wouldn't have been attacked. If I hadn't given my card to Sara, she wouldn't have called me.

The universe has a fucking sick sense of what is right and wrong.

"Room 4312?" I ask the nurse at the station in the ward where I'd been sent to get Sara's statement.

It should have happened earlier this week, but Sara's doctors had asked us to wait until she was done with multiple surgeries.

"Can I help you?" he asks, standing taller and crossing his arms over his chest.

I have to admire the way he protects his patient.

Pulling my ID from my pocket, I show him my badge and his posture relaxes.

"Sorry. Not the first time we've had someone show up and try to finish the job," he mutters and points in the direction.

None of the room numbers are labeled up here.

Is it sad there's an entire floor for domestic violence and sexual assault victims?

Yes.

But I appreciated the added security to include the person I'd had to show my badge to downstairs when I first asked about Sara's location.

Nodding, I head for the door, knocking several times before opening it slowly.

Sara is in the hospital bed, her eyes flying open at the sound of the click of the door as it opens. Brown eyes both black and blue, a white bandage on her cheek covers the gash I saw there on Monday.

Her cheeks and jawline are both swollen, and I second-guess whether she's up to providing her statement. But the doctor who left me a voicemail stating that Sara was asking for me assured me that she was when I returned his call.

But this is not the welcome distraction I need. I step into the light slowly, trying to put her at ease.

"Sara, it's Detective O'Connell. How are you feeling?"

"All things considered, I'm okay. Thanks to you." Her words are slurred but I don't know if it's from the swelling, pain medication, or something else.

I want to correct her, to tell her she's in here because I wasn't able to stop Ellis, but guilt—and experience—keeps my mouth shut.

"I had a message from you about your statement," I say instead.

Her nod is slight, like the movement is painful. It probably is given how bruised she is.

"I—my family is coming tomorrow from Virginia to take me home, and I wanted to get this done before they got here. To say they were surprised to hear from me—and where I was—is an understatement." Her grimace is laced with pain.

"Are you sure you're up to this?" I ask.

She nods again, moving her bed into a different position.

"He broke my jaw. And my cheekbone." She lifts her hand with an IV in it to the cheek covered by the bandage. "I…I was convinced I was going to die. He was going to…" she trails off because she and I both know what he was going to do. What I caught him in the act of doing. "I just remember wishing he would just kill me. That the pain would stop. Every time he said he was sorry. He promised it would never happen again. And I believed him. Every time."

Tears overflow, dripping down her cheeks, and I reach for the tissues on the table by her bed and hold them out for her.

"Thank you."

"I wish I could have done something sooner. Especially after the time before last when I gave you my card." I take the seat next to her bed, trying to understand.

It's not something I normally say, but this is not just another case.

She sighs.

"He made me believe I had nowhere to go. Isolated me from my family. Then my friends. He was all I had in Nashville. I…I left home and moved here when I was seventeen to try to make it as a country music singer. But he even took that from me. I couldn't go out and gig. I couldn't perform, because it would make him jealous. And he would get angry. At first it was words. But when those lost power it was more. So much more." She shudders and pulls the blankets tighter around her.

"Was the other day the first time he tried to sexually assault you?" How I get the question out, I have no idea. But it sits in the air between us as a tangible thing in the room.

The way her tears flow harder is all the answer I need, but the report is going to require her verbal confirmation. So I wait, allowing her time to process everything she's feeling.

"N-n-no."

Fuck.

The rest of my time with Sara is the whole horrific five years she spent with Ellis. A man I was responsible for bringing into Leigh's life.

This is why I am staying away.

This is why I need to continue to stay away, no matter how badly I want to call her when I slide into my driver's seat an hour later. I need her light to dispel the darkness. But I can't.

"It was my fault," I whisper in the empty car.

But it's a fight not to call her, not to drive to her house and drop to my knees on her front porch and ask her forgiveness. To explain everything I had seen. To tell her all the fucked-up emotions treating my body like their own personal amusement park.

Instead, I struggle through directions almost forgotten, pulling through the gates of the cemetery I haven't visited in a few years.

More than a few.

I refuse to stop at the office, driving along the winding roads until it starts to look familiar. Pulling over, I park the car and walk through the stone monuments until I find the one I know is there.

Sean William O'Connell.

"Hey, Dad," I whisper, staring at the dates on the headstone.

At the dash representing the words below the date.

Beloved husband and father.

The memory of my mom beside the casket at this site, hands gripping the hands of my two younger sisters while grief shook her shoulders swims to the surface, and I sit down quickly, tears burning the backs of my eyes.

I haven't cried in a long time.

But fuck if they're not there now.

I sit down, resting my arms on the tops of my knees and let them fall.

For women like Sara—the victim of a monster.

For Dad who was taken from us far too soon.

For Mom, Quinn, and Riley.

For Leigh.

And for me.

Even if I don't deserve to feel them for myself. Because it's my fault.

Sara.

Leigh.

Even falling in love.

Because I should have known better. I should have kept my promise.

"No woman ever deserves to feel pain because of me," I murmur.

It's poetic that the only thing to answer is the silent sentry of my father's headstone.

CHAPTER 30

LEIGH

What doesn't help with the antsy sensation?

Rage cleaning the house to a workout playlist I found on my music app.

I'm on my hands and knees scrubbing at a stubborn spot on a baseboard I just realized might have been paint when the text sound echoes through the speaker I have my phone connected to. I jump, the toothbrush I was using flying across the room.

"Chill out, Leigh," I mutter.

Unfolding from my position on the floor, I walk toward my phone and pick it up. A part of me hopes it's Murphy. A part of me doesn't care.

Liar, liar, pants on fire.

Okay, sue me. I do care.

But it's not Murphy.

It's Charlie.

He and I have texted a few times since the charity event. Once to let me know that his father has invited the CEO of Project Justice to Nashville for a charity golf event next month and asked if I want to go. I do, but it is the week after classes start in

Knoxville, and I can't leave classes for the day at the beginning of the semester.

The last time was to apologize for his dad—again—because he had overheard a conversation where his dad referred to me as Charlie's girlfriend. Charlie had shared with me that while he appreciated his dad's desire to see him move on, he couldn't understand Charlie was still grieving.

How was it so obvious to me when I had known Charlie for such a short time?

CHARLIE

Hey, what are you doing?

I avoid the full story and keep it short and sweet. He doesn't need to know I'm rage cleaning my house because my boyfriend —or is Murphy my ex-boyfriend now?—decided to ghost me.

Deep cleaning my house.

What about you?

There are lots of dancing dots as Charlie composes a message, but it doesn't come through until I start to set my cell back on the table.

CHARLIE

Today is Selene's birthday.

I hate this day.

My eyes burn with tears as they build up and I sit down on the couch, blinking the moisture away.

I'm so sorry, Charlie.

CHARLIE

To make matters worse, my dad picked today to tell me he set me up on a date next week.

What the hell? I can't imagine my parents being as clueless as Charlie's dad is.

You could tell him you're not going.

CHARLIE

I don't know what to tell him.

He's your dad.

CHARLIE

Exactly. He's not going to understand why I don't want to date.

You just have to talk to him.

CHARLIE

Maybe.

My phone stays silent for several breaths and I turn the music back on, putting away the cleaning supplies and checking Hannah Grace's garage for baseboard paint. It's dried out, so I take a picture of the brand and throw the dried-out can in the trash can before grabbing my keys and my phone.

Maybe if I stay busy enough, I'll stop thinking about Murphy. I'll stop feeling this overwhelming need to move. Which is how I find myself in the hardware store at four thirty in the afternoon in cutoffs and an old Iota Delta Kappa faded T-shirt with no makeup and a messy bun.

After the cashier tries to flirt with me and tells me he's off in ten minutes, I hightail it out of the store and toss the paint in the back floorboard of my car. As I'm about to pull out, my phone vibrates against my console, and I throw my car back in park and read the text.

CHARLIE

I could really use someone to talk to.

Any chance you're free?

I glance down at my shirt and cutoffs, chewing on my lip as I consider his request. I hadn't planned on going anywhere. Except back home. I'm not dressed to go anywhere else.

I'm not really dressed to go anywhere.

Hitting send, guilt rushes through my body and I quickly type another response.

I could meet you in an hour and a half or so? That'll give me time to shower and change since I've been cleaning all day.

There's the dance of Charlie's response before it vibrates in my hand.

CHARLIE

That would be great.

Thanks, Leigh.

Centennial Park? Is 7 okay?

Seven gives me more than enough time to get home and get a shower and something to eat before meeting him. It's also two hours before dark which means I might be able to take my camera and grab some other pictures.

That's perfect!

CHARLIE

Near the Parthenon?

I'll be there.

CHARLIE

See you then.

At ten minutes before seven, I pull into the parking lot I parked in before.

"It didn't take me long to get to the Parthenon from here, I think," I murmur, wishing I had gotten here a little sooner.

But a traffic accident had slowed traffic way down and I felt rushed, the impending doom of being late pressing in on me. My stomach flips and I take a deep breath to ease the nausea. I hate being late. Dark gray clouds rolled in while I drove from my house to the park, but it doesn't seem to deter anyone here. The parking lot is almost full, and I have to circle for a minute before I find a parking place.

I grab my phone and slide it into my back pocket and reach for my camera bag from the back, making sure the AirTag Sydney sent me when I moved to Nashville is in the bag. While she sent it for my purse, what is in there is less valuable than my camera bag. And since I have been known to set my camera bag down while taking pictures and walk off and forget it, this meant I could track the bag if I did that again.

I pass several people heading the opposite direction back to the parking lot as I speed walk toward the Parthenon, trying not to be late. Even this late in the evening, there are still people scattered along the trails, and the sounds of dogs barking and people talking are my soundtrack as I turn the corner and the Greek-like building comes into view.

Pulling out my phone, I check the time.

"Seven. Phew, I did it," I whisper to myself.

There's no sign of Charlie, so I grab my camera from the bag, attaching one of the lenses and snapping several images before I check my phone again.

7:15.

I don't know him well, but he didn't seem like the kind of person to be late. Opening our text thread, I send him a text.

Hey, are we still on for tonight?

I'm here, but don't see you.

His reply is almost instantaneous.

CHARLIE

Sorry, got a late start from my apartment and am still up the trail a bit. Can you meet me halfway?

A pin accompanies the text and it's almost ten minutes away.

What the fuck?

First, he's late, and now he drops me his location rather than just walking over here. My fingers hover over the keys, ready to tell him I'll wait the ten minutes. I'm not familiar enough with where he is in the park, and the charged feeling on my skin is going haywire.

He probably got a later start because it's Selene's birthday. How would you feel if the positions were reversed?

The itch along my skin has been there all day. How is now any different? The pin shows up clearly on the path, and if I get lost I can always do a search for the Parthenon in my maps and it will tell me how to get back here. Five minutes and I can meet up with him and we can walk the same loop we did before. It puts me at my car well before dark too.

Sure.

I start up the trail, the heat of the evening still simmering, but fading in the overgrown, shadowed trail Charlie had texted me he was on. The sounds are quieter, muted by the denser foliage, and I shiver, a chill chasing up my spine. The fine hairs along my arm stand up, the anxious electric-like sensations I've been experiencing all funneling to an alarm in my head warning me I should stop. Turn around. Do something other than continue walking.

I stop, feeling around my pockets for my pepper spray.

"Shit."

I never forget it. But I did today. Too much in a rush to get here.

There's still some distance between me and Charlie, and who knows who—or what—else is in the wooded areas.

"Stop being a scaredy-cat. It's still daylight. Charlie is just up the trail," I murmur.

He needs someone to talk to. If I can make his day easier, I want to help ease the burden. But better to be safe than sorry. Pulling my phone out, I confirm I shared my location with Sydney and shoot her the text.

Hey, are we still on for our rewatch of One Tree Hill tonight?

I'm really curious about how the football team does.

It may be an older show, but both Sydney and I love it and have binged several episodes on the phone with each other. She'll know the show isn't about a football team. It is our code for when we have a date gone wrong.

This may not be a date, but I really wish I had told Charlie no. Or waited on a more populated part of the trail.

"It's fine," I try to convince myself.

It is.

Right?

CHAPTER 31

MURPHY

Saturdays at the office are no different from any other day. Except I don't recognize most of the people milling at desks normally empty throughout the week.

But I needed to get Sara's statement and then get it typed up. The sooner Ellis is behind bars, the better. I still don't understand how he got bonded out after he was arrested on Monday. Rather than spending my time on trying to make sense of that, I need to get this done and make sure the report—the correct one—makes it in front of a judge who will throw him behind bars.

Focus, O'Connell.

Then maybe I can think about taking the rest of the day off. But what for? Days off used to be spent with Leigh. I doubt she is interested in seeing me after I blew her off this last week. It wasn't intentional, and it wasn't what I wanted.

It was what she needed.

It was what *I* needed to ensure she was safe.

Captain Overton pushes into the office, casually dressed in jeans and a short-sleeved sweater that shows off her recently acquired tan.

"O'Connell," she says as she passes my desk.

"Cap."

She turns then, head looking over her shoulder, and gives a slight nod at her office.

Mine is just as small, almost imperceptible, but she recognizes the movement and continues to her office. Sliding the documents I was working on into the file folder, I tap the file on the desk before locking it in my drawer.

I want to slam my chair under my desk and rush for her office. But if she wanted anyone else in our department to know she wanted to talk, she would have bellowed for me from her doorway.

This quiet request… This meant something. Something I don't want to name out loud.

I take a detour to the coffee pot for a refill before wandering toward her office. By all appearances, anyone would think it's a casual conversation.

Only my gut knows differently.

She has something. And she doesn't want anyone else to know.

"What are you doing here on the weekend, Captain?" I ask from her doorway, keeping up the pretense in case anyone is listening.

There's no heat between my shoulder blades, so I don't think anyone is.

But I have no idea who's been sabotaging me either, so it very well could be someone in the room right now.

"I just came in to tie up a few loose ends. I'd like to talk to you about your departure in two weeks. Close the door." Her words say one thing, but her expression says something else.

Once the door is closed, I drop into the chair on the other side of her desk, hoping my pose conveys a casual conversation despite the knot in my stomach.

Is the nightmare of the last few weeks finally coming to an end?

"Cap?" I ask, bracing myself for whatever it is she has to say.

Knowing—even if it's bad news—is better than the purgatory I've lived in for the last few weeks.

She nods.

"I have the results of the IA investigation. It took more time because the more IA uncovered, the more agencies had to get involved. State Prosecutor's Office. The FBI—not the special task forces you've been selected for, but our local guys."

What the fuck? What had IA found that all those organizations had to be looped in? I doubt it was anything against me since my badge is still in my pocket.

But this is big. Bigger than I had anticipated.

"What did they find?"

She sighs and leans forward, steepling her fingers in front of her chin.

"Turns out a clerk of the court was logging in after the files were submitted and changing them electronically before printing them and changing the hard copies. Your original hard copies were in the bottom drawer of her desk underneath a stack of other papers."

I rack my brain trying to think of any of the clerks I knew at the courthouse.

"I don't know any of them. What the hell did I do to her that she wanted to ruin my reputation?" I hiss.

Anger courses through my blood at some woman I've had zero interaction with who attempted to not only get me fired from NPD but also from the FBI.

I open my mouth to ask where she is and why she isn't already behind bars, but Overton holds up a hand and I snap my mouth closed, surprised the force doesn't shatter several teeth.

"She was a victim too, Murphy. She wasn't the mastermind."

Her words do very fucking little to assuage the anger. I've been in hell because of a court clerk. But I still don't even have enough of an answer, because there's still this shadow figure

I've been chasing like a goddamn ghost for the last several weeks.

"Who was?" I grit out through clenched teeth.

Aldridge? Warren? Who hated me that much?

"Our DA had to promise her immunity from prosecution and a transfer to a different position before she would admit to it. She was being blackmailed. Apparently, there are videos of her where she's engaged in...let's just say activities...with multiple people." Captain Overton grimaces, her disgust for whatever was in the videos obvious. "These videos, if they were leaked, would have cost her not only her job but, according to her, also her family."

A small part of me feels bad for her. But anger is still the primary emotion overwhelming me. Anger and frustration. Who would blackmail a court clerk to screw with my reports? Was I the only one involved? I still have more questions than answers.

And that fucking grates on my last nerve.

"Who?" I repeat, hand gripping my mug so hard I'm surprised it doesn't break.

"Kenneth Scott."

Of any name I had been expecting, his didn't even register. Why would he? He was nothing more than an annoyance to me even if I did still want to rip him limb from limb for what he had done to Leigh.

"What the fuck?" I roar, bolting out of my chair.

"Sit down, O'Connell," she says, also standing and pointing to my chair.

Air saws in and out of my lungs, the red haze coloring my vision receding slowly. Blood pounds through my veins, demanding revenge, but I finally exhale a longer breath and sit back down. Overton takes more time to take her seat, but eventually does after scanning the room. Belatedly, I realize my voice would have carried. I'm surprised no one is looking this direction when I crane my neck to check the window that shows the rest of the office behind me.

"Kenneth Scott? What the fuck did I ever do to him?" I hiss.

But I already know the answer.

Leigh.

I think back to when the trouble with my cases first started. Shortly after I showed up to Leigh's office with lunch. I'd run into Kenneth that day too. And I'd warned him to stay away from her.

So he had decided to sabotage me. All because he wanted something—someone—I was never going to let him have. Payback.

"I'm sure the clerk isn't the only one he's got videos on," I tell Captain Overton.

She raises an eyebrow into a perfect arch. "You know something I don't?"

"I don't know for sure, but I do know he's been harassing a… friend of mine." I stumble over the word because Leigh is so much more. Or at least she was. "She's an intern in their office and he came on to her."

Overton nods.

"Chief Bailey mentioned personnel issues but kept them vague. He did say they released Kenneth earlier this week. The warrant was issued yesterday, but Kenneth hasn't been back to his apartment. We've had units stationed at his condo since it was issued."

I snort.

"He's probably hanging with his BFF."

Water always finds its own level. And Kenneth's level is the likes of Vinny Ellis.

"Charles Vanderweel Senior?" Captain Overton asks.

What the fuck?

The record scratch echoes through my head as my gaze snaps to hers. Twice in five minutes, a name has caught me off guard.

"Vanderweel? I didn't realize he and Scott were close."

But even as I say it, I remember Kenneth's presence at the charity launch. And as the pieces click together, I realize he and

Vanderweel tend to run in the same circles despite Scott only making the salary of a public defender.

"What's the connection?" I murmur, but it's loud enough for Captain Overton to hear.

"Scott comes from family money. Apparently he and Vanderweel became friends as teenagers. We had to find the connection when the court clerk told us there were several times when Vanderweel would be at Scott's condo." The pointed look she gives me says more than her words.

The reasons for Vanderweel being at Scott's condo were not on the up-and-up.

My mind and my stomach are reeling as I try to process this latest information.

Charles Vanderweel is an upstanding citizen. He is a friend of the city. He cares about the police force. Kenneth Scott is lower than scum, helping filth get free and back on the streets.

Bile rises to my throat. If I've been wrong about Vanderweel, what else have I been wrong about?

"Fuck," I say, leaning forward and setting my cup on the desk and putting my head between my knees.

"IA has cleared your name. In fact, they called you an example for all the detectives to follow. When I shared you were leaving, they were sad to see you go," she says.

Well, that's a different message than the one I've been getting for the last few weeks.

Glancing up, I catch her half smile.

"I am too, you know. Right now, I have no one to keep Aldridge in line. Cocky little shit. I'm getting too old to deal with the arrogance," she says, rolling her eyes.

The relief flooding through me is like a cool breeze when I've been in the fires of hell for too long.

"Thank you," I tell her.

"For what?"

"I know you went to bat for me. I know it was your reputation on the line when you did," I tell her.

The nod she gives me is smaller than the one that called me into her office. But it's there.

We'd have both gone down if she wasn't able to figure this out.

"Get out of here, O'Connell. Go enjoy your Saturday. I've got to review some of the paperwork from IA but then that's what I'm doing too."

I open my mouth to argue that I don't want to go home, but she holds up a hand.

"Your cases will still be there Monday. That's an order, Detective."

"Yes, ma'am."

Fifteen minutes later, I'm in my car, but I'm not going home.

Or maybe I am.

It's been a while since I've driven the streets around my childhood home and guilt kicks me in the ass.

I need to visit Mom more often than I do.

But normally she stops in to see me and I don't have to.

I don't recognize the car in the driveway, and I grab my gun from the lockbox in my car, tucking it into the back of my pants, regretting I hadn't brought a holster with me.

I didn't think I would need it.

Who the fuck is here?

I don't knock, don't go through the front, but sneak around the side of the house, opening the back gate. I'm relieved the WD-40 I used last time I was here fixed the squeak and doesn't alert anyone to my presence.

Walking on the balls of my feet, I make my way around the house, the sliding glass door giving me a clear view of Mom's living room, where she's in the arms of a man I *do* recognize.

My dad's ex-partner.

Roberto De Luca. Rob for as long as I've known him. Uncle Rob when I was a kid.

I didn't think I could handle any more surprises today.

Then the universe said, "Hold my beer."

As I watch, he spins her out, then back to him in their dance, his face lowering to hers.

"What the fuck?" I ask, opening the sliding glass door, and the two break apart like guilty teenagers.

"Murphy James O'Connell!" My mother's triple name still has the ability to turn my ears flaming hot, her softer brogue after years in the United States still trilling over my name.

"Murphy, what brings you here?" Rob asks.

The question may be superficial, but the tone of the room is strained, embarrassment dancing around the three of us while the music still plays from the radio speakers.

"I could ask you the same thing. What the hell are you doing here with my mother?" I growl in his direction.

Suddenly the man who became like a second father to me is a stranger.

He has the courtesy to look sheepish, but it doesn't make him drop his hand where it's wrapped around Mom's waist.

I have the irrational urge to step between them, to sever the connection.

"The last time I checked, mo mhac, I was your mother and not the other way round," Mom says, using the nickname she's had for me since I was little.

The way her eyebrow arches, I know I am treading on dangerous ground.

But what the hell? Could the universe throw me for any bigger of a fucking loop?

First, Leigh. Then, Scott and Vanderweel. Now, this? Mom and Rob?

With a swallow, I realize a break might be best. I walk to the hall closet, finding the gun safe Dad installed all those years ago and put my own weapon inside, attempting to ignore there's another gun in there that isn't Dad's.

It's Rob's.

He may be retired, but I know he still carries. He and I just went to the range a few months ago to catch up. And he never mentioned dating my mother.

Is that what they're doing?

"Are you two a couple now?" I ask, shutting the safe and turning to face them.

Mom and Rob nod in unison.

Fuck.

It's like I've been sucker punched in the stomach.

"Do Quinn and Riley know?" I ask, protective big brother rising to the top of the swirling emotions resembling the tilt-a-whirl at the state fair.

Again, they nod.

Fuck. I was the last to know.

"They…they've given us their blessing, Murphy. We'd like yours as well," Rob says.

"Blessing? For what?" Because as much as my mind is whirling, I don't connect the dots.

Mom lifts her left hand, a shiny ring having replaced the wedding set Dad bought them when they were first married.

"Rob's asked me to marry him, Murphy. And I've agreed."

Ring. Marry. Agreed.

The world spins around me as I'm battered by waves of emotions. Surprise is understandable. But the sorrow zipping through me like a knife isn't.

Dad's been gone a long time.

But Mom never talked about finding someone else.

So it's a fresh wound on top of a scar—almost like I've been betrayed.

At least I can recognize enough to know I need to keep my mouth shut. I want to be happy for Mom and Rob. But I'm not there yet.

"I need some water," I mutter and spin on my heel for the kitchen.

The kitchen still looks the same as it did when I was a kid, but there are small changes. A second coffee cup next to Mom's. A new picture. A bottle of olive oil on the counter.

Mom joins me a few minutes later.

"How about some tea?" she asks, pushing me out of the way and already turning on the electric kettle and pulling down a plate for cookies.

The smell of her homemade chocolate chip cookies wafts up when she opens the jar and my mouth waters.

Traitor.

This isn't something to fix with cookies and tea. I'm not a teenager nursing a broken heart.

But cookies can't hurt.

She hands me the plate and I move to the kitchen table, sitting in my normal spot while Mom finishes preparing the tea.

How many times have I watched her do this? A hundred? A thousand? Anytime I had an issue and we needed to talk, this was our routine.

But it's not the same. Will it ever be again?

She finishes and brings both cups over to the table, handing me one before she slides into her spot.

I take a sip, scalding the roof of my mouth and wincing.

"You never did have the patience to let it cool. Ever since you were little," Mom says, smiling as she blows on her cup but doesn't take a sip.

I ease the burn with a cookie before focusing my attention on her.

"Why didn't you tell me? How long has this been going on?" I ask, not sure if I'm more angry or hurt that I'm the last to know.

She reaches over, laying her hand on mine, and squeezes.

"You know Rob and I have been friends since your Dad

passed. It wasn't until about six months ago he admitted he had developed feelings for me. He asked me out to dinner. But as a date rather than friends. And when he kissed me—"

"I don't want to know," I say, pulling my hand out from under hers to cover my ears.

She laughs.

"You act like you're still a boy, mo mhac, but don't forget it was me you admitted it to when you lost your virginity when you were sixteen. Not your father."

Fuck, that had been awkward. And as much as I'd thought about talking to Dad, Mom and I had sat at this table when I missed curfew because of what I had been doing.

"Now, as I was saying, when he kissed me, I realized I returned those feelings for him. They'd grown so gradually through the years neither of us noticed. Until it was the only thing we could see."

"What about Dad? Is this what he would want?" A lump sits on my vocal cords, making it hard to ask, my voice cracking over the words.

Mom's smile dims, growing wistful. Tears burn my nose and I have to blink to get rid of the moisture blurring my vision.

Fuck. Dad should still be here. He shouldn't have had to die.

"Did you know we talked about it before he passed? He used to tell me he didn't want me to be alone. He always wanted my happiness. Even if something happened to him. Bhí sé ina comhpháirtí anam."

He was the person of my soul.

Fuck. Lifting my hand to my heart, I rub at the ache there. Because I truly know what that means now.

"Rob makes me happy. He loves me. And I love him. He doesn't replace your dad. Not in here." She lifts a hand to her heart. "But my heart has more love to give."

Isn't that what I should want? Her happiness? She's the best woman I know. She deserves to be happy, and if Rob makes her happy, shouldn't I support them?

"You're sure he makes you happy?" I ask, studying her expression.

The love shining from her eyes is all the proof I need. The grief of Dad's death is still there, but softened. A dull ache versus the sharp one that existed when I first sat down.

She nods.

"I do."

"It's going to take me some time to get used to it, but if he makes you happy, that's what I want too, Mom. But if he hurts you, I'll kick his ass." I raise my voice.

"He went out to the porch to give us some privacy," she says.

"I'll still tell him the same thing," I mutter, and take a sip of my now-cool tea.

"He expects nothing less. Now what brings you here to see me? I know you've been busy with packing."

"I haven't been. Packing, that is. But I have been busy," I tell her.

Over four chocolate chip cookies and a cup of tea, I tell Mom everything. The wedding. Leigh. The errors on the reports. The situation with Ellis on Monday. She already knew about the officer who died in the line of duty, having heard from Rob, but her look of disappointment when I tell her I've decided I don't want the same fate for Leigh as for her is enough to have me second-guessing everything I've done to this point.

"Murphy, the world will bring trouble to your doorstep whether you look for it or not. Yet here you are borrowing trouble like you have a shortage of it. If you love her, fight for her. Love helps things work out the way they're meant to. I knew what I was getting when I signed on to be a policeman's wife. And even knowing everything I know now, I would not change it. Not for the world. I want that great love for you, mo mhac. Just as I want it for your sisters."

"But—"

"No more buts. If I let you, you could argue yourself out of anything. But love isn't meant to be argued with. It's meant to be embraced. Now take your dumb arse to her and apologize. Get on your knees and beg forgiveness. And, if you're smart, you'll marry her."

I jolt at the thought before allowing the idea to wrap me in a warm blanket.

Marry her.

Yeah, I think I could.

I just have to convince her to forgive me first.

CHAPTER 32

MURPHY

The drive to Leigh's is almost as familiar as the drive to my place.

She was the first person I wanted to talk to when Overton shared what IA had found. But I fought the sensation, heading to Mom's instead.

Yet here I am, nearly breaking the speed limit to get to her. To apologize. To beg for forgiveness. Exactly as my mother told me to do.

She may hate me.

I should probably just turn around.

But I can't.

I need to see her.

But I just pull into her driveway when her across the street neighbor calls out from the driver's side of his Jeep.

"She's not home. I saw her pull out about fifteen minutes ago," he calls out.

Suspicion has me narrowing my eyes as I study him. Who the hell is he to her and why does he know that?

"Who are you?"

"We met before. When you were looking into all that shit with Hannah Grace and Cole," he says.

As I scrutinize him, he does look familiar, and the tension eases somewhat, but doesn't disappear.

"I promised Cole and Hannah Grace I'd keep an eye on her this summer," he adds.

The tension fades as the memory of Cole mentioning him to me surfaces.

"Any idea where she was going?" I ask.

He shakes his head.

"I just happened to see her since I was mowing my yard before work." He points to the front yard with the diagonal lines of a fresh mow.

"Thanks, man, appreciate it," I tell him.

With a wave, he gets in his Jeep and drives off, leaving me alone.

I sit on the front stoop, considering my options. I could wait for her.

It's only seven twenty and I have no idea where she's gone.

Pulling up my text thread with her, I key out a text and press send.

I'm sorry.

I'm here at your place and would love to apologize in person.

The message shows as delivered but unread.

"You brought this on yourself, O'Connell," I murmur, willing the *Delivered* to turn to *Read*.

Five minutes pass.

Then ten.

Nothing.

"Fuck."

Standing, I'm almost to my car when it rings.

But it's not Leigh. It's another number.

One showing as Unknown.

Spam call.

I let it go to voicemail and get in my car, cranking the engine and letting the AC blow through the car.

The phone rings again, still with unknown as the caller ID.

"Hello?" I answer, bracing myself for some telemarketer or robotic recording.

Only it's not.

"Murphy?" the voice asks.

"This is Murphy. Who is this?" I ask, being careful not to answer *yes* since I had just read about a scam where criminals were using AI to use the word *yes* for access to a variety of things.

"It's Sydney. I'm not some AI bot who's going to steal your identity. Jesus Christ. Is Leigh with you?"

"No, I'm at her place. But she's not home."

"Fuck. That's what I was afraid of."

Warning bells clamor in my head. Fear and anxiety claw through my gut at the tone of Sydney's voice.

"Why? What's going on?"

"Leigh texted me a few minutes ago about a show we both like, but she changed the detail. It's a code phrase for when one of us is on a bad date and needs intervention. Usually it involves calling with an emergency or something like that."

"Leigh's on a date?" I ask.

Shit. Did I already miss my window to apologize?

In a week?

No, Leigh's not like that.

I'm letting fear control my thoughts and take several deep breaths, unsure what I'm more afraid of—Leigh leaving me or something happening to her.

"No. I said it's our code phrase for dates. She's still pining after your dumb ass."

That's twice in the span of two hours I've been called the same name.

"I—"

"I don't have time to argue with you. I think something is wrong. Otherwise she wouldn't have texted me that. I tracked her phone and it pinged to a place called Centennial Park. Do you know where it is?"

"Yeah, it's about thirty minutes from here. Maybe forty-five depending on traffic."

Maybe she had gone to take pictures—she had mentioned wanting to go back after her first visit there. We were supposed to go together and I was going to show her my favorite parts of the park.

But why would she text Sydney that code?

I'm already backing out of the driveway, keeping to the speed limit in the neighborhood until I'm on main streets where I speed up. The phone connects to the car via my speakers.

My heart starts to hammer against my chest, my gut agreeing with Sydney. Something is wrong.

And I need to get there. Now.

"The last ping is in a parking lot. It looks like a pretty big parking lot but it doesn't have any identification on it."

"Shit. There are a handful of parking lots around Centennial Park," I tell her, stomping on the accelerator.

My hands grip the steering wheel, knuckles whitening as the car shoots forward, through a stale yellow. The sound of horns and squealing tires echo behind me but I don't look back.

I can't.

Leigh needs me. Everything in my body is telling me so.

CHAPTER 33

LEIGH

Text sent to Sydney, I keep walking with no sign of anyone on this trail—it's almost like no one has ever been on this trail the way the weeds reach out onto the sidewalk.

I almost turn around, ready to text Charlie I'll meet him by the Parthenon like we agreed to when I hear him.

"Leigh, is that you?" It's Charlie, but off the trail, hidden by a large tree about a hundred feet in front of me.

See? Nothing to be worried about. No more bingeing true crime podcasts. They make you paranoid.

"Yeah, it's me. Are you okay?" I ask, hesitating in case he needs a minute to himself.

"I-I found a dog. It's hurt. Can you help me?"

I rush forward, my only thoughts on helping whatever injured dog Charlie has found. Poor baby, they must be scared and hurt and—

There's no injured animal on the other side of the tree. And the man who sounded like Charlie isn't.

The hair—while similarly styled—holds hints of gray that pick up the minimal sunlight managing to filter through the thick foliage as he turns, showing off dazzling blue eyes.

Exactly like his son's.

Not Charlie. Mr. Vanderweel.

What's going on?

He studies me for several moments, his eyes taking on a malicious glint. Ice cold travels through my body, sending a freezing chill to every extremity.

"Hello, Leigh, we've been waiting for you."

Twigs snap behind me and I jump, my heart racing as the presence of someone else registers, each step through the brush increasing my heartbeat until I'm sure the thing is going to pound out of my chest.

We. He said we. Why am I sticking around here?

Run!

Two rough hands reach out, holding my arms against my body. I struggle against the strong grip, thrashing around, desperate to get free.

But no matter how hard I try, I can't. The hold on my arms tightens, breaking through the adrenaline, and I cry out and stop struggling against the pressure that feels like any additional movement on my part is going to do some serious damage instead of the bruises I can already feel forming.

Fuck. What am I going to do?

My body is going haywire, my memory unhelpful as I try to focus on something—anything—from one of my self-defense classes to help right now.

Breathing is hard, my shallow breaths making me dizzy as I try to focus on any one of the techniques I learned. But they all scatter before I can land on one. Like any of them would help. None of the moves had focused on escaping multiple assailants. Let alone when at least one of them outweighs me by eighty pounds or more.

"Hello again, pretty."

My body reacts to the stench before I recognize the voice. I dry heave at the stale smell of alcohol mixing with notes of body odor and dirt.

Shit.

Vinny Ellis.

Fight!

Risk of broken bone or not, I struggle through the nausea, kicking back to try and catch his knee with my heel. He just laughs, shuffling me sideways until a third man comes into view.

The odds of me against Mr. Vanderweel and Ellis were almost impossible. But three? How can I fight against all three of them?

The blond-haired demon smiles as if he can read the resignation on my face.

"Really, Ms. Whittaker, you should know when you're outnumbered." Kenneth smirks.

I am. And I know it. But I'm not willing to give up so easily.

But something about Kenneth calling out the fact is like a physical blow.

My stomach somersaults, but all the adrenaline fades in a heartbeat, and tears burn the back of my nose.

"Let's go." Vanderweel nods deeper into the woods and fear claws at my throat.

Where are they taking me?

Vanderweel starts off first, with Ellis dragging me behind him. I try to set my feet, to hold back, but I might as well be a ragdoll for all the good it does. Tall weeds scratch my bare legs as I'm dragged through the foliage that grows thicker until it just stops.

A dark SUV is parked in front of us, and Mr. Vanderweel and Kenneth climb into the front while Ellis shoves me into the back.

"We could have some fun back here," he says, leering at me.

Bile rises to my throat and I shrink against the door as close as I can, shaking so hard my teeth chatter.

Kenneth turns around, freezing him with a glare.

"No touching." His voice is firm as he flicks a glance to me. "At least not yet."

Oh, God.

What the hell is going to happen to me?

My heart continues to pound against my chest, my palms sweaty when I try to grip the door handle where the child locks have been engaged.

Did you really want to throw yourself out of a moving car?

Anything would be better than whatever these three have planned.

Focus.

When I was a little girl, I used to love to stick my face in the fan and try to breathe. The feeling of having air all around me but unable to do anything with it is the same sensation I have now. Focusing is like trying to breathe against that fan.

Impossible.

"W-where are you taking me?" I ask, releasing my grip on the door handle as Ellis backs off.

"She parked in the same place as before?" Mr. Vanderweel ignores my question and directs one to Ellis.

"Yeah, I watched her, just like you told me to."

I remember the sensation of being watched the first time I was here with Charlie.

Was Ellis whose eyes I felt on me before?

"Is Charlie okay?" I ask.

Nobody answers me.

Is he okay?

My stomach is roiling and I bend over as I dry heave, my camera bag falling between my legs.

Camera bag!

The AirTag.

I want to cry as a kernel of hope lodges in my chest.

Ellis grabbed my phone from my back pocket when he shoved me into the backseat, but he left my camera bag around me.

I work the zipper open as quietly as possible, working my fingers into the bag while turning my attention to the windows. My fingers are shaking so hard, I'm amazed no one hears the zipper, but Mr. Vanderweel and Kenneth are deep in conversation, and Ellis is focused on them like a puppy.

We're back at the entrance of the park. If they're heading back to my car, I don't have much time, and I have no idea what's going to happen when we get there.

Nothing good.

My fingers brush the hard plastic of my extra lens and I push harder, wrapping around the metal circle of the keychain holding the AirTag. Hiding my hand behind the bag, I palm the keychain as we pull up behind my car.

"You know what to do?" Mr. Vanderweel asks.

"I got it. I got her phone. I just need her keys." Ellis looks at me with beady eyes.

My car keys are in the front pocket of my jean shorts.

"Give him your keys, Ms. Whittaker," Kenneth demands, turning to face me.

I open my mouth to argue. No fucking way am I going to make it easy for them to kidnap me.

"I would advise against arguing," Kenneth adds.

"I can always come get them if you don't give 'em to me." Ellis tries to waggle his brows.

Just the thought of his hands on me has bile rising to my throat. Shifting, I manage to yank the keys out of my pocket at the same time as I tuck the AirTag in. I hold my keys out, fighting everything in me that demands I tighten my grip, even as Ellis snatches them from my hand.

"Thanks, pretty," he says, blowing a kiss at me.

I have to fight the urge to gag.

"Take the bag too," Kenneth tells Ellis.

I shake my head, unwilling to give up the bag, even if the AirTag is now safely in my pocket.

"No." I shrink farther against the door, but there's nowhere else to go.

Ellis's fingers wrap around the strap close to my breast, and revulsion shivers through my blood like a poison. But I fight against the urge to release the bag, wrapping my own hand around the strap and holding on.

But I'm no match for brute strength.

He yanks it from around my neck, and I cry out as the strap scrapes the sensitive skin at my nape.

"When Vinny opens the door, you're not going to try anything stupid. Believe me when I say you will regret it." Mr. Vanderweel meets my gaze as he turns around, and all I see is horror.

My breathing shallows and I shake my head, biting my lip. Tears I refuse to shed burn my nose. I don't want to give them the satisfaction.

It's like I'm a watching a movie, seeing the heroine cower in the corner of her seat.

Ellis gets out, slamming his door with a vibrating thud before yanking my driver's side door open. He cranks the ignition and reverses out of the spot.

"That idiot is going to attract attention," Kenneth hisses to Mr. Vanderweel.

"We've already discussed this. We want him getting the attention," Mr. Vanderweel responds.

He continues to follow Ellis to a separate parking lot, and with some weird sort of detachment, I continue to watch as Ellis leaves my car unlocked, the keys, my phone, and my open camera bag on full display. Begging to be stolen.

Shit.

"W-where's Charlie?" I ask.

"My melodramatic wimp of an offspring is more than likely at his apartment, sobbing over his dead cunt of a fiancée," Mr. Vanderweel says with a snarl.

I swallow at the venom in his voice, unprepared for how intense it is.

Ellis gets back in the SUV and Mr. Vanderweel heads for the exit. I glance back once at my car.

Will I ever see it again?

Don't focus on that. Focus on where you're going.

Maybe I can figure out how to get away.

From three of them? Who are you? Batman?

CHAPTER 34

MURPHY

It takes forever to get to the park. For every red light I hit that I can't run, for every slow-ass motherfucker who can't get out of my way, I want to scream.

Anxiety crawls through my body, panic making it hard not to run every single red light I come across.

My fingers tighten on the steering wheel, my lips moving in silent prayers, willing Leigh to be okay.

Even Sydney is quiet on the phone, and from all the stories I've heard about her from Leigh and my own experiences—that's unlike her.

But what feels like hours is only about twenty-five minutes the way I speed around slower traffic and run through yellow lights I should stop for.

The first parking lot is smaller and I don't even have to drive through it to see there are no signs of Leigh's car.

The second parking lot is big enough—and full enough—I have to drive the rows, wasting precious minutes as I scan the aisles looking for her car.

Fuck.

No luck.

Pounding on my steering wheel, I head for the next lot, slamming on my brakes as a family crosses in front of me.

I'm about to give up after the third lot but I try one more.

And find it.

"Found her car," I tell Sydney, parking next to it where it overlooks a large pavilion.

"Is she there?" The hope in her voice is painful.

Or maybe that's my own heart when I have to say the words.

"No, there's no sign of her." I grab a napkin from the console in my car and get out, trying her door while trying to avoid contaminating the scene.

It opens easily. The keys are in the cupholder, her cell phone in plain sight, as is her camera poking out of a bag with several other lenses visible. Someone wanted her car to be taken.

"Shit."

"What? What is it?" Sydney asks in my ear, the earbud my ongoing connection to her.

I'd almost forgotten she was there.

"The keys and her phone are in her car. So is her camera with the bag. She wouldn't leave it if she had the choice. She cares about her camera too much to risk losing it," I say as terror ices through my veins.

Stóirín, where are you?

"Fuck, fuck, fuck." There's a flurry of computer keys on the other end of the phone.

I grab Leigh's cell phone and check it, but can't unlock it. Pocketing it, I stand, scanning the area for Leigh or any sign of her.

"There's no sign of her anywhere," I tell Sydney, spinning and checking for any clue in the car as to where she's gone. "Wait, the car seat is too far back for Leigh. Like almost all the way back."

She's too short to have driven her car anywhere in that position.

"Can you check her camera bag?" Sydney asks.

I open the back door, still using the rapidly disintegrating napkin, and flip the top on the bag.

"Why? What am I looking for?"

"Is there an Apple AirTag in there?" she asks. "It's a small gray circle in a keychain."

It's hard to see with the lenses, and after shifting them from one side of the small compartment to the other, I'm wasting precious seconds.

Fuck it.

Tossing the napkin on the seat, I lift one lens and then the other followed by her camera, coming up empty.

"Nothing," I say.

"Good girl," she crows with another flurry of keyboard activity.

"What the fuck does that mean?" I ask, helplessness clawing at my throat.

"Fuck, yes, it's finally updating and moving. I gave her an AirTag for her purse but she told me she put it in her camera bag. If it's not there and it's moving—"

"It means she managed to grab the AirTag before the bag got left here," I finish for Sydney, taking my first real breath in almost an hour.

"Exactly. And I can give you directions."

Relief is a tsunami warring with the ever-present fear.

Locking her car, I'm back in mine, and I clip my phone to the holder on the dashboard in under thirty seconds.

"What are we waiting for? Tell me how to find her."

CHAPTER 35

LEIGH

I try to keep track of the various turns, but since I'm not very familiar with Nashville, I end up more turned around than getting any clarity of where we are.

"W-Where are you taking me?" I ask.

Fuck, I wish my voice would stop shaking. It's showing weakness when none of these three deserve it.

I shouldn't be surprised when no one answers me. Ellis continues to stare at me, palming himself over his clothes and licking his lips when he sees I've noticed.

I cough, gagging, my stomach heaving.

"Don't puke in my car," Mr. Vanderweel mutters, taking another turn that only adds to the nausea.

Like I could help it if I did.

"I don't feel so good," I groan.

"Make sure she doesn't puke in my car," Mr. Vanderweel directs Ellis.

"It might help if he stopped fondling himself while looking at her," Kenneth says with a glance back at Ellis.

"Jesus Christ. Ellis, change of plans. You'll need to take this car and dump it. I don't need any DNA—from anyone—in this car," Mr. Vanderweel says curtly, taking another corner with a squeal of tires against asphalt.

Another ten minutes of driving and we pull through a garage door in the side of what looks to be an abandoned warehouse.

"W-where are we?" I ask, as the car stops with a jerk.

My stomach bubbles and I take several breaths.

"Out," Kenneth says.

He exits the passenger seat, opening my door and yanking me free. I stumble, almost falling to my knees before righting myself.

I'm not sure whose hands I don't like more—Ellis's rough grip or Kenneth's manicured hold.

Both make me sick to my stomach.

I shrug free of his grip, backing up against the car as the three men stand in various poses around me.

Mr. Vanderweel. On the surface he looks detached, but there's a hatred in his gaze creating a pit of terror in my stomach unlike any I've ever known. Kenneth stands near him, studying me like I'm a bug under a microscope. Ellis is farther away, twitching, his gaze bouncing between me and his boss.

"W-why am I here?" I clear my throat and try to keep the quiver out of my lip.

"You mean to tell me you don't know?" Mr. Vanderweel asks.

I shake my head, an errant tear falling, and I swipe it away from my face.

These bastards don't deserve my tears.

"N-n-no." I can fight my tears, but not the shake in my voice.

In this moment, I hate my own weakness. Scanning the almost empty building, I look for any way to escape. But there's nothing. All the windows are boarded up, and the only thing in the empty building is a dilapidated staircase leading to a separate room with gray-tinged windows.

The door we came through is already down, the steel heavy enough I can't lift it. I don't even know how they opened it.

Please let Sydney have understood my text.

But even if she does, will she think to track the AirTag?

"I picked you for him," Mr. Vanderweel snarls.

"Huh?" My attention snaps back to Mr. Vanderweel.

I don't understand. He picked me for who?

"Don't be stupid. You. You were meant to be the perfect society wife for Charlie. I saw the way you two interacted the day we met with you and your boss. So I had you investigated. And as soon as I got the results, I knew you were perfect for him. Exactly who I wanted for him. You were raised correctly. Your family is one of the founding members of one of the quaintest towns in all of Tennessee. Precisely what that sniveling little wimp needed. You have an almost impeccable college record, and law school is the crowning achievement. He was going to get the best crafted love story money could buy. He was going to continue the dynasty I've built from the ground up. She was never good enough for him." Mr. Vanderweel spits the words and they lie between us like a poison.

She.

"Selene? I ask.

"*Her*. She should have been perfect for him. She had the right pedigree. The right breeding. But in the end, she was nothing more than poor white trash. A gold-digging whore."

It sounds like he's referring to a dog versus a human being. Selene was from an upper middle-class family. Her file had said she went to Brown before coming back to Nashville to be close to her family when she got offered a job at Mr. Vanderweel's company. She and Charlie had met at a charity event for animals. Nothing I had read fit the narrative he was spouting.

"It-it was never like that between Charlie and me. We're friends. He loves Selene." I can't even use the past tense. Because the way he talked about her, the way he still grieved? It was still very much in the present.

Even if I hadn't fallen for Murphy. Even if I had been interested in Charlie.

He loves his fiancée.

It is obvious.

Isn't it?

"She didn't love him!" he explodes, pacing the length of the car and back. "She wanted to keep working once they were married. Charlie needed a wife who could uphold their social obligations. Not someone whose attention was divided. Even when I called her to my office to let her know her job would no longer be there when she and Charlie married, she had the nerve to stand up and tell me she would get a different job. With another company. That Charlie would support her. Would choose her. Not me. She was turning him against me. My own son!" he screams and it echoes around us.

Oh, God.

When did they have that conversation? Did Charlie know about it?

"I couldn't have that. I knew she would succeed. That little brat was always more his mother's son than mine. But I made sure he was going to follow in my footsteps. I had worked too long and too hard to get him where he was. And how did he repay me? By picking *her*!"

Rage mottles his throat, the red creeping up his face until he's breathing heavily, his motions exaggerated.

"She walked out and resigned the week before her wedding. I knew she was going to come between Charlie and me. So I went to visit her." He grows eerily calm. Like he's walking through a business report versus the vitriol he had just exhibited before.

He runs his hands through his hair before straightening a wrinkle in his shirt.

When did he visit her?

You already know.

But I don't want to believe it. So I force that voice to the back and watch Mr. Vanderweel's face return to a normal shade. Almost like his outburst never happened.

"She wasn't expecting me. She was expecting Charlie. They had a date that night."

A rock forms in the pit of my stomach and I want to cover my ears. To pretend I'm not hearing this.

I don't want to.

He looks up and a smile plays on his face. One that has my entire body flushing cold and chills ripping down my spine.

"I knew by the look in her eyes I wasn't going to get her to change her mind. So I changed tactics. I told her I was worried about Charlie. He'd been distracted that day at work. Not like himself. And I wanted to go talk to him but he and I always struggled with conversations. So I asked her to go with me. I told her I needed her help. For him."

He lifts his hands, staring at them like he's in some sort of trance.

It's a memory.

I jolt at the realization, trying to breathe through lungs that don't want to work as everything he's saying sinks in.

"It's a powerful feeling. Watching someone's light fade in their eyes because of your hands. More powerful than anything else I've experienced." He shares a glance with Kenneth and my stomach drops to my toes.

"You...you..." I can't say the words because then they'll be true.

They're still true whether you say them or not.

If Mr. Vanderweel has any reservations about saying the words, they're not evident.

He nods.

"I killed her. Then I paid some bum to dump her body in the water, but the asshole didn't light the car on fire the way I directed. Her DNA was still in the car. Charlie's car." He snaps his gaze to Ellis who nods.

I want to scream. To curl into a ball and cry. To run away from the monster who should only live in nightmares but is standing so calmly in front of me.

He killed his son's fiancée. The woman his son loved.

And I realize my fate is on the same trajectory.

Sydney, please send help.

"I know what I need to do," Ellis slurs.

Vanderweel's attention shifts back to me and he steps forward. I shrink back.

I need to buy some time.

"Was that the same person you convinced to take the fall for Selene's death?" I ask, hoping to keep him talking.

He shrugs, like he didn't ruin another life.

"It was the only thing he could do to make it right. I made sure his family was well compensated despite his idiocy," he says.

"Is that what you're going to do to me?" I ask.

Why I need the morbid confirmation, I don't know. But I can't resist asking.

His eyes light up and I want to throw up.

"It's poetic, isn't it? You're going to die in the same place she did. Back then the factory was fully functional. Another inheritance from my grandparents. I had to shut it down when workers kept quitting. They said it was haunted."

I shiver as the word echoes despite the quiet way he said it.

"I don't want to die," I say, unwilling to beg but needing to say the words.

His posture tells me he couldn't care less about what I want. About what I said.

"You've left me no choice. You embarrassed me." He says the words as if he's talking to a child.

I rack my brain, trying to think of something I could have done.

"W-what?" I say, the tremor returning to my voice.

"At the charity event. I made sure Charlie's cousin was busy with other plans. Which meant he had to take you. I made sure the opportunity to meet Project Justice was too good for you to pass up. It was a no-fail situation. I even spoke about you to all those people in that room, saying how happy I was Charlie had found someone again. You were his girlfriend. But then you had to practically fuck the detective by the bathrooms. Kenneth saw you. And your actions made me a laughingstock. I knew then no one would believe me if they saw the two of you together. Not after that."

"You tried to manipulate your son. And me. You can't make people do what you want."

Where the comment comes from, I have no idea. But it's like my backbone finally joins the fight.

Something that enrages Mr. Vanderweel.

"It's your fault!" he screams and takes a step toward me, raising his hand.

I shrink back against the car, sidestepping him, but have nowhere to run since Ellis and Kenneth close ranks.

"You promised," Ellis whines.

Mr. Vanderweel stops, lowering his arm as his attention shifts back to the short, dirty man next to him.

What did he promise?

Mr. Vanderweel rolls his eyes, but nods toward the office upstairs before stepping back.

"Fifteen minutes," he says.

Ellis and Kenneth both shift their focus to me. The evil burning in both their gazes has my stomach roiling.

I don't need to ask what he promised. Not anymore.

Ellis looks at me, licking his lips as he reaches for my arm, confirming my biggest fear.

Oh, fuck no.

I react on instinct, muscle memory taking over as I connect the punch, the satisfying crunch of bone followed by Ellis's roar.

"Fuck, she broke my fucking nose," he moans into his hands.

Blood pours between his fingers, hatred overcoming the lecherous gaze he's had on me all night. I rush past, heading for the door, but Kenneth snaps an arm out, snatching me by the hair. I struggle against his grip, trying to hit his instep with my heel.

"You fucking bitch." Ellis is in my face and I freeze, his backhand making my ears ring long enough for Kenneth to drag me over to the stairs.

Panic creates an adrenaline rush, overriding the dull ache in my head.

"No!" My scream echoes off the empty metal walls, and I fight every step they climb, Kenneth dragging me while Ellis follows behind, still cussing about me breaking his nose.

"Don't do this, Kenneth. Please," I tell him, on the verge of begging as I tug at each finger where it grips my wrist.

I know what waits for me in that dingy office.

I'd rather die.

But I don't intend for either thing to happen.

I'm going to figure this out. I have no choice.

My time is up.

"Hurry the fuck up." Ellis shoves Kenneth and we nearly trip up the stairs.

"Chill the fuck out," Kenneth says, looking over his shoulder at Ellis.

"He only gave me fifteen minutes."

"If I'm dragging her up here, you have to share."

Kenneth's statement causes the blood to freeze in my veins.

"What? That's not fucking fair," Ellis whines.

"I'm doing the fucking work. I get a little prize out of it."

I gag, choking on bile that rises to my throat, and struggle again.

"Shit. Stop struggling. You're going to make us fall down the stairs," Kenneth grumbles.

I scream, hoping someone will hear me and call the cops. Taking a breath, I get ready to scream again, but Kenneth's hand clamps on my mouth.

"Stop your fucking screaming or Chaz is going to speed up what he wants to do with you," Kenneth hisses in my ear.

Somehow I'd rather face that than what Kenneth and Ellis have planned. I fight against the grip Kenneth has over my mouth, my vision growing blurry at the edges as the oxygen ebbs. I can't pass out. I fight the darkness, my lungs burning, vision turning fuzzy until Kenneth finally releases me. Sweet oxygen fills my lungs, and I gulp in the musty smell of the old building.

We reach the top of the stairs and I trip over the final stair, dropping to the landing in front of the door. My hip takes the brunt of my fall and I cry out.

"Ten minutes!" Mr. Vanderweel yells from next to his SUV.

"No more funny business, bitch." Ellis leans over, mouth and teeth covered with drying blood. "I get to have my fun now."

I fight to my feet, dizzy from adrenaline and pain.

I refuse to let him look down on me. He may want to bully me, but I refuse to be the victim any more than I already have been.

There's a loud crash at the steel garage door and both Kenneth and Ellis look back, giving me the distraction I desperately need. I take advantage, pushing toward Ellis until he rocks back on the top step, surprised by the attack. Time slows down as he reaches for my arms to pull me with him, but I manage to evade his grasping fingers.

"You fucking—"

His words end on a scream as he falls the rest of the way, every thud as he hits the stairs ricocheting around us, making each sound much worse, and dragging out the dramatic fall. But what feels like minutes is over in a few breaths. Ellis lands awkwardly at the bottom, his lifeless eyes and body position confirmation that he isn't a threat anymore.

Slamming my eyes shut, I shake my head, the reality of what I just did sinking in.

I sink my teeth into my lip, my eyes filling with tears.

I killed him. I took his life. I'm a murderer.

Just like Mr. Vanderweel.

CHAPTER 36

LEIGH

I want to sob. To lie down and curl up as regret and relief form the strangest combination. That's the most fucked-up part of all of this—I'm relieved Ellis is dead. And the guilt that hits me in the stomach as soon as I recognize the small comfort is almost crippling.

"Oh my God, oh my God," I chant, hiding my eyes behind my hands as the dizziness increases, the small metal landing spinning beneath me.

"Good. I didn't want to share anyway. And this gets rid of the loose end," Kenneth says.

Opening my eyes, I witness his gaze move from Ellis's lifeless body at the bottom of the stairs to mine. It lights up and he reaches for me.

Another noise rattles the door and Kenneth and I both jolt, staring at the steel door as it shudders. Mr. Vanderweel rushes over to the bottom of the stairs, only sparing Ellis a cursory glance before he shifts his attention to us.

"Fuck. Bring her. We need to go," he tells Kenneth.

"But—"

"Now, Kenny."

Kenneth grumbles but does as he's instructed and leads me back down the stairs, his grip on my arm bruising even though I don't put up much of a fight.

I killed someone. Someone died because of me.

"Someone's trying to get in here. We need to go. We'll do this somewhere else," Mr. Vanderweel tells Kenneth.

"What about him?" Kenneth nods toward Ellis.

"Cops'll think it was a drug deal gone bad. We'll need to figure out a different fall guy," Mr. Vanderweel says.

I killed him.

He was going to rape you.

But I took a life.

What was he going to take from you?

The internal argument dies, locked behind the shock setting in after the traumatic events of the night.

"Not necessarily. We can make it look like he killed her before coming here. He can still be our murderer. But we have to hurry."

Kenneth opens the car door to shove me in, and a third noise rattles the door before it collapses inward. It was a crash. Someone has been ramming the garage door with their car.

Did Sydney send someone?

Fuck, I hope so.

Taking advantage of the latest distraction, I slam the door, Kenneth's hand caught between it and the frame of the car.

The scream is primal. High-pitched. Pain-filled. The shrill sound sends goose bumps down my body.

"Gah! Open the door, fuck, God, open the door! My hand! My fucking hand!"

With he and Mr. Vanderweel distracted by Kenneth's shouts, I'm free. I rush toward the collapsed door, a loud bang echoing around me.

"The next one's in you if you move," Mr. Vanderweel says from behind me.

Freezing, I glance over my shoulder to find a gun leveled in my direction with Mr. Vanderweel at the other end.

He opens the door and Kenneth crumples to the ground, cradling his broken hand.

"Get back here," Mr. Vanderweel demands.

If he thinks I'm listening, he's crazier than I thought possible. Which is saying something considering he's a fucking psychopath.

I shake my head.

"No. Shoot me if you have to, but I'm not going anywhere." A bravado I didn't know existed fills my voice.

But I already know he doesn't want my DNA here. He would have killed me already.

"Drop the weapon."

I want to drop to my knees as relief rushes through my body at the recognizable voice at the end of the command.

A welcome light in the darkness I've survived so far.

Murphy steps around the other side of his car, his weapon trained on Mr. Vanderweel while flicking a glance at Kenneth before his eyes clash with mine.

"You're here," I say, tears running down my face.

He nods.

"It's okay now, Stóirín. Come here," Murphy says gently.

Mr. Vanderweel cocks his weapon.

"If she moves I'm going to shoot her," he spits out.

"Drop the weapon, Vanderweel, it's over." Murphy turns his full attention back to Mr. Vanderweel whose hate-filled gaze stays glued to me.

"H-he killed Selene. He admitted to it. It was h-h-here." My teeth chatter and I can't stop shaking.

This nightmare is almost over. But I'm stuck in place, not sure if I should stay still or rush toward Murphy.

My attention shifts back to Murphy whose eyes soften when he looks at me.

"Dad? Is it true?" Charlie steps around the car, joining the weird circle we're forming.

Murphy's gaze sharpens and he shifts position until he can keep Charlie in front of him as well.

"What are you doing here?" Mr. Vanderweel asks, his eyes twitching between his son and me.

For the first time tonight, I see a weakness in the evil the man in front of me embodies.

"I found texts on my phone to Leigh and I remembered you asked to use my phone earlier. I went to the house to talk to you about them but you weren't home so I tracked the car." He points at the SUV. "Is what Leigh said true? Did you kill Selene?"

The question hangs in the silence wrapping around us, punctuated by the faraway echo of sirens.

"She was turning you against me!" Mr. Vanderweel shouts, his aim dropping as his attention shifts to his son.

The bellow of rage and grief is the only warning anyone gets before Charlie lunges for his father, knocking them both to the ground. Murphy rushes to me, pulling me into his arms and brushing a kiss against my hair before tucking me behind him.

"Let's get you outside."

"But Mr. Vanderweel—"

"I'll come back for him. But I want you safe."

I'm too cold to argue, relief swamping me as Murphy's cologne wraps around me.

I'm safe.

My fingers grip the soft cotton of his shirt and I try to focus on putting one foot in front of the other.

We're just past the SUV when another bang echoes through the factory. I jolt, losing contact with Murphy's shirt as fear locks my limbs.

"Charlie," I murmur.

"Stay here. Do you know how to use a gun?" Murphy asks, his eyes clashing with mine.

"Yes, but—"

"Here." He shoves his gun and cell phone at me and is back around the corner of the SUV before I can blink.

I want to call him back. He's unprotected. What if—

I can't think like that.

Time slows to a crawl as I wait. What has been incredibly loud and overwhelming the last few moments as the battle waged between father and son is now silent.

"Stóirín," Murphy calls my name and I want to cry as the adrenaline ebbs from my body again.

He's okay.

"Yes?"

"Call 911. We need an ambulance."

"Who?" I call out.

"Dad? Dad? Oh my God, I killed him. Dad?" Charlie's anguished cries fill the silence.

And for the first time since I started up that dark trail, I'm not sure how to feel anything at all.

CHAPTER 37

MURPHY

Blue and red lights flash against the industrial buildings, headlights lighting up the area until it almost looks like daylight in the small semicircle of police vehicles and several ambulances.

My car is a crunch of metal in the steel door, having rammed three times into the door in order to break it open.

"Are you sure you're okay?" Warren asks.

"I'm okay." The words are automatic, but I scan the remaining ambulances until I find the one where Leigh is being checked out.

"You're rubbing your neck. Sure you didn't get whiplash? Looks like your airbags deployed."

I drop my hand, not even realizing I had been rubbing at the ache I feel only when I think about it.

I shrug a shoulder, holding back the wince.

"I'm sore, but nothing a hot shower and some aspirin won't fix."

An ambulance takes off, lights and sirens blaring.

Must be Vanderweel Senior.

He's alive—barely.

"I hope he makes it." I say the words more to myself, but Warren responds.

"Really?" He seems surprised.

I nod.

"He needs to face what's he's done."

"Think he really killed Selene Gordon?" he asks.

I hadn't even been thinking about that. He needs to pay for what he did to Leigh.

"At this point? I don't know. I wouldn't put it past him. I never would have thought I'd watch him point a gun at someone with the intent to kill them. But I have no doubt he would have shot Leigh if she moved." I shudder at the memory, my eyes finding her again.

The EMT is checking out the cut on her lip and she winces.

"Are we done here? I'd like to..." I nod in the direction of Leigh's ambulance.

I've spent the last fifteen minutes talking to Warren about everything I know. Finding Leigh's car unlocked with her phone and keys, the way Sydney was able to track her with the AirTag—fuck, pride swells in my chest at how resourceful Leigh was to keep it with her. I might have been too late otherwise.

I almost was.

Even though she had disabled two of the three men who took her, Vanderweel was going to kill her. I know that with every fiber of my being.

"Yeah. Think she'd be up for coming to the station tomorrow to give her statement?"

I nod.

"I don't see why not. But if not, would Monday work?"

It's late. Hard to believe it's still Saturday night, but just barely. If she needs to go to the hospital, it'll be later still.

"Yeah, of course. I'm on shift on Monday too. Thanks, O'Connell." Warren pats me on the shoulder and heads for the uniform who waits with Charlie Vanderweel in the back of a squad car.

I walk toward Leigh with purpose, reaching her side as the EMT finishes checking her out.

"What is it about you that we keep meeting like this?" I tease her gently, not sure if it's the right thing to say.

Her lips lift in a smile, her arms opening until I step between them, pulling her to me.

"I'd say you were bad luck," she sasses back.

Fuck. This girl.

This woman.

Mine.

And I wouldn't have it any other way.

"Do you need to go to the hospital and get checked out?"

She shakes her head.

"No, she says I have a cut on my lip and some bruises and scrapes, but that's it."

I look at the female EMT who nods, confirming Leigh's statement. Not that I think Leigh would lie—more like stretch the truth a bit— but I know she's not the biggest fan of hospitals.

"I'd offer to drive you home, but I don't think I have a car anymore," I murmur.

If insurance doesn't total my car, it'll be a miracle. Not like I care. I'd make the same choice again and again. After trying the one door chained and padlocked several times over, I knew it would be my only way in to get to her.

I'd heard her first scream. My time was up.

Her eyes find mine, reflecting the lights.

"I-I killed someone." Her lip quivers with her statement, tears pooling in her eyes.

I lift a finger, running it along her jawline.

"It's going to be okay."

"B-b-but I pushed him and he fell…are they going to arrest me?" she asks, her gaze darting to the dozen or so officers milling around the scene.

"I very much doubt the DA is going to charge you. I don't

know for sure, since this isn't my case. But you were acting in self-defense, Stóirín. No jury in the world would convict you."

She leans her head back against my chest, her sigh blowing through the cotton of my shirt as the tension ebbs from her shoulders. Is that what she was worried about?

"I-is Charlie okay?"

I look for the car where Charlie was waiting, Warren now talking to him.

"He's not hurt." I can't really say if he's okay or not.

The gun Vanderweel Senior was holding had gone off as the two struggled for it. But it was Vanderweel Senior who had been hit.

"His dad killed his fiancée," she whispers, arms squeezing tighter around me.

But it's how she says the words that breaks my heart and has me holding her a little more carefully. She's lost more than a little bit of her belief in humanity tonight.

"I know, sweetheart."

We stand in silence for several breaths, letting the world rush around us. The coroner's van pulls up to collect Ellis, and it's not something I want her to see.

"Are you ready to go home?" I ask her.

"You don't have a car," she reminds me.

"So we'll get a uni to drive us."

Once we're in the back of a car and I give Leigh's address to the officer, I sit back and hand over her phone.

"You'll want to call Sydney. She helped track you down. That was smart thinking with the AirTag, by the way," I tell her.

Her soft smile might as well light up the night, because it lights up my whole world.

"You found my phone? And my camera bag?"

I nod, my smile growing at the mention of her beloved camera.

"And your car. I locked the car and they're going to get it to a lab to process it."

"They wanted it to get stolen."

"It probably would have been but I found it first," I assure her.

Her fingers fly on her screen for a moment before she puts the phone down in her lap.

"I just texted her to let her know I am okay. She made me promise to call her tomorrow."

My phone pings with a text and I tug it free from my pocket to read it.

SYDNEY

Good job, Detective McHottie. Maybe you deserve her after all.

I show the text to Leigh who laughs and leans against my side.

"That's Sydney," she says on a yawn.

"I wouldn't expect anything less."

"I'm still mad at you," she murmurs and glances up.

Her expression holds her hurt. The one I inflicted.

"I know. And I deserve your anger."

"We're going to talk about it tomorrow," she tells me. "I'm calling a truce for tonight."

"Whatever you say, Stóirín. So long as it means I get to hold you."

That's the only way I'll know peace tonight—holding her in my arms.

She snuggles back against me, and the only sound is her quiet breathing until we pull up in front of her house.

We use the keypad to get into her garage, and I lead her inside and into her bathroom, turning on the water in the shower.

"What are you doing?" she asks as I flip off the light in the bathroom.

There's still enough ambient light coming from her bedroom to see.

"*We*. We are going to take a shower and go to bed."

"Oh. Okay." The fact that she doesn't argue with me is proof she's reaching the end of her limit.

Tugging her under the warm spray, I shampoo her hair and rinse it before doing the same with the conditioner. Her body is marred with bruises still visible in the dim light, and my hands fist at my sides as red clouds my vision.

But rage doesn't belong in this moment with her.

Gratitude does.

I'm so fucking grateful I found her.

Taking several deep breaths, I relax my fingers, reaching for her soap and running gentle hands along her body until every trace of soap is gone. I'm reluctant to let her go, so worried she'll disappear if I'm not touching her. But eventually she's clean and I run soap over my own body quickly before cranking off the water.

Shivers rack her body and I grab a towel, wrapping her up and running my hands up and down her arms before I worry about myself. Convinced she's dry, I run a towel over myself before leading her into the bedroom. I pull back the covers and help her in, climbing in after her.

"You're exhausted," I murmur, brushing my lips against her hair where she lies curled in my arms.

"Aren't you?"

"Don't worry about me, sweetheart. Get some sleep."

Her breathing is already deepening as she continues to fight to stay awake.

"So tired," she murmurs.

"You have every right to be. Sleep, my love."

"'Kay."

Even after her even breaths wash against my chest consistently, I lie awake, holding her to me. Her weight is so slight, it amazes me she survived tonight with only a cut lip and bruises.

It could have been worse. So much worse.

But it's not.

Life has a way of working out.

Just like Mom said earlier.

And tonight, Leigh is safe.

My breath catches in my lungs, my arms tightening around her at how much of a miracle that is.

The other miracle?

She's mine.

And I don't have to let her go.

CHAPTER 38

LEIGH

Ordinarily, waking up occurs in waves for me.

A slow entry from my dreams into consciousness. The need to get up and do something pressing at me until I do.

But not this morning.

I move from a dreamless sleep to wakefulness in a rush, sitting up where I'm still curled in Murphy's arms.

"Stóirín?" Murphy sits up as well, his voice thick with sleep.

"Was it a dream?" I ask.

His eyes clear in an instant and he shakes his head, lifting his hand to cup my face.

"It wasn't a dream."

I knew it wasn't, but hearing him confirm it creates a burn in the back of my nose as tears blur my vision.

"Come here," he murmurs.

He pulls me into his arms, letting me cry while whispering words of comfort. I cry for me, for Charlie, for the woman I never met who lost her life because of Charlie's dad. I cry until there are no tears left. And through it all, Murphy's words are constant. The tears slow to hiccups and even those stop eventually.

"How do you feel?" Murphy whispers after several heartbeats of silence.

I'm not sure, but I don't feel as heavy as I did when I woke up.

"I—better, I think?"

My body is still sore, probably more so this morning than last night when we went to bed. He brushes a kiss on the top of my head.

"Good."

"Are you okay?" I ask, glancing up.

This time his lips find the tip of my nose.

"I'm okay. I'm so fucking glad you're okay," he tells me.

And I believe him. But with the morning also comes questions. Is he only glad because I'm an obligation? Something he promised Cole. And how does the whole ghosting thing work? Or almost-ghosting. Is that a thing?

He also hasn't repeated he loves you.

"I want to talk about us this morning," I tell him, the pit in my stomach widening as I put words to my thoughts.

If he doesn't want to be with me anymore, I want to know sooner rather than later. Rip the Band-Aid off while I'm already still reeling from everything else.

He doesn't seem surprised.

"I'm ready."

"Coffee?" I ask.

"I think that's a good idea," he says. "I'll meet you in the kitchen in five?"

Nerves fill my stomach. Instead of butterflies, it's like bumblebees buzzing back and forth. But I nod.

"Okay."

He leaves the bed, the sunlight coming through the blinds highlighting the muscles of his ass and the way the ink ripples along the skin as he tugs on pants. He looks back, catches me looking, and shoots me a wink.

"See you in the kitchen," he tells me before leaving the room.

I fall back against the pillows, lifting a hand to my pounding heart.

Does he have any idea what he does to me?

"Maybe I should tell him," I mutter to myself before getting up and throwing on an oversized T-shirt advertising the Mistletoe Creek Santa Run and a pair of sleep shorts.

After using the bathroom, I head to the kitchen and find Murphy lounging at the breakfast bar with two cups of coffee in front of him.

His eyes light up when he sees me and a smile tugs at my lips. Will this always be the way things are between us? This giddy sensation when we see each other?

"Here or the living room?" he asks.

"The living room."

We both sit on the couch, cups of coffee forgotten on the table in front of us. But he surprises me, turning to me and speaking before I can.

"I need to apologize. I locked you out."

"You ghosted me," I correct.

The anger and hurt are still there, but surprise joins the party. I hadn't expected him to admit to it, or apologize before I could say anything. But I'm not going to cut him any slack.

He grimaces, but nods.

"You're right. And I shouldn't have."

"What happened? You said you loved me and then decided you didn't?" I ask, curiosity and uncertainty warring through me.

Sucking in a breath, I hold it, bracing myself.

Do I really want to know the answer?

Yes and no.

But what if he doesn't?

It's not like I can just erase how I feel about him.

This time I've surprised him. His eyebrows shoot up, his eyes widening.

"What? Is that what you thought? Fuck. No. That's not what

this is about at all." He closes the distance, weaving his fingers through mine. "Every word I said that night is just as true as it was when I said them, Stóirín. Even more so now after I almost lost you. You are my chompánach anam."

The bumblebees quiet, soothed, but I still don't hesitate to call him out on his bullshit.

"You ghosted me less than forty-eight hours later; what was I supposed to think?" I ask, trying to yank my hands free.

He lets one go, but holds the other.

"I'm sorry. I'd like to explain. If you'll let me."

I cock my head, leveling him with a look. Whatever he has to say had better be good.

"Go ahead."

I knew part of it was because of the officer who died and he confirms it, but he also tells me about the run-in with Ellis on Monday. He describes the scene he walked into when he found him, and I shudder.

"Is she going to be okay?" I ask.

The regret in his gaze, the guilt… they speak to the guilt still crawling through my body and my heart hurts for him.

"She has a broken jaw and a fractured cheekbone. Bruised ribs. And a broken hand," he says with a sigh.

His eyes are shiny and he blinks several times before meeting my gaze.

I shudder, wondering if that would have been my fate.

"But she's alive," I say.

"She's alive. And you are too. Both instances I was almost too late. I…I hate I wasn't there. For either of you." He swallows and I see the struggle he's having with forgiving himself.

"But you were. You saved her just like you saved me."

"I kept thinking about what might have happened to you." He lifts his hands to my face, cupping my jaw and running his thumb lightly over the cut. "I kept thinking I wouldn't get the chance to tell you what an idiot I was. That I was sorry. I wanted to beg your forgiveness. And I almost lost my chance."

"What brought on this epiphany?" I ask, wrapping my hand around his wrist and holding him where he is.

His golden eyes search mine.

"My mom. After I found out who it was changing my reports—"

"You found out? Who? Who was it?"

"Kenneth. He was blackmailing a court clerk to change my reports. When I thought about it, I realized all my reports started having errors the day I brought lunch to your office. There was a warrant out for his arrest and he was fired from the public defender's office. And since they arrested him last night, the judge ordered that he be held without bond. The list of charges is massive, especially with the more serious ones from last night," he tells me.

Shock and relief filter through my body, washing away the stress built over the past several weeks.

"Holy shit! He was fired? When? You've been cleared?"

He nods.

"According to my captain, he was let go at the beginning of the week. And I've been completely cleared."

That explains why I hadn't seen him at the office. And it also means Murphy's job with the FBI in Washington, DC is still starting in just about two weeks.

From a high to a low in less than a heartbeat.

"I need to tell you something. Something my mom told me," he says.

"I still haven't met your mom," I say, sad because I'm probably not going to get the chance before he moves.

He barks out a laugh and tugs me into his arms.

"I'm going to remedy that soon. Now, can I tell you what she told me?" he asks.

"Okay."

He combs his fingers through my hair, cradling me as if I'm the most precious thing in the world to him.

"It's something she's said my whole life. But she reminded me that the world will bring plenty of trouble to our doorstep whether I'm looking for it or not. Then she accused me of borrowing trouble. She told me if I loved you then I needed to fight for you and love would help things work out the way they were meant to. And I love you, Stóirín. More than I ever thought possible. More than I can ever put the words to. I love you with all of me."

It's there. The truth. It exists in the depths of his eyes as his gaze stays locked with mine. In the gentle pressure of his fingers against my scalp. In the pounding of his heart next to mine.

He loves me. For me. Not because of obligation, not because he has to, not because he can't avoid it. He's embraced it, letting love bloom in a way I never would have thought possible the first night I kissed him after Hannah Grace and Cole's wedding.

"I love you," I tell him, meeting his gaze.

His mouth claims mine, his tongue licking along my lips to request entry. I moan, opening to him, as my legs straddle his hips. Need pounds through my blood, my core throbbing where his erection presses against it.

His lips trail along my jaw, words of love growled against my skin.

"Make love to me, Murphy," I murmur, pressing my chest against his as his hands grip my ass to drag me back and forth across his erection.

"With pleasure." His lips close over the spot on my neck where my pulse thrums frantically.

"Oh my God. Cole, close your eyes."

"Yeah, get it, girl."

"Fuck."

Three voices reach us from the doorway and we spring apart.

Holy shit!

Breathing heavily, my heart pounds in my throat as I yank my T-shirt back into place and look up to find Hannah Grace and Sydney standing in the doorway with huge grins on their faces. Cole is turned, facing the kitchen, mumbling about not needing to know things about his baby sister-in-law.

"What are you guys doing here?" I ask, rushing from the couch to hugs from Hannah Grace and Sydney.

"Apparently, cockblocking you," Sydney says, waggling her brows.

"Sydney told us what happened and we caught the first flight out of LA this morning. What the hell has been going on?" Hannah Grace asks, gaze shifting from me to Murphy and back again.

"It's a long story," I tell her.

"That's the best kind," Sydney says and pulls me into the kitchen. "But first…coffee."

CHAPTER 39

LEIGH

The salty air is tinged with the smells of coconut, sand, and sweetness as it melts together in the summer sun. I wiggle against the warmth of the beach towel on the sand, the sound of the rest of the beachgoers, sea birds, and the waves blending into a hypnotic soundtrack.

"This is perfect," I tell Sydney. "Almost perfect."

"Mmm." It's the sound of drowsy agreement.

We're lying on the warm sand of Manhattan Beach, where I've decided I'm going to camp for the rest of my trip.

"Why did we wait so long to come here?" I ask, rolling over and letting the sun warm my back while I nestle my head on my arms, breathing in the coconut of my own sunscreen.

I've been in California for five days and fly back tomorrow.

"We've been busy, girl," Sydney says on a yawn.

She's played tour guide the whole time. We've explored everything from Griffith Observatory, the Hollywood sign, Universal Studios—where we rode every roller coaster twice—and a variety of restaurants and clubs. We dragged Jessie along too.

Sydney was right. There were shadows in Jessie's eyes, demons chasing her that she wasn't saying anything about.

Instead she was throwing herself into dancing and flirting with any guy who approached her.

I frown.

That was the hardest part of this trip.

Leaving Murphy.

It was only for six days. I will see him tomorrow when he picks me up from the airport. There will be longer separations once he moves to DC and I am in Knoxville for law school.

But I miss him like crazy.

FaceTime isn't cutting it.

Texts aren't even close.

What am I going to do when he moves?

Opening my eyes, I reach for my phone, setting a reminder to look into law schools in DC again. I might have to wait until next semester, but that is as long as I am going to wait.

"Where are we going to dinner tonight?" I ask Sydney.

She turns her head in my direction, but her eyes are hidden behind dark sunglasses.

"I haven't given it much thought. What are you in the mood for?"

The sun is bright—even with my sunglasses—so I close my eyes to think. We've had sushi, steak, Italian, and one night just had ice cream for dinner.

Worth it.

That ice cream was some of the best I ever had. And it was just from a small shop around the corner from Sydney and Jessie's apartment.

For Sydney's part, everything she showed me she also tried to use to convince me to move to LA with them. Even Jessie had joined her bandwagon the last two nights out.

"I have no idea. I just want to lie here for a while longer," I murmur.

"Take your time. We're in no rush."

Sydney's phone buzzes with a text, and she responds before tossing her phone back on her towel.

"Was that Jessie? Where is she?"

"She was babysitting for her brother and sister-in-law. She said they were going on a day date."

"That's freaking adorable," I tell her, peeking one eye open.

"According to her, they say day dates are easier because then they're home at night for nighttime routines for their three kids. Especially since those routines change when Jax tours."

"I still can't believe you know Jax Bryant," I tell her.

We'd just heard one of his songs—an older one—on the radio on the way to the beach this morning.

"Jessie knows him better than I do," Sydney teases, sitting up and groaning. "God, don't look now but you're being ogled by another one."

I snort. "Whatever. They're looking at you."

With her red hair and flawless skin, she attracts attention wherever she goes. Or maybe it's the confident way she embraces life. Like the deep plum bikini she is wearing for the day. She is stunning.

"Not this one, babes," she says.

With a sigh, I sit up and look at where she's pointing.

He's standing at the edge of the beach in a pair of shorts and open button-down shirt, a pair of aviators covering his eyes, but I would recognize him in a crowd of a million.

I scramble up, running in his direction with Sydney laughing behind me.

"Murphy!" I squeal.

He meets me halfway, scooping me up and supporting my legs as I wrap them around his waist, peppering his face with kisses he returns as best he can while laughing.

"Did you miss me, Stóirín?" he asks.

I let my mouth do the talking, claiming his lips with mine and kissing him until several hoots nearby remind me we're not alone.

"Does that answer your question?" I ask.

He releases my legs and I slide down his body, the muscle in his jaw ticking with the delicious friction of my body against his.

"I'll have to show you later how much I missed you," he growls in my ear.

My fingers grip his shirt and I'm ready for us to find a place right now for him to show me how much he missed me. I hope he has a hotel room since I'm staying on Sydney's couch. Wait… Sydney.

I turn around and Sydney hands me my packed beach bag.

"That was the hardest secret I've ever had to keep," she confesses.

"Thank you!" I tell her, stepping away from Murphy long enough to wrap her in a hug.

"You're welcome." She hugs me back before turning toward Murphy. "Did Jessie get you into the apartment okay?"

He nods.

"She did. Thanks for setting that up. I stopped by Sydney's apartment to pick up your stuff before I came here. I hope you don't mind," he explains to me.

"I don't mind," I tell him, trying to hold back my excitement.

I mean, I love Sydney. She's my best friend.

But my hot as fuck boyfriend just surprised me in LA. One I haven't seen for five days.

It's a no-brainer decision.

"I wouldn't have minded either," Sydney speaks up from behind me.

At least we have her blessing.

"Call me later. Love you!" She hugs me again, waves at Murphy, and heads for her car, leaving the two of us alone.

Or as alone as we're going to be on a beach full of strangers.

"Want to go for a walk?" he asks.

He seems uncertain, slightly uncomfortable, and tension builds in my stomach. What's happened now?

I sink my teeth into my lower lip and he reaches up, running his finger along the flesh.

"Nothing bad, sweetheart. I promise," he murmurs. His sunglasses are gone, allowing me to see his eyes, and the truth is there.

I nod, the tension loosening, and follow him as he walks away from the pier, and the crowds thin. We walk to the edge of the water, continuing up the shoreline, his fingers woven with mine.

"What are you doing here? I thought you were going to spend this week packing."

He leaves next week for DC and his new job. I fight the burn of tears, staring out at the ocean and breathing in the fresh air until the burn fades.

"I'm all packed and ready for the moving company to drop the storage container on Monday."

I will not cry. I will not cry. Oh, who am I kidding? The tears blurring my vision release, and I'm glad for the dark sunglasses that somewhat hide them.

"Oh."

It's the only word I trust myself to say.

He stops walking and pulls me back to face him. I duck my head to the side, trying to sniffle inconspicuously which he ruins by pushing my sunglasses up my face.

"Why are you crying?" he asks, running his thumbs along my cheeks to clear the moisture.

"I'm going to miss you. This last week has been hard, and I know it was my choice to go, but I knew it was only for a few days and I would get to see you this weekend. You're leaving next week and who knows when we'll see each other again."

Dramatic? Yes.

Do I care? No.

He smiles, pulling me forward until I'm wrapped in his arms and his lips press a kiss to my forehead.

"Only I'm not leaving next week. I'm not moving to DC."

"What? What happened? I thought when IA cleared you the job was yours. Isn't that what the special agent in charge said?"

He's wanted the job for as long as he can remember—he told me so before. How dare they take it away from him when he was cleared of any wrongdoing with his cases.

"Sweetheart, take a breath. Fuck, I love you. One minute you're crying because I'm leaving and the next minute you're ready to do battle because you think I'm being treated unfairly."

He squeezes me to him, lifting my feet out of the waves lapping at our feet.

"Well, I know it's what you want. What you've wanted for forever."

"Wanted," he says.

"What?"

"You're right. It's what I wanted before. I called Agent Park and thanked her for the opportunity for the job, but told her my circumstances had changed and I could no longer accept it."

Confusion now joins the roller coaster of emotions I've experienced since I saw him standing on the beach.

"Why?"

He reaches up, smoothing his finger between my brows.

"You."

"Me? I don't want you to make a choice to make me happy and—"

"If you stop to take that breath we talked about, I can explain." He rolls his eyes, a smile playing on his lips.

"Sorry." Heat fills my chest, traveling up my neck.

"You're fine. And I didn't make a choice just to make you happy. I made the choice for us. If this week has been hard for you, it's been equally as hard on me. It only took me about three boxes before I realized I couldn't leave you. Not like I originally planned. I have zero doubt we could make long distance work, but that's not what I want for you. For me. For us. So I told the FBI thanks, but no thanks."

"You're staying in Nashville?" I ask, excitement building at the realization he's not moving.

"Not exactly."

Wrinkling my nose, I shake my head.

"Why not? Where are you going?"

"Well, for one, I don't have a job. The department has already selected my replacement. I could reapply but only when they have an opening. The second reason I'm not staying in Nashville is because my lease is up on my condo next week. But the biggest reason is you."

"Me?"

He nods.

"You're in Knoxville. And my home is where you are, Stóirín. I've lived without you for thirty-six years. I don't want to live without you anymore. Think you could handle a roommate in Knoxville?"

"Oh my God, yes!" I squeal, wrapping my arms around his neck and pressing a kiss against his lips, but pulling away just as he deepens it. "Wait. Was Knoxville PD hiring?"

He shrugs.

"I didn't check with them."

"You didn't?"

"Turns out, when he and Hannah Grace were in Nashville last week, Cole mentioned SAFE Haven was looking for a profiler. They've been using a retired FBI profiler for work on an ad hoc basis but he wants to fully retire. I flew out here this morning to meet with Sawyer and talk about the job. You're looking at the newest member of SAFE Haven Security."

"So you're not moving to DC?"

"Correct."

"You're moving to Knoxville. With me."

"Also correct."

"And you're going to go to work with Sydney and Cole?"

He nods. "Yes."

"Why is all of this so easy?" I ask, overwhelmed with happiness.

"Did anyone ever tell you that you ask too many questions?" he teases, lifting me until we're eye level.

"I am going to be a lawyer. Consider it practice," I tell him.

"So life with you is going to be full of questions?"

"Would you expect anything less?" I ask.

"No. Besides, I have a really good way of answering all of them." His gaze drifts to my mouth and my lips tingle in anticipation.

"You do?"

Our mouths collide, my question still echoing between us as his tongue dances with mine. My fingers thread through his hair, and I moan at the heat of his hand where it flexes against my hip. His other hand tangles in my ponytail, tugging my head to deepen the kiss, and goose bumps ripple along my skin, my nipples pebbling against the Lycra of my bikini top. We continue kissing until I have no idea where he ends and I begin.

"I have a question," I tell him, ripping my lips from his.

He moves to my jaw, pressing kisses in a line to my ear.

"Of course you do. What?"

"You mentioned earlier wanting to show me how much you missed me." It's hard to focus with the delicious things his mouth is doing to my ear.

"I did. Is that your question?"

"No. But can we go now? I'm ready for you to show me." The words are breathless, need blotting out every other emotion.

Except love.

It's a heady combination.

He lifts his head, his eyes finding mine. The golden depths

hold a fire I can't wait to explore. He studies me, eyes darkening as he does, until he nods.

"Just one more thing before we go," he tells me.

"What's that?"

"I love you, Leigh Whittaker."

I am a puddle of goo on the sand. The man knows how to light me on fire and make me melt in the same heartbeat.

"What was that for?"

"I'm always going to remember this moment. And I want it to be one where I told you so."

"I love you too."

"Now let's get out of here."

In the next instant, I'm over his shoulder and he's sprinting for the car.

"You're crazy," I tell him, laughing as he deposits me in the passenger seat of a rental car.

"Crazy for you," he says, snagging another kiss before closing my door. He rounds the hood, sliding into the driver's seat and cranking the engine in a fluid movement. "Now hang on tight."

"Why?"

"Because I'm about to bend several speeding laws on the way to the hotel."

EPILOGUE

MURPHY

"Thanks, Cap, I appreciate it," I say into the phone, ending the call as Leigh comes through the front door with the last box from her car.

"Who was that?" she asks, setting the box down.

When she turns around, I'm there to pull her into my arms.

"I'm all sweaty," she says, trying to pull away.

"Me too," I counter, tightening my hold until she relaxes against me.

"Who was on the phone?"

"Captain Overton."

She tenses, which is the reason I wanted her in my arms when I tell her. We've been waiting for this call since the night in the warehouse.

It feels like I've been holding my breath since that night. I can only imagine how stressful it's been for her.

"The DA made the formal decision. You're not being charged for anything related to the death of Ellis."

"Thank God," she whispers, releasing the same pent-up breath.

She was so fucking worried about it. But there was no way.

No way was she going to be charged when all she was doing was defending herself. It may not stop her nightmares, but at least she can rest a little easier now that the uncertainty isn't poised above her head.

"What about Mr. Vanderweel?" she asks.

"He's being charged for the murder of Selene Gordon as well as your kidnapping and attempted murder. Cap said the press has been going nuts. They're running all kinds of stories about Selene again, and every business deal and charity is being questioned.

Which sucks. Because Vanderweel had done some good.

But now everything is being questioned—good and bad.

She stays quiet so I keep going.

"Kenneth is also being charged with your kidnapping and attempted murder as well as extortion, obstruction of justice, and a whole other slew of charges based on things nobody knew he was doing."

My stomach turns at the memory of what Captain Overton had said.

Hard drives full of videos. Single encounters, multiple people, parties. Consensual…and not.

Hell is too good a place for the likes of Kenneth Scott and Charles Vanderweel.

She sniffles, her arms tightening around me, and I run my hands up and down her back, giving her time to process everything I've just told her.

I'm a seasoned detective and I still have a hard time processing it. Leigh wants to believe the best of everybody. And some people don't deserve it.

"What about Charlie?" The question is so quiet, I almost don't hear it.

"The DA didn't charge him," I tell her.

There's a more prolonged silence, one where the only sounds are our breaths and the gentle hum of the air conditioner.

"I called him," she murmurs, looking up at me.

Those Caribbean-blue eyes are stormy, moisture shining from their depths.

It's taken me this long—and finding the real killer—to realize Charlie was just as much a victim of his father as Selene or Leigh was.

"And?" I ask.

"You're not angry?" Her eyes widen in surprise, her mouth dropping into an O.

"Sweetheart, I knew you were going to. It was only a matter of time. I know you care about him. But I also know that it's only as his friend."

She nods.

"You're right. After what he found out—the way he found out…" She trails off with a shudder.

"What did he have to say?"

"We didn't talk for very long. I…I think he's trying to move on. Or at least as much as he can. He told me he's talking to someone. A therapist. For his grief and dealing with everything now that his dad admitted to Selene's murder. The board has put him in charge of the investment company and he's trying to learn the ropes. He did tell me that he still plans on honoring the commitments the company made for Shield 615 and the Wrongful Conviction Fund."

"That's amazing," I tell her, matching her small smile with one of my own.

Turns out, I had been wrong about Charlie Vanderweel. And his father.

"He asked me for help with the Wrongful Conviction Fund, but I politely declined. I need some time."

"You deserve that time," I tell her, pulling her back against me, loving the way her head feels against my chest.

"Will we have to testify?" she whispers.

I glance down to find her watching me.

"Probably. But the DA will reach out with those details when they're ready."

"I wish it were over already," she says.

I wish that for her.

"I'll be there with you the whole time," I tell her.

"Promise?"

"I'm not going anywhere, Stóirín," I tell her and drop a kiss to her forehead.

"You know, I've lived with my parents and sister and my sorority sisters. But this is different. Good different," she adds.

Her words make me smile. Fuck, I'm happy. Happier than I ever thought possible.

"Well, I've never lived with anyone ever. Not since I went to the academy," I admit.

"You didn't for college?" she asks.

That had been the plan, but after Dad died, I didn't want to leave Mom and the girls alone.

I shake my head.

"Nope. I commuted back and forth for classes, had family dinner if I wasn't working, and girls were forbidden in my room under Mom's roof."

"Awww, poor baby," she teases.

I find her ribcage with my fingers, finding all the ticklish spots that leave her breathless. She twists and folds in my arms but I don't let up, laughing at her infectious giggle until we're both smiling.

"Okay, okay, I give, I give," she pants.

"Just keep that in mind when you decide to tease. Turnabout is always fair play."

"You play dirty."

"Only when you ask me nicely," I tell her, tapping a finger against her nose.

"These boxes aren't going to unpack themselves," she tells me, pointing to the towers of cardboard.

"We could always unpack later," I offer, eyeing the couch after a dozen or so trips up three flights of stairs already today.

"If I left it up to you, we'd probably live out of boxes. How long did you have boxes in your condo?"

I raise my hands, giving up.

"Fine. You win."

"I like the sound of that," she murmurs, wrapping her arms around my neck. "Does that mean you'll unpack all these boxes?"

I bark out a laugh and shake my head.

"Not a chance. I still have a few things in my car too. So how about you get started and I'll finish and help unpack?"

Her lower lip pouts out and I steal a kiss.

"Fine," she says.

I release her—reluctantly—and make several trips to my car for the last few boxes.

I cuss every single stair on the last trip up, trying to recall the reason why we opted for the third floor.

Right.

Because Leigh had fallen in love with the third-floor apartment and the gas fireplace.

Which isn't going to be used for months since it is still ninety-plus degrees out. Fuck. It's hot. According to the weather app, it's the hottest day of the year—and one of the hottest in Knoxville's history.

"It's hotter than the hinges of hell out there. Whoever thought of the idea you need to move any time during the summer should be fucking shot," I grumble and set the last box down on the stack by the door before taking the three steps to the couch to crash on it.

Leigh pops out of the kitchen, her blonde hair up in a ponytail, looking cool and fresh and carrying two frosted bottles of water.

"You look way cooler than should be allowed."

She hands me a bottle and I guzzle the ice-cold water in one go, tossing the empty bottle toward the trash can at the doorway of the kitchen.

The glare she turns on me is cute. But I know better than to tell her so.

"That"—she points at the bottle sitting on the floor by the trash can— "is not okay."

With one hand on her hip and the other holding her open water bottle, I can't help myself. Reaching up, I yank her onto the couch next to me, her water spilling over the both of us. It feels amazing on my overheated skin, but she squeals.

"Holy crap, that's cold!"

Grabbing the water bottle before it can continue to spill, I set the now half-full bottle on the box next to the couch. She lifts her tank top from her stomach, fanning it in an effort to dry off.

"You made me wet!" she says, shivering.

"You've never complained before," I tease, waggling my brows and spinning us until she's under me on the couch.

"You're terrible." Her lips rub against mine with her words.

I close the distance, brushing my lips with hers for only a fraction of what I want to do before dragging my nose along her jaw.

"Terribly in love with you," I murmur against her skin before finding her lips with mine.

She opens immediately, her tongue dancing with mine as her hands roam my back, scraping through the thin cotton of my tee.

"You know the best thing about having our own place?" she asks, yanking her lips from mine.

"What?" I ask, reading the answer in her eyes but wanting her to say it.

"We get to christen every single room in our new apartment," she says with an impish grin.

"So the boxes can wait?" I ask.

"The boxes can wait. I can't."

My fingers find the snap of her shorts and flick them open.

"I'm done waiting, Stóirín. Our forever begins now."

And I seal the promise with a kiss.

The End

Thank you so much for reading!

Curious how Cole and Hannah Grace found their second chance? You can binge their happily ever after in bodyguard for the beauty queen available in KU or keep reading for a sneak peek of their story!

What happens when Murphy and Leigh head back to mistletoe creek? Turn the page to read their full circle extended epilogue!

BONUS EPILOGUE

LEIGH

ALMOST ONE YEAR LATER

"So what did you think of your official first event in Mistletoe Creek?" I ask, as we walk up the quiet street.

Tonight was so much fun. Hannah Grace and I had planned a surprise thirtieth wedding anniversary party for my parents and she, Cole, and Sydney had flown in for the occasion.

"What do you mean? I came to the wedding last year." He lags behind and I turn to look at him, seeing his brow furrow with his question.

"Yes, but as a guest. Tonight, you're one of us. Or dating one of us anyway," I explain.

"Does being a Mistletoe Creek insider give me any special privileges?" he asks, tugging me to him for a quick kiss shared under one of the streetlights.

"Only for me." I return the kiss, getting lost in the quiet summer night and the leisurely exploration of his kiss.

It's like we have all the time in the world.

And, I guess, for once this year, we do.

Between my second-year classes and Murphy's new job, we were constantly on the go. Then had come the trials for Kenneth Scott and Charles Vanderweel. Testifying in front of the two of them was one of the most terrifying things I've ever done. But all I had to do was look up in the courtroom and Murphy was there.

Exactly like he promised.

He breaks the kiss and starts walking toward the bed-and-breakfast again, but slower this time, like he's hesitant to end our walk from the civic building. It's hard to believe it's been almost a year since the last time we made this walk.

Back then I'd been a bundle of desire and nerves. Now, love was the foundation, desire was still there, and the nerves only showed up when he started acting weird.

Maybe he's tired.

The last week has been crazy with him finishing a job involving a missing woman, and I focused on finalizing the plans for tonight's party. God knows I'm exhausted.

"You know, this is the first time I haven't had a paper due since I started school last year?" I ask, breathing a sigh of relief.

"You worked your ass off this last year. Which is why I suggested taking the summer for yourself."

It's weird. I should be interning. Or applying for jobs. But Murphy had encouraged me to take the summer and recharge. And I loved the idea. I was still interested in working for Project Justice, but they weren't hiring interns this summer anyway. Lindsay had even called and offered me another internship with the public defender's office in Nashville.

But Murphy is in Knoxville. Our home is in Knoxville.

So my only plans for the summer involve taking lots of pictures—my camera has been feeling neglected after this last year—and spending time with Murphy when he isn't working.

"You've been working hard too," I remind him. "What about your summer break?"

He shrugs. Only I know better. This last case had impacted

him more than he cared to admit. They had found the missing girl, but it had been a close call.

"It doesn't really feel like work," he says.

He's said so more than once over this last year. He loves what he does—mostly. His passion for his job shines out of him, wrapping around the two of us in a bubble of contentment.

"Are we still heading to California next week?" I ask.

Murphy needs to fly to California next week but surprised me with a ticket at the end of the school year.

Another week of sea, sand, and Sydney.

Her coming out with Cole and Hannah Grace for tonight's party had been a surprise for me too. And this time we had left her at the civic building talking to Fern, Fawn, and Merry, who had managed to lock her in their matchmaking sights.

I don't feel bad for her though.

They are really good at it.

When I said goodbye, they were trying to convince her to go to breakfast with Fawn's nephew.

"What were you and my dad talking about for so long earlier?"

"I'm still trying to get myself out of the doghouse," he tells me.

I giggle.

"Daddy doesn't care you and I are living together. Hannah Grace and Cole did before they got married."

He snorts.

"That may be what he tells you. The man hasn't said more than six words to me since we moved into the apartment last summer, including when we spent Christmas weekend at your parents' house."

"He talked to you!"

Didn't he?

I'm trying to think back, but nothing flagged for me. It was another amazing Christmas in Mistletoe Creek.

"You and I have very different memories when it comes to

that weekend," he says, shooting me a look that tells me he's probably right about this.

"He looked like he said more than six words to you tonight."

They'd talked while I was telling Fern, Fawn, and Merry all about Murphy right after he met them for the first time.

Needless to say, they all approved.

We reach the gate of the bed-and-breakfast and Murphy opens it, ushering me inside before he closes the gate behind us.

"I don't know about you, but I'm ready for bed," I say on a yawn.

Trying to keep this a secret, while remotely planning from Knoxville, had been an exercise in patience as I had to keep reminding everyone this was a surprise party for Mom and Dad. I'm on the first stair when he pulls me back, tugging me into his arms.

My arms climb his chest automatically.

"You know where we are, right?" he asks.

I nod.

"It's the place where we had our first kiss," I answer.

The super hot kiss sent my life down a trajectory I had zero idea about. Followed by a rejection I didn't understand then.

At least now I know why he did it. The memory doesn't sting anymore; it's the memory of our beginning.

He leans down, teasing a kiss against my lips but then is gone before I'm ready for the kiss to end.

"Come back here," I demand, trying to pull him to my lips.

It's like trying to shift a statue.

"There's only one thing I regret about that night," he murmurs.

What the hell? I don't regret anything. Not if it led me to him. I try to pull away but he holds fast.

"Aren't you going to ask me what?" he asks.

"I don't regret anything about that night," I pout.

One side of his mouth quirks up in a smile.

Jerk. Glad I can make him smile when he's talking about regretting the night we met. Or connected. Or whatever you want to call it.

"What about my answer to your question? You don't regret that?" he asks.

I shake my head.

"No. Because it meant we became friends. Eventually. And that led to more. But you're still my friend too."

He studies me for several heartbeats.

"I love the way you look at things," he tells me, pulling me in for another kiss.

A longer one.

One that has me threading my fingers through his hair and ready to repeat my question.

"You make me forget what I was going to say," he tells me, teasing light kisses along my lips until he pulls away.

"Sorry, not sorry?"

His lips twitch with a smile and he closes his eyes, shaking his head, then taking a breath.

When he opens his eyes again, he's steady. Serious. And butterflies swirl in my belly with the fire burning in his gaze. For me.

"I was going to say I do regret the decision I made that night. But now I don't like that admission, because I like what you said more. It did lead to us being friends. I had to work at that, by the way. You didn't make it easy. When we talked the night of the wedding, I wasn't looking for anything. I wasn't looking for a relationship. But you turned out to be everything I never knew I needed. Everything I never knew I always wanted. Spending the last year with you has been the greatest adventure of my life. I called you Stóirín before I even realized it. And somewhere along the way I recognized you were so much more. You were my chompánach anam. My soulmate."

My heart is pounding in my chest with every word he whispers, the butterflies fluttering their wings in time to my heartbeat. But before I can say anything, he's stepping back, reaching into his pocket and dropping to one knee.

Breath saws in and out of my lungs at what's actually happening in this moment, the conversation I witnessed between him and my dad suddenly making perfect sense.

"And this feels like it's the perfect place to ask you to become something else. Mo bhean chéile. My wife. Laura Leigh Whittaker, grá mo chroí is mo anamchara thú—love of my heart and soulmate—I love you more than I ever thought possible. More than I ever could have imagined. Would you do me the honor of becoming my wife? Will you marry me?"

Time slows to a crawl as he holds out the ring. It's a pear-shaped emerald surrounded by diamonds, and smaller diamonds cover the band.

Holy shit! Breathing is impossible as I stare at him on his knee in front of me, holding a stunningly beautiful ring. And so much a symbol of the man holding it, my heart aches a little.

Do not pass out. Answer the man!

I'm nodding before I can make my mouth form the words.

"Yes! Yes, I'll marry you."

He surges up from the ground, capturing my lips before he breaks the kiss, sliding the ring on my finger.

A perfect fit.

A full circle.

"I love you, Stóirín."

"I love you too," I tell him, tugging him toward me.

He comes willingly this time and his mouth claims mine. His hands flex against my hips before tracing the curve to my ass and dragging me against him.

I moan and his mouth finds my jaw, dragging hot, open-mouthed kisses down my throat until he finds the pulse point at the base.

"Ask me," he growls against my skin.

I laugh, the combination of humor and lust zinging through my blood.

"Should we head to your room?" I ask, panting as his teeth find the tendon between my neck and shoulder.

Fuck.

My core throbs and I'm having trouble not ripping his clothes off right here.

I'm sure Fern, Fawn, and Merry would approve.

"Our room," he corrects and lifts me bridal style into his arms. "And I thought you'd never ask."

THE END

Want more Mistletoe Creek romance?

Read on for a sneak peek of Bodyguard for the Beauty Queen!

BODYGUARD FOR THE BEAUTY QUEEN

COLE

7 YEARS AGO

"What's the matter, Honey Girl?" I glance away from the windshield to spy my girlfriend curled up on the opposite side of the truck seat, clutching the door handle and looking like third runner-up in the Miss Mistletoe Creek County Fair Pageant.

But even me using a nickname for her that ordinarily makes her smile only creates a sigh.

Fuck.

I flip on the radio, tuning in to our favorite station as we wind the back roads through the foothills of the Smokies that surround our hometown of Mistletoe Creek, Tennessee. The reception is spotty the farther up we drive, but it fills the silence as I rack my brain and try to figure out how to make our last night together a happy memory rather than a sad one.

I'm going to need that memory to keep me going until I can see her again. Hopefully ten weeks from now when I'm finishing up basic. That's if she can make it out to South Carolina for my graduation.

She's still waiting on the information on when her freshmen move-in date is. I'm so fucking proud of my girl for getting into Vanderbilt.

"I'm fine," she says.

But the normal lyrical cadence to her voice is flat. Robotic.

"Sweetheart, it's been a long time since you weren't snuggled against my side. And the last time you were this quiet was the time you lost your voice at the football game we won against Devil Falls."

I find the turn that's little more than a gap between two of the trees. The path is clear, but only barely fits my old truck. Between the bumps and the trees I've skimmed with my fingers when my window is down, I can't watch for her response.

The trees finally spread out more until they're in my rearview and all that's left in front of us is a vista of Mistletoe Creek. The high school is on the edge of town, quiet now that school is out for the summer, and the rest of the little town nestles around it. It's idyllic and it's charming, but it's too small for what I want in my life. I've grown up here, but I'm not willing to just settle down and be a Volunteer before coming back to work in Dad's distillery. That plan might make sense for Justin and Jared, but I am not like my older brothers.

It's what makes the military so exciting—because it wasn't planned out for me.

I put the truck in park and reach for Hannah Grace's hand to tug her toward me.

"Han."

"Don't."

Fuck. Her voice is thick with tears, and proof of one drops on my hands.

"Sweetheart."

I pull her against my chest, rubbing my hand along her back while she sobs into the cotton of my T-shirt.

The scent of her citrus shampoo tickles my nose, and I take a deep breath.

"It's our last night together, baby. I don't want you to cry."

I don't want this memory.

Already the guilt is enough to have me second-guessing my choice.

"I don't want you to go," she mumbles, the words hard to understand through the tears and hiccuping breaths.

"I know." I drop my lips to her hair and keep the steady rhythm of my hand on her back.

She leans up, those cornflower-blue eyes shiny with tears.

"It didn't feel real before, Cole. I want this to be a dream. To wake up tomorrow and not have to say goodbye." Her lower lip trembles, and she sinks her teeth into it to stop the vibration.

I lift my hand and glide my thumb along the swollen flesh.

"It's not forever," I tell her.

More tears slide under my palm that rests against her cheek.

"I can call you…and write. And it's only ten weeks until graduation."

"It's not the same. I've seen you every day for as long as I can remember. I won't be able to do this"—she runs her hands up my chest— "when you're four hours away."

I try to ignore my body's natural reaction to her touch, but my dick jumps. And since she's almost on top of me, I can't hide it.

"Fuck, Hannah Grace, I'm sorry. I didn't bring you up here for this." I groan and lean my head back against the seat.

Even though *this* is something I've thought about since I hit puberty.

"I know. You've never…"

"No."

I respected Hannah Grace too much to push her to do something she wasn't ready for. I respected my own mama's hand upside the back of my head too. I didn't need any other reason to make her want to use it. Between five kids, she has plenty of her own reasons.

Her expression shifts, the tears only salty trails on her cheeks, while mischief tilts her lips.

"What's that look, Hannah Grace Whittaker?"

It's one that's never boded well for me.

In fact it normally results in one or both of us getting grounded.

It's not like Mom can ground me, since I'm leaving tomorrow morning.

It's an accurate statement, but I'm still hesitant to go along with anything involved in that particular expression on Hannah's face.

The last time had resulted in us launching over a thousand bouncy balls in the high school's auditorium during the county's beauty pageant that Hannah hadn't wanted to participate in. Turns out, it didn't stop the pageant. However, it did end up getting back to both our mamas.

Being grounded and voluntold into helping with the high school's locker clean-out day was a consequence I never wanted to live again. Several lockers hadn't been cleaned out all year—and the lunch bag/science experiments inside had proven it.

"Why did you bring me up here?"

"This is our spot, sweetheart. I couldn't imagine our last date happening anywhere else. My favorite view in this world is this view with you in it."

Reaching forward, I grab my phone off the dash and shake it toward her.

"Come with me," I tell her and open my door.

"No pictures. I'm a mess. I'm all splotchy." She tries to stay in the car, but our connected hands make it easy to tug her out.

"You're not splotchy; you'll always be beautiful to me," I murmur and brush a kiss on the tip of her nose.

Her hands come up and rest against my biceps, her fingers skimming the underside of my arms and coming close to my ticklish spot.

I shy away.

"No, you don't."

"It pays to have known you forever," she tells me and sneaks past my defenses to run her fingers up my side.

I giggle and clear my throat as I wrap my arms around her and hold her to my chest with her hands trapped between us.

"Gotcha," I say.

She moves to her tiptoes and puckers her lips in my direction, and I oblige by covering her mouth with mine.

"Would you please take a picture with me?" My lips tease hers with my question. "I want to have one with me that's recent. That's us. Not made-up for prom. But the real us."

"How do you always know what to say that makes me want to say yes?"

Her question is innocent enough, but I hope there's more truth to it since I have another question to ask her. One more important than to take a picture with me.

I position us so that she's still wrapped in one arm, the vista behind us, and lift the camera to capture one selfie of the two of us smiling.

"How about one with a kiss?" she suggests.

"Hannah Grace!" I hold my phone against my chest, pretending an affront that the older generation in our town has down pat.

Something I will never say to the leaders of that generation—Fern, Fawn, and Merry. Although deep down, I think they enjoy watching young couples in love.

"Stop pretending like you don't want to kiss me, Cole Strickland." She smacks my chest playfully.

I oblige her request for a kiss and lift my camera at just the right time to capture the two of us locked together. I manage to separate us before my hormones take over then pocket my phone.

My fingers brush the velvet box in my pocket, and I suck in a deep breath as Hannah turns in my arms to focus on the view at our feet.

I clear my throat again, swallowing the lump of nerves that wants to take up residence on my vocal cords.

"I'm going to miss you, sweetheart," I whisper.

She rotates in my arms and squeezes her arms around me.

"I'm going to miss you too."

"I love you."

It's not the first time I've said the words, but this is the moment when they take on the most meaning they've ever had.

"I love you," she murmurs and presses her lips against my heart.

"Hannah Grace, I've loved you for forever, and I'm going to love you for the rest of my life. Maybe even longer."

"Cole?" She looks up, her brows furrowed as she studies my expression.

I take advantage and drop my lips to hers again. She's where I find my strength and my peace. And I doubt she even realizes it.

"I've known I was going to marry you from the time I was ten years old. You walked into the community center Christmas dance in that red party dress with white lace—the one you told me you hated—and all I could think about was how soft it looked. And how nice you were to wear it because your mama wanted you to match the dress she had."

"What are you saying, Cole?"

"I won't ask you to marry me now, Hannah Grace. Partly because I haven't talked to your daddy for his permission, but mostly because I want to see you finish school, sweetheart. I'm so fucking proud of you for getting into Vanderbilt. And I refuse to let you give that up to follow me. You're going to be something, baby. And I'm going to be cheering you on. But until then, I won't ask you the question I really want and instead, I want to make you a promise. Someday, Hannah Grace, someday I'm going to ask you to marry me. With your daddy's blessing and when we're ready. Nothing is going to stop me." I pull the box from my pocket and flip up the lid. "It's not a ring, not yet. I want you to have one—the one you deserve—but I also wanted you to have something that sealed my promise."

I lift out the chain where a key rests next to a small heart with the initials C and H engraved in it.

"What I'm asking is if you'll accept my promise? If you'll let me love you forever and wait for me, for us, for the right time. To someday be my wife."

She nods furiously, throwing her arms around me as soon as I'm done with the speech I've rehearsed a thousand times.

"Yes!"

My arms tighten around her and I hold her to me, burying my head in her neck and breathing in her sweet citrus scent.

She said yes.

Her lips find mine, and she bounces in my arms until we break the kiss with a laugh.

"Put it on me, please?"

She spins again, and I lift the necklace over her head and wait for her to move her hair out of the way.

"There." Closing the clasp, I kiss the back of her neck and relish the shiver that works its way down her spine.

"Cold, sweetheart?" I ask, already knowing that even in the mountains, our June weather is hard to be cold in.

"Can we get back in the truck?" Her question catches me off guard.

"Sure. Sorry. I didn't think. It is colder up here..." I boost her into the truck and climb in behind her.

The door snicks shut and she straddles me, her mouth

claiming mine while her hands grip the hem of my T-shirt and tug. My dick hardens in a rush, pushing against the zipper of my shorts.

"Whoa, whoa, whoa, what's all this?" I ask, pulling away and holding her at arm's length when she appears ready to dive back in again.

"I want to, Cole. I—"

"I didn't make my promise for anything like this from you, Hannah Grace. We can wait."

"*I* can't wait. I want you. Right now."

She grinds her pelvis against my dick, and I can't hold back the moan that works its way out of my throat. Every part of my self-control is focused on being a gentleman even though she's telling me that's not what she wants.

Her lips find the pulse point in my neck and her tongue laves the spot, pleasure overwhelming every other conscious thought.

"Please. We just have tonight."

Apparently done fighting my shirt, she sits up and lifts hers over her head, displaying a perfect pair of tits clad in a light-pink lace bra.

I squeeze my eyes shut and fist my hands into the cotton of her shorts. She wiggles some more before grabbing my hands and lifting them to her now bare chest, and my eyes fly open to find my traitorous palms grazing the soft skin of her breasts, her nipples poking into the center of my palms.

"*Please.*"

Any chance I had of fighting against her temptation evaporates. With more strength than I think I have, I lift one hand and cup her nape to bring her lips back to mine and give in to the fire that burns us both until all that's left is the two of us…no longer two, but one.

WHAT HAPPENS AFTER COLE LEAVES? You can binge their second chance happily ever after, BODYGUARD FOR THE BEAUTY QUEEN, in KU!

WHO'S READY FOR SYDNEY?

I don't think you are...

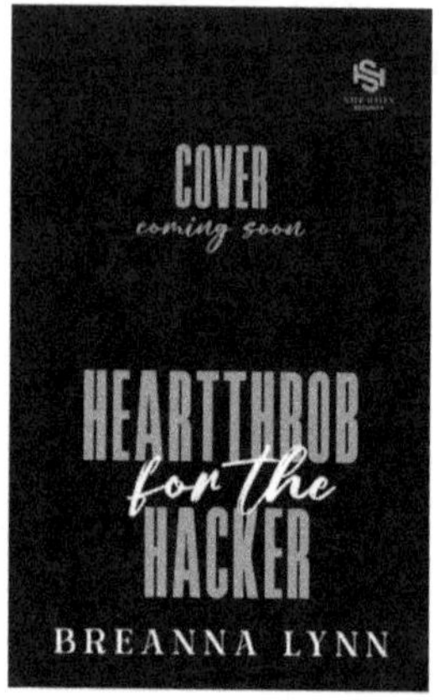

Coming 2026...

Scan the QR code to pre-order this first responder, age gap, romantic suspense happily ever after on Amazon!

PLAYLIST

The playlist for *Detective for the Debutante* is a mix of Leigh and Murphy—the wide eyed optimist and the seasoned detective. Music like "Too Sweet" by Hozier blends with Cole Swindell and Lainey Wilson's "Never Say Never" and "Drive" by the Cars. Their soundtrack weaves together their story of an undeniable chemistry and falling despite all the odds.

Want to listen to the music that inspired *Detective for the Debutante*? Check out the playlist on Spotify by searching for the "Detective for the Debutante" playlist or scan the QR code below.

You can both the playlist and the bonus tracks on my website:

https://www.breannalynnauthor.com

ACKNOWLEDGMENTS

To you. Yes, you. The one who just read Leigh and Murphy's story! Thank you for taking the chance on the two of them. I hadn't planned on these two…but they couldn't be ignored!

To Dennis—for being the person who keeps the house upright when I'm working or traveling. For being the person I want to share the world with. I love you. <3

To the Twinx—maybe someday you'll read this and maybe you won't. But if you do, know how much I love you.

Alina—Release day buddies once again! I tell anyone who will listen I would not be here without you. And, literally, I wouldn't! You have been my rock, my Vegas, and my uncontrollable laughter for the last five years! Love your face!!

To Dawn—thank you for helping me shape Leigh and Murphy into what they are. For continuing to ask the tough questions and for giving me suggestions and keeping me on the right path! And for brisket tacos…

To Shauna—thank you for letting me pick your brain for Gaelic phrases and helping bring life to Murphy's Irish ancestry!

To my ARC team—thank you for continuing to ask about the next release, for being excited about Leigh and Murphy as I painstakingly tried to give them the best story. I promise you won't have to wait as long for Sydney!

ALSO BY BREANNA LYNN

Heart Beats Series

Written in the Beat

In The Beat of the Moment

Keeping the Beat

Betting on the Beat

Embracing the Beat

Falling for the Beat

SAFE Haven Security

Soldier for the Starling

Bodyguard for the Beauty Queen

Detective for the Debutante

Stand alone novellas

Rockin' Around the Christmas Tree

Midnight in Mistletoe

Hating Mr. Write

One Weekend in Vegas

ABOUT THE AUTHOR

Breanna Lynn lives in Colorado with her two sets of twins (affectionately referred to as the Twinx), her boyfriend, his son, their two dogs, and three cats. A classy connoisseur of all things coffee, Breanna spends her free time keeping the Twinx from taking over the world. When not coordinating chaos, Breanna can be found binge reading, listening to music, or watching rom-coms with a giant bowl of popcorn.

Want to follow Breanna? Scan the QR code for all the ways to stay caught up!

www.ingramcontent.com/pod-product-compliance
Lightning Source LLC
Chambersburg PA
CBHW072108250626
47159CB00007B/2360

9781955359597